INTO WHISPERING SHADOWS

H.E. BAUMAN

First paperback edition September 2023

Cover design by MiblArt

Map by Cartographybird Maps

Jeanine Harrell of Indie Edits with Jeanine

ISBN 979-8-9888024-0-2 (paperback)

ISBN 979-8-9888024-1-9 (hardcover)

ISBN 978-1-7354553-9-6 (ebook)

www.hebauman.com

Content Warning

Thank you for picking up *Into Whispering Shadows*. This is a fantasy novel that follows Astrea Sovna, a 24-year-old librarian and mage, as she continues her journey to uncover the truth about void magic. The story includes themes and events that may not be suitable for some readers:

- Fantasy and magical violence

- Nightmares

- Stalking and threats

- Alcohol consumption

- Consensual sex scenes (two)

- Panic attacks and anxiety

- Insults by a mentor figure

- Forced drug use

- Physical and psychological torture

- References to parental death, current war, historical wars, and rebellion

If you need to put the book down at any time (including now), please do so and take care of yourself.

THE NORTH SEA
TALMARI
GRAND DUCHY OF NOVARIA
ZINDIR
THE ZAIKUD EMPIRE
MACADIAN MOUNTAINS
POSAN
FORT AVALON
NARIZON
FORT BLACKROCK
CORSYCA
FORT IRONWING
KINGDOM OF DELIA
SAPOI
THE WESTERN SEA
CAPITAL CITIES
CITIES
NOTABLE TOWNS
FORTS
MEMATOS
ILESOURIA

IRVINA
MOUNTAIRES MOUNTAINS
THE HELOSIAN EMPIRE
THE LOST ISLES
THE BADLANDS
RING OF FIRE
TINALE BAY
KALAMA
SEZIA
REPUBLIC OF TORNAMA
THASIA
KATAVENA
TAIPOLI ISLANDS
THE EASTERN SEA
THE SOUTHERN OCEAN

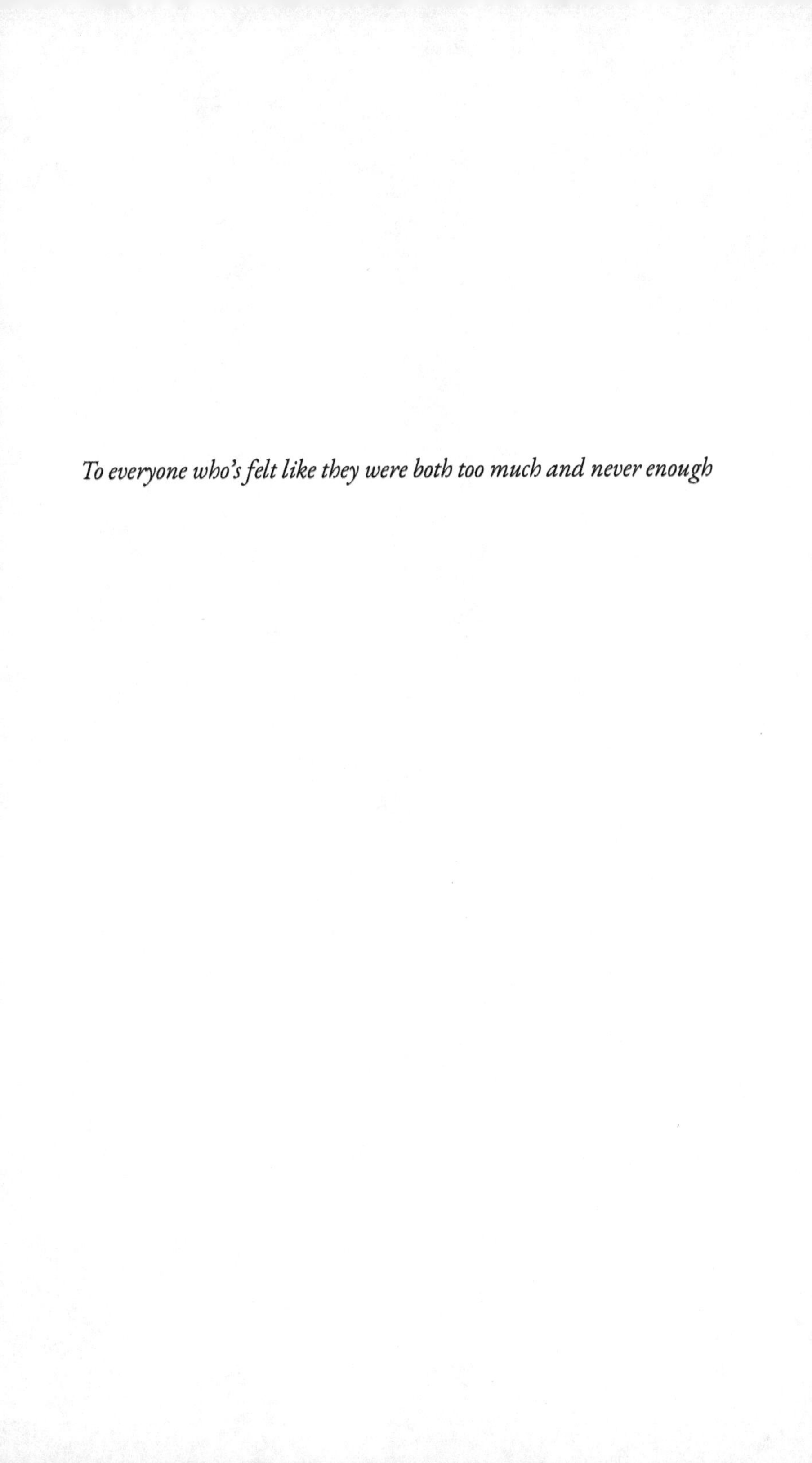

To everyone who's felt like they were both too much and never enough

CHAPTER 1

The last two days had been the worst of Astrea Sovna's life. In fact, the last few weeks had been some of the worst, too. She stared at her reflection in the mirror above the small bathroom sink, focusing on the familiar, almost comforting hum of the airship's engines.

Complete the mission.

Astrea forced her tears back. No good would come from more tears. She'd cried enough after leaving her uncle—her only blood family—behind in the Helosian capital. Leaving Kalama was the hardest thing she'd ever had to do. It had been far harder than her decision to reveal her Lightbringer magic.

Though she and her friends had fled the Helosian Empire, there had been no pursuit. The Helosians had, inexplicably, let them go. Since taking off from that Kalamian airfield, Astrea had expected a battle in the skies, her body constantly ready for another fight. But no fight came. Emperor Aelius Auris hadn't sent an armada of airships after them. Neither the Delians nor Zaikudi—enemies of Helosia—had given chase. No one had tried to shoot them out of the sky. Everything had been quiet.

Smoothing her hair, Astrea returned to her bedroom. It was barely big enough for one adult, let alone two, but she'd been sharing it with Jin since the day they fled Kalama. Astrea didn't know whether she was mad at him or not for hiding his tenuous connections to the Helosian rebels, but she wouldn't deny herself the one small comfort of sleeping in his arms.

A notebook, loose papers, and folios covered the low, hard mattress. All their evidence of void magic, contained in just a handful of pages. *Pathetic.*

None of it made much sense, no matter how much Astrea studied it. She could hazard a few guesses to try to fill in the gaps, but she had so many questions. At the top of that list was why she'd had a vision in Sezia when she was a Lightbringer, not a Stargazer. And why was a group called the Paragon looking for her? How were they connected to void magic? Astrea closed her notebook and tossed it on the empty side of the bed.

A metallic knock echoed through the tiny room. Astrea wanted to pull the covers over her head and pretend she wasn't there, but the knock came again. The urge to avoid everything was strong. Intoxicating. Almost impossible to resist.

"I know you're in there, Az!" called Eliana. A blend of excitement and anxiety rushed over Astrea's skin. "Come out here! I think you'll want to see this!"

Sighing, Astrea padded toward the door and pulled it open. Eliana was waiting outside, hands clasped over her heart. She still looked every bit the Helosian princess. Her hair fell in loose waves down to her shoulders, and her fashionable, knee-length red dress was better fit for a council meeting than whatever they were now after fleeing the country. Traitors? Rebels? If that bothered Eliana, she didn't let it show.

Eliana flashed a smile, her golden eyes twinkling. "Are you ready?"

"Ready for what?"

Eliana grabbed Astrea's hand and pulled her down the narrow stairs. "Ready for this!"

Cressida, Adi, and Jin were all in the airship's main cabin, clustered near one of the wide windows. Nicos, the only one missing from the scene, was still in the pilot's cabin, large headphones covering his ears. He'd barely looked at Astrea since she revealed her magic on the airfield.

Eliana pulled Astrea toward their friends and pointed out the window. "Welcome to Novaria."

Mountains stretched out beyond them as far as Astrea could see, a mix of green slopes and white-tipped caps. The sun shone through the few clouds that drifted through the brilliant blue sky. As the airship cleared the last of the mountain range, a smattering of lakes and rivers sparkled in the valley far below.

"We made it!" Adi said, bumping Astrea's shoulder with his. "We actually made it to skies damned Novaria, Astrea. Can you believe it?"

"No," she whispered. "I can't."

Because as everyone celebrated around her, Astrea had the sinking feeling they weren't going back to Helosia for a very long time. They couldn't, not if they really were rebels on the run. Eliana was intent on backing the Helosian rebels and actually trying to overthrow her father.

As everyone started moving away from the window—Adi returning to his post—Astrea stayed put. Far below, a river snaked through the thick clusters of green trees, the vegetation far different from anything back in Kalama. They were nearly as far north as they could get, had flown across the entire continent to get here. Had flown across the entire continent without their families.

She found Jin's eyes in the reflection of the window. He watched her, lips pressed into a thin line. Astrea focused on that faraway river again.

"Now that we're here," Eliana said, her voice carrying above the hum of the engines, "we need to start trying to contact Grand Duchess Ysabel."

"I'm still not convinced it's wise to go to her," Cressida said.

"We really don't have another choice, Cress." Eliana sighed. "All evidence about this . . . this Paragon group points here, right?"

Jin nodded. "It does."

"And it's not like Jin and I can just waltz into the country and do whatever we want," Eliana continued. "We need the grand duchess's permission to investigate, and frankly, I'm going to need to try to get support from some of the continental leaders if I'm actually going to take my father's throne. Ysabel may be the right place to start."

Eliana said it so simply, with such unwavering confidence. Astrea peeked over her shoulder. Only Eliana's aura revealed the truth. Orange anxiety tangled around the princess, as did red determination and light green focus.

"I wish there were an alternative." Cressida tucked a stray curl behind her ear.

"Well"—Eliana smoothed the front of her dress—"it's not like Ysabel is our father's ally."

"And that autumn summit with Novaria that Az and Jin were working on for him?" Cressida asked. "Wasn't that about an alliance?"

Eliana waved a hand. "A summit means nothing. It's a glorified meeting until both parties are at the negotiation table. If we present our case to Ysabel, there's no way she won't allow us to investigate."

"Jin?" Cressida asked. "What do you think?"

He ran a hand over his face, then blew out a long breath. "I think Ellie's right that our hands are tied. If we sneak in and either one of us is found out . . . that will be bad. We don't have to tell Ysabel everything, just enough to get permission to be here."

"You don't think she'll want void magic, just like your father?" Cressida asked.

"Ysabel's never done anything to suggest she wants such destructive power," Eliana said. "Besides, it's only a matter of time until the other continental leaders find out about void magic now that our father has it. Maybe we can sway her to our side first."

Astrea's stomach twisted. She could see Jin and Eliana's argument, just as she could see Cressida's. Neither choice felt like the right one. "Do you know anything else about Ysabel?" she asked.

"I've never met her, but her diplomats at the Novarian embassy are easy to work with," Eliana said. "She came into power over two decades ago. She's in her midfifties, unmarried, a non-mage, and her heir is her nephew, Crown Prince Veiko. Ysabel's foreign policy has always been neutrality."

"Neutral is good," Cressida murmured.

That last part didn't seem like the type of leader who would throw their support behind Eliana. But it was also someone who didn't seem keen on capturing void magic for their war efforts. And that was likely as good as it was going to get.

"Then let's try to get in touch with her, shall we?" Eliana didn't wait for a reply before she marched toward the front of the ship, where both Adi and Nicos now sat. Astrea had been only mildly surprised to learn they both knew how to fly an airship.

Jin glanced at Cressida, then Astrea. "It might be a while before we get in touch with Ysabel," he said. "Regardless, it'll be a few hours before we get close to the capital. Get some rest."

Rest was all they'd been getting on their flight across the continent. Astrea forced her jaw to relax. Jin didn't mean any harm. Besides, what else could they do? They were stuck thousands of feet in the air in a metal flying machine.

"Let us know when you hear from them," Astrea said. Then she slinked back to the narrow stairs in the far corner of the cabin and headed back to her room.

Astrea tried to go to sleep for a couple hours, but every time she closed her eyes, all she could see was Saros fighting Nazarov right outside the Kalamian palace doors. All she could see were those red eyes peering out at her from the darkness of the Sezian kitchen.

Complete the mission. Find the answers.

Burying her face in the pillows, Astrea breathed in deep. The bed smelled like Jin, like eucalyptus and sandalwood.

She couldn't just sit around anymore. Astrea climbed out of bed, shook the wrinkles out of her favorite lavender dress, and opened the bedroom door. Just across the hallway, Cressida's door was cracked open, and based on the anxiety grating on Astrea's skin, her best friend was in there.

Astrea knocked on the door. "Cress?"

It opened on silent hinges. Cressida remained in the middle of her bed, hugging a flat pillow to her chest with one arm. "One thing I love about being a Metalli on an airship," she quipped. Her fingers twitched as the door closed behind Astrea with a thunk. "I don't have to get up to get the door."

"Can we talk?" Astrea asked, despite the fact that she didn't want to talk about any of it.

"Is it about why you've been hiding in your room since we left Kalama?" Cressida scooted over, making room on the bed for Astrea.

"Yes and no." Astrea sat on the hard mattress and stared down at where her hands rested in her lap. She had no idea where to begin. "I'm sorry your parents didn't come. I really wanted them to."

Balthazar and Sarsali Nikaphoros were Cressida's parents, yes, but they were also Saros's close friends. Astrea had known them since she was just ten years old, and they were family. She'd so badly hoped they would leave Kalama while they had the opportunity, but they'd chosen to stay behind.

"My parents made their choice. So did Saros."

Astrea hadn't shown her uncle's note to anyone on the ship. *"I'm sorry. Forgive me."* She'd replayed their last conversation over and over in her head since leaving Kalama, trying to figure out what Saros meant about his visions of her being true. But Astrea had no way to ask him what those visions were or why she'd had a vision of her own in Sezia. Lightbringers didn't have visions. Stargazers did.

Saros had wanted her to leave Kalama for months. He'd warned them that something bad was coming. Even if his stargazing magic didn't give him exact dates or scenarios, Saros must have seen his choice to stay behind. He must have known what he was doing if he was choosing to stay in Kalama. If he'd had the foresight to leave her that note.

Astrea hadn't revealed that truth to her friends, though. She hadn't told them about her vision either. It all felt too heavy, too impossible to admit out loud. She knew she had to tell them. She had to. But she couldn't find the words.

"One way or another, we'll reconnect with everyone," Cressida continued. "We'll find a way to save them. But until then, you have to find some way to make peace with his choice."

"And you've made peace with your parents' choice?"

"Well . . ." Cressida shrugged, her jade eyes downcast. "I don't like it, but I trust them to take care of themselves and to help Saros if he needs it."

For all they knew, Saros could be in the emperor's dungeon or the Kalamian police station. He'd been there during their fight with the void mage Lord Victor Nazarov at the palace. He'd been holding Nazarov off while Astrea, Jin, Eliana, Adi, and Nicos escaped. But Astrea had used her magic to buy them time, too. There was no way someone at the palace hadn't seen that. And if they saw that, they would've reported it to the emperor because, as far as anyone at the palace knew, Astrea didn't have any magic. She was just supposed to be a librarian, not a Lightbringer. Nobody lied to the emperor and got away with it.

And besides, who was to say the Nikaphoroses wouldn't become Emperor Aelius's targets with Cressida on the run? It wouldn't be hard for him to figure out the Nikaphoroses had hidden Astrea's magic for years, too.

"When will we get to Talmaris?" Astrea asked. A change of subject seemed best.

Cressida shrugged again. "Soon, I suppose."

A small, narrow window near the ceiling revealed the first hints of sunset. The swatch of reds, oranges, and golds seemed out of place against the gray metal walls.

Hot anger rushed over Astrea's skin. She winced and pulled her magic back toward herself as much as she could. Cressida's gentle confusion followed.

Jumping to her feet, Astrea headed for the door. Even with her magic pulled back, and even with the roar of the airship engines, Eliana's anger was impossible to ignore. A string of curses floated up the stairs. Astrea started down them, Cressida right behind her.

"She wants us to sit and wait?" Eliana asked. "We tell her we have important information about our father's war plans, and now she wants us to *wait*?"

As Astrea reached the bottom of the stairs, she hesitated. The Auris siblings stood near the middle of the cabin, Jin's back to the stairs and Eliana facing them. His tall, wide frame nearly hid Eliana from sight.

"Why are you mad at me?" Jin's shoulders tightened. "I'm not the one who's telling you to wait. Of course Ysabel isn't just going to let us come into the city. We're lucky she's not making us go back to the border."

"Of course we're *lucky*. But what could she possibly have to consider?"

"Come on, Ellie," Jin said. "You have to admit it's suspicious for two of the Helosian emperor's children to show up, claiming to have information about their father. You'd be doing the same thing if your positions were reversed."

"Bad news?" Cressida called from where she still stood halfway up the stairs.

Eliana startled. Jin simply turned around, his arms crossed tightly over his chest.

"Ysabel wants us to land in a clearing on the outskirts of Talmaris, and she'll send someone out to talk to us." Eliana sighed. "Although I suppose Jin's right. I would be suspicious if I were her."

"At least she's not sending us away," Cressida said. "That's something, right?"

"Let's just land and talk to her people," Jin said. "It's our only option unless you want to go to Tornama and start the hunt over completely. If *they'll* even let us in."

"No, no." With another sigh, Eliana ran her hands through her dark wavy hair. "No, we'll do what Ysabel asks. We'll land. Hopefully we can get this cleared up tonight and go speak to her."

"I'll tell Adi to go ahead, then." Jin brushed past his sister as he headed for the front of the ship.

Astrea swallowed hard. At least they were allowed to land. Now they just needed to figure out how to convince the grand duchess to let them into her capital.

Chapter 2

Outside, night was beginning to fall. They'd just landed the airship in a forest outside of the Novarian capital of Talmaris, but nobody from the palace had come to meet them yet.

Astrea stared out the window, tracing the tall, shadowy trees with her eyes. The last remnants of the sunset were still visible through the foliage, hints of pink and orange almost completely overtaken by the darkening sky.

"Az?" Jin asked as he came up behind her.

"Yeah?" She peeked up at him.

"We're having a team meeting before the Novarians get here." He motioned toward the sitting area behind them. It was still empty, and above them, the ceiling creaked. Everyone else had gone upstairs to finish cleaning up.

"Oh. Alright."

The two of them hadn't spoken much since fleeing Kalama. Astrea had spent most of her time locked away in their shared room, and he'd spent most of his downstairs, doing whatever it was he had to do. She'd wanted to talk to him. She just didn't know what to say. Where to begin.

Rebel sympathies. Visions. Everything else.

Jin took half a step back, but he didn't completely walk away. "Are you mad at me for keeping my promise to Saros?" he asked. "I know how much his choosing to stay behind hurts you, and I'm sorry this is such a mess. And while there are a lot of things I regret, keeping that promise to Saros isn't one of them."

What did he regret, then? Astrea knew he regretted leaving Kalama all those years ago and not telling her. He'd made that clear after the dinner party at the palace. Did he regret kissing her that night? Did he regret kissing her in Sezia? He'd just said he didn't regret taking her away from Kalama, but what if he did? What if he regretted ever getting involved? Helping her?

Astrea wanted to ask him about all those things, but she couldn't. Instead, she said, "I don't know how to do this, Jin."

"Do what? Talk?"

"*This.*" Astrea motioned to the empty cabin. "The mission. The politics. The secrets."

Jin's eyebrows rose a fraction. "Secrets?"

When he'd first come home from Kalama after those eight long years, Astrea had declined his offer to talk about what happened for weeks. But when that conversation finally happened, something changed for them. Between them. She didn't want to talk to him—or anyone—right now, but this conversation needed to happen if they were going to complete the mission.

"I wish you'd told me about Zephyrine's connections." When he started to protest, Astrea said, "I know it probably wasn't a good idea for me to know, considering . . . But I just . . . I wish I'd known."

"I should've told all of you sooner. I probably should've enlisted Zephyrine's help sooner, too. I just never thought any of this would be so . . . complicated. It's hard to be objective when I'm trying to protect the people most important to me."

"You don't regret helping me?"

"Regret it?" Jin's eyes—that brilliant gold flecked with amber—stayed locked on hers. "I'd never regret that, Az. Never."

The knot in Astrea's chest loosened, then tightened again. Her friends couldn't walk into Ysabel's palace—ask for her aid—without knowing everything.

"I'm ready!" Eliana called down the stairs. Loud footsteps followed as her T-strap heels clanked against metal. "We're all ready."

As everyone returned to the cabin, Astrea swallowed hard. They all needed to know. They deserved the truth. She followed Jin to the sitting area, where their friends all dropped down onto the two long sofas. Astrea sat in the empty spot next to Cressida.

"Before the Novarians get here," Jin said, crossing his arms as he stood at the head of the group, "we need to figure out what we're going to tell them."

"The truth?" Nicos suggested. Rusty annoyance flickered around him, almost blending in with his auburn hair and his many freckles.

"Actually . . ." Astrea paused as everyone looked at her. "I need to tell you all something. Something I should've told you days ago."

"Alright," Jin said, voice steady. "What is it?"

"When we went to that house in Sezia, just the three of us, I . . ." Astrea huffed. Why was this so hard? She glanced at Adi, who was seated across from her, then up at Jin. "I had a vision."

Lavender surprise and gray confusion exploded around the cabin, so bright Astrea could barely make out the darkness beyond the windows.

"A vision?" Eliana echoed. "I thought you were a Lightbringer."

"I am."

"How could you have a vision when you're a Lightbringer?" Cressida asked.

"I don't know."

Cressida frowned. "Did you talk to Saros?"

"I tried. I tried, but all he would say was that his visions of me were true."

"His visions of *you*?" Jin asked.

"I don't know, Jin." Astrea traced a few wrinkles on her skirt with her pointer finger. "I don't know. And I wanted to wait until I had answers to tell you, because I didn't think you'd believe me." That voice in that house had even warned Astrea her friends wouldn't believe her about the vision she had. After all, a Lightbringer having a vision simply sounded . . . outrageous. "And I didn't want to make this more confusing than it already is, but now I have no way to *get* answers, and—"

"Why would he not tell you?" Nicos cut in, voice strained. Anger burned Astrea's skin. "Based on what I've gathered the last two days, your uncle is at the center of a lot of our problems."

"Nic." Eliana glared at him, her voice like the ice sheets that covered the mountains to the northwest.

"I'm sorry I didn't say anything," Astrea murmured. "I was trying to make sense of it."

"Well, you've told us now." Eliana offered Astrea a small smile. "What was your vision?"

"Kalama burning. The palace, the library, Cressida's home, everything."

"That certainly sounds ominous," Eliana said with an uneasy laugh.

Cressida and Adi had both remained quiet, but steel pain flared around Cressida. She grabbed Astrea's hand and squeezed it once.

This was going far better than Eliana's reaction when she'd found out Astrea was a Lightbringer. After healing her on Solstice Night, Astrea hadn't had a choice. She'd had to spill her secret after fourteen long years, and Eliana had been so upset. At least the only one who was annoyed now was Nicos.

"So, what does this mean about your magic?" Eliana asked. "Can Lightbringers and Stargazers . . . cross somehow?"

"I don't think so," Astrea said. She'd never heard of such a thing. All mages could control their base element, but those with more specialized powers—like Sparkcasters and Metalli—did not have unlimited magical abilities. It was unheard of for Lightbringers and Stargazers to cross, just as it was unheard of for someone to be both a Metalli and Greenkeeper. "I don't know."

"What do we tell the grand duchess?" Adi asked. "Does she need to know about this?"

"I had planned on being transparent." Eliana shifted, her fingers twisting the skirt of her red dress over and over again. "What do you want to do, Az?"

Not more secrets. That had gotten her into this mess in the first place. That was why the void mages were looking for her, right? Because she'd kept her magic a secret?

"I don't know," she said. "Wouldn't transparency be the best choice?"

"We're not telling Ysabel," Jin said, though it sounded more like a command than conversation among friends. "Az's magic, whatever that may be, doesn't concern the grand duchess."

Astrea sucked in a sharp breath. She couldn't really be a Lightbringer and a Stargazer, could she? Everything she knew about magic suggested that was impossible. The mere thought made her dizzy.

"Then what *do* we want to tell her?" Eliana asked. "If we're not being transparent, is there anything else we should be hiding?" Her jaw was set in that Auris way, tight and unyielding. "We need her support."

"And we'll get it," Jin said. "We'll tell her what she needs to know."

"And what is that?"

"That's why I wanted to have this meeting. To figure it out."

Eliana rolled her eyes. "Great."

"What do you want me to say, Ellie?" Jin asked. "Do you really want to tell Ysabel that not only does our father have access to void magic, but also that one of your best friends seems to control two branches of celestial magic?"

"Not really." Eliana huffed, her gaze flicking to Astrea again. "But it should be Az's choice, not yours."

Astrea didn't *want* to hide anything again. Not having to constantly watch what she said or did was freeing. But as anxiety slipped past Jin's wall, the faintest hint of orange bubbling around him, she frowned. "You really don't think we should tell her?" she asked.

"I think we should evaluate the situation before we give over everything we know," he said. "And it buys us a little time to find the answers Saros wouldn't give you."

Astrea nodded. Telling Ysabel about the situation with void magic and the emperor was already a calculated risk. Introducing another magical problem might just be a mistake.

"Then we won't tell her," Astrea agreed. "I don't care if she knows I'm a Lightbringer, though."

Rusty annoyance flared around Nicos, the heat of his anger following right after. Mint relief, however, bubbled around the others.

"Alright then," Eliana said with a nod. "What else are we taking off the table?"

"All she really needs to know is that void magic is real and that both our father and another group are after it," Jin said. "The Paragon seem to be connected to Novaria, so that's where we should begin. Once we get a better gauge on Ysabel and the situation, we can disclose more as needed."

As everyone agreed, static crackled to life in the cockpit. Adi jumped up first, Jin following close behind as they headed that way. Outside, airship engines rumbled. Bright lights lit up the forest from overhead.

"It's the Novarians," Jin called to the rest of them. "A man named Commander Lucian is here."

Everyone jumped to action as they hastily discussed the rest of their plans. Astrea would read the Novarians with her lightbringing, and Jin and Eliana would do the talking. And, with any luck, they'd be back on track in a matter of minutes.

Astrea let her friends exit the airship first. Everyone, that was, except for Jin. He'd stopped short of her, just an arm's length away. He watched her in that way he did, like he was trying to read her mind. Then he smiled at her.

"Ready?" he asked.

"Ready."

She went down the stairs first, trying to balance watching the Novarians on the opposite side of the clearing with watching her own steps. The two Novarian airships were compact, far smaller than what Astrea and her friends had flown in. Eliana, Cressida, Nicos, and Adi were already headed that way.

Jin's hand swept the small of Astrea's back as he moved around her to stand next to his sister at the front of their group. A shiver ran up her spine.

"Here we go," Eliana said as the doors of both Novarian airships opened.

Between the two ships, a dozen soldiers emerged into the clearing, their uniforms dark in the shadows of the night. As one Novarian closed the distance between his ships and their group, Astrea realized he had a dozen little pins attached to one side of his uniform, just above his heart. His dark hair was pulled up into a bun, and his beard was neatly trimmed.

"Princess Eliana," the man said in Helosian, his voice smooth and light as he offered a small bow. His complexion was nearly as pale as Astrea's. "Prince Varojin. Thank you for agreeing to the grand duchess's terms for entering Talmaris. I'm Commander Lucian Astor, the captain of her guard."

Commander Lucian was impossible to read with her magic, not in the way the void mages had been but the way Jin was. Astrea frowned. Whoever this Lucian was, he had tight control over his emotions. So did all the guards lining up behind him.

"We're just glad to see you, Commander," Eliana replied. "Thank you for agreeing to meet with us."

The commander nodded. "It's getting late, so I'll get straight to the point, Your Imperial Highnesses. Grand Duchess Ysabel wants to know exactly why you're here."

"We already told you on the radio," Jin said. "Not only are we here with information about our father's war plans, but we're looking for someone."

"Looking for someone?" Commander Lucian echoed. "And who might that be?"

"Someone we believe is connected to a series of murders back in Kalama."

The commander's thick eyebrows rose, but nothing slipped past his wall. He couldn't have been much taller than Cressida, and his tight, rigid posture made it impossible for Astrea to even guess what he was thinking.

"Murders." Commander Lucian nodded. "And information about your father. What could drive two Helosian heirs to betray their father like that?"

"Because we believe he's a threat to the continent, Commander," Eliana said.

"He's *already* a threat to the continent, Your Imperial Highness."

"And this will make him even more so." Eliana lifted her chin, red determination flaring around her. "I would be happy to discuss this with the grand duchess, but I will not be left to freeze in a Novarian forest while you try to mull over the decision for her." As if on cue, the wind kicked up, the chilly night air prickling Astrea's skin. "If the grand duchess doesn't want to hear us out, then my brother, myself, and our friends will simply leave."

Behind Commander Lucian, the Novarian guards shifted. Anxiety flared around Nicos. But Eliana remained steadfast, chin tilted up and shoulders pushed back.

"Should we leave, Commander?" Jin asked.

"No." Lucian shook his head. "No. We will escort you to an airfield, then bring you to the palace. The grand duchess will meet with you."

Chapter 3

Outside the ship, Talmaris came into view. It was a brilliant city, the buildings and roads glittering amid a sea of lights below. Astrea watched the approach through the main cabin windows, her attention focused on those beautiful lights. They were really in Novaria. They'd made it.

Somewhere down there were the answers she needed. The ones that would help her save Saros, Sarsali, and Balthazar, and everyone else back home.

"When we land," Eliana said, pulling Astrea's attention from the windows back to their little group, "let's be polite to our reluctant hosts, alright? Let's try to make a good first impression."

Adi's tinny voice crackled through the overhead speakers. "Landing in fifteen."

"And how do you suppose we do that?" Cressida asked.

"By being punctual and organized, and by presenting ourselves well." Eliana's gaze darted to Jin, dragging dramatically up and down his form. "Maybe we don't show up wearing military uniforms."

He looked down at his all-black fatigues and boots. Both Jin and Adi had taken to wearing them the last couple days. "It'll take me five minutes to change, Ellie."

"And Adi said you have just fifteen, and we're standing around talking."

Jin forced a smile. "Then let me go change. We should all make sure we're packed, too. Don't leave anything on the ship."

"You think we won't be coming back?" Cressida asked.

"I don't know, but I'd rather bring our things just in case." Jin nodded toward the stairs. "You too, Ellie. I'm sure your room's a mess."

"It is not," Eliana protested. Still, she followed the rest of them upstairs. "Be back down there in ten minutes tops!" she called over her shoulder as she disappeared into the room at the far end of the corridor.

Astrea went into her and Jin's room without saying a word. Jin said nothing, either, as he grabbed his knapsack and went into the bathroom. How he was going to change in there, Astrea wasn't sure. It was barely big enough to take two steps, let alone for an adult to get dressed.

Astrea set her suitcase on the hard mattress and opened it. She hadn't been able to pack much before they fled Kalama; she just had whatever it was she'd brought on their trip to Sezia and a few extra things she'd stuffed into her satchel. How had that trip been just a few days before? Everything else had happened so quickly.

She pulled out a white blouse and black skirt. Eliana had said to look presentable. It was an outfit she'd usually wear to her job at the Great Library, not something fit for a royal court, but it was the best she could do.

My old job, she corrected herself. Even if Grand Duchess Ysabel wasn't keen on letting them investigate in Talmaris, there would be no going back to Helosia anytime soon. Besides, Felix, Raela, Lena, and Serra would be fine, if not overwhelmed by the extra work they'd have to do in her absence. Astrea hoped they weren't too mad at her, or too worried since she'd simply disappeared from Kalama without any warning.

A loud bang echoed through the bedroom, and Jin muttered a curse. Ghost pain flared in Astrea's elbow, sharp and quick. "You alright?" she called to Jin.

"Fine," he muttered.

Astrea changed quickly, then folded her lavender dress and put it in her suitcase. After snapping the lid shut, she reached for the silver necklace she'd left on the narrow bedside table. The sapphire winked in the dim light of the room, and Astrea closed her fingers around it. Jin had gifted it to her before that dinner party just days earlier.

"Got everything?" Jin asked as he exited the bathroom. He'd changed into a black silk shirt, black trousers, and wingtip shoes. It was nearly the same outfit he'd worn that night at the Whiskey Dream.

"Yes." Astrea slipped the necklace on, clasping it behind her neck. Jin's lips quirked up as she moved past him to grab her satchel. She double-checked that her notebook, the *Myth and Magic* book from Felix, Mattina's letter, and the meteorite sample were tucked inside. So was Saros's note, which she hadn't opened since that awful day they left Kalama. "I have everything."

Jin took his knapsack and both of their suitcases. Astrea let him, doing one last visual sweep of the bedroom as she backed toward the door. It was empty. Cold.

Downstairs, both Eliana and Cressida were already waiting with their bags. And outside, the city had grown dark again, though a few lights came into view as they descended. Their airship landed smoothly, Astrea hardly noticing their arrival on solid ground if not for the metallic clunk of the ship against the airfield's paved ground.

"I'll be right back," Jin said before disappearing through a door behind the stairs.

"What's that about?" Cressida murmured, and Astrea shrugged. She hadn't even realized a door was there.

As the engines cut off, Adi and Nicos both left the pilot's cabin and headed for the stairs, calling out promises to be quick. Astrea meandered to the windows, watching as two airfield workers approached their ship.

Nearby, the two Novarian airships had also landed. Their doors were still closed.

As soon as they'd boarded their ship and gotten away from the Novarians, Astrea had told the others that Commander Lucian and his guards were unreadable. None of them had loved it, but they'd all agreed it was far better than the Novarians being void mages. Now, as Astrea watched the airfield, she let her magic stretch out wide. The two workers below were annoyed, but Astrea supposed she would be, too, if an airship unexpectedly showed up.

When Jin returned a moment later, he had an extra knapsack slung over his shoulder. Adi and Nicos joined them not long after.

"Stick together," Jin said. "Let me talk to the commander."

"But I—" Eliana started, and Jin cut her off.

"Ellie, I know you like to figure out the details, but empresses don't deal with that. If you want Ysabel to someday back up your claim to the throne, start projecting that image now, yeah?"

Eliana crossed her arms, but Jin had a point. Eliana could negotiate to her heart's content, but things like flight paths and schedules were typically left to the support staff. Astrea was glad she wasn't the one who'd pointed it out, though. If looks could kill, Eliana would've had Jin dead on the floor in a second.

Finally, Eliana huffed. "Alright."

Jin nodded. "Alright. Let's go."

Cressida opened the airship door again, air hissing out as it unsealed and chilly night air rushed inside. The breeze picked up as they descended the stairs one by one. Astrea shivered. The thin fabrics of her blouse and linen skirt were not suited to this kind of mild weather. Two black cars idled on the airfield, similar in style to those driven in Kalama.

Commander Lucian walked over, the silver trimmings of his uniform catching the moonlight as it filtered in between a few passing clouds. Two guards were at his heels, their postures rigid.

"Your Imperial Highnesses," he said, voice low. His gaze flicked to their suitcases and bags. "We'll have to take two cars to the palace. The grand duchess would like to be discreet about this, so we'll be bringing you in through a more . . . secluded entrance."

The wind gusted as Jin said, "Whatever we need to do, Commander. We're ready when you are."

As the Novarian royal guards drove Astrea, Jin, and Adi through Talmaris's streets, Astrea couldn't help but be amazed. Shining towers and new skyscrapers mixed with the beautiful, ornate architecture of buildings from decades and centuries past. Kalama had preserved most of its historical style, though some newer buildings had cropped up in recent years. The porticos and sidewalks they zoomed past were mostly deserted. Strange. In Kalama, some people would still be out and about, even at the late hour.

The three of them rode in silence. Nicos, Cressida, and Eliana were in the car ahead of them with Commander Lucian, which Astrea watched through the windshield of her own car. Anxiety buzzed off Adi in waves of orange. He tapped his long fingers against his thigh. On Astrea's other side, Jin sat still as stone.

Though Astrea had been born in Novaria, she'd lived in a town called Irvina, south of the capital city. It was farther inland and close to the Helosian border. Saros had lived in Talmaris for much of Astrea's childhood, having started university a couple years after she was born. He'd left everything behind to take care of her when her mother, Roxana, had died. Saros hadn't even been much older than Jin was now when he'd become Astrea's guardian.

Astrea leaned her head back against her seat. What would've happened to them if her mother hadn't died? Astrea assumed that both she and Saros would have stayed in Novaria. Perhaps he would've become a Stargazer for Ysabel, and Roxana would've been able to help Astrea master the Lightbringer magic they shared. *Surely I wouldn't be wrapped up in this conspiracy.*

As they barreled down the capital's quiet streets, Astrea's nerves began to settle—barely. The view outside grew darker as they edged away from downtown. The buildings thinned, giving way to wide expanses of what Astrea thought might be parks. After several turns down dark roads, the car eventually rolled to a stop. Massive gates swung open on silent hinges before the car started moving again.

"We're almost there, Your Imperial Highness," the guard in the passenger seat said in Novarian. "We're going in through the garage, then Commander Lucian will escort you to see Her Highness."

"Thank you," Jin said.

The car rolled on, passing large trees and gas lamps lighting the way. To their left, tall white towers occasionally came into view above the trees, only to disappear again. The driver turned right to a long, low building with two open bays. The front car pulled into one, and their driver pulled into the second. The doors swung shut behind them as the engine cut off.

"Here we are," the same guard said.

Jin opened his door and slid out of the car. Adi did the same on Astrea's other side. Astrea started toward Jin's open door, and when he offered her his hand, she took it. His fingers tightened around hers just for a moment, and when he tried to pull away, she gave his hand a quick squeeze.

"We'll leave your bags in the car," Commander Lucian said as everyone gathered around him. "Unless you need something now."

"My satchel," Astrea said. She didn't want what little evidence they had out of her sight.

Lucian waved a hand to one of the guards; they brought Astrea's satchel to her. She slung it across her body, smoothing her hand over the brown leather as she double-checked that every buckle was secure.

Instead of going into the open night air, Lucian led them through the garage, apologizing more than once to both Eliana and Jin for the circumstances. Astrea was sure they didn't mind. He unlocked a door, then ushered everyone through. A series of single lightbulbs hung overhead at even intervals, leading down a set of stairs. The walls here were gray brick, and the smooth stone floors did nothing to help with the echo.

"It's just a short walk to the palace," Lucian said over his shoulder.

Though the tunnels were empty except for the seven of them, Astrea kept her senses wide open. The only change came in the slope of the ground, which eventually began to angle up before they arrived at another set of stairs. More emotions and walls came into Astrea's awareness as they ascended into the palace.

Where Emperor Auris's palace was bright and alive, Grand Duchess Ysabel's was cool and calm. Instead of shades of white punctuated by red, gold, and orange, everything here was gray, blue, and purple. Even the ceilings here were higher, decorated with paintings of the night sky and what Astrea assumed was the Novarian countryside.

"This way, please," Lucian said as they headed down a wide corridor.

After several turns down long, empty hallways, they finally came to what seemed to be a main atrium. It was enormous, a glass dome rising high above them. Astrea was sure that on a clear night, they'd be able to see the stars. On opposite ends of the atrium were two sets of double doors. Lucian turned left.

"Wait here," he instructed as they stopped near the doors. "I will check that Grand Duchess Ysabel is ready for you."

As the commander disappeared inside, Astrea tried to push her magic out farther than she already had it. There was no way she'd be able to cover the entire palace, but Astrea wasn't sure she trusted that the void mages weren't already here, waiting. Her body ached with the effort, and she grabbed Jin's arm to steady herself. His muscles flexed under her hand.

"What is it?" he asked, voice low. Around them, their friends all shifted their attention to Astrea, a mix of anxiety and curiosity filling the immediate space.

She dropped her hand and pulled her magic back toward herself. "Just trying to feel things out. Pushed it too far."

Jin frowned. "Anything?"

Astrea shook her head.

Eliana had just opened her mouth to say something when the throne room doors opened again. Commander Lucian approached the group, his midnight blue eyes hard. In the light of the palace rather than the obscured moonlight, his pale skin looked warm and rosy.

"Her Highness is ready to see you," he said.

This was it. They were really in Talmaris, and they were really about to meet Grand Duchess Ysabel. If this didn't work out, Astrea didn't know what they'd do or where they'd go. Would she believe their stories of void magic? Would she turn Eliana away at whispers of civil war and rebellion?

The doors opened from the inside, and Astrea followed her friends into the Novarian throne room. The ceiling reached up three stories, another glass dome welcoming the cloudy night sky. The smooth gray-and-white marble floors contrasted against a dark blue rug running up the center of the room, right to the dais where a woman perched on a marble throne.

As they approached, the carpet muffled their footsteps. The woman—Grand Duchess Ysabel, Astrea assumed—stood. A silver crown was nestled among the dark hair swept on top of her head, and her black gown was a sharp contrast to her cool white skin.

"Princess Eliana Auris, Prince Varojin Auris," she said, voice light but stern. "Welcome to Novaria."

"Grand Duchess Ysabel," Eliana said, pausing at the foot of the dais and lowering her head. "Thank you for welcoming us. On a normal visit, I would exchange more pleasantries, but as I mentioned on the radio, we have urgent matters to discuss with you."

Six palace guards had spread out around the dais, hands clasped behind their backs. Lucian climbed the stairs to the platform, and he stood behind his grand duchess. It was exactly how Astrea imagined it would be if Eliana were empress; Nicos would, undoubtedly, still be stuck to her like glue.

"Urgent matters." The grand duchess smoothed a hand over the bodice of her gown. Closer now, Astrea could see strands of silver peppering the grand duchess's hair, and fine lines had formed around her purple eyes. "I should assume so, considering two of Emperor Auris's children have shown up in my capital with such a claim." Her gaze drifted over the group to where Jin still stood in the back with Astrea. "What could drive two of his heirs to arrive at a foreign palace unannounced?"

"We are here to warn of a threat that will impact every country on this continent," Eliana replied, voice and emotions steady. "I do not take fleeing Helosia lightly, Your Highness, and I understand the position this puts you in."

"Fleeing?" The grand duchess regarded Eliana for a moment. Her lips pursed. "If you have truly fled Helosia, then I am taking a great risk by allowing you to be in my city, let alone my palace. What could push you to flee?"

Eliana pushed her shoulders back. "Our father has discovered void magic and appears to have some kind of plan to harness it for his own gain."

Astrea's heart jumped to her throat. Eliana was wasting no time.

"Void magic?" the grand duchess asked. "What proof do you have of such a thing?"

As the grand duchess spoke the last words, something in the air around her changed. It was barely there, but a hint of curiosity—of knowing—brushed Astrea's skin, delicate like butterfly wings.

"We can name two void mages in Kalama," Eliana said. "Lord Victor Nazarov, who is in our father's custody, and our father's guard, a man named Caliban."

"Names are hardly proof, Princess Eliana."

"My brother spoke to several witnesses himself. Varojin and our friends were attacked by a void mage at the palace in the middle of the day."

"When we met in the clearing, Your Imperial Highnesses, you mentioned something about searching for a murderer here in Talmaris?" Commander Lucian cut in.

"And that," Jin said. "Your Highness, not only were we attacked at our father's palace, but Kalamian civilians have died at the hands of a void mage. We've seen it for ourselves. Shadows seem to cling to their bodies, almost like ink, even beyond death. It's disturbing."

That hint of knowing passed over Astrea's skin again. She brushed Jin's hand, and though he didn't look down at her, he returned the gesture. How could she tell her friends without the Novarians knowing what she'd picked up on?

"I have not yet heard about this palace attack," Ysabel said, "but I'm familiar with the murders. We've discovered a series of similar crimes right here in Talmaris."

Lavender surprise exploded around everyone but Jin. That was it. That was what Ysabel knew. Void mages were already in Talmaris, and whatever they were up to, it was connected to what had been happening in Kalama.

Astrea swallowed hard. It wasn't a total shock; that was why they'd come to the city in the first place. Lord Mattina's notebook—the one they'd found in Sezia—and his letter pointed them here, and he was connected to the void mages. But similar murders?

"You have?" Eliana asked.

"We have," Ysabel said. "Though we did not connect them back to . . . void magic, if such a thing exists."

"Did you connect the crimes to anything?" Jin asked.

Ysabel hesitated, but Lucian said, "No, we haven't been able to solve them, Your Imperial Highnesses. Every victim we've found has died from the same thing. A stab wound to the heart, and they seem to all be covered in strange . . . shadows."

Astrea's lungs tightened, memories of that poor woman behind the Kalamian history museum poking at the back of her mind.

"That's exactly what we've seen. That is void magic," Jin said. "We came to you because our investigation pointed to Talmaris. We'd like to continue investigating, and it sounds like we can help each other."

"Void mages," Ysabel mused. All hints of emotion were gone from her now, locked behind her own wall. "What would they be doing here in Talmaris?"

"Our father was searching for an artifact, a book. For the autumn summit with Novaria, actually," Jin said. When Ysabel's eyebrows furrowed, Jin explained the gala and exhibit he and Astrea had been tasked with putting together. "That book is somehow connected to the void."

"And you believe the void mages here are searching for this artifact?"

"I don't know why they're here, Your Highness," he said. "But doesn't that seem like too much of a coincidence?"

Ysabel pursed her lips, then nodded. "Indeed."

Silence stretched on in the throne room as Ysabel looked first at Commander Lucian, then back at their group. Her narrow eyebrows drew together. "What else do you know about this void magic?" she asked. "How can I best prepare my mages to handle it should it come to my palace?"

"What we've seen looks like black fire," Jin said. "We've also seen one of the void mages, Victor Nazarov, teleport within a small radius, and one . . . ."

"One what, Prince Varojin?"

He hesitated, but Astrea spoke first. "And one was able to negate my light, Your Highness. I'm a Lightbringer."

"A Lightbringer?" Ysabel asked Astrea. "You're a Lightbringer?"

"I am, Your Highness." Astrea hadn't planned on hiding that part of her magic from the grand duchess, but it felt strange to admit it so freely while standing in this throne room. She could never have said those words out loud in Kalama. "These void mages also feel hollow to my magic, like they have no emotion whatsoever."

"I thought Aelius was conscripting—"

"We've determined that not only does our father have at least one void mage under his command, but it seems like the others may belong to a different faction," Jin cut in.

Ysabel leaned back in her throne. "Who else knows about this?"

"Our brother Kaius," Eliana said. "We aren't sure if Prince Apelo is aware of any of this, nor am I sure what the council knows. I would assume the council knows some version of these events now. It would be hard for my father to hide this from them after the attack at the palace."

Ysabel steepled her fingers in front of her mouth. "My Stargazer foresaw the arrival of a foreign airship at my palace on a cloudy night. I cannot help but think this is what she saw."

Astrea glanced up at the glass dome above them. The clouds hadn't parted.

"As much as offering your group sanctuary in my city may be a risk to our tenuous relationship with Helosia, I believe our best option is working together," Ysabel continued. "You've already discovered far more than we have been able to in several months."

Just like that, Ysabel was offering to work with them? Astrea tried to school her features into that calm mask both Jin and Eliana seemed to slip into with ease.

"We have more details we can share," Eliana said. "Our father is looking for the same information, so if we can figure it out together, we can stop him."

"Stop him?" Ysabel asked.

"We certainly can't let him continue," Eliana said. "Everyone here knows that whatever power he's after won't be good for the rest of the continent."

"And what does stopping him look like?"

Eliana pushed her shoulders back. "I intend to dethrone him."

"A Helosian civil war." Ysabel stood, a hint of a smile pulling at her thin lips. Behind her, Lucian shifted. "While I want to solve this . . . problem . . . in my city, the most I can offer right now is merely sanctuary and shared information. Supporting your claim to the Helosian throne will have to be an . . . ongoing conversation."

"If you can see the kind of threat my father poses to Novaria, and if you've seen evidence of void magic for yourself, why not support my claim now?" Eliana asked, rusty annoyance dancing around her.

"It's a complex situation. There are . . . dynamics to consider. Optics."

"And what would those be?" Eliana asked. "The autumn summit in Kalama? Surely you wouldn't still consider attending."

"This may be a conversation best left for a smaller audience," Ysabel said.

"Whatever you want to say to us, you can say to our friends. We don't hide things from them."

Ysabel nodded at Lucian. He passed some silent command to the guards on the dais, and they disappeared through a door near the back of the room. It was just Astrea, her friends, Lucian, and the grand duchess now. Astrea's stomach tightened. What did Ysabel have to tell them?

The grand duchess sighed. "Having the heir to two thrones involved makes this complicated."

"The heir to two thrones?" Eliana echoed. "My mother was from a Helosian noble family, not another royal house."

"I don't mean you, Eliana." Ysabel barely moved a muscle as her gaze fell to Jin. "I was talking about your brother."

"Me?" Jin asked.

"You are the only Auris sibling of different parentage, are you not?"

He shifted. "So? That's no secret."

"Caliste didn't tell you?" Ysabel's tone was cool, but her confusion prickled Astrea's limbs.

"Tell me what?"

"Your mother was my cousin."

"What?" he asked, voice hoarse.

"Your mother, Caliste Seviya, was my cousin."

Icy blue shock and steel pain exploded from Jin. It was almost like Astrea could see his wall now, colorful emotion bursting through the cracks ray by ray. Emotion crashed into her from every direction around the throne room—Ysabel, Lucian, her friends—but Astrea couldn't take her eyes off Jin.

Your mother was my cousin. The words replayed in Astrea's head as she watched Jin, his jaw tightening and relaxing several times before he finally focused on the grand duchess. Astrea swallowed.

Jin didn't know his mother was from a royal line? Did Emperor Aelius know? Was *that* why Ysabel was so willing to work with them after a single conversation?

The same icy blue shock and gray confusion danced around Eliana.

"Caliste was my first cousin," Ysabel said. "Our mothers were sisters, daughters of Grand Duke Ero. Caliste's paternal side was . . . technically nobility, but her royal blood came from her mother."

Jin sucked in a breath. "So that makes me . . ."

"A prince of Helosia, yes, but you're also a prince of Novaria. You are one of the last descendants of our royal house."

Jin's attention shot to Astrea, the first time he'd looked her way in several minutes. "Is she lying?"

"I . . ."

"Is she lying?" His voice was desperate, pleading.

"Lightbringers cannot distinguish truth from lie, Your Imperial Highness," Lucian said from his spot on the dais.

"I didn't ask you, Commander," he snapped, attention glued to Astrea. "Is she lying?"

"I can't tell, Jin," Astrea whispered. She could no longer sense anything from Ysabel, but it wouldn't have mattered if she could. There was no magic to tell a truth from a lie, not really. The best Astrea could do was guess based on whatever emotions people put out into the world. "I'm sorry."

"Our father is not exactly forthcoming with information," Eliana said slowly. Gray confusion and crimson rage pulsed around her in sharp, quick spikes. "I don't believe anyone in Kalama was aware of Caliste's . . . connections. Our father certainly never mentioned it."

How is that possible? Astrea wondered. For a Novarian noblewoman—a princess, technically—to go unnoticed by Aelius or anyone at the Helosian court was nearly unimaginable.

"Just as you have more information to give me about void magic, I have proof of our familial connection," Ysabel offered. "Your grandfather, Lord Tanel Seviya, was exiled from court before your mother's—"

Jin's chest heaved. "I need time to think."

Ysabel frowned, confusion leaking from her again in a slow, steady drip. "Varojin," she said, "I apologize if I've upset you. She asked me to keep it a secret, but I always assumed your mother had at least told *you.*"

The torrent of emotions around Jin, so many colors Astrea could no longer separate them, barely calmed as he sucked in a breath. "I'd like to talk to you about it more . . . another day. I just need to think."

The grand duchess nodded, then focused on Eliana as she said, "I hope this does not change your desire to work together."

Eliana shook her head. "It does not, but you were right, Your Highness. It complicates things."

"Commander Lucian will escort you to the guest house at the back of the palace compound. You can stay there for the time being. Lucian"—Ysabel turned back to her guard—"provide them with anything they need. I will speak with you all again tomorrow."

Astrea couldn't focus on anything besides Jin's chaotic emotions as they walked back through the quiet palace. The air around him crackled with energy. Lavender surprise, blue sadness, crimson rage, and more mingled together like paints on a canvas. When one emotion receded, another spiked, round and around, until it was too much for Astrea to take in anymore. She sucked in a shuddering breath and forced herself to look away.

Astrea almost reached for his hand, but she resisted. Whatever Jin was feeling, he needed time to sort through it all.

Chapter 4

By the time they exited the palace and started through the gardens, Astrea wanted to close her eyes and put distance between herself and her friends. Cressida, Adi, Nicos, and Eliana were barely in better shape than Jin, their emotions flickering brightly in the darkness. Astrea's skin ached from the intensity of it all.

"We will store your airship in a hangar," Lucian said as they started down a path lined with ornate gas lamps. "My people should already be bringing your luggage to the guest house. You'll have everything you need tonight, including a security team stationed outside."

"Thank you, Commander," Nicos said. "I'd like to talk with you more about security in the morning."

In front of them, at the edge of the half-circle driveway, a symmetrical three-story building made of cream stone rose into the darkness. It reminded Astrea of the Nikaphoroses' vacation home in Sezia, only this was larger. Behind them was Ysabel's palace, farther away than Astrea had anticipated it would be.

"Here we are," Lucian said. One of the front double doors opened, and a Novarian guard slipped outside, murmuring something about their luggage. "Do you need anything else this evening, Your Imperial Highnesses?"

"I think we're alright, Commander," Eliana said. "Thank you."

"Well, if you do, there's a phone in the foyer that connects directly to the housekeeper. Just call, and she'll pass your request on to the right people. You can also just tell one of the guards." He surveyed their group before giving a small nod. "I'll come by in the morning. We have much to discuss about these void mages. Goodnight."

As Lucian started back toward the palace, Jin brushed past their group and the guards now taking up their posts near the front doors. He pushed inside, disappearing into the bright hallway beyond.

"Should we go after him?" Eliana asked as she stared at the doors. Uncertainty scraped Astrea's arms, rough and unpleasant. "I wasn't expecting that."

"None of us were," Nicos said.

As much as it hurt to see Jin in so much turmoil, Astrea didn't think he needed them breathing down his neck. If she were that upset, she'd want a few moments to think first.

"Let's just go inside and get settled," Eliana said. "We'll figure it out in the morning."

The inside of the guest house was decorated as grandly as the palace back in Kalama, its sleek wood floors, heavy carpets, and gold-framed art the first things to catch Astrea's eye. The front hall opened into a larger foyer, the ceiling extending up to the height of the second floor. A wide staircase ascended to the next level, its thick wood railings carved with intricate designs.

"You good?" Cressida whispered as they both followed Eliana and Nicos toward an open door on the right side of the foyer.

Astrea shook her head. "That was . . ."

"Intense?"

"That's an understatement," Adi said from behind them both.

Prince Varojin Auris of Helosia and Novaria. Jin, not just descended from one royal house but two. Jin, who despised his father and court politics. It seemed almost more like a cruel joke than anything, but Ysabel had dismissed her guards. She'd claimed to have proof. Why lie?

This was not what they needed. They already had too much to sort through.

The parlor they entered, though sizable, wasn't quite as large as the ones back in the Kalamian palace. The muted color scheme—blues, grays, and dark, glossy wood—matched Ysabel's palace. A fireplace took up the middle of one wall, serving as a centerpiece for the adjacent sitting area. A sofa faced the door, and four plush armchairs made up the rest of the space. Stacked neatly on the sofa were their suitcases and bags.

"You think we're safe here?" Cressida asked as she walked the perimeter of the room. When she reached the dove gray drapes covering the windows on the far wall, she peeked outside, then shook her head.

"Ysabel won't risk anything happening to us," Eliana said.

Grand Duchess Ysabel certainly wouldn't risk anything happening to one of the last descendants of her own royal family, Astrea was sure of that.

"Let's just get some rest," Adi suggested. Though he'd been quiet for the entire meeting with Ysabel, orange anxiety now coated his entire body. "I think we can all use it."

Astrea approached the stack of luggage, then adjusted her satchel. She slung Jin's military knapsack over one shoulder, then grabbed his second pack and slung it over the other. With that settled, she took both her and Jin's suitcases.

"Want some help?" Adi asked. "I can bring them up to him."

"That's alright," Astrea said. "I'll go check on him."

"You're sure?"

"I'm sure."

Luggage in hand, Astrea followed the others out of the foyer and up the stairs. The second floor was really just a long, wide hallway. Several doors lined each side, and paintings and tapestries hung in the blank spaces on the walls. A long blue rug stretching the length of the corridor led to a staircase ascending to the third floor.

Just one door on the second floor was closed, and the energy coming from behind it nearly knocked Astrea off her feet. Nicos and Eliana walked past it to one of the doors at the far end of the hall. Cressida went into the one across from them, and she nodded at Astrea before disappearing inside. Adi, however, lingered across the hallway from Jin's closed door.

Those peculiar, mismatched eyes of his flicked from Astrea to the door and back again before he said, "I'm here if either of you need me."

Astrea forced herself to smile. "Thanks, Adi. I'll let him know."

Only when Adi, too, disappeared into a bedroom, did Astrea turn back toward the closed door. She steeled herself, then knocked. "Jin?" she called. "May I come in?"

Silence.

But a few moments later, the door opened. Midnight blue grief and steel pain wavered around Jin in the darkness, crimson rage occasionally snapping into the air. The emotions pressed in against Astrea, but they weren't disorienting like they had been on the walk to the house.

"You really can't distinguish truth from lie?" he asked.

"I wish I could, but no."

Jin took both suitcases from Astrea, then walked back into the room. Taking that as an invitation, Astrea followed him and shut the door behind her. The room, decorated in shades of blue and white, was nearly double the size of Astrea's old bedroom in Kalama. To her left was a fireplace, small sitting area, and wardrobe. On the wall to her right was a dark wood credenza filled with bottles of what she guessed was alcohol, a writing desk, and another door. A wide canopy bed sat against the middle of the far wall. Windows flanked both sides of the bed, and the thick drapes pulled closed over them fluttered occasionally. Had Jin opened the windows?

After setting their luggage down next to the wardrobe, Jin dropped onto the edge of the bed. "I can't fucking believe it, Az."

Astrea dropped the knapsacks and her satchel down, then sat next to him on the soft mattress. "I know." She folded her hands in her lap. Astrea wanted to reach out to touch him so badly, to let him know he wasn't alone, but it felt like an intrusion with so much color still dancing around him. When she was that upset, she didn't always appreciate someone else's touch, even if well-intentioned. "I know how much it hurts."

Saros wasn't Astrea's parent, but in the last month, she had learned he was hiding so much from her. And it hurt knowing that he was doing it because he thought it would protect her when in the end, it now only seemed to be making things more confusing.

"Yes," Jin said after a moment. "I suppose you do. I can't believe my father kept this from me."

"Maybe he didn't know either," Astrea offered. Disbelief pressed into her bones.

"How could he not know my mother was . . ." He sighed and closed his eyes. Jin sighed again, a harsh, heavy sound as rage flared around him. "I just can't believe—" His back heaved as he blew out another breath.

Disgust and confusion rolled off him, the two shades of gray twining as blue grief spiked again. Astrea had never seen so much emotion from him, from anyone that she could remember. Astrea unclasped her hands and reached out, brushing Jin's forearm.

"Why wouldn't she tell me that? Why not at least tell me before she died?"

Astrea's heart ached, but she forced her eyes to stay open as his emotions threatened to bury her again. "I don't know," she whispered. "I'm sorry, Jin. I don't know."

Just like how Astrea had no idea why Saros had kept things from her.

"Why did she leave me with him?" Jin whispered.

It was a question Astrea had asked about her own family, not because she hated Saros but because she missed her mother so deeply sometimes. That pain had lessened over the years, but it was still there. Why, indeed, had they left? Astrea knew her mother had gotten sick, but what about Caliste?

"I don't think she would have if she'd had a choice," Astrea said past the lump in her throat.

Jin closed his eyes, his body still as he breathed. He lay down. "The wind," he murmured. "My heartbeat. Footsteps."

"What?" Astrea asked. Then she realized he was doing the same exercise he'd had her do that night in the palace, after she woke up with a nightmare. Naming things he could see, smell, and hear to calm himself. She sat frozen in place.

"Laundry soap. Astrea's shampoo. Lavender. The window. The bedroom door." He paused, then gazed up at her. "Silver eyes."

As Jin blew out a final breath, the air around him calmed, though his iron grip on his wall hadn't returned. Grief and anger still scraped against Astrea's skin, but it was less. It was manageable.

"Sorry," he muttered.

"Why are you apologizing?"

"I can't lose control," Jin said. "I have to see the mission through."

She swallowed. Wasn't that what he'd told her in Kalama, that she had to stay focused to complete the mission? Was that even the right mindset if all it was doing for him was burying his old wounds?

"You can't keep it all inside, Jin."

Jin sat up and ran a hand through his chestnut curls. "No, but losing control in my . . . my *cousin's* throne room doesn't seem ideal, either. I need to go downstairs and help."

"There's nothing to help with. Everyone else went to bed," Astrea said gently. "You need to rest."

"Soldiers don't rest."

"You're not on a battlefield right now."

"I might as well be. We all are."

"Do you remember what you said to me in Sezia?" Astrea asked. "I wanted to go find Mattina right away, but you said we needed to be rested when we went."

"That was different."

"How was that different?"

"It just was."

Astrea glared at him. "Was it because you weren't the only one affected?"

Jin had always been hard on himself, even when they were just kids. A few years after she moved to Kalama, Astrea had seen him and Eliana training with their mage teacher. Jin had insisted he was fine to keep training even when he was obviously exhausted. It was only when Eliana admitted to her own fatigue that he'd insisted the lesson end.

"No."

"You're a terrible liar, Jin."

A fleeting wisp of amusement tickled the end of her nose, but Jin simply flopped back against the pillows. "Skies, I forgot how annoying you are when you want something."

"When it's for your own good," she muttered, then yelped. Strong arms pulled her down, her cheek meeting Jin's hard chest. "What are you doing?"

"I can be annoying when I want something, too," he said. "Stay with me, or I'm going downstairs to find something to do."

"You're holding me hostage?"

"If I have to." Jin relaxed his hold on her, then shifted so they were lying face to face. "Thank you for coming to check on me."

Astrea didn't know what to say. Whatever words she could think of sounded so contrived, so she settled on saying nothing at all. Instead, she reached for his hand. Jin smiled weakly at her as he twined their fingers together. She didn't know how long they lay like that in the dark, but the energy surrounding Jin slowed from an intense boil to a slow, steady drip. Manageable, not just for herself but for him, too.

"Az?" Jin whispered.

"Yeah?"

"Will you stay here tonight? I can't pretend I don't want you in my bed."

She swallowed, her belly curling with a mix of flattery and uncertainty. They'd shared a bed for the last few nights, but . . . "Is that even allowed here?"

"Is what allowed?" Jin asked, his eyebrows drawing together.

"You know. Sharing a bed."

"I'm sure plenty of people share beds in Talmaris."

Astrea huffed. She didn't want to dredge up his feelings again. Still, she said, "Those people aren't . . . royalty."

"You think Ysabel will care how I spend my nights and who I spend them with?" Jin asked after a moment. "I don't really give a shit what she thinks. As I said, I'm too tired to pretend. Do you want to stay? I won't be offended if you say no."

Astrea was too tired to pretend, too. "I want to stay. I just also don't want to break any rules."

"Of course you don't," he said with a soft chuckle. Amusement danced over Astrea's skin. "Fuck whatever strange rules Ysabel might have, right?"

"You're never going to get me to say that," Astrea whispered.

Jin laughed, the sound tired but genuine, before rolling onto his back with a groan. "Alright. Are we unpacking tonight or in the morning?"

"Morning. I can feel how tired you are."

"Alright." Jin yawned, then pushed himself out of bed and turned on the bedside lamp.

They moved around in the low light, grabbing whatever they needed for the night. As Jin crossed the room to another door—the bathroom—Astrea wiggled out of her clothes and tossed them on one of the chairs near the fireplace. She slid on her nightgown, the cool, silky fabric stopping halfway down her thick thighs. Jin took longer than expected in the bathroom, but the remaining rage, regret, and pain slipping past his wall had finally quieted all the way. When he was done, Astrea made quick work of cleaning herself up for the night. Jin was already in bed, and he lifted the blankets for her as she climbed in.

The lamp switched off. Jin rolled over, draping one arm over her side as he settled in next to her.

"Jin?" Astrea whispered.

"Hm?"

"Do you really think we're safe here?"

"Safe enough."

As Jin's breathing slowed, Astrea leaned back into him. She closed her eyes, willing herself to sleep. They were both going to need at least a few hours of rest before they started their hunt for the book again and tried to unravel whatever web they were stuck in.

CHAPTER 5

Astrea awoke to a hint of morning twilight filtering through the windows. The curtains fluttered, bringing cool air into the room. At least they were alive, safe behind Ysabel's palace gates. The guest house was still, and as Astrea stretched her magic out, she only sensed one other person awake in the house.

Jin rolled onto his side. The blankets were barely pulled up to his waist, revealing the wide, muscular expanse of his back.

A jagged array of fine white lines skittered down the left side of Jin's back, the branches dipping below the blankets. She'd first seen them in Sezia, and the scars were hard to ignore, as was the round, puckered mark near his left shoulder. But Astrea's sleepy eyes kept drifting to the one on the right side of his back. She reached out, tracing the white line on Jin's shoulder. It was smooth like the rest of his skin, though it wasn't quite a straight line like she'd first thought. The right side of the scar twisted up toward the top of his back. Most healers could fix wounds without leaving a scar if they got to the injury early enough. What had happened that all of this remained on his body?

Pulling her hand away, Astrea rolled over until her back was to his. Maybe she could go back to sleep for another hour. Her traitorous mind wouldn't allow that, though. It was waking up and running through a dozen questions. When would Ysabel call on them today? What evidence did she have to add to their pile of clues? Was this actually going to get them somewhere, or were they just wasting time? Astrea burrowed into the pillows.

Heat enveloped Astrea as Jin slung an arm over her waist. "Go back to sleep," he rasped in her ear.

"I can't."

"Why not?"

Once she was awake in the morning, she was awake. It was almost impossible for her to go back to sleep.

"I just can't."

He sighed as he snuggled closer to her, warm satisfaction pressing into Astrea's chest. Other than the occasional hint of curiosity or confusion coming from across the hall, it was the only thing Astrea could feel. No anger. No rage. No pain.

"Alright," Jin said. "No going back to sleep. Now what?"

"We could unpack."

Jin let out something between a laugh and a groan as his hold on her tightened. "Skies, do you never just laze around in bed?"

"No, though I suppose I can't be surprised you still do," she quipped. "Used to take forever to get you out of the palace some days, especially if we had lessons."

"That was simply because I didn't like school, not because I had a soft, warm woman in my bed." Astrea's entire face burned, but Jin simply said, "Alright, let's get up. I'm sure Commander Lucian's going to be here soon. He doesn't strike me as the type to let things wait."

Astrea slipped out of bed first, regretting it as soon as the cool morning air wafting through the windows met her bare skin. Maybe Jin was right about lazing around in bed. Still, she scurried to the bathroom.

One thing was for sure: The grand duchess's guest house was nothing if not luxurious. The bathroom was just as grand as what Eliana had back at the Kalamian palace—black and white hexagon tiles on the floor, a long marble vanity with wood cabinets underneath, an ornate mirror, a large shower, and a separate wide bathtub. Even the toilet, in a separate water closet, was ornate, the porcelain decorated with some kind of floral pattern.

Why go through all the trouble? Astrea wondered. She supposed this was where many important people had slept before them, but it still seemed unnecessary to do so much in this one space.

After brushing her teeth and taking care of her immediate needs, she returned to the bedroom. Jin had tugged on his trousers from the day before, though he hadn't put a shirt back on. He'd made the bed, too, with such precision Astrea couldn't help but be impressed. Even their bags were lined up, ready to be unpacked. His wall had returned, steady and unyielding in the new day.

Jin pulled a stack of wooden hangers from the wardrobe, and as he turned around, his gaze flicked up and down Astrea's body just once. She resisted the urge to tug at the hem of her nightgown. Instead, she joined him near the bed and opened her suitcase. Taking a hanger, she slid her lavender dress onto it and brought it to the wardrobe. They continued on like that in silence until the only things left in their bags were bundles of undergarments.

Would this be what life could look like for them if they weren't about to embark on this quest? Some normal, domestic scene? That had been them once, as much as it could be for two teenagers, for a Stargazer's niece and a bastard prince.

Astrea looked down at the green linen dress she'd set to the side. Hopefully Ysabel didn't take offense by her casual wardrobe. Eliana would be the only one with anything remotely court appropriate.

"Have you ever considered why my father chose you for his stupid project?" Jin asked.

"I asked myself why," Astrea said as she fingered the material of her nightgown. "Cressida said it was because I was smart and qualified, but . . . Something about it just felt off."

"I agree," Jin said. "Not because you aren't both of those things—you very much are—but he was just using you to manipulate me." When Astrea's eyebrows furrowed, Jin continued, "You were worried about any missteps reflecting poorly on you or Raela, but he said it right in front of us. 'You don't want your insolence to reflect poorly on Miss Sovna.' He knew I would do what he asked because you were involved."

Astrea blew out a harsh breath. She'd forgotten that conversation, but as Jin said it, she could practically hear the emperor saying it in her mind. Of course. Of course that was why Emperor Aelius had assigned her to that project. That was probably also why he'd asked Cressida to look at the meteorite, or at least part of the reason. Because they were deeply connected to his children, and he could pull the puppeteer strings if and when he needed to.

That was what Emperor Aelius always did. He pushed people, manipulated the rules, and did whatever he must to get what he wanted. Eliana had explained that to Astrea a dozen times before.

"He's awful," Astrea muttered.

Jin finally looked at her, his golden eyes burning. "There's a lot I never told you about him, Az."

She swallowed hard. "Like what?"

"It was about a week before my eighteenth birthday," Jin said. "I'd finally been invited to an imperial council meeting. Kaius and I both were. My father wanted us to listen, to behave. I asked a question when I shouldn't have, challenged some plan they'd come up with. When the meeting was over and nothing happened, I thought he may have forgiven me for speaking out of turn. I thought that maybe I got one free pass.

But later that night, well." Jin breathed a laugh, then turned so his back was to her. There they were again, those scars. "I didn't get a free pass."

"He did this to you?" Astrea whispered.

"The ones that look like lightning, yes. He did, and he wouldn't let me see the palace healer after. And then for my birthday a week later, he broke the news that he was sending me away."

Astrea knew Emperor Aelius was not a kind man, though he often pretended like he was. She'd seen enough of his hot and cold behavior over the years, either at a distance or, more recently, up close and personal. But turning his Sparkcaster magic on his own son *and* denying him a healer? That was a different level of cruel.

Astrea's fingers trailed down his back, following the nearly smooth skin. There were lots of times when they were younger when Astrea had felt ghost pain from Jin, and on the few occasions she'd found an excuse to ask, he'd always said it was from mage training. But had it been? Or had some of that been because of his father?

"That is who my mother left me with," Jin said, sighing as he faced her again. Pain ghosted over her body, just a whisper as it managed to get past his wall. "She died in a boating accident when I was ten, but even before that . . . she left the palace when I was so young. Maybe three or four. She left me there with him."

That had all happened long before Astrea's time in Kalama. Jin had barely mentioned Caliste when they were younger; he'd only told Astrea that his mother had died.

"It wasn't the first time my father did something like that, but it was the worst," Jin said. "And I just can't help but wonder if things would have been different if she hadn't left me with him. If she had told me about Ysabel and this place."

Astrea pulled Jin toward her, wrapping her arms around his neck as she hugged him tight. "I'm sorry," she said. His arms slipped around her waist, holding her close. "I wish I'd known. Sometimes I could feel—"

"I didn't want you to know," he said. "Even if you'd asked me, I wouldn't have told you."

"Still." As she tried to pull away, Jin's grip on her waist tightened. "Are you going to let me go?" she whispered.

"Never." Astrea's heart fluttered. But after another moment, Jin pressed a kiss to the top of her head and took just half a step back. "I'm going to get cleaned up."

As he started to squeeze past her, Astrea grabbed Jin's hand. Faint lavender surprise flickered around him as he stopped. "We'll figure it out," Astrea said. "Together."

"Together," he agreed. "We'll figure all of it out together."

Sleep, a hot shower, and fresh coffee could do wonders for a person. Though Astrea still didn't know how they were going to fix any of the problems staring them in the face, she felt almost like a real person again.

"Thank you for agreeing to meet with us so early in the day," Ysabel said, her voice smooth and light.

Meeting with the Novarian grand duchess was not unexpected. What *was* unexpected was the fact that Ysabel had come all the way to the guest house for the meeting. The dining room had a table that could seat ten, perfect for their group. Ysabel sat at the head, a selection of pastries, coffee, and tea spread out before them. Morning sunlight filtered in through the open windows, and the scene was almost cheerful.

Eliana sat at the end directly opposite Ysabel, the rest of their friends flanking either side of the table. Astrea was already on her second cup of coffee, being careful not to spill it on the stack of books and folders she had in front of her. Before they'd left Kalama, Jin had grabbed the old police reports and notes he had about the murders from his apartment, including the map where he'd mark the locations of everything. He'd only given her the documents that morning, but she was just glad he'd had the foresight to bring them. Even stacked up with the *Myth and Magic* book, Mattina's journal, and the letters, it seemed like an impossibly small amount of evidence.

"I thought it best for us to get started as soon as possible," the grand duchess continued, "and meet away from prying eyes and ears. I will try to keep the courtiers and ambassadors away from my palace, but doing so for too long will raise suspicions."

"You think we need to hide?" Eliana asked as she set her coffee cup on a saucer painted with delicate pink flowers.

"I think we need to be discreet," Ysabel corrected. She looked so different in the soft morning light of the guest house, almost younger. "I would actually like you and Varojin to speak with my council after this meeting. They're aware of your arrival and have questions."

"Of course," Eliana said. "We'll answer as much as we can."

Unlike Emperor Aelius, Grand Duchess Ysabel actually needed the approval of the majority of her council to take certain action. What those actions were, Astrea wasn't sure. The politics of it all hurt her head. Hopefully it wouldn't impact their ability to investigate.

Jin, seated to Astrea's left, was surprisingly relaxed. His emotions were locked up behind that wall of his, but he seemed to be taking Ysabel's news and presence better than Astrea had expected.

"Let's move on to why we're really here this morning," Ysabel said. "Lucian?"

The commander circled the table as he handed folders to each of them. Astrea flipped hers open. *Police reports,* she realized as she skimmed the stack of papers inside. The words "shadows" and "stab wound" jumped out at her immediately.

"As the grand duchess said last night," Lucian began as he returned to his seat, "a series of murders in Talmaris appear to be connected to the ones in Kalama. In the last six months, we've found six victims with the same types of wounds and strange marks on their bodies. We've not been able to make a connection between the victims, so I cannot tell you why they were targeted."

Astrea and Jin hadn't really figured out why the people in Kalama were murdered. The museum employee made some sense; she was connected to Mattina. Mattina made sense, too, since he'd apparently had what the murderer wanted. But what about that man in the southern part of the city? The witness she and Jin had interviewed had said the victim was originally from Novaria. And what about the woman found on the border of Nobleman's Hill and the Market District? They hadn't been Lightbringers like Astrea. Had they somehow known something about void magic? Or just been caught in the wrong place at the wrong time?

"I was only able to connect three murders in Kalama to the void mages," Jin said as he reached for the files tucked under Astrea's books. She slid them toward him, and Jin stood and brought the files to Ysabel. "There were also the murders in Sezia that occurred the same way. We didn't have time to look into the backgrounds of the first few victims."

"So many murders in just three cities," Ysabel mused as she flipped open Jin's files. "I do not like this."

"The last one in Sezia wasn't just a single murder," Jin said slowly as he returned to his seat next to Astrea. "There were at least a dozen victims in one house."

The grand duchess heaved a sigh as she shut the folders again. "Truly?" Jin nodded. "Well. You said evidence you found in Sezia pointed you to Talmaris. What was that evidence?"

Astrea reached for Mattina's journal and the letter tucked inside. She passed them to Jin, who again started to stand, but Lucian waved him off.

"I'll take them, Your Highness," the commander said.

Jin's jaw tightened, but he nodded as he passed the items to Lucian. "We found this journal with our lead suspect, the man we thought stole the artifact my father wants. He didn't have the object with him, but if you open to the marked page, you'll see two addresses. The address listed there in Sezia is where we found the other victims. The letter mentions a meeting in Talmaris, and we assumed the address listed there was connected to that meeting."

Lucian opened the journal as he walked it back to the grand duchess, his eyebrows pulling together. He passed the letter to her before flipping through the journal's empty pages. After Ysabel read the letter, she and Lucian switched items.

Astrea's friends were tense, their anxiety grating on her magic as they continued eating their breakfast. Cressida, seated on Astrea's right, pushed a scone in Astrea's direction, but she had no appetite. The thought of food was enough to make her stomach tighten unpleasantly.

"This address is in the Garden District," Lucian said. "Just a few miles from the palace, actually."

One of the murders in Kalama had happened close to Emperor Aelius's palace, too. Could that be a coincidence?

"There was a tattoo we saw on several people, including some of the murder victims and some of the void mages," Jin said when Ysabel remained quiet. "It was also painted on the house where we saw void mages gathering before their deaths. We believe it may be connected to a group called the Paragon."

It hadn't been a huge leap in logic to assume the Paragon was some kind of void mage organization. It was what Nazarov had shouted about in Kalama, and he shared that tattoo with so many connected to the void. What the Paragon wanted, however, was a different question. Nazarov had mentioned balance, but that was it. And who was the "boss" the void mage from Solstice Night had said wanted to talk to Astrea? Certainly someone with the Paragon, right?

"The Paragon?" Ysabel echoed.

"Yes. Do you know that name?"

"It hasn't come up in our investigation," Ysabel said as she finally set Mattina's journal on the table. "Nor has any kind of symbol. What does it look like?"

Astrea passed the drawing of the tattoo to Lucian. His eyebrows furrowed again, as did Ysabel's when he offered the sketch to her.

"We should take this to Mariya, Your Highness," Lucian said.

"Who's Mariya?" Eliana asked as she looked up from the Novarian police reports.

"My Stargazer," Ysabel said. "I will see if she's had any more visions since your arrival. Perhaps she's seen this before."

"Your Highness," Astrea said, and everyone's attention jumped to her. "My uncle is Emperor Aelius's Stargazer." Lavender surprise arced out from the grand duchess, but she said nothing. Just the mention of Saros made Astrea's throat tighten. "He had a vision of the tattoo."

"And he is not with you?" Ysabel asked.

"No, Your Highness."

"Saros stayed behind so we could flee," Eliana said. "He actually held off one of the void mages."

"I see." Ysabel nodded at Lucian. "We most definitely need to show this to Mariya."

Astrea wished that they'd brought the meteorite. Giving it to the grand duchess's Stargazer might've given them more information about it and whatever Emperor Aelius was doing in the Badlands. But Jin had thought they needed to hold some cards close to their chest, and that was one of them.

"Murders, mythology, and history." Ysabel tapped her fingers on the dining table. "It's messier than I'd hoped."

Astrea almost laughed. Had Ysabel thought this would be easy?

"I don't know what to make of it," the grand duchess continued, "but I agree that your father should not have control of void magic. Is there more?"

"Some minor details, but that's the bulk of it," Jin said.

They were only skipping over the meteorite, the fact that the Paragon were hunting Astrea, and the vision she'd had. *Details.*

After taking a sip of coffee, Ysabel set her cup down and nodded. "We can go over details later. We still need to meet with my council. Are you willing to share this information with them?"

"If it would help," Eliana said.

"I believe it will."

"Then we will tell them."

"And I believe you and I need to have a conversation, Varojin," Ysabel said. "Sooner rather than later."

Jin stiffened in his seat, then asked, "Today?"

"Today," Ysabel agreed. "And then you can continue your investigation. But before you do, I'd like to bring my tailors here to sort out a more . . . fitting wardrobe." Her narrow nose wrinkled slightly. "I need you working with Lucian on this, which may mean going outside the palace. Your clothing does not exactly suit Novarian style. None of you will blend in dressed like that."

Astrea glanced down at the green linen dress she wore and frowned. She hated tailors. She'd only been to see them a few times over the years, but very few of them respected her desired look and were always trying to convince her to wear more fitted pieces. Plus, their pins always seemed to poke her. Both were like waking nightmares with the way the world pressed against her senses every day.

"While that's a generous offer," Eliana said, "won't that take too long? I assumed we would want to sort this out as soon as possible."

"What would you suggest? Going to a department store?" Ysabel asked with a chuckle. "Eliana, surely you know that will not be fitting for someone of our status."

"I don't mind," Eliana said. "If it means we can get back to work, I'll wear anything."

The grand duchess was silent for a few moments as she watched Eliana. Then she sighed. "I'll have someone go get you some new things this afternoon. Will that be enough time to put together a list and your measurements?"

Astrea hated the idea of someone shopping for clothes for her. Eliana, Cressida, and Sarsali were the only three people in the world she'd trust to do that; they knew exactly how particular she was about certain things, from fabric to the way seams were sewn. This situation was already awful enough. Uncomfortable clothing might just send her over the edge.

But Astrea kept her mouth shut. Now didn't seem like the time to start making a fuss.

"Yes, it will be," Eliana said.

"And of course, you will have use of my facilities," Ysabel said. "Laundry, kitchen—it'll be provided for you while you're our guests. Do you want staff?"

"No staff," Eliana and Jin said at the same time. When Ysabel's eyebrows furrowed, Jin said, "Aside from security and the basics, we don't need anything else."

"Actually . . ." Adi cut in, the first time he'd said anything all morning. "If it's not too much trouble, Your Highness, is there someplace we may be able to train? I don't want to startle anyone with unsanctioned magic."

"By all means. One of the guards will show you to the lake. Nobody ever goes down there. And if there's nothing else," Ysabel said, "I will have Lucian return shortly to escort Princess Eliana and Prince Varojin to the council chambers."

"We'll be ready," Eliana said.

Once Ysabel and Lucian had left the dining room and the echo of the guest house's front door closing had faded, Eliana pressed her lips into a thin line. "Well," she said, "I suppose it's time to get started. Are you sure you're comfortable being here, Jin?"

"It's not like we have a choice," he said. "This is bigger than my feelings. Let's just do what we need to do and get Ysabel to back you."

"Alright." Eliana nodded, then pushed her chair back before she stood. "I'm going to get ready for the council meeting. I suggest you do the same. And don't forget to make lists, too, for Ysabel's staff."

Nicos followed Eliana out of the room, annoyance flickering around him. Astrea ran a hand over her face. Just one more day, then they could get back to work. They could get back to the mission.

"Adi, while my sister and I are meeting with Ysabel's people, have one of the guards take you to the lake," Jin said. He looked at Astrea, then Cressida. "I'd like you two to go with him and start learning how to fight."

Fight. Astrea was definitely not a fighter. In fact, Saros had prohibited her from fighting for fourteen years.

"Start learning?" Cressida laughed. "I already know how, or did you forget about all those lessons my parents paid for, Jin?"

"Right, the years when you were determined to get drafted into the mage sports leagues," Jin mused. Cressida had long since given up on that path, but she was one of the most talented mages Astrea knew.

"You can help me teach Astrea, then," Adi said. "Two teachers are better than one, right?"

"I'm—" Astrea started, but Jin cut her off.

"You two saw what those void mages could do," Jin said. "We don't know when we're going to run into that kind of magic again. All of us need to practice."

"I know we do." Astrea huffed. "I'm just . . . Me? Fighting?" She couldn't imagine it.

Jin smiled at her. "Anyone can learn with a good teacher and some patience, Az. You'll do great."

Chapter 6

In Astrea's wildest dreams, she never would've imagined learning how to punch someone.

"And you open your hips and shoulders like this," Adi said as he twisted his body with his punch. "It's easy."

One of Ysabel's guards had shown them to a quiet spot in the gardens near a wide, sparkling lake just a short walk from the guest house. A paved path circled the shoreline. Her entire property was littered with sky-high trees, weeping willows, and flowering bushes of all kinds. Peony, lavender, and azalea scented the breeze. To the north of the lake was a towering wall marking the edge of Ysabel's property. To the south and east were the palace and guest house. It was peaceful despite the fact that Adi was trying to teach Astrea how to fight.

Cressida had flopped on the soft grassy spot between two trees, and she'd spent the last five minutes observing.

Astrea plucked at the fabric of her tight black pants, the same ones Cressida had given her to wear on that skies forsaken night in Sezia when they found all those dead void mages.

"Easy for *you*," Astrea said.

"Just try it," Adi insisted. "Copy my stance."

Astrea tried to mimic the way Adi was standing. Feet shoulder width apart, her left foot half a step in front of the right.

"Good," he said. "Hands up, like this."

She brought her hands up next, her left fist blocking the front of her face and the right one near the same cheek.

"And now, light on your feet." Adi bounced back and forth a couple times, and Astrea copied that, too. "See, you're a natural."

Cressida snorted. "You should see her hand-eye coordination; it's not very good."

"Rude," Astrea muttered, but Cressida grinned at her. "And also very true."

"Repetition and practice will help," Adi said. "You really never had a mage teacher?"

"My mother taught me some before she died," Astrea said, her hands falling to her sides. "And I used to practice on my own, especially healing, but the last time I had any kind of formal lesson was when I was ten."

She'd watched Eliana and Jin sometimes when they worked with their mage trainers at the palace as children, and she'd seen Cressida work with her mage trainer at her parents' home for years. Astrea had learned what she could only through observation, and she'd practiced summoning her light by herself in that little closet in the observatory. While healing was natural for her, working with her light had always been difficult. Saros hadn't even tried to teach her more than what she needed to control her magic.

Now, Astrea really regretted not pushing him harder for lessons or for answers. But Saros had always been stubborn and avoidant. Pushing him usually just made things worse.

Adi smacked her hands, and she glared at him. "Part of practice is holding your stance," he said. "Hands up until I tell you to put them down." Astrea brought her hands back up the way he'd shown her. "We'll start with the basics, then we'll try adding your magic. Sound good?"

"Sounds great."

"Is that sarcasm I sense?" he asked, peach amusement bubbling around him.

"I don't think you need to be a Lightbringer to sense sarcasm," Astrea quipped.

He laughed. "Okay, I see how it's going to be."

Adi taught her what he called jabs first. She punched out with her left hand, her torso and hips turning just like he'd shown her. She did it again. Then he showed her crosses, and she punched out with her right fist, again turning her entire body as instructed. They continued on like that until her muscles screamed with the effort.

"You weren't kidding about repetition," she muttered.

"Still up for adding some magic?" Adi asked.

"Sure." Astrea may have been tired, but she needed to learn.

"Of course, you can throw a punch without magic," he said as he took up his stance next to her, "but adding magic makes it hurt that much more. Go ahead and relax while I show you."

Astrea finally dropped her hands from her face, and even Cressida pushed herself off the ground to join them.

"Care to demonstrate with me, Cress?" Adi asked.

"Now you want to make things interesting?" Cressida moved into position in front of Adi. Her movements were so natural, fluid even, as she assumed the stance Astrea had just been practicing.

"Focus on what I'm doing," Adi said, and Astrea nodded. "When you call on your magic, imagine it going out with your punch." The ground rumbled as a chunk of rock shot into the air and floated in front of Adi's fist. "Obviously this will look different for you, but watch how it goes out with my movement."

Adi punched with his right fist. The rock flew toward Cressida. She pulled her hands apart like she was opening a set of double doors. The rock broke in two, the pieces thumping as they hit the ground.

"Just try doing what I did with your light," Adi said.

"That's not how it works."

His thick eyebrows drew together. "What do you mean? I saw you on the airfield back in Kalama, and I fought a Lightbringer once in Corsyca."

"You fought a Lightbringer?" Cressida asked. "I didn't realize they were being sent out on missions."

"Yeah . . . that's new since the war started," Adi said. Heavy regret pressed against Astrea, and he focused on his boots as he said, "I'm sorry to say I had to take him out."

"It's okay," Astrea said. "I know you regret it. War is war."

War may have been war, and Adi surely hadn't had a choice, just like many of the soldiers shipped out by their governments. But Astrea didn't love hearing that Lightbringers were being sent into fights now. She'd always heard of them going in *after* battles, ordered to help the dying and injured.

He gave her a small smile. "So, the lesson?"

Astrea nodded. Right. The lesson. "I don't do it like *that*, the way you want me to."

Green curiosity bubbled around Adi. "Then show me how you do it."

"Cress, can you make me a target or something?" Astrea asked. She could've just used one of the towering oaks or weeping willows, but she didn't want to damage the beautiful gardens if she could avoid it.

Cressida simply nodded. The ground rumbled as a chunk of earth shot into the air. It hovered about a dozen feet away.

Astrea let light build over her right hand. She sucked in a breath, then pushed her light out like she had in Kalama. It shot forward, but it missed Cressida's target by more than a few inches.

Adi pivoted toward Astrea, his arms crossed over his chest. "I have one concern."

"My terrible aim?" she asked. "We warned you."

He laughed. "No, that comes with practice. When you do that, it leaves your front entirely vulnerable to another mage's attacks."

Well, she certainly didn't want that. "How do I avoid that?"

"Get back in your stance." Astrea assumed the position again, and only then did Adi continue. "Punch forward, like this," he said. He brought his right fist forward, rotating so his closed fingers were parallel to the ground. "And when you do, think about your magic. Think about sending it out with the punch."

Blowing out a harsh breath, Astrea rolled her shoulders. She bounced back and forth, just as he'd shown her, then copied his motion. *Send your magic out with the punch.*

She repeated the motion, focusing this time on the energy buzzing under her skin. It reacted, bursting to life around her closed hand. But the magic didn't go *out* with the punch like Adi had suggested.

"Try again," Adi said, cool patience radiating from him. "It's alright."

Astrea tried again, and again, and again, but she still got the same results. Her magic simply seemed to stop, too heavy for her to keep pushing.

"Maybe you're not meant to do it that way," Adi said.

"But you said the other way isn't as good."

"It's not." Adi frowned. "You can always burn people if they get close."

Astrea's shoulders sagged as she finally broke her stance, and she didn't care if Adi scolded her again. "What, I'm supposed to fight close quarters all the time?" That seemed less than ideal.

"Hopefully you won't be fighting at all," Adi replied.

"She needs to be able to do this," Cressida said. "Just in case."

"I know I do." Astrea's teeth ground together. "I'm trying. It's just . . . Why is this so hard for me?"

"It's not easy for every mage," Adi said. "Maybe it was the rush of the fight back in Kalama. Lightbringers are healers, after all. Maybe it's not in your magic's nature to be aggressive."

"You talk about it like it's alive," Cressida said.

Adi shrugged. "Sometimes it feels like it is."

"Alive or not, that doesn't help our situation." Cressida lowered the floating target back to the ground. "We all need to be able to fight when we go home. She's got to find a way."

"And she will," Adi said. "Be patient."

"Patient, right." Cressida nodded. Rusty annoyance flared around her. "That's all anyone asks nowadays. Be patient while Ysabel considers our problem. Be patient while Jin and Ellie talk to the council. Be patient while my parents are stuck in that skies damned city."

The cool patience radiating off Adi twisted into steely pain. "You think I don't have people I'm worried about?"

"You're not from Kalama."

"You think the capital is the only place in danger? You think I don't have people there I care about?"

Astrea dropped to the ground. Pain and anxiety twined around both Adi and Cressida, the weight of both pressing into Astrea's bones.

"It's the place in the most danger right now," Cressida said.

"Maybe," Adi agreed. "But that's going to change very quickly if we don't get back there and get Eliana on the throne."

"Who, exactly, are you worried about?"

Astrea frowned. Cressida had a sharp tongue, but that was only when people deserved it. This was just rude. "We all have people we're worried about, Cress."

Cressida's jade eyes flicked to her, then back to Adi.

"My little sister." The muscle in his jaw tightened. "My little sister, Noemi. We grew up about half a days' train ride from the capital. She's on summer break from university, but she's heading back to Kalama in a few months."

"What about your parents?" Cressida asked.

"I'm all she has." That steel pain flashed around Adi again, cobalt regret mingling with it.

Cressida's shoulders loosened as her arms dropped to her sides. "Why are you in the—"

"The military paid well," Adi said. "My father left a lot of gambling debt behind. I was nineteen when he passed and joined as soon as I came of age. I had to find a way to take care of both of us."

Just how many lives had the emperor's wars turned upside down? How many had they ruined? Twenty was barely adulthood, and yet Adi had enlisted as soon as he'd been legally allowed. Jin had been forced in by his own father even younger. Nicos's father had died on a mission near the Macadian Mountains several years earlier. Even Astrea's life had been impacted; those wars were why Saros had instructed her to hide her abilities, to prevent the inevitable enlistment that came with healing magic.

"I didn't realize . . ." Astrea started.

"Neither of you would know," Adi said. "I don't exactly talk about it, and it's not like we've known each other that long."

"I'm sorry," Cressida said. "I shouldn't take my anxieties out on you. I just . . . I'm sorry."

"None of us exactly feel good about this," Astrea said. "Trust me."

The pain surrounding Adi dimmed, replaced by his bright smile. "The good news is that like it or not, I'm your trainer," he quipped. "That means I can get back at you however I see fit."

Cressida nudged his shoulder with hers. "Gee, thanks."

That buzz under Astrea's skin was still palpable, begging for attention. She sighed and summoned a ball of light over her palm, the white light dancing and flickering in the afternoon sun.

Was there even time for her to learn how to fight? Astrea wasn't sure what timeline her friends were planning for a return to Helosia, but anything less than several months didn't seem like enough time for Astrea to gain any semblance of mastery over her magic. She let the light die, the last few sparkles of stardust drifting away with the breeze.

"Do you think they're done with their meeting yet?" Adi asked, scanning the path leading back to the guest house. "I know we have work to do, but I don't feel like being out here."

"I vote we go back," Cressida replied. "A long bath sounds like the perfect way to end the afternoon."

"Astrea?" Adi asked.

"You can go," Astrea said. "I'll be there in just a few moments."

"You sure?" Cressida asked. "I can stay with you."

"No, really. It's alright." When Cressida still didn't look convinced, Astrea smiled. "I just need a few moments."

Pausing, Cressida searched Astrea's face. "Alright, but I'm coming to find you if you aren't back in ten minutes."

"Ten minutes," Astrea agreed. It was more time than she needed anyway. She just wanted a few minutes alone to clear her mind.

Adi and Cressida started back toward the guest house, their voices fading as they disappeared over the hill and around a large rose bush. Astrea pushed to her feet. She walked closer to the edge of the lake, her eyes trained on the water as it sparkled in the sun. It was almost disorienting.

She forced the thought away. She also forced away the thought of Jin's body pressed against hers while they slept, the thought of training, and even the thought of being here in Novaria.

Focus, Astrea reminded herself. *Complete the mission. Find the answers.*

They were here to find the missing book and get answers about the void. *That* was her mission. The others could figure out the logistics of returning to the Helosian capital. Eliana would figure out how to take down her father. Astrea would do her best to learn what she could about this other side of her lightbringing, but her true power was in her healing. And aside from that, the one place she could truly be useful was in figuring out what was going on with the void. She had to do this. She had to figure it out.

"You look glum."

Astrea flinched as she looked up. "Commander Lucian?"

Lucian smiled. Up close and in the daylight, Astrea realized he was younger than she'd previously thought. He was closer to her uncle's age than Ysabel's. The commander couldn't have been older than forty.

"I hope I wasn't disturbing you," he said. "Prince Varojin asked me to speak with Mister Kuwat, but I saw you down here."

"Oh." Astrea had no idea what to say to that, nor did she know why he'd want to speak with her of all people. "I hope everything's alright."

"Everything's fine. Their Imperial Highnesses are meeting with Ysabel and her council right now."

"That's good."

"Admittedly," Lucian continued as he looked out over the lake, "I was also watching you train with your friends."

Great. Just what she needed: one more person to witness her failure.

"I didn't have much formal training." The admission was easier than Astrea expected, but her gut still tightened. The grand duchess would have no reason to conscript Astrea based on her magic. There was no more reason to hide it.

"I assumed as much."

Her cheeks burned, and Astrea crossed her arms.

Lucian laughed, a light, clear sound. "It's alright, Astrea. I'm a Light-bringer, too."

Her gaze snapped up to him, but the commander was relaxed as he watched the lake. "You are?" she asked. "I thought Lightbringers only served as healers."

"Perhaps in Helosia. Not here. Anyone can be anything they want here, regardless of their mage status."

Astrea pressed her lips together. No emotion danced around him, but he offered her a small smile. "Why are you telling me this?" she asked.

"I believe in what your friends are trying to do," Lucian said. "Void threat or not, I'm glad Their Imperial Highnesses are trying to take down their father. And I assume you're going to help them, or that you want to."

"I plan to." It was all Astrea wanted right now. She wanted to save Saros, Sarsali, and Balthazar. She wanted to stop Nazarov, Theo, and the emperor. She wanted Eliana to be on the throne. She wanted to go home and pretend none of this had happened.

"While you're in Talmaris, I can teach you."

If Astrea had been embarrassed before, she was now stunned into silence. She watched the commander, trying to read anything she could from him, but his emotions remained elusive. Hidden.

"Why do you want to help me?" Astrea finally asked. "It's not like you know me."

"As I said, Astrea, I believe in what your friends are doing. If giving you even just a small boost in your magical knowledge helps, it's worth my time."

Astrea swallowed. Could he really mean that? Had Ysabel given him approval? She must have, otherwise there was no way the commander of her guard would be making such an offer. But Ysabel hadn't seen her training. Ysabel hadn't seen her failure.

Astrea looked up at Lucian again. Could she accept his help? Adi was trying his best, but he clearly knew nothing about lightbringing. That wasn't his fault. None of her friends did. When would she get this kind of opportunity again? And was it right to take it when Eliana and Jin wanted to keep so much information from the Novarians?

"Do you need an answer today?" Astrea asked. "I'd like to think about it."

Lucian smiled, the corners of his dark blue eyes crinkling. "No, I don't need an answer today. Let me know when you've made a decision."

"Thank you, Commander."

After they said their goodbyes, Astrea followed the same path her friends had walked just a few minutes before. When she got to the top of the hill and rounded the corner, she nearly collided with Cressida.

"Oh!" She caught Astrea by her shoulders. "There you are."

"Here I am," Astrea said, forcing a smile. "I told you I'd be back."

"That you did." Cressida looped her arm through Astrea's and dragged her toward the guest house looming at the end of the path. "Did you get the time you needed?"

Astrea glanced over her shoulder, but she couldn't see the commander around the thick foliage of the garden. "Yes," she murmured. "I think I did."

Chapter 7

One of the perks of staying at the grand duchess's guest house was that her chef was also sending meals there. Astrea supposed it was an unusual arrangement, hosting a runaway foreign princess and her friends, but she was still grateful they had someplace to go.

As Astrea placed silverware at each seat, Cressida laid out the covered serving dishes the palace staff had brought over. There were even several bottles of wine and carafes of water, too. After their first day at Ysabel's palace, Astrea was sure they could all use a drink.

It was almost normal, like the hundreds of times she'd set the table for dinner at the Nikaphoroses' home. Their group would fill just half of the long table. The Nikaphoroses also had a large dining room, but it had never felt empty like this one did.

"You want wine now?" Cressida asked as she passed a corkscrew to Astrea. "Or at least want to pour for everyone?"

"Sure." That, too, felt normal, like the dozens of times she'd opened wine for Sarsali before dinner.

"How much longer are they going to be?" Adi asked as he lifted a lid off one of the dishes. The smell of grilled meat and roasted potatoes made Astrea's stomach growl.

Her lightbringing may have overwhelmed her sometimes, but Astrea appreciated being able to sense when people were on the move. Jin's wall was headed their way, as were myriad emotions from Eliana and Nicos.

"They're coming," Astrea said as she uncorked the first bottle of wine.

Jin strode through the dining room door first, followed by Eliana, then Nicos. Before Astrea could begin pouring drinks, Jin offered to take the bottle from her. She passed it to him, then uncorked a second while he filled everyone's wine glasses and Cressida finished pulling the lids off the serving dishes.

As her friends began taking their seats—Eliana at the head of the table, Jin to her right, and Nicos to her left—Astrea hesitated. She hadn't seen either of the imperial siblings since they left that morning to join Ysabel at the palace. They were both so calm. *Unexpected.*

When Astrea dropped into the chair next to Jin and across from Cressida, peach amusement bubbled in the air. Cressida's gaze flicked dramatically from Astrea to Jin. Had she been able to reach, Astrea would've kicked her under the table.

"So," Jin said, breaking the silence as everyone passed dishes around and began filling their plates, "Ysabel's council has agreed that we should stay to help them figure out their void problem."

"Did we expect them to say otherwise?" Adi asked as he passed a dish of roasted potatoes to Cressida.

"Well, not exactly," Eliana said. She accepted a platter from Nicos and plucked out two pieces of dark, thick bread. "But it was certainly a possibility."

"We'll proceed as we first planned," Jin said. "Keep our training sharp, investigate this void issue with Lucian's help, and figure out what to do about our father. Ysabel has also agreed to look out for communication from Zephyrine and grant her permission to enter the country."

"You think she'll get out of Kalama?" Adi asked.

Astrea knew very little about Jin's time in the military, but General Zephyrine Kanakos had once been both Jin and Adi's commanding officer.

"That was her plan," Jin said. "I don't know how long it'll take her, but she was going to get the rest of the team and come after us."

"Hopefully it's soon," Eliana said. "I'd like to know what news she has to share about both the council and Father."

"She's on the council?" Astrea asked.

"She retired from the military a few years ago when our father offered her a position on his council," Eliana said. "Zephyrine's a noblewoman by birth. He couldn't turn down a general *and* noble's perspective. If anyone else is ready to back the rebels, she'll know."

Maybe she'll know what happened to Saros, Astrea thought, her throat tightening as she pushed a small potato around her plate.

"And of course," Jin said as he set his fork and knife down, "Ysabel and I spoke about her claim from last night."

"Are you . . . ?" Adi's silent question hung in the air.

"Actually related to Ysabel?" Jin asked. "Yes. She showed us genealogy charts as well as letters from my mother dating back to when I was an infant. There was a photograph of us—my mother and I—that I'd never seen before, taken at the palace back home. Apparently my grandfather's family—the Seviya family—was ostracized from court after he secretly married my grandmother. My mother didn't spend much time in Novarian high society."

"I'm surprised they were allowed to keep their titles and status at all," Eliana said. "That wouldn't go over well back home."

"Sounds messy," Cressida murmured.

Astrea reached for her water. There were all kinds of social and political ranks among the various noble families in Helosia, drama that Astrea had never been interested in but that Eliana knew all about. To think that Jin's mother was not just ostracized from her own family's royal court but then again in Helosia when she became the emperor's mistress . . . *That's certainly reason to hide your heritage.*

"And are you . . . ?" Adi asked, another silent question heavy in the room.

"Her niece, nephew, and that nephew's two young children are all in line before me," Jin said. "I fall fifth in line. And though I'm technically a prince in this country regardless of my Helosian rank, my Helosian rank complicates things. Since my father never formally barred me from claiming that throne, the Novarian Grand Council might bar me from this one."

"Complicated," Adi muttered.

"It doesn't matter anyway. I never wanted the Helosian throne, so why would I want this one?"

Eliana popped a roasted carrot into her mouth, then chewed and swallowed before saying, "Though it would be nice if Helosia and Novaria could be ruled by two Aurises. Not in an empire way, just in an . . ." She pursed her lips. "In that it would make foreign relations run a little more smoothly."

"Yes, well, maybe Ysabel will take your familial connection into consideration in the future," Jin said.

Eliana rolled her eyes. "Maybe."

"You wouldn't want it even if you could have it?" Nicos asked.

"No." Jin's answer was quick, simple. "I'm not suited for the job."

As Astrea and Jin had gotten older, he'd confided that to her many times. He'd never been interested in that kind of power. He'd talked to her about it just before his eighteenth birthday. Just before he'd been sent away.

"Why would your mother get in touch with Ysabel but not tell your father about who she was or what that meant for you?" Cressida asked. "Wasn't that a risk on her part?"

"Your guess is as good as mine, Cress." Jin sighed. "I don't know what my mother was thinking or how she hid it, but it seems she did. She asked Ysabel not to tell the family. Nobody knew."

Even if Caliste hid her heritage from Emperor Aelius, why would Ysabel agree to keep that secret? Wouldn't it have been beneficial to both countries, help them secure some kind of formal alliance? *Unless Caliste didn't want Jin to be sucked into that. I wouldn't want my children to become political pawns.*

"Regardless of all that," Eliana said, "Commander Lucian wants to go to the Mattina address tomorrow. We spent a few hours going over everything with him in more detail, and he agrees that's the next best step in solving this mystery."

Rusty annoyance burst to life around Nicos as he took a long sip of wine. Magenta embarrassment followed, then steel pain joined the mix.

"Nicos?" Astrea asked. "What's wrong?"

The magenta and rust spiked higher. "Nothing's wrong," he said, slamming his glass down so hard Astrea thought the stem might snap.

The Nicos she knew was calm. The only time she'd seen his aura so bright and chaotic was after Solstice Night, when Eliana had practically run away from him. He'd been so upset, a mix of anger and fear, as he saw Eliana in rough shape after what he *thought* was an attempted robbery. He now knew the truth, though, that a void mage had attacked them that night. A void mage looking for Astrea.

"I mean, of course you know I'm lying," Nicos continued. "I'm sure you're reading me right now. I'm sure you've been reading all of us for years."

Astrea's face heated. "I can't control it."

"Oh, I'm sure you can't."

"Nic—" Eliana started, but he waved a hand.

"It's fine," he said. "It's all fine."

"Well, now *I* know you're lying," Eliana said, the words strained. "What's wrong?"

"We had all day to tell the grand duchess that someone was stalking Astrea," Nicos said as he focused in on the royal siblings. "Jin told them things I didn't even know happened until he brought them up today, but nobody thought it might be a good idea to tell them a murderer is looking for one of our own."

Astrea glanced at Cressida, then Adi.

"And there's a very good reason I'm not telling Ysabel that," Jin said, but Nicos laughed.

"Just like you won't tell her about Astrea's visions?"

"One vision," Astrea said, the defense sounding lame as it left her. "It was one."

"Because that's so much better," Nicos muttered. "Astrea keeping her magic a secret almost got Ellie *killed* that night." His nostrils flared as he finally looked Astrea in the eye. She forced herself to hold his gaze. "You're supposed to be her best friend, you and Cressida both, and yet you both kept information from her that ultimately put her in harm's way."

"That's hardly Astrea's fault," Eliana said. "We talked about this, Nic. You know I was the one who—"

"Who walked off, I know. It doesn't change that Astrea's magic makes her a target right now. And that makes all of us targets."

"Nicos," Jin said, "you need to watch your—"

"No." Astrea's heart thudded wildly, her breathing shallow. "Let him say it."

Nicos's jaw flexed, his light brown eyes sharp and focused. "I have a job to do, and I have to be able to trust the people around her. I can't keep Eliana safe if you're hiding things. Lucian can't keep his people safe if we're keeping secrets from him."

Emotions exploded around the table again. Magenta embarrassment around Eliana, the scrape of anger coming from Cressida, confusion from Adi. Jin's wall, though, remained solid.

"That's fair," Astrea said, forcing herself to look at Nicos. "You're right. You're right, and I hope you know I didn't mean for that to happen. I didn't *know* it would happen. I truly thought only Cress and her parents knew about my magic."

The anger and pain spiking around Nicos cut off, lavender surprise replacing them both. But he didn't have a chance to say anything.

"We don't know why the Paragon are looking for her," Jin said. "But if Ysabel finds out about that, or the vision, she might sideline Az, and we need her. She can identify void mages, Nicos, whether they work for the Paragon or our father. She *is* our best shot at keeping Ellie safe from that threat right now."

Astrea was glad Lucian wasn't with them. She was sure her own aura was bursting with embarrassment as Jin's words washed over her.

"I don't know about that," she said. "Just ask Adi. My aim this morning was terrible."

Eliana laughed, an uneasy sound. "I'm not surprised."

"We may be keeping this from Ysabel," Jin said, "but we won't keep things from each other from here on in, alright? Whatever we learn, whether it's about my fucked up family, those skies damned void mages, or even Az's magic, we share with each other first, Ysabel *maybe* second."

The others murmured their agreement, though Nicos was still stiff in his chair. Astrea twisted the napkin in her lap. "Actually, uhm." She cleared her throat. "Commander Lucian saw me training with Adi and Cress this morning."

"He did?" Adi asked.

"Apparently." Astrea shrugged, focusing on her wine glass as she rotated it on the smooth white tablecloth. "He's a Lightbringer, too." Surprise, shock, confusion—all of it pushed against Astrea, painful almost. "I'm guessing neither he nor Ysabel told you that?"

"No," Jin said. "They didn't."

"Well, Lucian knows I don't have any formal training, and he's offered to teach me while we're here."

"What did you tell him?" Eliana asked.

"I said I had to think about it. I wanted to talk to you all first. I didn't know if it was a good idea since we're . . . since we're not telling them everything."

"Why would he want to train you?" Nicos asked. "I don't mean that to sound harsh, but he's the captain of Ysabel's guard. He's busy."

"He said he believes in what Ellie's trying to do," Astrea said. "He thought it would help us. Help her."

Nicos's lips pressed into a thin line, and Eliana frowned. "He said that?" she asked.

"He did."

"You should train with him," Jin said. "I don't really care why he wants to help. We've come this far, and we've trusted Ysabel this much. Learn what you can from Lucian and let us teach you the rest."

"I know you said we're keeping my vision quiet, but should I tell him more about how void mages feel to my magic?" Astrea asked. She'd briefly mentioned it the night before at their first meeting with the Novarians, but she doubted that was a good enough explanation.

Jin nodded. "Yes. As Nicos said, Lucian has people he needs to keep safe. That will help him do his job."

Nicos's shoulders finally loosened, and everyone's emotions calmed as silence fell over the room. Astrea just hoped Jin was right. She hoped training with Commander Lucian would be worth her time, and she hoped teaching him about the void mages would help them stay safe.

Astrea stared up at the ceiling of Cressida's bedroom. Unlike the one she and Jin had picked, this bed didn't have a canopy, so Astrea traced the box beam ceiling with her eyes. Adi and Jin had gone out to the lake after dinner, and Eliana had excused herself for the night. Nicos, of course, had followed her. Which left Astrea and Cressida to their own devices.

They'd spent some time going through the shopping bags Ysabel's staff had dropped off after dinner. Much to Astrea's surprise and delight, they'd actually followed the careful instructions she'd written about fabrics and garment cuts. Now, she had several new dresses, plus several sweaters, blouses, and skirts, to wear around Talmaris.

But the staff hadn't just brought those. They'd also delivered bags with black sporting clothes, not unlike the fatigues Adi and Jin wore. And boots, too. Gear, Astrea assumed, to train in. She was going to wear them the next morning when she went for her next lesson with Adi. That was the plan: training every morning with him until . . . until they went home, Astrea supposed.

"You're quiet." Cressida plopped onto the mattress next to Astrea and leaned back into her pillows.

"Sorry, just thinking."

"About?"

"Nothing important." Astrea pushed up on her elbows and shifted so she could look at Cressida. "How are you feeling? Really feeling, I mean."

After the tiff between Cressida and Adi at the lake, Cressida had apologized to him a second time before dinner. But even now, the faintest sheen of anxiety swirled around Cressida, the orange color almost impossible to see.

"Not great, honestly." Cressida sighed. "I hope Emperor Aelius isn't taking my absence out on my parents."

"Do you think he would?" Astrea asked. She certainly did.

"Maybe. But he might also be making my dad work on that meteorite project in my stead."

"I thought you'd kept it hidden from them until that lunch."

"I had, but there are few people the emperor would ask to handle the task. My father's likely one of the alternatives to me."

"Is there anything you can do with it here?" Astrea asked. "Keep studying it?"

"I don't see how. I just have the one piece. I don't want to do anything to it that ruins the sample."

Astrea nodded. Ruining the sample would certainly be worse than leaving it be. Who knew when they'd get another chance to examine the larger piece?

"We'll figure it out. Now, I don't want to keep talking about all this." Cressida gestured vaguely above them. "Let's talk about something else."

"Like what?"

"Like you and Jin sharing a room."

Astrea flopped back down against the pillows. "There's nothing to talk about."

There was, of course, a lot to talk about. But Astrea didn't know where to begin. Their kiss at the dinner party? Their kiss in Sezia? The way her heart fluttered every time Jin wrapped his arms around her? Back in Kalama, Cressida had tried to press the issue and had even said she'd support something happening between Astrea and Jin, but Astrea just . . . wasn't sure. She and Jin needed to talk.

"Bullshit." Cressida leaned over and poked Astrea's upper arm. "What's going on with you two?"

"We just like sleeping in the same bed."

"Sleeping, right." Amusement tickled the end of Astrea's nose, almost making her sneeze. "I'm sure that's all it is."

"Really. I swear."

"I don't know how you haven't jumped his bones," Cressida said. "At dinner, he looked like he wanted to jump yours."

Astrea's entire body heated. After they'd discussed their situation and Astrea's training with Lucian, the group had moved on to other subjects Astrea hadn't paid much attention to. Innocuous things, just attempts at distracting themselves. She hadn't even noticed Jin looking at her.

"I'm not talking about this, Cress."

"Fine, fine. But I'll tell you what I told you in Kalama. I'd be happy for you if that's what you want."

"What I want is to go to bed," Astrea quipped as she stood. She knew Cressida meant well, but Astrea simply didn't have the mental energy to discuss . . . any of that with her. Another day, perhaps. "See you in the morning."

Cressida called her goodbyes as Astrea left her bedroom. The hallway beyond was silent, though now, as Astrea let her magic widen out, she realized two more people were in the house. Adi and Jin, she guessed.

She opened her bedroom door, half expecting Jin to meet her there. But he was walking out of the bathroom and running a towel over his wet hair.

"I was wondering where you'd gone," Jin said as he tossed the towel on the bed.

Astrea swallowed as she shut the door behind her. He was in nothing but his underwear, his muscled body on full display. "I was just with Cress," she said as she moved toward the desk.

She didn't actually need to do anything at the desk, but she straightened up some of their folders and papers anyway. Sneaking a glance over her shoulder, Astrea found Jin watching her.

"Why are you so shy right now?" he asked with a chuckle.

"I'm not shy."

Another laugh. "Would you like me to put some clothes on? I was going to go to bed, but I'll get dressed if you want me to."

It wasn't anything Astrea hadn't seen before—technically. She'd shared a bed with Jin for multiple nights now. But there was something so intimate, so personal about seeing him like this. Whether it was the dampness of his curls, the way even the room smelled like that eucalyptus soap he used, or the way he was so relaxed, she wasn't sure. *He looked like he wanted to jump your bones at dinner.*

"That's alright," Astrea said as she finished straightening the void evidence she had stacked in a neat pile on the desk. "I was going to go to bed, too."

Astrea had never been so quick to grab her pajamas in her life. She closed the bathroom door behind her. Why was this so different? Why *was* she so shy? It was Jin. Jin, who she'd known for years. Jin, who she'd kissed twice in recent days, one of those times almost leading to something more. Jin, whom she *wanted* more with.

Forcing the thought away, Astrea cleaned up for the night and changed into her nightgown. When she returned to the room, only one of the bedside lamps lit the space. Jin stretched out on his side of the bed, a blanket barely draped over his lap like he was modeling for some kind of painting.

Astrea huffed. "Well, now you're just making it awkward."

He grinned at her. "Does my lack of modesty offend you?"

"You never used to be like that." Astrea tossed her clothes on one of the chairs; she'd deal with them in the morning.

"Is that a bad thing?"

"No, it's just different."

"Military life doesn't exactly allow for modesty. You're hardly the first person to see me like this."

"Oh, so Adi's seen you in your underwear?"

"He's seen a lot more than that."

Astrea's whole face burned as she yanked the covers back and climbed into bed next to him.

"I forgot how fun it is to see if I can make you turn ten different shades of red," Jin teased.

It was true. Back when they were just teenagers, Jin had teased her all the time. And she'd often turned red, though his teasing never crossed a line.

"And I forgot how annoying you can be." Amusement reached out to her magic first, then that sweet approval coated her tongue as Astrea scooted closer to Jin. "Are you alright?" she asked. "I can't imagine today was easy."

"I'm alright."

"Really?" She couldn't imagine trying to figure out that kind of news.

"It wasn't easy by any means, but there's nothing I can do to change the choices my parents made. I've been dealing with the fallout for years. This is more shocking than it is bad news." Jin scratched his beard and let out a heavy breath. "There's a lot I need to tell you about the last eight years, Az. Not just about my father, but everything else."

"You can tell me when you're ready." Astrea had so many questions about his time away from home, starting with the mission Adi had told her about back at the house in Sezia. Whatever he wanted to share, she would listen.

"Tonight, I'm very tired." Jin shifted, and Astrea moved back onto her own pillows as he leaned over her. "And I also want to finish our conversation from Sezia."

"I don't remember our conversation," she whispered. His wide frame blocked out most of the light from the lamp.

The faintest whisper of amusement tickled her nose as he lowered himself and said, "You are *such* a bad liar."

Of course Astrea remembered. In that Sezian bedroom, Jin had said he'd wanted to do things the right way. That as much as he'd wanted her right then and there, he thought talking with clear heads was the right course of action.

"So . . . when do you want to talk?" she asked as she gazed into his half-closed eyes. He hadn't moved, and his mouth was just inches from hers.

"When we aren't exhausted, maybe."

Astrea's breath caught in her chest, but she still managed to ask, "Does that mean I can't kiss you until we finish that conversation?"

Lavender surprise and peach amusement, almost transparent, spiked around Jin. "You want to kiss me?"

"Why would you think I don't? I'm sleeping in the same bed as you, and you practically sleep naked. That means something, doesn't it?"

As the corners of Jin's mouth pulled up into a smile, Astrea threaded her arms behind his neck and pulled him as close as she could. Then, she kissed him. He groaned, sweet approval exploding on her tongue. The way Jin's mouth moved against hers, the way his hand slid from her cheek to caress the base of her throat, made Astrea lose her train of thought.

When he pulled away, he huffed and said, "Perhaps that conversation needs to happen sooner rather than later." After pressing one more kiss to her forehead, Jin rolled back onto his side of the bed. "Goodnight, Az."

"Goodnight, Jin."

CHAPTER 8

Having coffee brought straight to her room was an incredible luxury, and Astrea willed herself to stay in bed as she sipped on the surprisingly bold liquid. She still had time before she needed to meet Adi for training. After that, they'd coordinate the investigation with Lucian.

It was going to be another long day, and Astrea still wasn't sleeping well. Though no nightmares had come the night before, she still found herself waking up every few hours. Staying in bed while she drank coffee might just make the day a little more bearable.

Jin was already awake, dressed in his fatigues and rifling through his military pack. He set several pieces of his gear on the settee near the fireplace.

"What are you looking for?" she asked.

He finally pulled something out of the bag, a stack of papers tied together with ribbon. Orange anxiety bubbled up around him, followed by shame hollowing out her insides. *So much for coffee in bed.* Astrea set her half-empty cup on the bedside table and straightened just as Jin sat near her. He looked down at the bundle again as he handed it to her. Astrea took it. It was a stack of envelopes, at least a dozen but probably more.

"What's this?" she asked.

Jin was silent for so long that Astrea wasn't sure he'd answer, but finally, he nodded. "When my father sent me away, you wrote me six letters."

"This is a lot more than six," she muttered. Surely he wouldn't ask her to read the letters she'd written him when she was just sixteen, would he? When he'd first left for the military, Astrea had written him one letter a month for the first six months he was gone. She'd never gotten a reply even though he'd written to Eliana a few times.

"After my father's dinner party, I told you I had thought, very wrongly, that it would be easier to not be friends in case something happened to me while I was gone." Astrea watched Jin now, wary as he continued. "The first few years were the hardest for me. And maybe it was foolish or even wrong, but I wrote to you. I just never sent them."

Astrea stared down at the stack in her hand.

"You don't have to read them if you don't want to," he said. "I honestly never planned on showing you but . . ." He sighed. "I don't know. It just seems right to offer you the choice. It doesn't replace all the things I want to tell you, but they're a starting point."

The envelopes doubled in weight, impossibly heavy. He'd written to her? After that dinner, Astrea and Jin had finally talked about why he'd left Kalama without saying goodbye. He'd told her that he thought it would be easier on both of them that way, and he'd also taken responsibility for the fact that he'd been very wrong. Jin had alluded to trying to write back to her, but this was . . . this was more than she'd imagined. There were a lot of letters in her hands.

"Are you sure?" Astrea hesitated. That fear and shame pulsed around him, bright even in the early morning light. "I can see you're nervous about it."

He half smiled. "I'm positive."

"Then I'll start reading them later."

"Good." That half smile remained, as did his anxiety. "I'm going to go speak with Lucian about the plans for later. Have fun with Adi."

"Thanks."

Once Jin left the bedroom, Astrea pushed herself out of bed and took the letters to the desk. All their void evidence was there. Astrea looked down at the envelopes in her hand again. She was tempted to rip into them now, but there wasn't time for that before training with Adi. She'd have to wait, and Astrea hated waiting.

Books could be frustrating on any given day, but Astrea wanted to chuck Mattina's journal straight into the fireplace behind her. Training with Adi had been tiring, and now this.

Fingers threading through her hair, she tugged at the roots and glared down at the journal spread out on the desk in her and Jin's room. Why would this journal be empty except for the two addresses? They were scribbled on a page in the middle of the book. Had Mattina simply opened up to that random page when he wrote them down? She'd done that plenty of times while at work and in a hurry to take notes.

Perhaps it was a coincidence, but none of what was happening around them seemed to be random. The tattoos hadn't been a coincidence, nor had Theo Kadis's connection to Novarian artifacts or his offering that mysterious manuscript in the first place. Not even the meteorite was a coincidence. The connections weren't obvious, but they were there. Astrea had to find them.

She slid her old work notebook toward herself and flipped to the next blank page. What did she already know? Murder victims in three cities. Tattoos. Theo's missing book. The emperor's strange research topics, from mythology to history to meteorites, most of which she still had her notes on. Void magic. Saros and Astrea's visions.

Astrea flipped open the *Myth and Magic* book to some of the stories Saros had talked about with her. Stories about the old beliefs, how the elements balanced each other. She summoned faint starlight over her hand, letting the magic weave between her fingers. Water and fire, air and earth—they balanced each other and themselves. But what about her magic? Celestial magic?

"So you fucked a Lightbringer and brought her in to balance the fight." That was what Kaius had yelled at Jin on the airfield in Kalama. *"The Paragon will restore balance."* Victor Nazarov's words from their fight at the palace.

Water and fire. Air and earth. Celestial and void.

That was it.

The Paragon wanted to restore balance to magic.

"How did I not think of that before?" Astrea muttered as she tugged at her hair again. It seemed so obvious now, looking at everything in front of her. But in the few days they'd been in Novaria—in their short time since fleeing Helosia—Astrea had barely been able to think straight. She'd been so scattered from . . . everything.

A knock echoed through the room, then the bedroom door opened. Astrea turned just in time to see Jin poking his head inside.

"Can I come in?"

"You don't have to ask," she said.

Smiling, he stepped inside and closed the door. "I didn't want to bother you. You've been up here for hours."

"What time is it?" Training with Adi had been fine, though Astrea still wasn't able to throw her light out the way he wanted her to. Afterward, she'd taken a shower and locked herself in the bedroom, trying to find some skies damned connection between everything that had happened.

The sooner they could figure it out, the sooner they could go back home. "Does Lucian want to leave soon?"

"We have a little time, but soon." Jin crossed the distance to the desk in a few long strides, then leaned over her shoulder as he surveyed the papers and books. "This is what you've been doing?"

"Yes." She looked back down at that list she'd written out and pressed her lips together. "I think the Paragon want to restore balance to magic."

"What?"

Astrea explained the stories Saros had shown her, as well as what Nazarov had said. And when she repeated Kaius's words, heat traveled from her neck to the tips of her ears. Even Jin's cheeks flushed pink, too.

"It makes sense," Jin said when she was finished. "Although I wonder why they want to do so now."

"Do you really think my magic is different? Is that why the Paragon were looking for me on Solstice Night?"

"Maybe," Jin said as he scanned the list. "I don't know."

"The men on Solstice Night said their boss wanted me. Do you think that's the leader Mattina mentioned in his letter?"

"Maybe." Jin's hand landed on her shoulder, his touch somehow both soft and achingly heavy. "Let's just see what we find at that house, then we'll revisit the list, alright?"

Astrea huffed. "Alright."

More evidence might start filling in the picture. Not just about what the emperor wanted but what the Paragon wanted, too. How they planned to restore balance. Why they wanted to. Maybe then her head wouldn't hurt so much.

Pushing the chair back, Astrea stood and made her way to the wardrobe. "Let me get changed. Are Cress and Adi ready to go?"

Astrea had pushed the drapes back earlier in the afternoon, leaving just the thin, sheer curtains over the windows. Outside, the sun had started to set, painting the sky a brilliant mix of orange and pink. She hadn't realized she'd been upstairs for so long.

"They're waiting in the parlor."

She finally looked up at Jin, really looked at him. He'd followed her toward the bed but stopped near the middle of the room, hands shoved into his pockets. He'd changed at some point. He now wore street clothes: a silky forest green shirt tucked into fitted black slacks.

"When did you change clothes?" she asked as he watched her.

"I came up about two hours ago."

"You did?"

"You didn't notice?"

"I—" Had she noticed? She didn't think so. "I've been focused."

"Focused and not realizing someone is in the same room as you are two very different things."

"Sometimes I . . . fixate."

His eyebrows quirked up. "Fixate?" Jin echoed, a hint of amusement brushing her senses. "I think that's an understatement."

Astrea shrugged. She'd always done that for as long as she could remember. Saros had never stopped her from doing it as a child. In fact, he did the same thing. That was probably part of why he'd spent so many damn hours in his office the last few months.

"You did this on the airship, too," he said. "Cress is worried about you. She said you forget to eat when you get like this."

Saros also did that. Astrea ran a hand across her forehead.

"Do I need to wear something special?" she asked. She'd had to wear something special in Sezia when Jin and Adi agreed to take her to that house marked with the Paragon's symbol.

"Street clothes are fine. Lucian wants this whole thing to be subtle." Jin finally moved from his spot in the middle of the room and joined her near the bed. He took her hands and pulled her closer. "Don't burn yourself out trying to find the answers. We'll find them as a team."

Saros had said something like that, too, when Astrea used so much of her magic on Solstice Night. Her eyes stung, but she forced the tears down. Tears would not help her find answers. Tears would not make the ache in her heart go away.

"Something normal," she said. "Alright."

She rummaged through the wardrobe until she found a deep blue blouse and a pleated black skirt. Good enough. Astrea took her clothes to the bathroom and closed the door behind her.

By the time she finished braiding her hair, changed, and re-emerged into the bedroom, Jin had sprawled out on the bed. "Ready?" he asked.

"Ready."

"Alright. Let's not keep them waiting."

As they headed into the hallway, Astrea's hand brushed Jin's. He took hers gently, squeezing once. Astrea squeezed back, and she didn't let go. Holding Jin's hand was . . . nice. Calming, even as a dozen thoughts ran circles in her mind.

Jin didn't try to pull away. He didn't even let go of her hand when they reached the bottom of the stairs where everyone was waiting for them. The fact that they'd been sharing a room for days was no secret to their friends—though only Cressida had brought it up—but Commander Lucian's heavy eyebrows shot up, and gray confusion bubbled up around Nicos. Astrea pulled away from Jin and clasped both hands behind her back.

"Now that we're all here," Lucian drawled, "the goal is to return to the palace before midnight so my people can properly lock down for the night. We'll be walking to the address."

"Not taking a car?" Eliana asked. She wasn't going with them, but Eliana liked to be involved.

"I scouted the location earlier in the afternoon, and it looks deserted, but I'd still like to be cautious," Lucian said. Even he was in civilian clothes, loose midnight blue slacks and a gray shirt. "Walking will allow us to blend in more in this part of the city."

"And what part is that?" Eliana asked.

"The Garden District, according to the evidence you provided," the commander said. "And—"

"Before we go, Commander," Astrea said. He raised an eyebrow at her. She hadn't had a chance to speak to him about her training yet, but she needed to at least tell him this before they went out in search of the Paragon. "I mentioned the other night that void mages feel different to my magic. They're hollow, like there's nothing there but should be."

Lucian frowned. "Not like we're being blocked out?"

"No, hollow. And very cold."

"Alright." His gaze shifted back to Jin. "As I was saying, if we're prioritizing discretion, I must be honest, I think too many of us are going."

"You haven't seen the void mages," Jin said. "If we're unlucky enough to cross paths with them, you'll want all of us there."

"The grand duchess isn't sure about allowing a member of her family to walk into such a situation. She would prefer that you stay behind, Prince Varojin."

"And I would prefer to go."

Lucian lifted his chin. "It's not a request, Your Highness."

"You've got to be fucking kidding me."

"If I'm speaking freely," Lucian continued, "I had hoped you would see the logic in it so that I didn't have to give an order. Surely you understand."

Based on the annoyance scraping over Astrea's skin, she guessed her friends agreed with Jin. So did Astrea. If they were unlucky enough to find a void mage tonight, Jin was one of the few people there who had experience fighting them.

"Just let them go, Jin," Eliana said. "They're in good hands. I'm sure they'll be able to handle whatever they find." Even as she said it, though, orange anxiety blossomed around her.

Jin's jaw tightened, but Lucian simply folded his arms over his chest. If it was on Ysabel's order, Jin and Eliana didn't really have any right to go against it. But did the grand duchess really have a right to order them around?

"Fine," Jin muttered. "They'll join you outside in a moment, Commander."

"Make it quick," Lucian said as he started down the hall. "We need to leave soon."

Once Lucian was outside, Jin said, "Follow Adi's lead. Get there, look around, and come straight back. I do not want you three gone longer than you need to be."

"Oh, I think the commander's going to keep us on a tight schedule," Adi said as he nodded toward the front door. "He doesn't mess around."

After a quick goodbye, Eliana excused herself, and Nicos followed her up the stairs. As Astrea watched them go, she didn't miss the way Nicos reached for Eliana's hand, then pulled back. She glanced at the rest of her friends, but they didn't seem to be paying attention.

"Be careful," Jin said. He looked at Adi first, then Cressida, and finally, Astrea. "I'll be waiting."

Chapter 9

Talmaris wasn't as quiet as Astrea had expected it might be in the evening. That first night they'd landed at the airfield, the city had been a silent maze of bright lights and tall buildings. Now, though, it looked almost like Kalama. The wide road, wide sidewalks, and endless flow of people all reminded Astrea of home. Passing pedestrians spoke Delian and Tornamian, and one woman walking in the opposite direction was speaking Zaikudi to her companion. A teenager on the corner of the road was hawking newspapers, shouting about the Corsycan War. Cars still traveled up and down the streets, and a raised train system snaked through the city. They'd even passed a few staircases leading up to platforms where passengers could board.

The most important part, though, was that Astrea had yet to run into any voids. Like Kalama, Talmaris was full of life and emotion, a spectrum ranging from those closed off like Jin to those projecting it all out into the world.

Lucian remained quiet as he led them through the city, though Adi tried—and failed—to strike up a conversation with him several times.

"A few more blocks," Lucian called over his shoulder, "then we take a left."

"We're making good time," Cressida said as they got the signal to cross the street. A few cars idled at the stop light, and Astrea pushed her magic out toward them. No voids in the drivers.

They passed a café with tables spilling into the sidewalk. Most of them were occupied by people eating their late dinners. Something smelled rich and savory, and Astrea's stomach growled. She'd accidentally skipped lunch and dinner. She reached up and fiddled with her necklace, running her fingers over the small sapphire. She liked the feeling of the silver chain on her skin, and every time she wore it, Jin's eyes lit up.

"I still can't believe we're here," Cressida said. "It's just nice not to be stuck in that airship."

"Or the guest house," Adi quipped as they came to a pedestrian street.

If he was trying to get a rise out of Lucian, it didn't work. Instead, Lucian simply turned left at the next corner.

Back in Kalama, before all this had started, Astrea had sometimes struggled with her magic in a crowd. She couldn't block out people's emotions and reactions; the few times she had tried, it had given her a headache. But she'd learned how to tune out the more mundane things, and she had some control over how far out her senses reached.

Now, as she tried to keep her senses wide open in search of the void, she found herself almost disoriented. Other pedestrians were pausing, turning, crossing the street, or ducking into some of the stores still open, and whatever emotions she felt from them dispersed and moved constantly. Trying to pick out a void in this was going to be difficult.

"How much farther?" Cressida asked.

"Another block," Lucian said, "and then we'll be close."

Astrea wasn't sure she was ready for whatever they might find. More murder victims? Perhaps another den of void mages? The murderer themself? The manuscript? Any of that—and none of that—was possible, she supposed. Maybe it wouldn't even be connected to the void at all. Maybe it was just the location of one of the antiquities dealers Mattina sourced artifacts from.

"Alright," Lucian said as they approached a plaza. He stopped and spun around to face them. "We go in, we look around, and we go back to the palace. Kindly follow my orders tonight, and we'll keep this simple."

Adi's eyes narrowed, but he nodded. "Of course."

Astrea glanced at Cressida but said nothing as they followed Lucian toward a pedestrian road marked Juniper Way. She'd memorized the address for this damn location in the last few days. *Number 564, Juniper Way, Garden District, Talmaris.*

The buildings here seemed to be a mix of shops, restaurants, and homes. Based on the clotheslines zigzagging across the street, most of the homes were on the second or third floors of the rows of buildings. The shops all appeared closed. A few of the restaurants were open, but they weren't nearly as crowded as the ones back near the main road.

As they rounded a bend, Lucian nodded toward a light blue building. Long shadows cast by the nearby street lamp nearly obscured the numbers hanging above the door, but there they were: 564. It was the exact address from Mattina's notebook.

"Looks empty," Adi said as they passed it.

Indeed, the windows for the shop on the first floor were dark. Astrea pushed her magic out that way, but it came up empty. She forced it higher, wider, but her magic still found nothing.

Lucian led them to a break in the street and buildings, an alley that ran perpendicular to the road they were now on. They turned down it, then turned again to follow it behind the buildings. The buildings blocked the light from the street lamps, and the moon was hiding behind the clouds. The only blessing was that the alley wasn't dirty or muddy or gross; it was simply narrow, the cobblestones here more uneven.

"This one?" Cressida asked as they approached a blue building. There was a single window on the back of the building—shutters blocked the view inside—and a single door.

"Yes," Lucian said. "If you would . . .?"

Cressida's hand snapped out, and she closed her fist. The door's lock tumbled free with a soft click, then Cressida reached for the handle. She opened it, stepping to the side as Lucian went in first. The floorboards creaked with his weight. He stilled just inside the doorway, then continued moving.

Adi tilted his head toward the commander, then nodded. Astrea crept in after Lucian, then Adi and Cressida followed. The door locked again with another soft click.

Pitch black surrounded them. Lucian summoned a bit of light, a mere pinprick among the darkness. But it was just enough to make out the empty room.

If anyone had told Astrea weeks ago that she'd be used to breaking into buildings and sneaking around in the darkness, she would've laughed in their face. She'd broken into Mattina's Kalamian home with Jin. Then, in Sezia, she and her friends had broken into Mattina's second home and the void house. And here she was again.

Lucian cut off his light as soon as they were in view of the front windows. It didn't look like anyone was outside, nor did Astrea's magic brush up against anything, but the streetlight filtering inside was just enough to show them the space.

It had clearly been some kind of store at another time. A counter lined one wall, empty shelves behind it gathering dust. A few drop cloths and discarded tools were also laid out in one corner, but otherwise, it was empty.

"Well, fuck," Adi muttered, unease prickling Astrea's limbs.

She turned. A massive four-point star was painted on the opposite wall. Two haphazard concentric circles surrounded it, almost like someone hadn't had time to do a better job.

Astrea's blood chilled. *Paragon.*

"So, it would seem your letter was indeed referring to the void mages," Lucian said as he stared up at the wall. "And this hollow feeling you mentioned, Astrea? You don't feel it now?"

"No," she said. Her magic pushed out again and again, but still, it came up empty. "I believe you would recognize it, Commander. It's like nothing I've ever felt before."

Lucian pressed his lips together, then nodded. "Let's look around, then return to the palace. The grand duchess was clear that she didn't want us to be gone for too long."

They checked behind the old counter, in a small closet Adi found under the stairs, and even returned to the back room, but there was nothing except for paint cans, a few spare boards, boxes of nails, and even a ladder.

Lucian was silent as he started to climb the stairs, and Adi and Cressida followed him wordlessly. Astrea wasn't so sure about going up there. Nobody was in the building now, but what if they came back? There was no easy escape from the second story.

Still, she followed them up the creaky stairs. As Astrea climbed, she couldn't help but envision that narrow staircase in Mattina's house. What if there was a dead void mage here, too? She'd seen enough death in the past few weeks to last her a lifetime.

The hallway at the top of the stairs had no windows, and Lucian summoned a brighter ball of light this time. Three doors lined the hall, and it seemed the only way up to the third floor was a ladder that would pull down from the ceiling.

"If you three can handle checking the rooms," Lucian said, "I'll go into the attic."

As Lucian pulled the ladder down from the ceiling and started his ascent, Astrea summoned her own light for her friends. All three doors were locked, but that didn't stop Cressida. With each door she opened,

Astrea held her breath, but it was more of the same as downstairs: a few tools and paint cans. Until they got to the room at the end of the hallway. Its windows were boarded, and a large crate sat against one wall.

"What is that?" Cressida asked.

Adi crept toward it, then lifted the already loosened lid. Gray confusion spiked around him as he said, "It's just paper."

Astrea joined him, then leaned into the crate and pushed more energy into her light. There had to be hundreds of pieces of paper, all blank. She lifted a single sheet off the top of one of the piles and pulled it out of the crate.

"What would they want with paint and blank paper?" Cressida asked.

"Maybe they're starting an art project," Adi said, earning him a glare from Cressida.

"Let me try something." Astrea never had been one to gamble at the clubs in Kalama, but she'd bet a whole pile of money that something would show up on these pages. The void mages back in Sezia had been flashing papers and their strange dark flames at the man standing guard outside their meeting.

Astrea ran her light over one side of the paper. She pushed more energy into it until the tiny ball put off heat. A smidge of dark detail started to form on the paper. It wasn't vibrant, but it was the same symbol as Nazarov's tattoo. The same tattoo Theo, Mattina, and all of those other void mages had, and the same symbol painted on the wall downstairs.

"Well, fuck," Adi muttered for the second time that night.

He pulled out a few more pages, handing them to Astrea one at a time. She repeated the process on at least twenty pages, but all of them showed the same symbol.

"It might be some kind of invitation," Astrea said. "At the house in Sezia, Cress and I saw the void mages flashing paper at the guard before they could go inside."

"There must be hundreds of them," Cressida said. "Maybe thousands."

That didn't bode well for . . . for whatever this was. Hundreds of some kind of invitation related to the void? Just how large was this Paragon organization?

"Did you find something?" Lucian asked, the floor creaking with his steps. "The attic was empty other than the cobwebs."

Adi took a few of the papers from Astrea and brought them to the commander. "The crate is full of these," he said. "Only the paper looks blank until Astrea runs her light over it."

Lucian's eyebrows furrowed, long shadows cast over his face. Then he walked to the crate and pulled out a blank page, flashing his own light behind it. It, too, had the Paragon's symbol emblazoned in faint ink. "Well, that's certainly something."

Mattina's journal, Astrea realized. She thought those pages were blank, but what if that was what she'd been missing these last few days? What if she needed to use her light? Invisible ink had fallen out of favor in recent years, or at least she'd thought it had.

"Let's take more of these back to the palace with us," Lucian said. "I'd like a few that appear blank so we can demonstrate this for Her Highness. We should go back."

Astrea folded up a few of the pages she'd used her light on, then grabbed a few 'blank' sheets and folded them up. She slid them into her skirt's deep pocket. Adi, Cressida, and Lucian all grabbed a few extra papers as well.

Leading the way downstairs, Astrea dismissed her light as soon as she got close to the last few steps. The papers were practically burning a hole in her pocket. She needed to get back to that damn guest house and go over every inch of that journal. She'd stay up all night if she had to.

Astrea reached for the handle on the back door, but it pulled open before she could even make contact with the metal.

"Astrea, wait—" Lucian called as she stumbled forward a step, awareness bursting over her magic. How had she not noticed them coming? Gray confusion bubbled in the darkness of the alley.

"What—" a deep voice started in Novarian.

Astrea didn't think. She just pulled her fist back and slammed it right into the person's face. Pain burst over Astrea's senses, but she didn't know if it was hers or theirs. The person stumbled backward, clutching their nose and cheek.

"What the fuck?" they shouted.

"Oh, for skies sake," Adi muttered as he grabbed Astrea's shoulder and hauled her backward.

Astrea tried to focus on her awareness, on anything but the pain now pulsing in her hand. Lucian grabbed the person by their collar and dragged them into the dark back room of the house. Her face throbbed, too, and even Lucian let out a heavy sigh.

"Why the fuck did she do that?" that stranger—he sounded like a man—asked in Novarian again.

"Why are you here?" White light flared to life over Lucian's palm. Long shadows stretched through the room.

"I'm the contractor overseeing the renovation here," the man said, his voice nasal as he doubled over and lifted a hand to his face. "Fuck, did she break my nose?"

Cressida suppressed a laugh, peach amusement bubbling brightly around her.

"You need to come with us," Lucian told the man.

"Why? Who are you?"

"It doesn't matter who I am," Lucian said. "Come with me and you won't have to pay for a healer to fix that very painful break."

Though it sounded like an offer, and though pain exploded in her bones again and again, Astrea knew what Lucian really meant. It was a command.

The nasal man sighed. "Alright. Alright, I'll come with you."

Lucian forced the man out the back door, then Adi, Cressida, and Astrea followed them into the night. The stranger was no taller than Astrea, and his skin was the same color of the sand at the beach in Kalama.

"Lucian," Adi said. "Check his wrists for the tattoo."

The commander paused, then nodded and grabbed the man's arms.

"I'll show you," he protested. Now that they were under the moonlight, Astrea realized his nose was crooked and bleeding. "Just give me a moment."

The man pushed up the sleeves of his rough cotton shirt and offered his upturned wrists to Lucian. His tan skin was smooth, unmarked except for a sprinkle of freckles. There was no Paragon tattoo.

"Let's go," Lucian barked. "I'll get us a cab when we get to the main road."

As they retraced their steps through the back alley and onto Juniper Way, Astrea winced. There wasn't any bruising, but her fingers were starting to swell.

"Well, you sure hit him hard," Cressida said.

"Let me see." Adi took Astrea's hand as they trailed after Lucian. His touch was gentle as he brushed his fingers over hers. "Can you heal it?"

"I'll wait," she said. "I don't want to do it here." Because even though the man Lucian was hauling back toward the main streets of the capital wasn't a void mage, Astrea couldn't shake the feeling that something about that building wasn't quite what it seemed.

Chapter 10

By the time they reached the palace gates, it was nearing the tenth evening bell. As he'd hauled the stranger into the guard house near the front of the palace, Lucian had told Astrea and Cressida to go back to the guest house. Astrea had wanted to stay and see what the stranger had to say, but Adi had convinced them to go back. Now, as they walked through the dark, silent gardens, Cressida laughed.

"What could possibly be funny right now?" Astrea asked.

"I can't wait to see Ellie's reaction when I tell her you broke some guy's nose."

"And managed to break my own hand in the process," Astrea muttered. She'd broken two fingers, which she'd healed on the cab ride back to the palace. Lucian had healed the stranger's nose then, too.

"That's why you don't go right for the face," Cressida said as they passed the guards stationed outside the guest house and opened the front doors. "You go for the throat."

"You couldn't have told me that earlier?"

"I didn't think you'd need to know so soon."

"Forget that," Astrea said. The house was quiet, almost too quiet. Fatigue clouded Astrea's mind, but she pushed her magic out again. "I think they're upstairs. I need to look at the journal."

"Why?" Cressida asked as they started up. "You think it's like those papers we found?"

"We have to try it." Astrea jogged the last few stairs and headed right for her bedroom door. "Get Ellie for me?" she called over her shoulder.

Cressida marched toward the end of the hall. "Already on it."

Astrea didn't bother knocking on her and Jin's door. She flung it open, and he jumped up from where he was sprawled on the bed.

"I didn't hear you come back," he said. "How was it?"

"Adi's with Lucian."

"Alright . . ." Jin hesitated, then asked, "Doing what?"

"Questioning someone." Astrea made a beeline for the desk, where all her notes and books were still spread out. Jin hadn't touched them. She opened Mattina's journal, light flaring over her other hand. She pulled her magic back until the light was small but warm.

"What do you mean questioning someone?" Jin asked. "Az? What happened?"

"She punched someone in the fucking face!" Cressida announced. Surprise washed over Astrea, and Eliana's smooth, tinkling laugh followed.

"You *what*?" The horror in Jin's voice was obvious, but she couldn't focus on that.

"Can you all be quiet?" Astrea asked, her back to them as she hunched over the desk. "I need to focus."

"On what?" Jin asked.

Astrea didn't answer, nor did Cressida. They could explain after she tried this. Sucking in a deep breath, Astrea held her hand a few inches away from the first page of the journal, trying to keep her light steady and not too hot. Brown text began spreading over the page as she pulled her light over it. She stopped when she got to the last corner.

What was *that*? It wasn't the Paragon's symbol, nor was it any language Astrea knew. All the continental languages used the same alphabet, but the symbols on the page before her looped in strange, unfamiliar ways. She could pick out punctuation—the same as the alphabet she knew—but whatever it actually said, she couldn't read it.

"Fuck," she muttered as her light drifted away into a sprinkle of stardust. This was supposed to be her answer. This was supposed to fill in some of the gaps in her understanding. "Skies damn it."

"What is going—" Jin started as his hand landed on Astrea's shoulder. "What the fuck is that?"

Astrea shoved the journal at him and marched over to the bed. Heavy, oppressive confusion and anxiety pushed into her bones.

"What happened?" Nicos asked.

Reaching into her skirt pocket, Astrea grabbed the papers they'd taken from the house. Cressida pulled several from her pocket and passed them to Eliana and Nicos.

"There were no void mages," Astrea said. "But we found the Paragon's symbol, and there was a crate full of blank papers. Cress and I saw the void mages showing papers to the guard at that house in Sezia, and I just . . . I should've thought of it sooner."

How much evidence and information had they left behind at Mattina's home in Sezia? Astrea remembered combing through his bookshelves, finding a mix of novels and other blank notebooks. How much of that paper had been covered in invisible ink, too?

"Invisible ink?" Eliana asked. "Seriously? I thought this had fallen out of use."

"You'd be surprised, El," Nicos said. "Lots of people use it to write to their love—" Eliana glared at Nicos, jealousy flaring bright and hot around her. "Well, it doesn't matter," he finished. "Some people still use it."

Astrea shoved some of the papers at Jin. "We think it might be some kind of invitation, at least if it's what Cress and I saw them using in Sezia. I really should've thought of it sooner."

Jin's eyebrows drew together as he took the wad of papers from her. He sorted through them, then set down the stack that already had the Paragon symbol revealed. "These blank ones," he said. "Can I try?"

Astrea shrugged. "Just save a few to show the grand duchess."

A flame burst to life over Jin's hand. Near the door, Nicos, too, summoned his fire and held it to one of the blank sheets Cressida had passed him. As they did, the Paragon symbol bloomed to life on the paper.

"And who are Lucian and Adi questioning?" Jin asked.

"The guy Az punched," Cressida said. "Claimed to be renovating the space. He didn't have the tattoo, and he's not a void mage."

"And they have him where, exactly?" Jin asked.

"The guard house near the front gate."

"Nicos," Jin said. "Let's go see what he has to say."

"I don't know . . ." Nicos pressed his lips together.

"Go, Nic," Eliana said. "You've been hovering too much. I will be perfectly safe. Or have you forgotten that I'm also a trained mage, surrounded by other trained mages?"

Something silent passed between them, unreadable even to Astrea. Finally, Nicos nodded. "Alright," he said to Jin.

The two men left the room without another word. Astrea flopped back on the bed and covered her face with her hands as her own disappointment flooded her body.

"Hey." The bed dipped as Cressida sat next to her. "What's wrong?"

"What's wrong?" Astrea asked, her voice cracking. "We just keep running into more questions. How am I . . . how are we supposed to figure this out, Cress?"

"With patience."

"Oh, great," Astrea deadpanned as she forced herself to sit up. "Patience. That's going to help Saros and your parents."

Eliana plopped down on Astrea's other side. "Would it help to know that if we haven't figured it out, my father probably hasn't yet, either?" she asked. "We're probably closer to the answer than he is."

That didn't make Astrea feel any better at all. Emperor Aelius was still looking, and he had far more resources than Astrea did. He probably had more resources than Ysabel, too. If nothing else, he would force people to do the research for him.

Sighing, Astrea pushed herself off the bed and went back to the desk. Jin had abandoned the journal there, so she picked it up and summoned her light again before flipping to the second page.

"What are you doing?" Cressida asked.

"We at least need to know if the whole book is like this," Astrea said.

"That can't wait until the morning?"

"No."

"Do *you* want to try knocking some sense into her?" Cressida asked Eliana.

"Absolutely not. I know how she gets," Eliana said. "But I *am* going to go make some tea, if either of you want any."

"Sure," Astrea said, but her eyes were trained on the strange language now filling up the second page of the notebook. She flipped to the third and repeated the process, then the fourth.

"Bring up something to eat too, Ellie!" Cressida called as Eliana made her way down the hallway.

"The whole skies damned thing is full of it," Astrea said as she haphazardly started lighting up the pages. "What are we supposed to do with this, Cress?"

"We'll find a translator," she said. "Or maybe one of the museums or universities here will have some artifact with the same language. There's got to be a connection somewhere. Following the letter and journal here has gotten us this far. Have a little faith."

Faith. Faith and patience weren't going to get Astrea anywhere right now. She needed evidence. She needed information. But Cressida was right. Someone in the city had to know something about this language. Now, Astrea just needed to find them.

"There you are, little Lightbringer."

Astrea turned in a circle, seeking the source of the voice. But darkness pressed in around her, and she couldn't pull on her magic. She tried to speak, but no sound came out.

"Just open your eyes, and soon you'll discover the truth."

She'd thought her eyes were open. She tried to open them again. A familiar bedroom came into view. Jin was asleep in bed. So was she.

"Have you found what you're looking for?" the voice asked.

Astrea spun around. Shadows wavered in the corner of the room near the wardrobe. They danced closer to her.

"You're too late. The wheels were set in motion many moons ago. You will fail here just as you failed in Kalama, little Lightbringer."

"This isn't real," Astrea seemed to say, even though she was sure she hadn't spoken.

"Isn't it?" The shadows moved closer still. "I told you the shadows have so much to offer. In fact, I believe I told you twice."

"This isn't real."

"You'll learn the truth, if you would just open your eyes. You will not stop the Paragon."

Astrea pulled on her magic, pulling and pulling despite the mere trickle of energy it gave her. When she finally summoned her light, the shadows retreated, revealing an unwelcome pair of copper eyes.

"Open your eyes, Miss Sovna."

Astrea's eyes opened.

That light still floated over her palm, only now, she was in bed with Jin again. And Victor Nazarov's lithe form, half obscured in shadows, grinned at her from a few feet away. He raised a shadow-tipped finger to his mouth as he circled around to Jin's side of the bed.

Astrea tried to scream, but she couldn't. She couldn't move or do anything. Something held her down, something strong and invisible.

That same shadow-tipped finger traced over Jin's face, down his neck and to the spot on his chest just above his heart. Jin didn't move. He didn't even seem to notice Nazarov touching him. His breathing was even, his body still, as he continued to sleep.

See you soon, little Lightbringer, Nazarov's voice echoed in her head as he dissolved into a hundred tiny shadows. They drifted into the air, some of them landing on Jin's skin. *Tell your friends I said hello.*

Even after he disappeared, Astrea couldn't move. She tried, muscles tightening and relaxing as she tried to move over and over again. A scream finally tore from her throat.

"Let me go!" Astrea thrashed, her magic building in her veins. It pushed and pushed against her, painful and too hot.

"Fuck, it's me! Az, it's me!"

Warm hands cupped her face. Golden eyes illuminated by white light stared down at her. Astrea's chest heaved. Something soft tangled around her legs.

"Az." Jin's voice cut through the fog, raspy and heavy with sleep. "Can we cut the lights?" When she still didn't respond, he said, "Your magic."

Astrea squeezed her eyes shut, then opened them again. Her magic built around her hands, uncontrolled. She forced it back, deep down inside of her as her breath came in raggedly.

"No," she whispered, burying her hands in her tangled hair. It had come loose from the braid she'd put it in before going to bed. How had

Nazarov spoken to her in her dreams like that? It was too real. "Why is this happening?"

Jin tried pulling her back down, but she wiggled away from him and jumped out of bed. Cool air drifted in through the open windows. Electricity buzzed through her. Her heart raced. Astrea needed to do something. She needed to leave, find the source of the shadows and what the Paragon—

"Az."

"Did I burn you?" she asked, whipping around toward Jin. He was pushed up on one elbow, still buried under the blankets. "Did I hurt you?"

"No, but you're a lot stronger than I gave you credit for."

"But I didn't hurt you?"

"No, I'm fine."

"What about the shadows?"

"What shadows?" Sighing, Jin lifted the blankets a little. "Will you come here?"

"I can't."

"Why not?"

"What if I summon my magic again?" she asked. "What if I burn you? Or set the bed on fire?"

Sighing again, Jin pushed himself up and out of bed. He wasn't wearing anything except his underwear, his body on full display. There wasn't a single inky shadow on his body, just the shadows one would expect to see in the middle of the night.

"You're not going to set the bed on fire," Jin said gently. "You're not going to hurt me. And you need to sleep."

"Then we need to drug me. Sedatives . . . Ysabel's healers should have those, right?"

"I'm sure they do."

"Then I need that."

"You don't need that."

"I'm dangerous."

His hands brushed her upper arms before landing on her shoulders. "You're hardly dangerous." He paused, then added, "No offense."

Astrea leaned forward, resting her forehead against his bare chest. Her body warmed as Jin wrapped his arms around her back and tugged her closer. She focused on the sound of his heart thumping steadily under her ear.

"What was that one about?" he asked.

"What they're always about," she croaked. This time was different, though. Different in a way she couldn't explain to him. There was something wrong with her mind if it was showing her Nazarov so realistically.

"Come on," Jin whispered before pressing a kiss to her forehead. "It's the middle of the night. Come back to bed."

This time, Astrea didn't resist. She climbed into bed next to Jin, leaning into him as he pulled her close. As his breathing slowed, his body heavy and limp behind hers, Astrea kept her eyes open. Because even now, even when she knew it wasn't a dream, the shadows lurking around the edges of the room seemed darker than usual.

CHAPTER 11

Astrea paced the length of the parlor. Her friends were all still upstairs, a mix of fatigue, confusion, and curiosity perceptible even through the walls. What was taking them so long?

She hadn't slept much after the nightmare. *It's the stress getting to me,* Astrea reasoned as she walked. *This is what hardship does to one's mind.* Nightmares, hallucinations, fatigue—they were all things soldiers coming home from the war reported. In a way, she was at war, too.

That skies damned journal. What if it didn't actually have any information for them? Could it be a false lead? What if the language wasn't even real but simply made up to confuse whoever might have been trying to get information? She'd heard of such hoaxes before, collectors who had purchased fake items.

Astrea shook her head. Writing it in invisible ink? That wouldn't make much sense if it were a hoax.

What she needed was a plan to decode the journal. And one was already forming in her mind.

"Az?" Cressida asked as she poked her head into the room. "You want some coffee? There's some ready in the dining room."

Astrea wordlessly followed Cressida across the foyer and into the next room, where everyone was beginning to gather for breakfast. They plopped unceremoniously into plush dining chairs and reached for pastries and empty coffee cups. Astrea loitered at the head of the table.

"I know what to do with the journal," Astrea said once they started pouring their coffee.

"What?" Eliana asked.

"Either we find someone who already knows the language, someone like Mattina," Astrea said, "or we find a linguist who can help us decode it."

"Who would speak the language besides someone from the Paragon?" Adi asked.

"It could be a dead language," Astrea said. "Some researchers and scholars know them. And if we can't find someone like that, then we need to get a linguist."

"Didn't you study languages at university?" Nicos asked before stuffing half a muffin into his mouth. Then he pointed at Jin and Eliana. "Don't you two speak the continental languages? Can't one of you figure it out?"

"I only studied Tornamian," Astrea said. "It doesn't work like that. If we go that route, we need translations to work with. A basis for decoding it. Something."

"Hence a linguist," Cressida said.

Jin glanced at the empty chair next to him, then Astrea, then the chair again. An invitation. She didn't move.

"Do you think the grand duchess will let us talk to someone at the university?" Astrea asked. "That's probably the best place to start."

"Lucian's supposed to come by this morning," Jin said. "The man last night was no threat, but Lucian was going to have his teams dig into his background more anyway. He said he'd have something for us this morning."

Astrea huffed. She wanted to *do* something. Needed to do something. As she considered protesting, a new wall entered Astrea's awareness. She turned around in time to see Lucian pause at the dining room's open door.

"Good, you're all here," he said.

"We were just talking about you, Commander," Eliana said. "You have news?"

"Just that the man from last night was clean. Everything checked out." As he looked at Astrea, Lucian's eyebrows furrowed. "I hope I wasn't interrupting something?"

"We were just talking about the journal," Astrea said. "We need to find someone who can help us translate it. Someone at the university."

Lucian nodded once and crossed his arms behind his back. "How about we start at the palace library instead?" he suggested. "Tomas, the palace librarian, has all sorts of connections. He might know who to send us to."

That sounded perfect to Astrea. "When can we go?"

"Whenever you're ready."

"I just need to get the journal, then I can go."

"I'll go with you," Cressida said.

"Do you need us there?" Jin asked. "Adi and I were going to review some training plans for the group."

"And I was going to look over a few things I'm preparing for Ysabel," Eliana said.

"That's fine." Astrea didn't want it to sound rude, so she smiled as she added, "Really. Cress and I can handle it."

And she was sure they could. After all, books were her domain.

After a quick cup of coffee, Astrea grabbed Mattina's journal from upstairs, then joined Cressida and Commander Lucian outside. The morning sunshine made Astrea squint. The mild air was somehow both warm and cool, but Astrea didn't mind.

"Speaking of training . . ." Lucian's voice trailed off as they followed the path curving through the palace gardens. "Have you given more thought to my offer, Astrea?"

"I actually meant to talk to you about it last night, but with everything going on . . ." Well, with everything else that had happened, she'd simply forgotten to tell the commander. "But yes, I want to train with you."

"Excellent. Perhaps we can begin today? I have a break in my schedule at the third afternoon bell."

"That sounds great." Astrea actually had no idea what to expect from Lucian, but she was eager to start.

"Good," Lucian said. "Let's meet by the lake."

All around them, lush green foliage lined the walkways. Towering trees and weeping willows dotted the landscape. The occasional marble statue peeked out from between leaves, and somewhere up ahead, a fountain bubbled and splashed. Gravel crunched under Astrea's brogues as Lucian led them toward the palace. She hadn't noticed the details of the palace grounds the night they'd first arrived, and she hadn't been back to this part of the compound since. It was beautiful. Serene.

Lucian led them to a shallow stone veranda flanked by guards dressed in midnight blue and silver. They entered the palace, though none of it was familiar. Aside from the occasional guard, the corridors were empty. Ysabel *had* said she would try to keep the palace free from visitors for a while. Still, it was strange to see such a cavernous building so empty.

"This," Lucian said as he stopped in front of two enormous mahogany doors, "is the palace library. You are welcome here at any time during your stay."

"Any time?" Cressida asked.

"Yes, Miss Nikaphoros. Any time, day or night."

They followed him through the double doors. Inside was a spacious two-story room, the vaulted ceiling painted a dazzling mix of midnight blue and gold. Spiral staircases led to a mezzanine, where more books lined the walls. The fireplace at the far end of the room was unlit, though the chandeliers provided plenty of light. Several tables and seating areas took up the middle of the room. Though it was merely a fraction of the Great Library's size, it was the perfect place to start. Astrea's mind buzzed with the possibilities.

"Tomas?" Lucian called as he led them deeper inside. Silence loomed. "Tomas, you have guests!"

Astrea watched the balconies and bookcases disappearing underneath them.

"Tomas!" Lucian called again.

This time, a mop of bright blond hair popped out from between some of the shelves on the second story. "Coming!" Rushed footsteps followed, and then a short, stout fellow hurried downstairs.

"Ladies," Lucian said as the man finally stopped in front of them, "this is Tomas, our librarian."

Tomas had to be older than Saros by at least a decade. He was close to Astrea in height, and his pale cheeks flushed pink. As he smiled and pushed his round spectacles up the bridge of his small nose, the wrinkles around his blue eyes multiplied.

"Nice to meet you . . . ?"

"I'm Cressida Nikaphoros," Cressida said, sticking out her hand. He shook it.

"And I'm Astrea Sovna." She extended her hand out, too, and Tomas took it in his.

"Cressida and Astrea," he mused before turning his attention to Lucian. "Are these the young folks the grand duchess mentioned?"

"Two of them, yes," the commander replied. "There's been a development, and we were hoping you might have some insights."

"A development?" Tomas asked, curiosity tickling Astrea's nose. "Would you like to sit?" He motioned to the closest table, round and able to seat six.

Astrea and Cressida sat down first, then Lucian joined them. Tomas smiled as he set down a book Astrea hadn't realized was tucked under his arm. Warm, steady friendliness permeated the space around him.

"Well, I'm not sure how much you already know . . ." Astrea said as the silence stretched on.

"Grand Duchess Ysabel has explained some," Tomas said. "Is it true that you've encountered void mages? Her Highness said you fought them in Kalama?"

Astrea didn't feel like explaining this again, the mere thought of what happened in the Helosian capital sending goose bumps across her skin. Still, she managed to say, "Yes, it's true."

"Unfortunately," Cressida said. "And we didn't learn much from them. People trying to kill you aren't usually forthcoming."

"Indeed." Tomas chuckled, but the friendliness around him cooled to discomfort. "So, what can *I* help you with?"

Astrea set Mattina's journal on the table. She flipped it open to a random page, then slid it toward Tomas. "To make a very long story short," she said, "we confiscated this from a man associated with a void mage group called the Paragon. Do you recognize the language or that name?"

Leaning forward, Tomas brushed his fingers over the page. "I've never seen anything like it," he murmured, "and I speak all the main languages on the continent."

That was quite the feat. There were five main languages: Delian, Zaikudi, Novarian, Tornamian, and Helosian. Novarian, Helosian, and

Tornamian all shared a number of similarities, but still, few people were fluent in all five. Jin and Eliana only spoke all five because of their royal status.

"Do you know someone who can tell us more?" Lucian asked.

Tomas's thinning eyebrows furrowed. "Indeed, I may, but I will need to track her down. Lili is not always . . . so readily available. You know the flighty type."

Astrea definitely knew that type. Raela Zornovski, the head librarian at the Great Library and Astrea's old boss, was certainly flighty. But Astrea could always find Raela when she needed to. She could always rely on her.

"And who is this Lili?" Lucian asked.

"A professor at the university. I'll get in touch with her as soon as we're done here, Commander."

"Do just that," Lucian said.

Tomas gestured to the notebook as he asked, "May I copy down a bit of this text in case she wants to see it?"

"Of course." If Astrea wasn't paranoid about losing the notebook, she'd give the damn thing to Tomas if it helped them figure out what it said. "Copy as much as you'd like."

"I need to check on a few things before I'm to escort Her Highness to a meeting," Lucian said as he stood. "Will you ladies be able to find your way back to the guest house?"

"We will," Cressida said. "Don't worry about us."

Lucian nodded. "Tomas, please help them however you can. Anything they need. That's the grand duchess's order."

Tomas pushed his glasses back up his nose. "Of course. I'll make sure of it."

As Lucian bid them farewell, Tomas excused himself to get paper and a pencil to make his copy. He disappeared back up the winding staircase, his footsteps just as hurried as before.

Orange anxiety sparkled around Cressida for a moment, then disappeared. "You think he'll be able to help us?" she asked, voice low as she leaned toward Astrea.

"Maybe."

Pulling Mattina's journal back toward herself, Astrea began flipping through the pages. She'd spent an hour going through each page of that journal the night before, meticulous as she pushed her magical stamina and tried to find every strange, invisible letter Mattina had written down. The entire journal was filled with that strange language except for the page with the addresses.

She traced the foreign shapes on the page with her pointer finger. She blinked, then leaned in closer. The strange, looping letters looked like they were moving. No, not just moving. Dancing, the way Nazarov's shadows danced in Kalama and in her nightmare.

"Az?" Cressida asked. "You good?"

Astrea blinked again. The letters went still. She blinked again, but the page remained unmoving.

"Fine . . ." Astrea shook her head. "I'm just tired."

"Should've had more coffee."

"Here we are!" Tomas called as he clambered back down the stairs, waving several sheets of paper above his head. He slid back into his seat and nodded. "Right. A strange language, indeed," he mused as he examined the notebook again.

"There's actually more we need help with," Astrea said. Tomas nodded. "To make another long story short, there are some things I need to research that may be related to void magic. The old beliefs, as well as Novarian and Helosian history from the Great Wars, and mythology."

"Oh, my." Tomas let out a chuckle, half amused and half uneasy. "Well, you've come to the right place, I suppose. We can find you something on the topics."

"Thank you."

"Of course." Tomas smiled. "Let's get to work, shall we?"

Running wasn't what Astrea had in mind when she thought about training.

She'd been trailing after Adi for what seemed like forever, her pace slowing with every step she took. Tomas had promised to get back to Astrea within a couple days with news from his friend Lili. Both she and Cressida had spent a good chunk of the morning and afternoon in the library, reading the few books Tomas was able to immediately pull on their requested topics. He was going to take the next day to pull more books once Astrea brought him a list of everything she'd already read.

Then Tomas had to move on to some of his other duties, and Astrea had to meet with Lucian, anyway. When Adi heard she was going to be training with Lucian, he'd pounced on the opportunity to continue *his* version of training while they waited for the commander.

And now, Astrea was cursing herself for agreeing to go along with this at all. Running was the worst.

When they were kids, Astrea, Jin, Eliana, and Cressida had all run laps in the Kalamian palace gardens, playing whatever games they could until Eliana and Jin were summoned by their governess. But that was a long time ago, and it was for play, not whatever the skies this was.

"Come on!" Adi called from in front of her, light on his feet despite the several laps they'd already run.

"This is a very specific form of torture!" Astrea called back, rounding the corner he'd just disappeared around.

Adi grinned at her as he jogged backward down the lakeside path. "It's not that bad."

"Someone needs to examine your head," she muttered, pushing her legs to keep going. Adi's pace slowed as he matched her stride, his amusement warm and bright against her skin, just like the afternoon sunshine.

"I think you're both slow," Cressida called as she passed both Astrea and Adi. She'd already done two more laps than Astrea, but she was trying not to think about that.

Astrea ignored both of her friends, focusing instead on finishing this lap. Even if she hated running, Astrea couldn't think about anything other than putting one foot in front of the other. No Saros, no Kalama, no emperor, no bad dreams. That made it almost worthwhile.

Almost.

Up ahead, near the path that would lead them back to the guest house, Cressida stopped. She hunched over, her hands on her knees. Adi reached her first, and even he seemed winded, but that didn't stop him. As soon as Astrea reached them, Adi faced her.

"Ready to practice?" he asked.

Astrea huffed. "No."

"Which means it's the perfect time to test your limits. Get in your stance." As Astrea assumed her position, Adi said, "And after breaking that guy's nose last night, I'd suggest being careful. Don't need you healing any more broken hands, alright?"

Astrea groaned. "Are you ever going to let me live that down?"

"Not a chance!" Cressida called.

"I panicked," Astrea muttered, to which Adi simply chuckled.

Adi adjusted her stance twice before he was satisfied, then had her practice a series of jabs and crosses. He showed her how to throw something called a hook and explained more about where she should be punching people should the situation ever arise again. She was very much a beginner, but Adi said she had good form.

The sun sank lower and lower in the sky, and Lucian still wasn't there. He'd promised to join her by the lake no later than the third afternoon bell, but by the looks of the sun's position, it had to be at least the fourth bell. Lucian was late.

Adi had just started to show Astrea how to dodge a punch when the commander finally crested the hill leading back to the palace. Despite Adi's protests, Astrea dropped her stance immediately.

"Apologies," Lucian said as he joined them. "Her Highness's meetings ran late. Do you still want to begin today, Astrea?"

"I do." Learning how to fight was fine, but what she really needed was to learn more about lightbringing. She didn't want to get up close and personal with any void mages, and Adi's exercises definitely required close quarters.

"I, for one, am done for the day," Cressida said. "I'll see you back at the house for dinner?"

"See you both," Astrea replied as Adi joined Cressida. "Where do we begin, Commander?"

"Unfortunately, I don't have much time to spare since I'm so late," Lucian said. He motioned for her to sit on the ground. "But we can begin with what you already know or any questions you might have."

Questions. She had so many questions.

"I know I can heal physical injuries," Astrea said as she finally dropped into the grass. Lucian sat across from her. "I can summon some light, though doing so can be difficult for me, and I can sense emotions and pain."

"Lightbringing is different from other magics," he said. "So is stargazing, actually. You said your uncle is a Stargazer, right?" Astrea nodded. "I'm surprised he wasn't able to teach you more."

Astrea shrugged. Saros had always been paranoid about someone finding out the truth. She knew without a doubt he could teach her more, at least about the light they shared.

"Take Cressida's magic, for example," Lucian continued when she didn't answer. "There is nothing so passive about a Metalli's power. If she wants to manipulate metal, she has to do so with thought, with purpose."

This seemed like an elementary place to begin the lesson, but Astrea kept quiet. He was the expert.

"Stargazers and Lightbringers both have more passive abilities than this. Without training to do otherwise, it's hard for us to ignore the energy we sense around us, like people's emotions. We can sense things beyond ourselves, usually without even trying to do so."

"Is there a way I can control that?" Astrea asked. "I've figured out how to control how far out my senses reach, at least to an extent. But I've never been able to shut off my connection to what people are feeling. It's overwhelming."

"There is, in fact, a way. Relax as much as you can."

Easier said than done. The commander was kind enough, but she could barely relax around her friends lately, let alone a stranger. Still, Astrea rested her hands on her knees and sucked in a deep breath.

Lucian had assumed the same position as her. "Now, I want you to become aware of your body."

"What?" Was she not already aware of her body? She was in it, after all.

"Slow your breathing," Lucian said. "Focus on that first. Then start to notice sensations in and around your body."

This didn't sound like magic at all. Even in the limited lessons Saros and her mother had given Astrea, they'd never suggested anything like this.

"Trust me, Astrea," Lucian said again. "This is where you need to begin."

She nodded, then focused on her breathing. She breathed in as deep as she could, then pushed the breath out slowly. In and out she breathed, her eyes drifting closed.

"Now focus on your body and the space around you," Lucian said. "Feel the energy in you *and* around you."

What was the energy around her like? What was she feeling now, in her own body?

Pain was the first thing Astrea noticed. Bone-deep pain, her limbs almost growing heavier as she let it wash over her. Memories of Saros and Roxana, Sarsali and Balthazar, even Raela, came to her mind uninvited. Astrea's breaths grew shallow.

"It's alright," Lucian said.

"You could see that?"

"Yes. Just notice this energy for now, then move on."

"Notice it and move on." Astrea nodded. She needed to get through this if this was just the basis for everything else, the more important things she was going to need when they went back to Helosia. "I'll try again."

They repeated the exercise three more times before Astrea was finally able to 'notice and move on,' as Lucian had instructed. It didn't make her heart hurt any less, nor did it ease her homesickness, but it was manageable.

"Now I want you to feel the energy you're projecting into the world," Lucian said.

"What?"

"You said you taught yourself how to adjust the radius of your empathic senses, right?" When Astrea nodded, he said, "All emotions generate energy. All of our bodies do. To create this barrier around yourself, you need to find where your energy extends, then pull it back in toward yourself."

She scrubbed at her face. Was this how Jin—and countless other people in the world—created their walls, or did he do it without realizing it? Could he even sense his own energy that way? She'd never considered it that closely. It wasn't like she could simply ask people back in Kalama, and her family had never kept themselves closed off.

"I know you're frustrated, but just try the exercise before you write me off."

Astrea forced her shoulders down and back as she took a deep breath. This shouldn't be hard. She'd pulled on energy in and around herself dozens of times before, like when she healed Eliana back on Solstice Night or even when she'd healed her broken fingers just the night before. Why would this be much different? *Come on, Az.*

She wasn't sure how long it took, but as the ground grew harder and more uncomfortable underneath her, Astrea finally felt it. The energy surrounding her drifted out, stretching toward Lucian. He was calm. Cool curiosity radiated off him. This was different from when she healed, and it was different from when she controlled how far her lightbringing senses spread. She couldn't quite explain it. Still, Astrea imagined herself pulling her energy back toward her body. It was almost like she was pulling her magic and something more back toward herself, and it only followed her command with great effort on her part.

"How do you feel?" Lucian asked.

"It's difficult." And it was, like holding back an animal eager for freedom. It was almost like her senses didn't want to be controlled.

"It will be at first," he agreed. "How do *I* feel?"

"You feel . . ." Beyond that wall of invisible energy, she didn't feel much of anything. No colors flashed across Lucian's aura. No extra tastes coated Astrea's tongue. Nothing pressed against her skin or settled in her bones. The only thing she could feel was the cotton of her training shirt. It wasn't the wrongness of the void mages, either. The world simply grew quieter. Softer. "Did you—"

"I did nothing," Lucian said. "I am still letting my energy flow out toward you."

Part of her almost didn't believe Lucian. *I'll try it when I'm with Cress later.*

"It will take practice," the commander continued, either unaware of her distrust or simply ignoring it. "This becomes easier with time, to the point that you won't have to think about it nearly so much. Your magic and your control over it gets stronger the more you practice."

Practice. She could do that.

"What about using my magic in a fight?" Astrea asked. "I've been attacked by void mages twice now and could barely defend myself."

"That's a lesson for another day." Lucian pushed to his feet, then offered his hand to Astrea. She took it, letting the older Lightbringer pull her up.

She almost protested, then thought better of it. He was going out of his way, taking time out of his day and away from his duties to the grand duchess, to teach her anything at all. She should be grateful.

"Can you meet me again tomorrow afternoon?" Lucian asked.

"Yes, of course," she said quickly. "I'll be here."

"Good. Meet me at the third afternoon bell, and practice what we just discussed in the meantime."

As Lucian started back up the hill toward the palace, Astrea pushed her sore legs into a jog as she headed for the guest house. She needed a shower, and as her stomach rumbled, she really hoped Cressida would have that dinner she'd promised.

Chapter 12

For just a moment, Astrea wondered if she'd be able to skip Adi's future lessons. Every muscle in her body ached, and even the long, hot shower she'd taken before dinner hadn't helped.

White light drifted over her fingers, gentle as her magic explored the pain in her thighs. Would it be worth it to actually try healing this? Astrea didn't think so.

Jin had just returned from a run with Adi. How the Earthmover was able to go twice in one day, Astrea didn't know. The shower in the bathroom had been on for a good ten minutes already. It was still too early for Astrea to go to bed, and she didn't want to look at Mattina's journal anymore, nor did she want to look at the mythology book Felix had given her. She just wanted to stop thinking about the void for ten skies damned minutes.

Groaning as she pushed herself off the sofa near the fireplace, Astrea forced her legs to take her to the desk on the opposite side of the room. The journal, book of myths, Novarian police files, and Jin's old Kalamian files were stacked in the top left corner of the desk. Below that were the papers marked with the Paragon's symbol, though Jin had folded them so the symbol wasn't visible. And in the top right corner was a bundle Astrea hadn't looked at in almost two days.

Jin's letters.

He wanted her to read them, and Astrea wanted to know about what had happened in his life those eight long years, but she hesitated as she reached for them. Was she ready for this? *Yes,* she decided as she grabbed the envelopes and returned to the sofa.

Astrea sucked in a sharp breath as she untied the blue ribbon holding the bundle together. The first envelope, dated for the year Jin first left Kalama, wasn't even sealed. She pulled out a single sheet of folded paper. He wanted her to read them, and if he thought it was time, then it was time. Jin always had his reasons. She could do this. Astrea unfolded the letter.

Az,

I'm sorry I'm not writing back to you. Well, I am, but you won't ever know that. I can't send you this.

Leaving Kalama has been so difficult. Fort Ironwing is awful.

I've been to the healers four times this week already. I think one of the mage trainers here has something against me. It's not that he doesn't take it easy on me. I don't expect him to do that. But he pushes me harder than he does anyone else I've seen here. It's not even pushing . . . it's bullying.

I hope you don't mind that I'm writing to you like this. We aren't allowed much at the fort, but I have access to paper, and this makes not getting to see you easier. Maybe I'm selfish. I don't know. I hope you understand. You've always been so understanding, but I don't deserve that anymore.

I miss you. I'm sorry.

Jin

Astrea stared at the letter, then at the other envelopes sitting next to her. Some seemed to hold a single sheet like this; they were so thin. Others were so thick she couldn't begin to guess how much he'd written.

She reached for the second.

Then the third.

Then the fourth and fifth. They'd all detailed Jin's opportunity to leave Fort Ironwing with Zephyrine Kanakos, the noblewoman and former general now supporting Eliana's desire to take the throne. Jin's descriptions made Zephyrine sound kind, if not a bit aloof.

The letters didn't get truly difficult to read until the sixth.

Az,

I got your last letter. I know you don't consider us friends anymore. You probably wouldn't believe me, but it hurts me just as much as it hurts you. I wish I could hug you right now.

I also wish I could tell you about my new team in person. I learned that Zephyrine recruited me because the last Fireweaver on her team died on a mission.

This is why we can't be friends. That's going to be me someday, and I can't do that to you.

I'm sorry.

Jin

Astrea's heart ached. She remembered that final letter she'd sent him. She'd been so angry with Jin for leaving without saying goodbye. She'd been so confused. And in that time, his mage trainers had been impossibly hard on him. He'd been brought onto Zephyrine's team to replace a dead mage. How had that felt to him when he was just eighteen? That had been his fear, dying in the field. He'd told her that after the imperial dinner.

The next few letters detailed Jin's first mission and the first time he'd taken someone's life, how horrible he felt about it. His frustration about his father sending him away before he was even of legal service age. Training in the Macadian Mountains and how he was trying to get used to life at Fort Avalon. How much better things were for him serving under Zephyrine.

As Astrea reached for the next letter, the fireplace lit up with a small flame. She jumped, then turned to see Jin walking out of the bathroom.

"It's cold in here," he said.

Astrea had opened the windows earlier. A strong breeze pushed the drapes away from the wall every so often. Talmaris's nights were far colder than Astrea had expected, but she didn't mind. It was a nice change from Kalama's humidity.

Jin paused when he approached the sofa, his head tilting to one side. "You started reading them?"

"I thought you wanted me to." Astrea set down the envelope she was holding. "I can stop."

"No, I do want you to," Jin said. "I don't know. I'm just surprised."

"Surprised I'd read them?"

A wry smile tugged at his lips. "I suppose I shouldn't be surprised by you reading anything, should I?"

He circled the sofa, gathered the letters, and sat down next to her. Shame and regret pushed against her chest, suffocating even as his wall held most of it back.

What had Adi told her in Sezia? That Jin had always been there for his team, doing whatever he could to help and protect them. That he shouldered much of the responsibility for the things his father had ordered—forced—them to do. That he'd done things he didn't like just to protect them. Just what hadn't she read about yet?

"What do you think so far?" he asked.

"I didn't get through that many."

"Is my writing that boring?"

"No." She smiled at him. "You just have bad timing."

"Do you want me to leave you alone so you can keep reading?"

Astrea wanted to read every page he'd written to her over the years, but she reached for his hands, those envelopes still clutched tightly between them. "Maybe you can just tell me about some of it . . . if you want to."

Jin tossed the stack of letters onto the armchair next to him, took one of her hands and tangled his fingers with hers. Shame and regret still pulsed out from him in a slow, steady rhythm.

"What do you want to know?" Jin asked.

"Anything. Everything."

"How far did you get reading?"

Astrea swallowed. "Your first mission in Delia. You said you were brought onto Zephyrine's team as a replacement for another Fireweaver."

Staring down at their joined hands, Jin nodded. "I was. Some of the ones after that just talk about my training with my original team."

He half smiled. "Mostly that's just me complaining about them. Skies, Lando was so annoying."

"Lando?" she asked.

"One of my teammates on my very first team," he said. "Lando, Rasa, and Dorin. Zephyrine sometimes went on missions with us, too. They were all at least a decade older than me. Lando gave me a hard time when I joined, but he could also see through my bullshit, just like you always could."

"You do know I could see through it because I used to be able to feel so many of your emotions, right?" Astrea asked.

"Oh, I think it was more than that. I think you just always knew. And Lando always knew somehow, too. But he also pushed me, and he pushed me hard. He wasn't always the nicest, but . . ." Midnight blue grief thudded around him.

"What happened to him?"

Jin started drawing smooth, slow circles on the top of her hand with his thumb. "Do you remember the attacks on civilian ships during the Delian-Helosian War?"

The Corsycan War was not the first time Delia and Helosia had fought in recent years. The Kingdom of Delia had been politically unstable for nearly two decades, their royal family infighting and military leaders trying to take advantage of the chaos. The Delian-Helosian War had started five years prior and lasted almost two years. The only thing Emperor Aelius got out of it in the end was control over the island of Ilesouria.

"I remember," Astrea said. The summer of that war, civilian ships, both merchant and leisure, had been attacked by the Delians. It had enraged the Helosian public.

"My team and I were sent to Ilesouria to take out the general ordering those attacks. Our mission was to go in and take him out. And we did."

Astrea wasn't naive enough to think Jin hadn't taken lives during a war, but it was hard to imagine him in that position. In all the years she'd known him, Jin had been gentle. The only time he ever got angry was with Kaius, and Kaius had been even more of a bully when they were children.

"We'd cleared the entire fort before we went after him. But on our way out, we were ambushed. Four Delians, though we thought there were just three."

Astrea swallowed.

"The fourth was behind me, and I was covering our rear. That scar you were touching the other morning—"

"You felt that?"

Chuckling, Jin finally looked up from where their hands were joined. "I did."

"Sorry, I thought you were asleep."

"It's alright." He sighed. "The fourth Delian was behind me. That scar is where he stabbed me. I nearly bled out." Astrea's stomach twisted as steely pain spiked high around Jin. "I don't remember much of what happened, but I will never forget that moment. When I realized what happened . . . the look on Lando's face was just"—Jin swallowed—"pure terror. They'd lost their last Fireweaver in a similar situation."

"Oh, Jin—" Astrea started, but he flashed a weak smile.

"Obviously my team got me out of there. They got me back to our airship and a healer in time, but it was hard. It took me a long time to recover, even after being healed. I've had other close calls, but none like that."

That was exactly what Jin had been afraid of. That was why he'd tried to shut Astrea out all those years ago, and it had almost come to pass. What if something *had* happened to him? What if he hadn't come home?

Astrea forced herself to breathe. He *had* come home. He had. He'd nearly died, but he was there now.

"At the tail end of the war," he continued, "we were ordered to take out one of the last Delian generals that wouldn't surrender. He had Helosian prisoners of war and a half dozen war airships right near the Helosian border. The worry was that he'd either try to take more prisoners or attack some of the border towns, or both. When we got to his camp, Lando, Dorin, and I were to take out the general."

Was this what awaited them when they finally went back to Helosia? Covert missions, assassinations, and prisoners of war? Could Eliana somehow convince her father to step down without a fight? Astrea hoped so, but it didn't seem likely.

As Jin sucked in a heavy breath, Astrea edged closer to him. He didn't ask her to move away. He just focused on their joined hands again, his shoulders tight.

"Lando had always been overconfident in himself, but it got worse toward the end of the war. We were supposed to be the best of the best. The strongest mages Helosia had to offer. And that confidence was the end of him. A sword to the gut before we could react or get Lando to back off."

"Jin," she whispered as grief and regret swirled blue around him. "I'm sorry."

"The worst part was that I just . . . lost it."

"What?"

"I still don't even know exactly how to explain it," he muttered. "It's something with my magic. I can . . . turn my fireweaving into a bomb, I suppose. The only people who know about it are my old teammates—Dorin and Rasa—as well as Zephyrine and Adi. Zephyrine and I kept it out of our reports. Even Ellie doesn't know. Zephyrine and I just couldn't imagine what my father would do if he knew I was capable of generating so much power."

"A bomb?" Astrea looked down at where their fingers were intertwined, trying to imagine what that would even look like. She'd seen Cressida experiment with dozens of tiny explosives in her workshop over the years, but a fireweaving bomb sounded . . . impossible. "Is that normal?"

"That's your question?" Jin breathed a laugh. "If it's normal."

"I mean . . ." Astrea trailed off, her cheeks warming. "What else would you have me ask?"

"I don't think you understand." Shame leaked from him now, rough and suffocating. "I destroyed almost the entire Delian camp on my own, and I didn't even realize what I was doing."

Astrea's eyes followed the bursts of blue shame, cobalt regret, and steely pain as they flashed around him. "You think I would judge you for that?"

"You wouldn't?"

"No. I can see how much it hurts you."

As Jin sucked in a deep breath, the colors dancing around him subsided. "There's a lot more, but . . ."

"You don't have to tell me all at once." Astrea had so many questions for him, but she could feel his weariness. She could barely talk about her nightmares, and those weren't even real. She wouldn't push him just to satisfy her curiosity. "I can read more if that's easier."

"I want to tell you, but I think that's all I have in me for tonight."

Astrea followed his gaze to the fire still crackling, low and warm. She couldn't imagine what he'd seen. When they were children and had played in the gardens, he'd hated causing any pain, even by accident. What was that like to be able to cause so much destruction, then, and not even realize he was doing it?

"Thank you for telling me."

"I've wanted to tell you for a long time," he said. "Though I'm surprised you're still here. I'm just glad you're giving me a chance to make things right, even after all I've done."

"All you've done?" she asked, hoping he could hear the teasing in her voice. "That's a bit dramatic, don't you think?"

Jin's smile was sad as he finally peeked up at her. "There's a lot you don't know."

"Maybe, but just based on what I've read and what you've told me, it sounds like you did what you had to do to survive. It was war, Jin, and you didn't even want to go. You can't blame yourself for that."

"But?" he asked. "I've seen and done some terrible things."

"There is no but." Astrea's mind wandered to the way he'd saved her and her friends on Solstice Night. The way he'd talked her through those episodes in Kalama. The way he was now trying to save Helosia from his father and protect her from the Paragon. "I don't think it's that simple, that either you were good or bad. Besides, I know what you've done for me, and what you're trying to do for Ellie and everyone else and Helosia, and I think that counts for something. For a lot."

Jin exhaled, his shoulders slumping as he leaned his forehead against hers. "Thank you," he whispered. "Thank you, Az."

As she wrapped her arms around his neck, Jin pulled her into his lap, somehow holding onto her even tighter than she held onto him. Astrea didn't know how long they sat like that, tangled around each other on that ridiculously tiny sofa, but the shame, pain, and regret leaking from behind Jin's wall slowly receded, replaced by something much calmer Astrea couldn't name.

She glanced at the letters, long forgotten on the nearby armchair. What else had Jin been through the last eight years?

Chapter 13

Astrea pulled at the sleeves of her new blouse, a plum-colored option with delicate lace details on the collar and cuffs. The sleeves were longer than she liked, falling halfway down her hands. She settled on rolling them up to her elbows and was working on the second as she headed for the stairs.

She needed coffee, and then she needed to go back to the library to talk with Tomas. Hopefully Cressida would go with her again; she wasn't the fastest reader, but two sets of eyes were better than one.

When she was halfway down the stairs, voices echoed through the foyer. Astrea stopped mid-step.

"There's been *what*?" Eliana asked. Astrea let her senses spread out, only to be rewarded by harsh, grating anxiety—a lot of it. "When? Who?"

Astrea ran back upstairs. She knocked on Adi and Cressida's bedroom doors, then hurried across the hall to grab Jin. Only as she reached for the handle, ready to push inside, it opened. She stumbled, and Jin caught her.

"Whoa." He set her back on her feet. "What's the rush?"

"Ysabel's here," she said as both Adi and Cressida's doors opened, "and it sounds like she has bad news."

"Well, shit," Cressida muttered.

The four of them rushed downstairs, and Jin wasted no time bursting into the parlor. Grand Duchess Ysabel was perched on the sofa next to Eliana. Orange anxiety pulsed around her, but Ysabel's walls were strong. On the far side of the room near the windows, Lucian stood with his arms crossed behind his back, and Nicos had assumed a similar pose near the fireplace.

"Good, Varojin, you're here," Ysabel said.

When Astrea caught Nicos's eye, he shrugged almost imperceptibly. They hadn't talked much since that dinner a few nights before when he'd blown up about them keeping secrets. They probably needed to, but both of them seemed to be avoiding it.

"There's bad news, I'm afraid," Eliana said.

Astrea's heart jumped to her throat. Had something happened in Kalama? No, that couldn't be right. Eliana would be more than anxious if something had happened back home.

Ysabel motioned for Astrea, Jin, Adi, and Cressida to take seats. Only when they were all settled did she say, "I hate to start the morning off with this, but there's been another murder."

"In Talmaris?" Jin asked.

"Yes. Last night, based on my conversation earlier with the chief of police."

"Who was it?" he asked.

That orange anxiety sparked bright around Eliana again, her hands folded tightly in her lap. "The man Commander Lucian questioned."

Astrea was very glad she didn't have coffee. If she did, she might've spit it out or dropped the cup onto the beautiful carpet underfoot.

The man from the void house was dead?

"But we just saw him," Astrea said. "We just saw him."

Was he dead because she had been at that house? *My fault,* her mind whispered. Back in Kalama, when Astrea had told Jin this was all her fault, he'd said it wasn't, that the void mages were the only ones responsible. But she *was* connected. That man likely wouldn't have died if she hadn't gone there. Astrea barely swallowed the bile surging up her throat.

"I'd like to take Prince Varojin and Adi to the crime scene this morning," Lucian said. "I'm hoping you might have more insight that our police do not have. Anything that might help."

Jin glanced at Ysabel. "I thought I wasn't supposed to go into the city."

"Commander Lucian does not believe there is any danger at present," she said. "It will be safe for you to go."

"With all due respect, I'm perfectly capable of taking care of myself. We spoke about my work in the Helosian army."

"That we did, but I would still prefer to be cautious."

Jin huffed. "When do we leave, Commander?"

"Now, Your Imperial Highness." He turned to Astrea and said, "I believe our next lesson may have to wait."

She nodded. Lightbringing lessons were important, but figuring out why the Paragon was murdering civilians was important, too.

Lucian led Adi and Jin out the door. Astrea stared at their retreating forms, her fingers playing with the pleats in her skirt. Skies, she hoped they were careful.

"What now?" Eliana asked.

"I'm going to speak with my Stargazer." Ysabel stood and smoothed the skirt of her dark gray dress. "You're welcome to join me if you wish."

"Az? Cress?" Eliana asked. "What do you think?"

"I need to speak with Tomas this morning, Your Highness," Astrea said, more to Ysabel than Eliana. "And Cressida was going to go with me. He's helping us continue the research we started in Kalama."

Ysabel nodded. Not one hair moved out of place. "Excellent. If we split up, we'll be able to learn more. Make sure Tomas gives you whatever you need."

"Thank you, Your Highness. We will."

As Ysabel strode out the parlor door, Nicos followed her. Eliana, though, hesitated as she neared Cressida and Astrea. "If you need anything, let me know. I'll meet you back here soon?"

"Soon, Ellie," Astrea agreed. "Go meet this Stargazer."

Eliana hurried after Nicos and Ysabel, orange anxiety and red determination wavering around her as she went. And though Astrea knew there was only a chance the Stargazer would have insight, she hoped they did. They needed to put an end to things before someone else died.

After several wrong turns through the palace and speaking to one of the guards inside, Astrea and Cressida found their way to the library. The mahogany double doors seemed larger that morning, but Astrea pushed them open and led Cressida inside. This was her space—books. She didn't know much about magic or fighting or solving murders, but she knew books.

The library wasn't empty like it had been last time. Tomas was on the far side of the room near the fireplace, speaking in hushed tones with a buxom ginger-haired woman. Lavender surprise flickered around Tomas when he glanced at the door. He nodded at Astrea, then returned to his conversation.

"Well, well," Cressida murmured.

Whatever Tomas was talking about with the woman, it seemed pleasant. She even leaned over to place a quick kiss to Tomas's cheek before hurrying out of the room. Now *that* was a surprise. The stranger hurried past Astrea and Cressida, her blushing cheeks the only thing Astrea needed to know.

"Astrea, Cressida," Tomas said as he walked toward them, his own face flushed. He cleared his throat. "You're back."

"We are, and we were hoping you had something for us," Astrea said. "Have you heard back from Lili?"

"Ah. Straight to the point." Tomas smiled and pushed his glasses up his nose, the gesture an unwelcome reminder of Theo Kadis. "I haven't, but I came in early and found a dozen books that should fit the parameters you provided."

A dozen? That was amazing, but it was also going to be a lot of work. "Do you have them ready now? I'd love to start going through them."

"Have a seat. I'll go get them."

As Tomas headed for the spiral staircase in the corner, his steps rushed just like last time, Astrea and Cressida took seats at one of the round tables near the middle of the room.

"Who was that woman?" Cressida whispered despite Tomas being nowhere in sight.

"I don't know," Astrea said. Tomas didn't have bands on either of his ring fingers, so he likely wasn't engaged or married.

"Well, good for him," Cressida said. "I might even be a little jealous."

Astrea had to stifle her laugh as Tomas's hurried steps returned. The librarian dropped a heap of books on the table, all different sizes and colors. Some were thick; others were narrow. And while some had colorful cloth covers, others were bound with dark leather.

"These are the immediate texts I thought of," Tomas said. "Will this be sufficient to start?"

"That's perfect," Astrea said, standing and moving to join him on his side of the table. "May I take some of these back to the guest house with me?"

"I don't know . . ." Tomas said, his hesitation scraping on Astrea's skin.

She was supposed to be practicing what Lucian had taught her, but when she wasn't in a crowd and nobody was overwhelmed, it felt better to keep her senses open. Natural. Still, Astrea reached for that edge of her magic and pulled it back toward herself. It was difficult, like she was trying to hold on to one side of a rope while someone pulled on the other end with all their strength.

"Back in Kalama, I worked at the city's main library," Astrea said.

Tomas's eyebrows shot up. "Really?"

"Yes, I worked there for just over two years before we left." Even the thought of her old job made Astrea's lungs tighten, but she pushed the thoughts away. Worrying about that would do no good right now.

Tomas hesitated for another second, then nodded. "I think that would be alright, yes. As long as you're careful with them and bring them back."

"Thank you." Ysabel's palace was beautiful, but Astrea didn't want to be locked inside this room with Tomas for hours upon hours. "And you'll let us know when you hear back from your friend? It's really important that we speak with her."

"Of course," Tomas said. "I'll follow up with her this afternoon."

"Thank you, Tomas," Astrea said. "Thank you, really. Oh, and here." She reached into her skirt's deep pocket and pulled out a folded sheet of paper. "Here's what I've already reviewed in my earlier research."

He took the paper from Astrea. "I'll keep looking so long as you're careful with my books."

"Librarian's promise," Astrea replied, earning her a smile.

She split the stack of books with Cressida, and they headed back out into the winding palace corridors. When they finally reached the gardens again, Cressida laughed.

"What?" Astrea asked.

"And here I was worried I wouldn't have anything to do but sit around all day while we waited for the others," she said, lifting her books higher. "Let's put on some coffee and get to work."

With a groan, Astrea stretched and cracked her back. Though she and Cressida had been in the guest house parlor reading for hours, none of their friends had returned. Not even Eliana.

Tomas hadn't supplied them with many mythology books; most of what she'd read about so far was just more history. Battles that seemed unimportant, the wartime strategies of various groups from the Great Wars, and bland descriptions of long-dead rulers with no apparent connection to the void.

Astrea was sure, though, that there had to be some crossover between the myths and history. Back in Kalama, before she'd known Theo was associated with the Paragon, he'd told her that his lost manuscript had both firsthand accounts of the Great Wars *and* mythology. Why else would Emperor Aelius want that manuscript if not for some history disguised as legend? Could it be that what many deemed mythology was actually something that had happened? And the *Myth and Magic* book still in Astrea's room upstairs had interested Theo greatly despite it being largely filled with old beliefs.

But where was the overlap? What was true? That was what she needed to pinpoint.

"Anything?" Cressida asked as she finally tore her attention away from the thick book settled in her lap. Though she'd started their research session sitting on the sofa, she'd long since moved to the empty spot on the floor in front of the fireplace.

"Nothing that seems particularly useful." Astrea rubbed her temples. Her head hurt. Her eyes strained to take in even the smallest details of the parlor. "I need a break."

"Walk?" Cressida suggested as she pushed to her feet.

"Sure."

"I don't know how you do it, Az," Cressida said as they started for the foyer.

"Do what?"

"Back home, working at the library. I'm going mad not being able to bake or take something apart."

Astrea shrugged. She'd loved working at the library, even when they were short-staffed. She liked helping patrons find books, and she liked the quiet of the whole place. "It was easy on my magic, honestly."

Cressida hummed her understanding as they exited the guest house's front door, only to cut herself off as a car pulled up on the circular drive. It was already late afternoon, and the sun had inched westward. Astrea squinted as three people stepped out of the car.

Jin, Adi, and Lucian had returned. The commander exchanged just a few words with Jin and Adi, then climbed back into the car and headed off again. Orange anxiety tangled around Adi in a tight knot as he and Jin approached the front door.

"We need to talk," was all Jin said.

Swallowing hard, Astrea spun on her heel and headed right back into the guest house. Whatever Jin wanted to discuss, she highly doubted the nearby Novarian guards needed to be privy to the conversation.

"So much for a walk," Cressida muttered as she kept pace with Astrea.

"Upstairs," Jin said.

They went to Jin and Astrea's room, and once inside, Jin closed the door. Why was he being so secretive?

"Ellie's not here, is she?" he asked as he strode into the room. Astrea perched on the edge of their bed, and Adi and Cressida both stayed standing in the middle of the room.

"No, she went with Ysabel to talk to the grand duchess's Stargazer," Cressida said. "We thought she would've been back by now, but . . . she isn't."

Jin ran a hand through his hair, tugging at some of his curls before he sighed. "Alright. I'll fill her in later. You already know the murder victim was the man we interrogated."

"And?" Astrea asked.

"And he was definitely killed by void mages. Stab wound to the heart. Those shadows all over his body. But that's not all."

Astrea looked from Jin to Adi, then back again. It was just like the other murders back home.

"They've escalated," Adi said. "The Paragon have escalated."

"How?" Cressida asked. "I'd say murdering all these people is already pretty damn escalated."

"They dumped his body at that abandoned shop in the Garden District," Jin said. "And they painted the Paragon's symbol on the front window."

"Why the fuck would they do that?" Cressida asked. "Aren't they supposed to be all secretive?"

"Adi and I think it's a message." Jin lowered his voice as he added, "They have to know we're here and that we're working with the Novarians. Lucian said every other victim they'd found had been dumped somewhere secluded, and no symbols had shown up before this. There's no other reason to try to get our attention like this."

Goose bumps prickled Astrea's arms. The murder victims in Kalama hadn't been dumped in secluded areas, and the Paragon had graffitied at least one symbol in the Market District.

"Is the shadow man here?" Astrea asked. "Is he the one who killed all of those people in Sezia, then came here to the same address as us? For the leader or whomever Mattina's letter was talking about?"

"We don't know," Adi said. "We're obviously not detectives, but the crime scene didn't have anything else that jumped out at us. Nothing to suggest it's the same exact person who was looking for you in Kalama. It could be the same murderer who'd already been at work here."

"What about witnesses?" Cressida asked. "Someone must've seen something."

Jin shook his head. "So far, no one's come forward."

Astrea played with one of the pleats in her skirt. "Why kill him? Just because he spoke to us? I thought he wasn't connected."

"As far as we know, he wasn't," Jin said. "It's probably meant to be a threat toward us, and he was just caught in the crossfire."

Cressida folded her arms over her chest, wrinkling her rose red blouse. "So . . . now what? Do we switch our focus to this?"

"I don't think so. We can let Lucian's people handle it," Jin said. "Did you two find anything today?"

"Tomas didn't have an update on the language from Mattina's journal," Astrea said, "but he gave Cress and me a dozen books on the Great Wars and Novarian mythology."

"You think there's something there?" Adi asked.

Astrea shrugged. "Theo said something to me about his book, the missing one. He said it had both firsthand accounts of the Great Wars and Novarian myths. But why would a book have both? They're entirely separate topics."

"Unless they're not," Adi said, and Astrea nodded. "You think some of these myths are true, then? Is that what the emperor wants? Some more proof or information about void magic from the Great Wars?"

"That might explain why the Paragon wants that book, too," Jin said. "If it contains some information they all need. Maybe some wartime tactic or void power."

Astrea's mind hurt just thinking about it all.

"I think what's important right now is the fact that the book probably contains documented proof of void magic." The mattress dipped as Jin sat next to Astrea. "And the fact that neither the Paragon nor my father has it, either. Someone took it, and now we have to find them."

"You're right," Cressida said.

"Wow," Jin quipped. "How many times have you agreed with me in the last couple weeks? This might be a new record."

"Careful," she warned, "or I might start disagreeing just for the sake of it."

"Astrea," Adi said, rolling his eyes, "how many books do you still need to read through?"

"Eight," she said. "Cress and I planned to split them between us."

"How about we each take a couple tonight?" Jin offered. "Get through as much as we can and flag anything that might be related to the void. If you think dividing it up between us is helpful."

When Jin didn't continue, Astrea looked up. He was watching her, one eyebrow raised. "Who, me?" she asked.

"Yes, you." He laughed. "Who else would I be asking? You're the expert when it comes to this stuff."

Astrea shrugged. She didn't consider herself an expert at much of anything. If she was, maybe they could've already figured this out. Still, she said, "It would be faster. Everyone just needs to read carefully. I'll give you lists of what to look for."

"Everything's downstairs," Cressida called over her shoulder as she headed for the door. "You two are in for a treat. Really riveting stuff."

Adi followed her, mentioning something about his love for history. Slowly, Astrea pushed herself off the bed. Jin stood with her.

"You alright?" he asked as he reached for her hand.

"Fine," Astrea lied. Not only was her mind exhausted, but so was her body. Nightmares, staying up late reading Jin's letters, the exercises Adi had started putting her through. It was all weighing on her. But she didn't have the luxury of time, especially not if the Paragon were still out there killing civilians. "Let's just get back to work."

Chapter 14

Despite the clear, sunny morning, lightning and fire flashed through the Novarian palace gardens.

"Is that all you've got, Nic?" Eliana called. "Where's your bite?"

Eliana, dressed in uncharacteristic black sporting gear, moved in toward Nicos. He circled her, fists protecting his face. Amusement danced off him in warm, light waves of peach. Astrea's entire body tensed as Eliana lashed out with a right hook, blue lightning flaring around her fist. Nicos pivoted just one step, but it was enough. Eliana missed. She punched again, and again Nicos pivoted.

"Astrea?" Adi asked.

"Huh?" Astrea blinked and turned to find Adi watching her. Behind him, the guest house's roof barely rose over the hill. Jin sauntered down it, late but dressed in his fatigues.

"I asked if you're ready to start," Adi said.

"Oh. Sure."

Despite having Adi and Jin's help the evening before, Astrea, Cressida, and the two men had only managed to get through four more of the books Tomas had provided. Astrea had considered skimming them, but she doubted the information they needed would be highlighted by a chapter titled "Void Magic During the Great Wars and Why It's Been Hidden Since." No, she was sure it would be something subtle. Something small. And so they had to take their time and read carefully.

Eliana and Nicos hadn't returned to the guest house until supper. The grand duchess's Stargazer hadn't had news to share about the murders or the Paragon, and then Eliana had spent a good portion of the day discussing Helosian policy changes if she ascended the throne. Grand Duchess Ysabel was, according to both Eliana and Nicos, pleased with Eliana's ideas. She'd also invited their group to dine with her privately.

Now, they were taking advantage of the nice morning weather to fit in training before they had to get ready for this dinner. Lucian was supposed to join them eventually and give Astrea another lightbringing lesson, but he hadn't specified what time.

"I was thinking we'd start with something easy," Adi said.

Turning to follow him, Astrea tried to ignore Eliana's laughter and Nicos's grunt of pain behind her. "And what's—" she started to ask, but the question died on her tongue.

Cressida stood a dozen feet away. With a grin, she shot her hands out to either side of her body. The earth rumbled, and two wide targets rose from the ground.

"Basic target practice," Adi said.

"I thought we were letting Lucian handle my lightbringing training."

"Well, sure, but it doesn't hurt to practice even when he's not here."

"I still don't know how to send light out with a punch. We didn't get that far."

Adi smiled down at her, a dimple forming under his green eye. "I'd rather you know how to do *anything* with your light, honestly. Just do it your own way."

"Whenever you're ready!" Cressida called.

Energy swirled under Astrea's skin. Starlight twinkled over her palms, warm and low. Eliana laughed again. The breeze kicked up, tugging at the loose strands of hair escaping Astrea's braid. *Just focus.* She hadn't hit a single target last time she did this with Adi. But she'd hit Nazarov in Kalama when he'd attacked her at the palace. She could do this.

Light pulsed out from Astrea's hand and zipped toward the target on the right. It missed by more than a few inches.

"Not bad," Adi said. "Try again."

More light exploded over Astrea's palm, hotter and brighter. She aimed for the left target. It wasn't a clean shot and only caught the edge. Astrea tried again, and again, her light didn't hit quite where she wanted it.

Astrea huffed. "I'm looking right at it. Why won't it go where I want?"

"Your hips aren't turning enough." Jin's voice made Astrea jump. He circled around in front of her. "Watch me."

He assumed a stance similar to hers, with his body mostly open to Cressida and the targets. Fire burst to life over his hand. He even copied Astrea's motion, sending his fire right toward the target. It hit, leaving nothing but a scorch of black on the dirt as the flames died.

"You make it look so easy," Astrea muttered.

He chuckled. "Just try again. It's all about repetition anyway. Adi and I have done this tens of thousands of times."

"Something to look forward to," Adi quipped from behind Astrea. "Lots and lots of practice."

As Jin joined Adi, Astrea resumed her stance. She pulled on her light again, trying to copy Jin's movement as she shot it toward the right-side target. And just like before, her light barely hit the edge.

"Here." Jin came up behind her, his hands resting on her wide hips. Even though his touch was all business, Astrea's entire body warmed. She was sure even the tips of her ears were bright red. "I'll guide you, if that's alright."

"Sure," Astrea squeaked as she ignored Cressida's knowing smile. Her magic still buzzed just underneath her skin, eager.

"When you're ready," Jin said. His right hand stayed on her hip while the left moved to her shoulder. "Your arm and hips both need to turn more to the left."

Light shot out from Astrea's palm. She aimed left, as instructed. As she did, Jin guided her body the slightest bit. Her light still didn't hit the center of the target, but it was that much closer.

"See?" he asked, his grip still firm. "Simple."

"Right. Simple." Astrea swallowed hard, an unfamiliar mix of satisfaction and shyness swirling in her chest. That *had* been much better. But why did Jin's touch have to make her so nervous and giddy at the same time? "Thanks."

Jin sucked in a breath, almost like he was going to say something. His hands dropped away. "I'm going to go watch Ellie. I need to evaluate where she's at."

And then he was gone.

Cressida lowered the targets back to the ground. Peach amusement danced in the air, but Astrea didn't have time to consider it. Adi clapped a hand on her shoulder.

"Let's keep going, yeah?" When Astrea nodded, Adi called to Cressida, "How about four smaller ones this time? We'll make it a little more interesting."

Astrea may not have been a natural fighter, but Adi was a natural teacher. He was so encouraging and reassuring. By the time Lucian finally showed up, Adi had Astrea feeling that much more confident in her magic. No, she couldn't hit the centers of his targets very often, not like Cressida. And no, she couldn't quite use her light the way he hoped. She still had to do things her self-taught way. But she was doing them. It was something.

"So, I see Adi has already put you to work," Lucian said as Astrea followed him away from her friends toward a quieter area of the garden. Nearby, Adi and Cressida were sparring while Jin watched. Nicos and Eliana had returned to the guest house half an hour before. "Hopefully you've still got some energy."

"I do," Astrea said despite the fatigue settling into her bones.

"Good." As he turned toward her, the silver stitching of his captain of the guard uniform sparkled in the sun. "Though if it's not too forward of me to say so, it seems you have a lot on your mind. Have you been practicing with your barrier?

"Some," Astrea said, "but it's uncomfortable, actually."

"It gets easier with time. Keep practicing."

"I will."

Lucian pressed his lips together, then said, "I know going up against the Helosian Empire must seem impossible. And this Paragon, too."

"Have the police found any leads on the murder?" Astrea asked. Last she'd heard, they hadn't, but maybe they'd found something overnight.

"No, they have not."

Astrea sighed. "Great."

"Let's just move on to today's lesson, alright?" Lucian suggested. "Let's talk about the offensive side of your lightbringing. Emotions are just one type of energy, correct?"

"Yes," Astrea said. She already knew that.

"Well, we can use our emotions as fuel."

"I know. I've felt it before." Astrea had recognized the correlation years ago, first after a bad day at university and, more recently, during their short fight with Prince Kaius. "I've even used it a bit."

"Recognizing it is different than practicing it." A ball of light burst to life over Lucian's outstretched hand, like a miniature star come to life. "Go ahead, do the same."

Astrea was exhausted after everything that had happened since the start of the summer. Digging around the library with Tomas. Staying up late to talk to Jin. Training. Trying to find a way to save her family. Now, even summoning light felt like a chore. But her own tiny star hovered over her palm, the white light a contrast to Lucian's blue.

"As a Lightbringer, your strength comes from feeling your emotions, not suppressing them," Lucian said. "That's the core of your power. So, think about everything that's bothering you. What's making you angry, Astrea? What's causing you so much pain?"

That was a simple answer. She opened her mouth to speak, but Lucian shook his head and pointed at her light with his free hand.

"Don't tell me. Tell your magic. Close your eyes and focus on all of that energy in you."

Breathing in deep, Astrea followed Lucian's instructions. She pulled on how she'd felt most days since receiving the emperor's letter—the helplessness, the frustration with Saros, the fear of the shadow man, the blame she laid on her own shoulders—and searched for the energy in her mind's eye. It danced and flickered like a flame, angry and hot.

That was how she wanted her light to be. Angry. Hot. Dangerous.

"Remember what you're doing," Lucian said, satisfied, "because it's working."

Astrea squinted as she opened her eyes. Her light had nearly tripled in size, white-hot. It reminded her of one of the balls she saw children in Kalama playing with at the beach, only this one was angry and vibrant.

"Now kill it off," Lucian instructed.

She pulled back on her magic as she often did to dismiss the little light she usually summoned, but it didn't react. She tried again.

"Find the opposite of your anger, Astrea. That is just as powerful."

What soothed her?

Eliana and Cressida's laughter that morning when they were teasing Nicos about spilling coffee on himself. Every time Jin smiled at her, that secret smile he only showed her. The first time Saros had bought Astrea cinnamon pancakes when she was just ten years old. Sarsali and Balthazar's warm hugs.

The light dimmed, disintegrating into a dust of twinkling stars as Astrea's heart calmed again.

"Very good," Lucian said. "You're a quick study."

She shrugged. "I already knew some of it."

"Even so." He ran a pale hand over his hair, smoothing back a few pieces that had escaped his bun. "Let's work on that for the rest of the lesson, shall we? We can talk about healing another day."

"Whatever you think is best," Astrea said. She already knew how to heal, but she would study whatever Lucian asked her to. It would help her take on Helosia, and it would help her take on the Paragon. It was worth it.

By the time Astrea finished training with Lucian, she was the last of their group to make it back to the guest house. While everyone else had already cleaned up and eaten lunch, Astrea had showered. She'd just scarfed down some leftovers Cressida saved for her, and now, she needed to get back to work. She had half a day to kill before the grand duchess's dinner, and she was sure she could make it through another one of Tomas's books if she was quick.

The problem was, she'd left it in the parlor. Which wasn't a problem, exactly, but Astrea's tired body protested at the thought of walking up and down the guest house's staircase again.

Still, she made her way down the quiet second-floor hallway and descended the stairs. Jin had gone to talk to Eliana about Ysabel's dinner invitation, and Cressida had mentioned something about trying to study the meteorite some more. Adi was in his room, reading another one of Tomas's books. The quiet settling over the house actually helped Astrea's nerves settle, too. She used to crave this kind of silence. Silence she hadn't had since fleeing Kalama.

The parlor door was already ajar. Astrea nudged it open, only to stop short.

"Oh," she said. "Sorry."

Nicos sat on the sofa, an array of papers and folios spread out on the coffee table. Unexpected. He was always stuck to Eliana's side.

"Hey, Astrea." He glanced up at her, his light brown eyes clear and focused. "Do you need something? Is Ellie alright?"

"Ellie's fine." Astrea shifted her weight to her right leg and crossed her arms behind her back. "I was just looking for a book I left in here . . . I was going to try to do some more research before we have to go to this dinner."

"Ah." Nicos gestured toward a narrow side table to the right of the sofa. "I put one over there when I came in."

"Thanks." Astrea hurried over to it and snatched the thick blue book from the table.

Nicos simply returned to his paperwork, shuffling through a few loose sheets he held in his hand. She hated feeling awkward around Nicos, but after he'd snapped at all of them—at her—at dinner earlier in the week, she didn't know what to think. He hadn't been hostile toward her since then. He wasn't even annoyed or upset now, at least not according to her magic. But he also hadn't been his usual friendly self. They also hadn't seen much of each other at all.

"Listen, Nicos . . ." Astrea clutched the book to her chest. "I hope you know I'm really sorry about what happened on Solstice Night. I didn't mean for Ellie to get dragged into this."

He sighed, a heavy, tired sound, as he set down the papers he'd been holding. Nicos ran a freckled hand over his equally freckled face, then scratched at his beard. "It's not your fault," he said. "I shouldn't have snapped at you like that."

Astrea shrugged. "I'd be upset if the positions were reversed."

"Still. That's not the way to bring it up, and I owe you more than that. Besides," he said, finally meeting her gaze, "you saved her life that night even though it put yours in danger."

"I would do it again," Astrea said. "I would never hesitate to do that for her."

"I know." The corners of his mouth quirked up, the first time he'd smiled at Astrea in days. "Thank you for keeping her safe."

As Nicos resumed his work, Astrea asked, "What is all of this, anyway?" He didn't exactly strike her as the type to get involved in bureaucracy of any kind.

"Ellie's plans for when she takes over Helosia," he said.

"When did she have time to make all this?"

"Well . . ." Nicos hesitated before he finally said, "She's been working on it for a while."

"What?" The word barely left Astrea.

"A couple of months, actually."

That . . . that wasn't just a reaction to Emperor Aelius's void connection. That was . . . planning. Back in Kalama, right before Solstice Night, Eliana had mentioned that she thought the rebels had some good points. She'd often disagreed with her father's policies. But . . .

"Plans for if she was named heir or plans for the rebellion?" Astrea asked.

"A little of both. I've been helping her, actually. As it turns out, growing up in a military family means I have a lot of perspective. Or so Ellie says."

"I thought Ellie wanted to end the wars."

"Oh, she does, and so do I. But my parents were stationed all over Helosia," Nicos said. "I saw a lot of the empire. Met a lot of people."

Astrea nodded. "Well . . . that's helpful."

Nicos chuckled. It was warm, friendly. "It is. Granted, I've been in Kalama for years now, but still. As Ellie says, I've got more real-world experience with the empire than she does. We're hoping to have a revised version ready sometime soon to present to the grand duchess."

"Good luck."

He smiled again. "You too."

As Astrea returned to the foyer, she let out a relieved breath. At least she and Nicos were on the same page. About a lot of things, it turned out. She'd always known he was devoted to Eliana, but to know he'd been helping her plan for something like this—even just a small bit—was a relief.

But Nicos had his work cut out for him for the afternoon. *And so do I,* Astrea thought as she trudged back upstairs. *So do I.*

CHAPTER 15

Dark flames burned, burned, burned. A dark laugh, deep and low, echoed everywhere and nowhere.

"Where do you think you're going, little Lightbringer? Trying to run away from me?"

A hand yanked her hair. Pain seared across her shoulder, snaking down to her sternum. Around her, everything burned hot and cold.

"You can't hide from me, little Lightbringer. I will find you."

Astrea gasped as her eyes opened, her heart pounding so fast she thought it might explode. She summoned light over one hand, staring as the Novarian bedroom came into focus around her. Why was it so dark?

The drapes, Astrea realized. Jin must have drawn the thick velvet drapes over the window while she was asleep.

In fact, something heavy weighed her down. Astrea dismissed her light and leaned back into the pillows. Jin was asleep next to her, his head tucked near hers and his arm wrapped tightly around her waist.

When had she fallen asleep? After chatting with Nicos, she'd started making an outline of myths from Tomas's books as well as *Myth and Magic.* She'd hoped to use it later to narrow down what they needed to be delving into.

She reached for the switch on the lamp beside the bed. Warm light filled the room. Her books and notes were stacked neatly on the bedside table; Jin must've done that, too. But Astrea nearly jumped out of bed as she read the clock. It was already past the fourth afternoon bell, and they had to meet with Ysabel for dinner at six.

Skies, Astrea was tired. Between training and staying up late the night before to read, she wanted nothing more than to stay in bed with Jin.

Next to her, Jin yawned. "Az?"

"We need to get up," she said. "We have to get ready for dinner."

"What time is it?"

"Quarter after the fourth bell."

He kissed her cheek and said, "Then we have a little time."

Astrea's entire body heated pleasantly. She peeked up through her lashes only to find Jin watching her, his expression sleepy and soft. Yes, she needed to get out of bed to get ready, but Astrea still found herself melting into his arms.

"How long was I out?" she asked.

"Just a couple hours." Jin played with the end of her braid, twisting it gently between his fingers.

"I didn't mean to fall asleep."

"Hm." He tugged on her braid gently and said, "If you're falling asleep while working, you might be overdoing it."

"The bed's just very comfortable."

"Still. Your body's not used to training. That, plus all of this studying, is going to wear you down."

"I'm fine."

"I just don't want you to push yourself too hard. Let us help. It's what teams are for."

"Adi was helping. He was just in the other room."

Jin rolled his eyes even as he smiled. Astrea couldn't help herself. She stared at his mouth, taking in the shape of his smooth, light pink lips. Her belly tightened, then tightened again when he whispered, "What are you looking at?"

"Nothing."

"Liar." Jin dropped her braid and reached for her face. When his thumb brushed the apple of her cheek, Astrea swallowed hard. "Can I kiss you?"

"You really don't have to ask."

With a chuckle, Jin pressed his mouth to hers. Though it was soft—almost chaste—Astrea's entire body buzzed. They pulled apart, but Jin pulled her back in, harder this time. Astrea opened her mouth to his, and Jin's teeth pulled at her lower lip. She hummed, and Jin smiled against her mouth.

"Isn't this better than immediately getting out of bed?" he asked.

Astrea was about to answer him with another kiss when someone pounded on their door. Both of them startled.

"Az! Jin!" Eliana called. "You didn't forget about dinner, did you?"

Pressing his forehead against Astrea's, Jin sighed. Then he pulled away and yelled, "No, we didn't!"

"Can I come in?" Eliana paused, a mix of soft curiosity, sweet approval, and nauseating disgust making Astrea's stomach turn. "Oh, skies, you're not naked, are you? Gross."

"Ellie, just come in!" Astrea yelled as she scrambled out of bed. Jin followed.

One heartbeat passed, then another, and another. Finally, the door creaked open. Eliana stuck her head inside, her hair already swept up in a chic bun. "Oh, good, you *are* clothed," she said as she pushed the door open wider. "Here." Eliana held up two black garment bags. "From Ysabel."

"What is it?" Jin asked as he met his sister near the door and took both bags from her.

"I told her no tailors, and yet her staff took the measurements we gave them for the store and made us a few things anyway," Eliana said. "For tonight. And other nights, I suppose. There should be two things for both of you."

"Thanks, Ellie," Astrea said.

"Yes, well." Eliana smiled at them as she smoothed the front of her blouse. "I should go finish getting ready. Want me to do your hair, Az?"

"If you don't mind."

"I don't. Come on, Cress is already waiting." Eliana snatched one of the bags back from Jin without so much as a single word, then grabbed Astrea's hand. "Be ready in an hour, Jin!" Eliana called over her shoulder as she dragged Astrea out the door.

"Can you slow down?" Astrea asked, snatching her hand away. "Skies."

Eliana wasted no time, scurrying down the hallway and into the room at the far end. It was nearly a mirror image of Jin and Astrea's, though instead of the same cool blue color scheme, this one had shades of pink and gold. As promised, Cressida was already inside and laying out her own garment bag on Eliana's bed.

"Let's see what they gave you, shall we?" Eliana asked as she tossed Astrea's bag on the bed and began unbuttoning the front.

Scrubbing at her face, Astrea tried to get rid of both the fatigue still lingering in her body and the feeling of Jin's hands on her skin out of her mind. She really just needed to talk to him. Finally finish that conversation they'd started in Sezia. Everything else just felt more important.

"Oh!" Eliana's aura lit up with teal approval as she took out one dress, then another. "These are nice. Which one do you want to wear?"

Astrea padded over to the bed. Two dresses had been laid out for her: one forest green and the other midnight blue. They weren't exactly Astrea's preferred style, especially with the plunging necklines and thick fabric, but they were pretty. The green one had subtle beading along the hem and neck, and a silver lace overlay finished off the blue option.

"I'll wear the blue," she said.

Eliana nodded and shoved the garment at Astrea.

"What do you think?" Cressida held up a champagne gown and another that was topaz and red. "I think I'm feeling the champagne."

"Do it." Eliana nodded. "Not bad since they've had, what, a week?"

Astrea folded her dress over her arm, then slunk off toward the bathroom while Cressida and Eliana discussed fashion. It wasn't that Astrea didn't care for the conversation; the three of them had talked about mundane things like that all the time back home. Astrea just needed another moment to collect herself.

She closed the door behind her and wiggled out of her linen dress. As she slid on the blue one, she realized her brassiere wasn't the right cut for the neckline. With a sigh, she took it off. It was fine, though. The dress's bodice held her small bust perfectly.

Astrea, however, couldn't secure the last few buttons on the back. As she started for the bathroom door, a razor on the counter caught her eye. And when Astrea actually surveyed the bathroom, she realized that half the items on the counter weren't Eliana's.

Eliana liked very specific things. She'd used the same moisturizer and cosmetics for years, always going back to the same shops to ensure she got what she liked. Half the reason Eliana even liked them was that they were beautifully crafted and kept in pretty gold containers. And the plain wood and metal jars mixed in with the gold were definitely not Eliana's.

Which means . . . Nicos. Of course. Astrea didn't know why she was surprised. Surprised, maybe, to see the two of them be so careless about it. They'd been trying to hide whatever was going on between them since Solstice Night, Astrea was sure.

She went back into the bedroom, only to find both Cressida and Eliana in various states of undress. Not unusual for situations like this. "Can one of you help me get the last few buttons?" Astrea asked.

"I'll do yours if you do mine," Cressida said as she fixed the straps on her dress. Then she joined Astrea and buttoned everything. As Astrea worked on the back of Cressida's dress, the Metalli said, "Why dress up, though? It's just us and Ysabel, right?"

"It is," Eliana said, "but you know how this works. There's a certain image to uphold."

"Even to just one person?"

"Yes." Eliana turned around as she finished adjusting her crimson dress, then smiled at Astrea. "Good choice. Goes with the necklace Jin gave you."

"And all those simple grooming products really go with your collection, Ellie," Astrea quipped.

"What—" Magenta embarrassment burned through the room, almost blinding.

"Oh, shit, really?" Cressida asked as she made a beeline for the bathroom.

"Hey!" Eliana called. "You weren't supposed to see that."

"Then maybe don't leave everything out like that." Cressida grinned as she returned. "What's the deal?"

"I'm not ready to talk about it." Eliana stalked toward the narrow desk tucked in the corner of the room. There, she began spreading out tubes of lipstick and kohl pencils.

"Talk about Nicos?" Cressida asked. Eliana nodded as orange anxiety curled around her curvy frame. "Why? We like him. What's the big deal?"

"I know, but . . . it wasn't supposed to happen. I'm still trying to figure it out."

"Well, whatever you want, Ellie," Astrea said, "Cress and I just want you to be happy."

Though that orange anxiety remained in Eliana's aura, mint relief mixed with it. Her shoulders dropped. "So, what do you two want to do with your hair?"

Ysabel's private dining room was exactly what Astrea expected: the same cool color scheme as the rest of the palace, paintings of landscapes and deceased ancestors on the walls, and a table large enough to seat a dozen people. Several trays and bottles of wine already sat on the table.

A member of Ysabel's staff guided each of them to their seats. Eliana sat to Ysabel's right, Nicos and Adi on the same side of the table as her. Jin was to the grand duchess's left, Astrea was next to him, and Cressida filled the last spot on their side. Astrea thought Lucian might join them, but once everyone was settled, he positioned himself near the door, arms held behind his back.

The dinner started with the same pomp of meals in the Helosian palace: shows made out of wine being poured, plates being set, and dishes being brought out. It seemed pointless to Astrea, but the food smelled incredible. There were dumplings, roasted vegetables, and slices of the fluffiest bread Astrea had ever seen to start with. One of the palace staff even started up an ornate gramophone. A soft waltz echoed through the room.

"While this last week has seen its challenges," Ysabel said as the servants retreated from the room, "I'm very glad to have you both here, Eliana and Varojin." The grand duchess lifted her wine glass, and Astrea reached for hers to join the toast. "To the next generation. I look forward to further uniting our families."

What did that mean? Astrea fiddled with her necklace as she watched Eliana's aura. It revealed no hint about what Ysabel's words might mean; Eliana was calm.

"We look forward to the same," Eliana said. Jin offered a small smile, but he didn't say anything. "Thank you for inviting us tonight, Ysabel."

"It's my pleasure, Eliana," Ysabel said. If Eliana and the grand duchess were on a first-name basis, that had to be a good sign, right? "I'm eager to learn more about your friends." Her purple eyes flicked to Jin. "And you, Varojin. We haven't discussed much outside of your time in the military."

"There isn't much to add." Jin picked up his crystalline goblet. "Unless you want to hear about my teenage years."

Ysabel's lips pursed as she looked around the table. "Miss Nikaphoros. Let's start with you then, shall we? What do you do back home?"

"I'm an engineer for my father's company, Your Highness," Cressida said. "My mother's a Greenkeeper for the city."

Ysabel nodded thoughtfully. "I always wanted to be a Greenkeeper when I was a little girl. While I was not gifted with magic, at least I am able to employ Greenkeepers to do the work for me."

"My mother would love your gardens, I'm sure. They're beautiful," Cressida said.

Ysabel smiled at her. Not the practiced smile of a public figure but a real smile, genuine and warm. "Thank you very much. They are my pride." She turned to Adi next. "And you, Mister Kuwat? Varojin said you served with him during the Corsycan War?"

"And earlier than that, too, Your Highness," Adi said.

"What about your family?"

"My younger sister's studying in Kalama," he said as he brought a forkful of roasted potatoes to his mouth.

"And what does she study?"

Adi chewed, then swallowed before answering. "Archaeology and Helosian history."

"Two degrees at once? That must keep her busy," Ysabel said.

"Oh, it does. I'm very proud of her, Your Highness."

"And you, Miss Sovna?" Ysabel asked. "I'm still curious how a Light-bringer escaped Emperor Aelius's front lines."

Astrea tried to school her features into calm, but she hadn't been practicing her barrier like Lucian had taught her. She was sure he could sense her anxiety. He even glanced in her direction for a moment.

"Oh, well . . ." Astrea pushed a glazed carrot around on her plate. They hadn't explicitly agreed they weren't telling Ysabel about Astrea's past. They just weren't telling her about the vision she'd had. Under the table, Jin's hand brushed Astrea's. When she peeked up at him, he nodded. "Well, Your Highness, you know my uncle is a Stargazer. When I was very young, he had a vision of me dying in battle. He had me hide my magic."

"Indeed?" Ysabel's eyebrows rose.

"Yes, and so instead, I got my degrees in Helosian literature and the Tornamian language. I started working in Kalama's public library." There. Ysabel could do with that information whatever she wanted.

"Impressive," Ysabel said. "That must be so interesting. Did you get to meet many patrons during your time there?"

"Oh, yes, Your Highness. All kinds."

"Tomas has always claimed he prefers working here at the palace library because he has to deal with far fewer people," Ysabel said. "Though I'm sure he still gets his fair share of visitors."

Astrea smiled tightly before biting into a dumpling. Eliana cut in before Ysabel could get started on a tangent about literature, instead directing the grand duchess's attention to the palace's architecture. Astrea tried to follow the conversation as it shifted to the antique furniture collection

Ysabel had in one of the other wings of the palace. But she couldn't stop thinking about the hundred things they still needed answers for.

Void magic, the Paragon, the rebellion, the Great Wars. *I need to see Tomas first thing in the morning and start narrowing down our focus.* She had a plan, but when she wasn't thinking about those things, her mind jumped to her lessons with Adi and Lucian. Why wasn't she progressing more quickly? Was she not cut out to fight? Was she not strong enough? Astrea wished she could just turn her mind off the way she could switch a lamp off.

By the time dessert—cups of espresso and individual fruit tarts made with red berries—was brought to the table, Astrea wanted nothing more than to go back to the guest house and take a long, hot shower.

"Now that we'll be alone for a while," Ysabel said once the last servant had left the dining room, "there's something I would like to discuss."

"And what might that be?" Eliana asked.

"I've received new intelligence on the Corsycan War, and it doesn't look good."

Of course. Astrea's stomach dropped, spoiling her appetite more than it already had. *More bad news.*

"The Delians are reporting an attack by the Helosians that resulted in three hundred casualties," Ysabel said.

Beside Astrea, Jin stiffened. "Not unusual for Corsyca, unfortunately. I've seen worse numbers."

"It's not the number of casualties that has me and the Delians concerned," Ysabel said. "It's the way they were killed."

"And how was that?" Eliana asked.

"Several survivors reported black flames, not from bombs but from mages."

"I don't know that it's unexpected to learn my father has void mages in his army," Jin said, but the hairs on Astrea's arms prickled.

"We certainly didn't know of any, though," Adi said. "Not even a whisper, and news like that usually spreads through the ranks. We haven't been gone from Ironwing for that long."

"Maybe your father has hidden away these mages until he deemed the timing right," Nicos said. "I still can't believe he had one at the palace and I didn't know."

Astrea frowned. Emperor Aelius would have the resources to hide such mages, yes, but why would he deploy them now? The only consolation was that the Delians didn't seem to know it was void magic specifically that they were up against. But that information couldn't stay hidden forever, and if Emperor Aelius really had deployed void mage troops, the timetable for that information spreading had just shortened considerably.

"Whatever the case may be," Ysabel said, "it's disconcerting to know void magic has spread to Emperor Aelius's army. It was exactly as you said you feared, Eliana."

Eliana's red-painted lips pressed into a thin line. "It won't be good."

"I plan on speaking with my council tomorrow about this development," Ysabel said. "I know both myself and my advisors have been reluctant to support you in an official capacity, Eliana, but perhaps it's a discussion we need to have sooner rather than later."

Lavender surprise flickered around the table. "That would be wonderful, Your Highness," Eliana said.

"Although, based on what I've been told," the grand duchess continued as she lifted her espresso cup, "you may want to rethink your return to Helosia until you know more about the changes in your father's army."

Wait longer to go home? They'd never had a timeline for that, not officially. Astrea knew this wouldn't be over in a single week, perhaps not even a few weeks, but how long would it be before she got to go back to Kalama?

"We have no plans at present," Jin said. "We need to know the full extent of support Eliana has before we can even begin to think about making the trip back."

"Actually . . ." Ysabel's lips pulled into a tight smile. "While it is not the same as hearing from your friend, the general, my people were able to get the information you requested, Varojin."

"What information?" Eliana asked.

"Varojin requested that they find out about the Stargazer, Saros," the grand duchess said. "And Miss Nikaphoros's parents as well."

Astrea's attention snapped from her plate to the grand duchess. Under the table, Jin squeezed her hand again. Astrea reached for Cressida's on her other side.

"It appears your uncle is still at the observatory," Ysabel explained. "Apparently he's being hailed as some kind of hero for helping to unearth that void mage, the one you fought at the palace . . . Victor Nazarov?"

Astrea tried to blink her tears away. Not only did she not want to cry in front of Ysabel and Lucian, but the kohl Eliana had so delicately lined Astrea's eyes with would get everywhere.

Saros was being called a hero? He *had* been trying to stop Nazarov when the palace guards descended on them; he'd just also been lying to the emperor for over a decade. Was stopping Nazarov enough to outweigh that crime?

"As for the Nikaphoroses," Ysabel said, "they're at their home in Kalama. My people have tracked them at home and around the city. They're moving about freely, unhindered by any Helosian guards or troops."

"Thank fuck," Cressida whispered, so low even Astrea almost didn't hear it. Relief. Relief was the only thing rolling off Cressida now in bright, minty waves. It coated Astrea's skin and tongue, cool and crisp and so, so welcome.

Astrea picked up her water glass and took a sip, trying to will the fresh tears away. Though she didn't know Ysabel well, the fact that it was *the* Novarian grand duchess's people providing the information made it real. Saros and the Nikaphoroses weren't safe—nobody was in Kalama, or even on the continent—but they weren't in prison. Saros was at home, at the observatory. The Nikaphoroses were at home. And right now, that was good enough for Astrea.

"You alright?" Jin's voice was low, and everyone else at the table had started discussing how to get more information about void magic in Corsyca.

"Thank you," Astrea whispered. "Thank you for asking Ysabel to do that."

Jin smiled that soft, secret smile. "Anything for you, Az."

Chapter 16

By the time dinner was over, the sun had completely set and the stars were out in force. Adi, Cressida, Eliana, and Nicos were walking ahead of Astrea and Jin. Something Adi said made the others laugh. Though the news about Emperor Aelius's army wasn't good, Astrea couldn't focus on anything other than the fact that her family was okay. They were as okay as they could be given the situation, given their decision to stay behind. The weight that had pressed so heavily on her chest the last few days had finally lifted, not fully but enough to let Astrea breathe.

"I thought we could go for a walk before we go back to the house," Jin said. "If you want to."

"A walk?" She nodded. "Let's go for a walk."

"Hey!" Jin called, and Adi and Nicos turned around. "We're going for a walk."

"Do you want company?" Cressida yelled back.

"Absolutely not."

Peach amusement lit up the night as Jin pulled Astrea toward the path that would lead them down to the lake. He laced his fingers through hers, his pace slow as they moved through the darkness.

"Thank you," Astrea said as they approached the lake, the same one she now spent so much time running circles around.

"For what?" Jin asked.

"For asking Ysabel to find out what she could about Saros, Sarsali, and Balthazar."

"You already thanked me for that."

"I know, but I really mean it. Thank you."

Jin squeezed her hand. "And I meant what I said, too."

"Anything for you." His words echoed in her mind as they strolled toward the water. Just ahead, near the spot where Astrea usually trained with Adi and Cressida, small lanterns sat on the ground, spread equal distances apart to make a rectangle. As they got closer, Astrea realized they marked the four corners of a blanket.

"What's this?" Astrea asked as Jin led her toward it.

"A surprise," he said. "I have nine birthdays and two graduations to make up for, remember? I know it's not much, and it doesn't really make up for anything, but I thought it'd be nice to actually be alone for a while."

"You didn't have to do that," she murmured, though she couldn't suppress her smile. No one had ever done something like this for her, as small of a gesture as it was.

"Yes, I do. And much more than this, too."

As they reached the blanket, Astrea took another step forward. At night, the lake was like a galaxy coming to life, hundreds of stars reflected on the black surface of the water. Astrea sat down next to Jin, her focus trained on the sparkling light.

What would life be like if they were just two old friends with no conspiracies or wars or thrones to worry about? What if Astrea hadn't had to keep her truth hidden for so long? What if Jin hadn't been born into two royal houses?

"What are you thinking?" he asked as he tucked a stray piece of hair behind her ear.

"That I wish we didn't have to worry about all this," she said. "I can't help but wonder what our lives would've been like if I hadn't hidden my magic and you hadn't been sent to war."

"I've wondered that before, too." Jin nudged her shoulder with his. "What *would* it have been like if I'd been home? What trouble would we have caused?"

"Trouble?" Astrea laughed. "Remember what Cress said after Solstice Night, about how I'd be the last person in the room to have enemies? Well, it's true."

"Oh?"

"My life's been boring."

"I'm sure you've done something fun in eight years." Jin shrugged off his suit jacket and unbuttoned the top few buttons of his shirt.

"Well." Where did Astrea begin? "For a few summers, I worked at Lodestar as a secretary for Balthazar."

"Work isn't fun," Jin said. "That doesn't count."

"Right, well . . . The spring I turned eighteen, Sarsali finally convinced me to try working in the garden with her. I was always afraid to do so since she's so particular about those flower beds, but she really wanted me to. I was no Greenkeeper, but she taught me how to tend to her rose bushes the non-magical way."

"I don't think I've touched a rose bush a single day in my life," Jin said.

Astrea smiled, her gaze fixed on the lake. The tendrils of the nearby weeping willow rustled in the breeze. Here, with the mix of floral scents hanging on the cool night wind, she could almost imagine being back in Sarsali's garden. The dirt. The soft petals and leaves. The thorns and bugs, too.

"Cress never would garden with her," Astrea said. "She always wanted to spend time in the workshop with Balthazar, so I think inviting me into the garden was as much for Sarsali as it was for me. It was nice."

"And you never wanted to work in Balthazar's workshop?"

"Skies, no. Have you ever been in there?" Astrea asked. Jin laughed, his chuckle warm and deep as amusement tickled her nose. "It's a nightmare. I tried several times, but either Cress or her dad would accidentally set something on fire."

"I suppose accidental fires aren't very fun."

"Definitely not." She glanced sidelong, only to find Jin watching her. "I would give anything to be at their house right now. I miss both of them and Saros."

Jin angled his body toward hers. "I'd give anything to take you back."

"Do you think we can go soon? Do you think Ysabel's council will support Ellie?"

"They're fools if they don't." Jin ran a hand over the back of his neck. "Ysabel didn't mention it at dinner tonight, but she thinks I should meet the rest of the family."

"Oh." Was that what Ysabel had meant when she mentioned 'uniting' the two families? "You don't sound so sure about it."

"I know it could be a good thing, especially since we need them to support Ellie and they'll hold sway with the council." He sighed. "But I know it's more than that. It's a side of my family I know nothing about. They didn't even know about our connection for twenty-six years. And it makes things . . . complicated."

"Things are already complicated," Astrea said quietly. "Everything back home, the Paragon, the void . . ."

"And us?" Jin reached for her hand. He glanced down at their twined fingers before saying, "I'd be lying if I said I wasn't worried about how this affects you. Us."

Astrea swallowed. "Whether you're a member of one royal family or two, I think it's complicated either way."

Jin was a skies damned prince, not just of one country but two. Two crowns, even if he would likely never accept power, let alone be put in that position in the first place. It didn't change that it was complicated. There were rules and expectations for royalty. And while Helosians weren't shy about all things romantic, they still had rules about marriage and partnership. Astrea was sure the Novarians did, too.

And she knew she was getting ahead of herself. Skies, she was getting so far ahead of herself, but Astrea didn't think she could handle losing Jin again. There was no way she would be strong enough to be with him now, to be his partner in every way, only for it to be ripped away from her down the road. That would be too much. They could never go back to a friendship after that.

At least, I could never. Astrea stared down at their hands. Jealousy surged in her veins as she thought about Jin marrying some aristocrat, some Helosian or Novarian noblewoman, just to appease the powers that be. She squashed it down. *Ahead of myself.*

"I'd change it if I could. I don't want this life."

"I don't want you to change who you are." Astrea swallowed. "Just because it's complicated doesn't mean you have to change it."

Jin half laughed. "But I've *always* wanted to change it, Az."

"I know."

"And as much as I hated the wars, the last eight years showed me that I don't have to be defined by this bullshit. I got to figure out who I really was and what I really wanted, all away from the palace and whatever influence it had over me."

His letters had mentioned the barest of details in that regard. Jin had discovered that he really liked the mountains near Fort Avalon, and he'd found that working with his magic and body every day helped him feel more grounded. But he'd never written about what he really wanted, as he put it. Or maybe she hadn't gotten to those letters yet.

"And what did you discover about yourself?" Astrea asked.

"Beyond the obvious of preferring to be away from palace life," he said, "all kinds of things. That I could survive being away from El-lie—and you—even if it was lonely and painful. That some people could actually see past my invisible crown and just see a normal kid."

"Your team?"

Jin nodded. "It took them a while, but we were all equals. It was nice, not having to pretend to be something I'm not."

That must have been a relief for Jin.

"Of course, I learned about the true limits of my magic. And I also realized that I couldn't wait to say what I wanted to say or do what I wanted to do. I nearly died. Lando did die. And as scary as it is to not know what's coming next, I realized I just had to keep pushing forward." He sighed. "Do you remember my eighteenth birthday party?"

Astrea's eyebrows furrowed. He'd asked her the same thing after the dinner party back in Kalama. "Yes . . . you've already explained that was the night your father told you he was sending you away."

"Do you remember when we snuck off and you gave me that book?"

"A novel," Astrea said. Jin had always liked novels, even if he had never been attentive during their lessons with their tutors. "One about a pirate queen."

"I so badly wanted to tell you everything, Az. I just couldn't find the words or figure out how to make it stop hurting. My shoulder, the one where my father attacked me, had only been healed that morning. Every part of me hurt, and I didn't let myself tell my best friend."

"I knew you were sad about something. I hadn't wanted to ask and make it worse." Should she have, though? Would that have saved them years of heartache?

"I wouldn't have told you even if you'd pushed." Jin ran one hand over her hair before stopping at the base of her neck. His touch was warm, gentle. "What I'm doing a very poor job of saying is that even before I left home, I started shutting out the people I care about most, and I can't do that. I have to let them in, and I have to tell them what I want, no matter how terrifying that might be."

Astrea swallowed hard, her breath coming in shallow bursts.

"I know we have a long way to go, and I have a lot to make up for—"

"Eight birthdays and two graduations."

Jin laughed, half amused and half uneasy. "I thought it was nine birthdays."

"And here I was, ready to let you off the hook for one. At least you're honest."

"If I weren't trying to tell you something important right now, I'd kiss you."

"Sorry," Astrea whispered as butterflies danced in her belly.

"Don't be." Jin's hand, still on the back of her neck, slid to her shoulder, then down her arm until he was gripping both of her hands in his. "What I'm trying to tell you is that when I say I want to try this—us—I'm being entirely serious. I've lost so much in the last eight years, Az, including time. I don't want to lose any more. I don't want to wait."

Nothing was going to change in the next few weeks. Astrea wasn't foolish enough to think they'd get Aelius to abdicate peacefully so soon, if at all. The situation was only about to get more dangerous, especially with the Helosian void mages moving into Corsyca. What was the point of waiting when she felt this way? What was the point of worrying about royal titles and claims to thrones when they first needed to get through a war? What was the point of worrying about it at all when Jin would walk away from royal life simply because he'd always wanted to?

"And I know this is complicated," Jin continued when she said nothing, "and I know how much I hurt you back then, so I'll understand if you don't want to now or ever."

She'd only grown more fond of Jin the more time she spent with him. Even if he'd made mistakes. Even if things were complicated. Even if she didn't know how things would end. Astrea didn't care. She knew who he was, and she knew what she wanted. She just had to give herself permission to see what happened.

Astrea leaned forward, her hands grabbing the sides of Jin's face as she pulled him toward her. His arms wrapped around her waist, pulling her halfway into his lap as their lips met.

Jin tasted like the wine they'd been drinking at dinner, his lips still a bit sticky from the sugar-coated dessert. Or was that her? It didn't matter. Astrea pushed herself as close to him as she could, her fingers threading through his hair as Jin started trailing kisses across her cheek, her jaw, her throat.

"You and me," he said as he finally pulled away. Astrea's skin throbbed every place his lips had been, and she desperately wanted him to do that again. "It's not just one night for me, Az. I'm really serious about—"

"Yes."

"You didn't let me—"

"I want to try, too." Astrea's heart thundered as the words floated between them. At the start of the summer, she never would have believed she would say those words. She never would have believed she would see this new Jin, both who he used to be and who he'd become. "I want to try."

Jin's eyebrows rose. "Really?"

"Yes."

"Even with everything going on?"

"Yes."

"Even with everything that's happened in the past?"

"Yes." When Jin leaned in to kiss her again, Astrea pulled away. She needed to get this out. "I'm serious about it too," she said. "I want to see where this goes. It's not just one night for me, either."

When Jin leaned toward her again, Astrea met him halfway. His kiss was gentler this time, soft and sweet. They could take their time here, under this canopy of stars, like they hadn't been able to before. No Prince Kaius around the corner. No hunt for clues in Sezia. No running away from void mages or Emperor Aelius. No Eliana knocking on the skies damned door.

"We should go back," Jin whispered.

Astrea frowned as he pulled away from her. "Do we have to?"

"I didn't say we had to stop." Something else skittered over Astrea's tongue, sour and sweet all at once.

"Really?"

"Come on."

Jin waved one hand toward the lanterns, and the candle flames extinguished. Astrea's entire body tightened as Jin practically hauled her back toward the guest house. That sour and sweet taste teasing her magic suddenly made sense. It was lust, and its heat pressed against every fiber of her being.

They went back to the guest house, giving the guards nothing more than a quick nod. After pulling her inside, Jin locked the door.

"Come on," he whispered.

The chandeliers in the foyer and front hallway still glowed. The door to the parlor was cracked open, and Eliana's loud laugh made Astrea look back over her shoulder.

Jin put a finger to his lips and tilted his head toward the stairs. Smart, considering they'd either get cornered into talking or finishing whatever bottle of wine Cressida had probably opened. The thick rugs lining the stairs muffled their hurried steps, and they made it to the second floor without anyone stopping them.

Were they really going to do this? Astrea's confidence began bleeding away as they took the last few steps to their room. She believed Jin and what he wanted. She knew what she wanted. But her mind kept going back to the fact that she might lose him all over again.

What would she do if they tried this and something happened to him? She'd just gotten him back. *Barely* gotten him back based on the few stories she had from his time in the military. If his royal obligations didn't steal him from her, what if something else did?

"Hey," Jin said, turning back to her after he locked the door. "What's wrong?"

She swallowed. "Just . . ."

"We don't have to do anything you don't want to do. I didn't mean to rush—"

"No, it's not that . . ."

"Are you worried about me taking mavustro? I take it every day."

Astrea hadn't even considered asking him about mavustro—the bitter herb used as contraception—before. She couldn't imagine trying to face the void or Emperor Aelius if she got pregnant.

"I'm glad," she said, "but that's not it either."

Astrea loitered halfway between the door and the bed. Even if their relationship progressed no further, she couldn't pretend she didn't care about Jin. No matter what, losing him would hurt more than she could bear.

"Talk to me, Az."

"People I care about leave." Astrea barely forced the words out past the lump in her throat.

"You think I'll leave?"

"It's foolish."

He guided her toward the bed, sitting her down on its edge before he squatted in front of her. "I don't have the best track record, I know, but I swear, I'm going to show you that you don't have to worry about that," he whispered, his thumb drawing circles on her knee.

"But what if it's not your choice? What if . . ."

He smiled. "I came home once already, didn't I?"

Astrea's breath caught in her chest. Deep purple reverence, red determination, and pink desire vibrated around Jin's body. His wall had shattered again, but this time, it wasn't a torrent of rage and regret. It wasn't in reaction to terrible news or a gossiping duchess. The colors lit up the darkness of the room, and for a moment, Astrea couldn't help but think how unfair it was that Jin couldn't see it, too.

It was beautiful, bright, unwavering.

And it was all for her.

Chapter 17

"Can I kiss you now?" Jin asked, his voice rough.

"I'll really hate you if you don't."

Jin laughed as he stood and pulled her up toward him. His kiss was urgent, and Astrea couldn't focus on anything but the way he felt against her, hands roaming around her waist and hips. She couldn't focus on anything but the maddening flurry of kisses and heavy breathing, the desperate way she clung to him, trying to bring him closer.

He picked her up, her legs wrapping around his waist as he moved her backward on the mattress. "Is this alright?" he asked as he crawled toward her.

"Just get over here," Astrea said, hating the way she sounded so desperate. But she was desperate to have him kissing her again, to have his hands on her, to finally find out what else he could make her feel.

He laughed as he hovered over her, eyes searching hers. Astrea wasn't sure he was going to move. But then he brought his lips to hers again, the motion gentler this time, delicate, so achingly soft. Astrea threaded her fingers through his hair. Jin groaned as he started peppering kisses down her cheek, her jaw, her neck. He stopped when he got to the bodice of her dress, his gaze flicking up to hers with a silent question.

"Please," she whispered. "I want to feel you touch me."

He groaned again, retracing his trail of kisses up to her mouth. "You will be the death of me." A ghost of a smile passed across his face as he pulled away. "Let's get that dress off, then."

Jin climbed off the bed first, then helped Astrea.

"Buttons," she said. "On the back."

She turned around, summoning a hint of light in her palm so Jin could see the tiny buttons better in the dark. Her heart pounded wildly as the bodice loosened. Jin's fingers trailed down her spine, stopping when he reached the small of her back.

"Take it off," he said, the order sending a shiver down Astrea's entire body.

Without turning around, Astrea dismissed her light, then let go of the bodice and pushed the skirt off her full hips. She kicked off the flat shoes she'd worn to dinner, too. Her entire body tightened with the coldness of the room, but she stepped out of the dress and peeked over her shoulder at Jin. That lust was back, sour and sweet and flashing raspberry in the dark.

"Lie down," he said.

Astrea swallowed hard. Her chest heaved. There was no safety in peeling clothes off layer by layer; all she had on now was her bloomers, but the silky little things didn't offer much in terms of modesty. She hadn't been so shy with the two partners she'd had before him, so why was she being shy now? Yes, it had been a long time since she'd been intimate with anyone, but she couldn't let her shyness get in the way. Jin's lust and desire pushed and pushed against her, overwhelming in the best way. Reassuring, even. They both wanted this. There was no reason to be shy.

Astrea climbed back onto the bed, not turning around until the last second. Jin had already undone the buttons of his shirt, revealing a sliver of his chest and the light dusting of hair that traveled from his belly button to below the waistline of his pants. It wasn't anything she hadn't seen before after sharing a room for so many nights, but this was different.

And Jin was watching her in that way he did, raspberry lust flaring brighter as he took in her bare torso. He shrugged off his shirt first, tossing it somewhere on the floor behind him, then took off the rest.

Astrea scooted back on the bed as Jin climbed in with her, his body warm as he inched closer.

"You still want to do this?" Jin asked, his lips impossibly close. She nodded, leaning forward to kiss him. But he pulled back, smiling as he whispered, "I need you to say it."

"Yes," Astrea breathed. She was so tired of overthinking things, trying to plan out and ward off every potential consequence. She just wanted to feel good. She just wanted to be happy. And being right here with Jin? Well, this was everything. "Yes."

Jin paused for just a beat before settling himself among the pillows near the headboard. "Then come here. Let me see you."

Astrea straddled his lap, clumsy at first. He steadied her, though, as his eyes roamed her face, her neck, her breasts.

His chest swelled just before he whispered, "Skies, Az—"

Cutting himself off, Jin dug his fingers into her hair and pulled her down for another kiss. Moaning, Astrea opened her mouth to him just as his tongue swiped her bottom lip. When her bare chest pressed against his, Jin tensed, then left a trail of warm, aching kisses along her jaw, her throat, her collarbones. Head rolling back, Astrea ground her hips against his.

That raspberry lust danced around him again, bright and pulsing and mesmerizing as it mixed with his reverence, his joy, his desire. When she ground against him again, the lust spiked higher, making her head swim in the best way.

"Fuck, Az."

Astrea's breath caught as Jin's hands worked their way around her torso and up her back, his skin impossibly warm. She couldn't take it.

"Please," Astrea whispered.

He smirked, that skies damned smirk she both hated and adored. "Please what?"

"Just take me." She might've been embarrassed by how needy she sounded, but she did need this. Wanted this. Desperately.

He rolled them over. Astrea's back hit the mass of pillows as Jin hovered over her. The gold chain he'd worn to dinner dangled from his neck. His lips ghosted over her skin as the tips of his fingers trailed between her breasts. "It's our first time, and I want to focus on you. Please? I meant what I said in Sezia."

"I don't remember what you said."

He laughed and nipped at her neck. "Liar."

"Remind me." Of course Astrea remembered. She couldn't forget. But she wanted to hear him say those promises again, to feel what he did as the words left him.

"I said I wanted to take my time." Jin leaned down and kissed one breast as raspberry lust sparkled around him. "I said I wanted to do this right." He kissed the other, peach amusement pulsing with what she thought might be his heartbeat. "I said I wanted to make love to you." He kissed her sternum, right between her breasts, as that purple reverence joined the mix again.

"And?" she asked.

"And I'm going to stick to that plan."

Astrea kissed him, breathing in as much of that sandalwood soap as she could. His hardness pressed into her as he cupped one of her breasts, massaging gently before tracing a circle around her nipple with his thumb. She moaned into his mouth.

Sex had never been like this for her before. The energy swirling around Astrea made her head spin, like how she felt after a glass of wine. It was pleasant. The slightest bit intoxicating. Neither of her past partners had ever projected so much energy out. Maybe she hadn't let them, or maybe she'd just never been that into it herself. It didn't matter. Jin's hands and tongue on her skin brought Astrea back to him, the bed, the moment.

As Jin pulled away, his hand trailed over her stomach right to the waistband of her bloomers. One finger barely dipped under the fabric. "May I—" he started, but she cut him off.

"Yes."

"You don't even know what I was going to ask."

She threw her head back into the pillows. "Damn it, Jin."

He laughed again. "Shall I take these off?"

"Could you possibly ask any more questions?"

"They say patience is a virtue, you know," he mused as his fingers hooked into her bloomers and pulled them down to her knees. Pulling them the rest of the way off, Jin tossed them over his shoulder without taking his eyes off her.

"I never claimed to be virtuous."

"Noted."

Laid out bare before him, the last of Astrea's shyness bled away. She sucked in a sharp breath as his hands began to wander, first along her thighs and then between them. His fingers were gentle as they explored, featherlight and perfect. Astrea tried to reach for his underwear, but he smirked again and batted her away.

"We can play later." Jin pulled his hand away from her, and Astrea instantly missed the contact. He pinned her wrists down playfully. Delicately. "We're focusing on you, remember? Now . . ." Jin let go of her wrists, one hand tangling with hers as his other went back down to caress her thigh. Jealousy scraped over her skin as he said, "Show me how you like to be touched."

Astrea guided his hand up her vulva once, twice, then up to her clit. As soon as his fingers hit it, she gasped. His touch was so different than her own, gentle but firm, intense but soft.

Jin made slow circles at first, and with every gasp and little affirmation she whispered, he went faster. Pleasure jolted through her as she melted into his touch. What she wouldn't give to just lay there like that forever as he studied what she liked.

He slid one finger down right to her entrance, then stopped. "Good?"

Astrea nodded, unable to force out anything other than a little huff as Jin dipped his finger inside her. Then he slid in another, moving so purposefully, deliciously slow as he ran his thumb over her clit again. Jin's mouth traveled back down to her throat, kissing and sucking on the delicate flesh there.

Skies, she wasn't going to last long if he kept doing that. Astrea ground down against his hand, and that sweet approval washed over her when she did it again. And when he started lavishing attention on her breasts, Astrea was sure she was going to arch her back so high that both of them would end up flying off the bed.

"Good?" Jin asked.

"Don't stop." Her body coiled tighter as she gripped at the sheets on either side of her.

The pressure was too much, her muscles so tight she was afraid it might hurt when the tension was finally set free. Astrea's face heated, but she was already spiraling, tightening around his fingers as her release came. Her body quivered. Her legs trembled. When Jin pulled his hand away from her, she both missed the feeling of his fingers in her and was grateful for the pause as the last of her shudders subsided.

"Jin," she whispered, opening her eyes to find him watching her with pupils so dilated she almost lost sight of that gold. In fact, the colors around him had expanded, so bright it was like he was lighting up the entire room. Astrea's blood buzzed, electrified. "I just want you to be in me. Please."

Jin smiled. "Well, you did say please." He smacked the outside of her thigh. "Move back."

Astrea settled herself in the middle of the bed, her head cushioned by the pillows. Jin sat up and took off his underwear, his length bouncing as he freed it. Astrea took in everything she could about his body: his broad shoulders, tight abs, strong arms, and thick erection. The heat burning in her belly doubled.

"Are you sure you want to do this?" Jin asked as he climbed on top of her.

"Yes." Skies, did she ever. "Do you?"

"More than anything."

Jin lined up with her entrance as she lifted her legs to his waist, his fingers trailing over her again. With a shuddering breath, she arched up into his touch. His lids were half-closed, his expression soft. He stroked himself a few times, then groaned as he guided himself into her, deeper, deeper, until he finally stopped.

Astrea sighed, her eyes fluttering closed as she reveled in the feeling of Jin inside her. She couldn't focus on anything but how good this felt, how right it felt. How right they felt together, not just now, but always. They always had. It made her nervous and giddy at the same time.

"Good?" he asked.

"Great."

He moved slowly at first as they found their rhythm, hands and lips exploring every inch of each other's bodies. Astrea couldn't think about anything else even if she wanted to. All Astrea could do was focus on the way Jin rocked his hips against hers, the way his calloused fingertips felt when he started circling that sensitive spot again, the way his energy seemed to pulse against her magic in time with his thrusts.

He sat up slightly, rhythm slowing as he peered down at her. Every movement was tantalizingly slow and steady. Hot, bright pressure built within her again. Astrea tightened her legs around Jin's waist and tilted her hips higher.

"Fuck," he gasped. "Do that again."

She tilted her hips up. Astrea's hands explored the width of his back, brushing over the knotted scar on his left shoulder. Her nails dug into his skin as he hit the right spot over and over again.

"Wait," he said as she tried to pull him closer. "I want to see you."

Astrea held his gaze as the pressure in her belly built. Her entire body was tight, and her mind spun in the best way.

"Fuck, you feel so good, Az." Jin swore again, his smile faltering. "Where do you want me to—" he started, breathless as he pumped in and out of her, but Astrea cut him off.

"In me," she managed to say. That felt right, too.

He leaned down, kissing her hard and deep. "Fuck, you really will be the death of me."

Stars danced behind Astrea's eyelids as Jin pounded into her again and again. He pinned her wrists among the pillows with just one hand, his other drifting back down to her clit. She didn't know if she needed less or more or faster or slower, but she needed to hold on to something. It was like Jin knew. That light grip on her wrists lifted, and he threaded his fingers through hers. Just as Astrea grabbed his shoulders with her free hand, release tore through her a second time, hard and fast and so achingly good.

She was still trembling underneath him when Jin sped up. He buried his face in the crook of her neck, his breath hot and humid. His thrusts were uneven, frantic as he chased his own high. Clinging to him, Astrea ran her hands through his hair and tightened her legs around his waist. Jin tumbled over the edge after her, warm bliss exploding in her chest.

That euphoria washed over her, wave after wave, as Jin collapsed on top of her. Astrea could barely catch her breath, not just from his body crushing hers but the way her magic still spun out of control. She closed her eyes, reveling in it as it slowly subsided and the pressure building in her bones eased.

Slowly, Jin rolled off to one side and kissed her shoulder. "Are you alright?" he asked as he pulled her against him. A light layer of sweat dampened his skin.

She barely nodded. "Are you?"

"I'm wonderful." He sat up with a grunt. "Do you want to lie here for a moment or clean up first?"

Astrea wanted to lay there forever, in the warmth of the bed, wrapped around Jin. She could barely think straight. She doubted she could put weight on her legs, weak as they were, let alone decide what she wanted to do first. Her eyelids fluttered as she melted into the bed.

"I think we should clean up first," Jin whispered into her ear. "You're already falling asleep."

Astrea couldn't remember the last time her body had relaxed so completely. "Sure," she said, eyes still half-closed.

The bed dipped, the chill from the window greeting her as Jin got up. She heard his footsteps as he crossed the room. The sound of running water. A closet door closing. Then she was being picked up, and she let him carry her to the bathroom.

"It's alright," she said as he tried to walk into the wide shower with her. "I can stand."

He set her down and motioned for her to get in first. The blissfully hot water turned Astrea pink. Jin wrapped his arms around her waist as they let the water hit them. There was much they still needed to talk about, but Astrea laughed once, the soft sound muffled by the water.

"What are you giggling about?" Jin placed a kiss behind her ear.

"This," she admitted. "I never thought—"

"I only dreamed."

Astrea was glad the steam and water had already tinged her pink. Her cheeks heated up, those three words somehow making her more shy than what they'd just done.

But Jin carried on like nothing had happened. "Shall I wash you?" he asked, already lathering a bar of soap in his hands.

"Sure."

Jin took his time washing her, directing her when to lift her arms or turn around to rinse off one side. She tried to ignore how delicately he touched her now, hands skimming every part of her body again. Part of her could take him again right there, and she didn't miss his length hardening against her backside either. But she was tired, and Jin's fatigue pressed against her.

When he was done, she reached for the soap, but his hand found hers. "I'll shower properly in the morning," he said. "Let's just go to bed."

She hadn't thought about what came next, but the steam was clearing her head. They'd agreed they were going to try—that meant a relationship, right? And what about Ysabel?

"Oh no," Jin said, reaching around her to turn off the water. "There's that look again."

"What look?" she asked, frowning.

"The one when you're overthinking something." He leaned out of the shower and passed a fluffy towel back to her. She wrapped it around herself. "Your eyes lose focus."

"Oh."

But when he straightened again, wrapping a towel around his waist, he smiled. "So, what were you thinking about?"

"Just . . . I hadn't thought about what comes after."

"After?" Jin moved out of the shower, offering her his hand to help her out. She followed him. "After sex?"

Astrea nodded, cheeks burning again. She silently cursed herself, unsure why it was so hard to say that. She'd had sex with Jin. And she wanted to do it again, as soon as possible.

"Is something supposed to be different?" he asked as he used a spare towel to dry off his hair.

"I don't know. That's why I was thinking about it. Is this . . . inappropriate?"

"Inappropriate?"

"I wasn't sure if something . . ." She paused, trying to find the right word. "Changed."

"Changed?" His eyebrows knitted together, but teal understanding blossomed around him for just a moment. "You're truly worried the Novarians will care?"

She shrugged. For all the empire's flaws, Helosians weren't shy about sex, not even for the imperial heirs. Astrea knew Eliana had already had several partners of different genders. Kaius always flaunted his latest bed buddy around the city. Jin definitely seemed to know what he was doing. Jealousy surged forward with that last thought, but Astrea shoved it deep, deep down.

"I don't want to do something improper," she said, "now that we know you're . . ."

Jin closed the distance between them and set his hands on her shoulders. "I really, truly do not give a damn what Ysabel or her courtiers think," he said. "Regardless of whatever my status might be here, our relationship is none of their business. If this is what *we* want, that's what matters, and we'll figure out the rest. Together. As partners."

"Partners," she whispered.

He laughed. "You don't sound so sure. Changed your mind already?"

"No, of course not. I just . . . I wasn't expecting that, I guess."

"Wasn't expecting . . . ?"

"You to use that word."

"Should I not?"

"No," she whispered again. "I like it."

That beautiful purple reverence swirled around Jin's body. It mingled with the faint raspberry lust still lingering from before, golden joy weaving its way through both colors. It was still unfair that he couldn't see her colors, which she was sure would match. Astrea reached up, grabbing his face with both hands and kissing him as deeply as she could.

"What was that for?" he asked as they pulled apart.

"Just because."

Jin smiled, then helped her finish toweling off before disappearing into the bedroom. She'd just started braiding her hair when he returned.

"Here." He handed her a shirt and another pair of bloomers. "It's too cold to sleep naked."

"I never sleep naked," she said as she took the clothes. "You know that."

"It's never too late to try something new."

"Nice try."

He grinned. "It was worth a shot."

Sticking her tongue out, Astrea turned her back on him and slipped the bloomers on first. The shirt was one of the tunics she'd seen him sparring in, the fabric light and sleeves long. It smelled like his soap, or maybe she did. As she followed Jin into the dark bedroom, that same blissfully deep fatigue returned.

Once they settled back in bed, Jin's hands snaked around her waist and pulled her body flush against his, her back to his chest. This part, she was familiar with. This part, they'd done before.

"Relax, Az," Jin whispered into her neck. "I know you're tired. Just go to sleep."

Astrea closed her eyes, breathing in deeply. She was tired. So very, very tired and so very, very happy.

CHAPTER 18

Astrea was proud. She'd managed to find her way back to the palace library entirely on her own.

She was disappointed that neither Cressida nor Adi was going with her, but everyone else had things to do. Adi and Jin wanted to discuss training plans, and Cressida had asked to be part of that discussion. Eliana and Nicos had gone to see Ysabel.

By the time Astrea had finished cleaning up for the day, everyone else had already left the guest house. Getting her day started had taken longer than she'd anticipated, thanks to Jin's extra attention. Warmth flooded Astrea as she stood alone outside the palace library, a few of the borrowed books and Mattina's journal cradled in her arms. Jin had woken her up in ways she'd never been woken up before. She needed to focus, and thinking about how she'd been tangled up with him only an hour before wasn't helping.

Their group had managed to get through almost all the dozen books in the last couple days. While none of them had yielded information about the Paragon, Astrea had finished her list of myths to get more information on. Surely Tomas would have *something* else for them, too, now that he'd had additional time to search his collection. Even if it was just more subjects and battles to rule out, that would be some kind of progress.

Astrea didn't have any more time to consider the possibilities. Tomas was just inside the doors.

"Oh, excuse me!" he cried as he jumped back.

"I'm so sorry!" Astrea nearly dropped the books, but the older librarian stepped forward and took half the stack from her. "Thanks."

"I wasn't expecting you to come by so early, Astrea," he said. "Visitors rarely come by the library before lunchtime."

"Do you want me to come back later?"

"No, no. I'm glad you're here."

"Really?"

Astrea followed him through the collection of tables until he stopped at one near the middle of the grand room. They both set their stacks down, and he motioned for her to take a seat.

"Would you like some tea?" Tomas asked. "I can ring for tea."

"No, I'm fine." Astrea really just wanted to know why he was glad to see her back so soon. That had to mean he had news, right?

"Very well." He frowned, his forehead wrinkling. "Were the books helpful?"

"Nothing specific in these, but I have a list of myths I'd like to get more information on." Adi had found several references to the void, as had Cressida, but everything pointed to it as the emptiness between the stars that they knew rather than another branch of magic. "Oh, and I need more information about a war between a Fireweaver king and Novarian queen." That was one bit of history Emperor Aelius had been particularly interested in, but he'd only told Astrea and Jin about it a couple days before everything else went awry.

"We can look for that after," Tomas said. "The good news is that I finally heard back from Lili. She's usually quite responsive to my calls, but I had to track her down in her office—was only there during her so-called office hours, if you can believe it—and I showed her that page of symbols I copied from your notebook."

Astrea sat up straighter. "Could she read it?"

"No, she couldn't, but she has seen similar markings before in an archaeologist colleague's notes."

Astrea deflated. A librarian's friend's colleague's 'similar' notes? That was a weak connection. Still, a lead was a lead.

"Can we speak with her?" Astrea asked.

"She actually recommended you go straight to the source. Professor Kostas Shalysko. He also works at the university."

"When can we speak with him?"

"When would it be good for you to meet with him?"

"Tomorrow would be ideal," Astrea said. At dinner the night before, Ysabel had mentioned the imperial siblings needed to speak to her council, and lately, at least for Eliana, political meetings seemed endless. Still, they needed answers. *Maybe Cress, Adi, and I can go with Lucian like we did for the void house.* That could work.

"I'll be right back!" Tomas called as he hurried back up the spiral staircase in the far corner. "Let me call him to confirm!"

Astrea sighed and looked back at the books on the table. It was a shame none of them had yielded anything specific, but she wasn't all that surprised. The Paragon had been hiding. Void mages had been hiding for a very long time. Why they'd been hiding, and how long they'd existed, she didn't know. But as Astrea knew firsthand, if someone wanted to keep something secret, they usually could. And with how fractured the continent had been during the Great Wars, as well as the way victors emerged, all it would've taken was a few key people to rid the history books of void magic.

Pulling Mattina's journal toward herself, Astrea opened it to a random page. She examined the peculiar letters and the way they swirled and curved at strange angles. What was this language? And where did Mattina learn it?

Tomas's heavy footfalls returned. Why was that man always in a rush? Raela usually strolled around the Great Library as if she had all the time in the world.

"Astrea!" he called over the mezzanine's railing.

"Yes?"

"Will the day after tomorrow work?"

"No!" she yelled back. "We need to talk to the professor as soon as possible!"

"Alright . . . let me see what I can do."

How busy could one professor be? Back when she was in university, Astrea's professors had always made time to answer questions, not just from students but from all kinds of people. Did this Professor Shalysko not want to help them?

Astrea examined the notebook again. The shapes didn't look even remotely similar to any letters of the alphabet she knew. Patterns jumped out at her, the same letters repeated in the same sequences, but she couldn't even hazard a guess as to what the words were. Someone in the world had to know what this said besides the Paragon, right?

"He put me on hold!" Tomas called over the railing again. Astrea rolled her eyes. "There's another book I was going to give you today, on the row capped by the bust of the late Grand Duke Vytas. It's *Queens of the Great Wars.*"

"I'll look for it, thanks, Tomas."

Pushing to her feet, Astrea started toward the left side of the library. Busts capped several different rows, and she had no idea who Grand Duke Vytas was. Astrea checked each one for names, then went to the other half of the library before she finally found the right place.

Halfway down the dimly lit aisle, Astrea stumbled. Sharp pain scratched between her shoulder blades. Her head pounded. Astrea tried to right herself, but when she blinked, a pair of copper eyes stared back at her.

"What—" she started, the question dying on her tongue when she realized she couldn't see the Novarian palace anymore. Darkness rushed past her, an all-consuming storm as she seemed to move through the nothingness.

Kalama took shape around Astrea, slathered in shadows and consumed by deafening silence. The history museum towered behind her, and as something pulled her forward, all she could focus on was the alley. Jin's motorcycle. The flickering street light. The museum's ticketer lying in a puddle of shadow, her skin graying and ashen.

"Oh, little Lightbringer," Victor Nazarov purred. Astrea couldn't see him anywhere. "I knew we'd see each other again."

"This isn't real," Astrea whispered. It was another vision. It had to be.

"What do you want me to do to prove it's real?" he asked.

"This *can't* be real." She'd just been in Novaria. She'd just been in Ysabel's palace.

"Perhaps the scene is in the past," Nazarov drawled, "but our conversation is very, very real."

If it was a vision, why was Nazarov answering her questions? Would her mind make up something so complicated? Would she even be thinking about her mind making it up if she was, in fact, imagining it all? That didn't seem likely, but why, why was she back here, to the first night she failed?

Astrea tried to look anywhere but the dead woman on the ground. But it seemed, no matter how hard she tried, she couldn't stop looking at the woman. *I'm sorry. I'm so sorry.* That night had been the start of everything, of them really beginning to understand what was happening. Why would Nazarov bring her back to this moment?

"What do you want?" Astrea finally gritted out to the darkness enveloping her.

"To warn you."

She almost laughed. "To warn me?"

"Believe it or not, yes, little Lightbringer."

"About what?"

"About the emperor. He knows more than you think."

"What do you mean he—"

"You have something that is mine," Nazarov snapped from somewhere in the darkness, his voice swift and cold. "In exchange for the warning, you will give it to me. And you will also stop telling the Novarians about this. I know the other Lightbringer has been to the house in Talmaris. We have friends everywhere."

Astrea's blood chilled, but she forced herself to ask, "Why would I do that?"

"If you don't, your uncle will regret ever bringing you to Kalama."

The image of the dead woman by the museum faded, replaced by Saros in a crumpled heap on the ground. Astrea tried to run to him, but her muscles seized. He held some small object in one hand, a sheet of paper in the other. Astrea strained to see what exactly he was holding, but that sharp pain between her shoulders returned, the same she'd had in her dreams before. The one that made it feel like something was leaking from her chest.

"I'll see you soon, little Lightbringer," Nazarov whispered.

Saros's image burst into flames. All the buildings around them caught fire, too, the flames tinged with shadow. Kalama burned down around her, and Astrea couldn't move. It was just like the vision she'd had in Sezia, the one from her very last night in Helosia.

"You'd better have what's mine when I return. Oh, and tell that princeling of yours I said hello."

The darkness returned, and Astrea rushed backward even though she knew her feet weren't moving. Then the shadows receded. Warm lights shone overhead. Shelves and shelves of books surrounded her. She was standing in the middle of the aisle in Tomas's library, hands shaking.

"Astrea?" a familiar voice asked. Tomas. "Are you alright?"

Astrea looked back at Tomas, who stood just a few feet behind her. Gray confusion undulated in the air around him. "I'm fine," she muttered. "Excuse me."

She pushed past him, her legs moving without thought as she dashed through the library. She grabbed her satchel and Mattina's journal, then sprinted for the door.

"What about that book?" Tomas called after her. More confusion washed over Astrea, unrelenting. Disorienting. "And the appointment tomorrow?"

"Send it all to the guest house!" Astrea yelled over her shoulder just before bursting through the library's doors and into the palace hallway beyond.

There was no way that was something her mind had made up. There was no way her own psyche would torture her with that. And there was no way that was just a vision. No, Nazarov really was trying to talk to her. He really was trying to find her. To find all of them.

Mattina's journal, Astrea realized as she shoved past a group of guards. One of them shouted at Astrea, but she ignored them. It had to be Mattina's notebook. It was connected to the void, and so was Nazarov. And Astrea had the journal, so did that mean Nazarov was connected to her? Was that what he wanted from her?

Astrea's head started to ache as she burst into the sunshine outside the palace. Several guards looked at her funny, and one even called in

Helosian for her to slow down, but Astrea kept running toward the guest house.

"He knows more than you think." What, exactly, did the emperor know? And when was Nazarov coming back? An hour? A week? Would he really kill Saros if he didn't get what he wanted? He had to want the notebook, right?

Astrea forced her body to go faster still, her legs and abdomen cramping as she rushed through the gardens. She needed to tell her friends.

Why did these things always seem to fall on her? Why did Nazarov have to fixate on her? She wasn't special. She couldn't even save a dying woman. She couldn't even save her family or the city she called home. She couldn't figure out this puzzle. Astrea was no match for Nazarov. She was no match for the emperor. She was barely a real Lightbringer.

The guards stationed outside the guest house tried to greet Astrea, but she ignored them, tearing open the front doors. She sprinted into the front hall as the doors slammed shut behind her.

"Cress?" Astrea shouted as she stumbled into the foyer. She tried to catch her breath, but her lungs burned. "Cress? Ellie?"

Silence.

"Jin? Adi? Nicos?"

Astrea turned in a circle, looking for any sign of her friends. The parlor door was open, the inside silent. The door to the dining room was open and quiet, too.

"Is anyone here?" she called.

Silence.

Astrea backed toward the stairs. Darkness crept in around the edges of her vision. Was Nazarov back already? She hadn't had enough time to figure out what he wanted. That wasn't fair. He couldn't be back already, could he?

"Jin?" Astrea called again, her chest so tight she couldn't focus. She couldn't breathe. That spot between her shoulders burned. She was going to die, right in the skies damned guest house, because she didn't know how to get Nazarov what he wanted. "Please!"

Muffled footsteps sounded behind her. Astrea whirled, but her vision was just a blur of shadow.

"Astrea?" Adi. Confusion and concern crashed against her, rough and cold, but she couldn't see the colors. "What's wrong? Hey—"

"Adi!" She lunged for him, grabbing onto his outstretched arms as she lurched up the stairs. "He's coming!"

"Who?"

"Nazarov, he's—"

"Skies, Astrea, come here." Adi's hands gripped her tight, but Astrea couldn't see straight. She couldn't see through the shadows. What was taking Nazarov so long this time? "Come on, sit down."

"You have to believe me," she begged as Adi's confusion slammed against her body again and again. "The dream . . . then the book . . . and the library . . . and he's coming *now*—"

"I believe you, Astrea. I believe you, but you need to breathe," he said.

The cold, icy shock of terror drowned out that rough confusion. She really was going to die, wasn't she? This was it.

"Come on, deep breath in. You're alright. Just one deep breath, please."

Astrea knew they were moving, could even see part of the foyer through the blur—a bit of the pale blue paint, one of the gold picture frames—but this felt less real than that time back in Kalama. Was Nazarov playing with her now, too? All Astrea could feel was Adi's fear mixing with her own. All she could feel was the stabbing in her back and the way it seemed to burn a hole straight through her heart.

"Jin?" Adi shouted. "Jin! Oh, for fuck's sake, the one time I *actually* need him . . ."

Astrea fell down into something soft. She dug her fingers into the sofa cushion to stop her hands from trembling so hard. Her whole body felt like it was going to burn away, like *she* was going to burn away. The darkness surged in closer. It was going to swallow her whole.

"Adi, why the fuck are you—"

More of that same icy terror crashed into Astrea's awareness, nearly toppling her over. Terror and pain and rage and confusion wrapped around her and pulled tighter. She could shut it down, maybe even shut Nazarov out, like Lucian taught her, if she could just focus . . .

"Hey." Hands brushed against her face and hair. "Az, *please* look at me. Please open your eyes."

Had she closed them? Astrea tried to force them open, past the pain still burning in her back and the emotions slamming into her from two directions. Everything hurt. Everything was still blurry. But there were no shadows. No Nazarov. No Kalama burning around her.

Jin crouched in front of her. Behind him, near the parlor door, Adi watched on, mint relief dancing with that pure white terror.

"Three things," Jin said, his voice tight.

Some part of Astrea's mind knew what he was asking of her. "You. Adi. The door."

"Breathe, Az." Jin squeezed her thigh. "You're alright. Just breathe." She breathed in.

"Good, now push it out." She breathed out.

"Again." She breathed in. And out.

Jin reached up, wiping some of the tears from her cheeks. The air around Adi had calmed, gray confusion mixing with his relief.

"I'm sorry," Astrea whispered, falling forward against Jin. His arms wrapped around her as she slid onto the floor in front of him. "I'm sorry."

"Why are you apologizing?" he asked, one hand stroking her head. "Skies, you don't have to apologize."

Astrea buried her face in the crook of his neck. Why couldn't she hold it together? She had important information, and she couldn't get it out past her tears. Jin had been so happy just a couple hours before—*she* had been so happy—and she was ruining it.

She didn't want to pull away from Jin. But she had to. As she did, Astrea wiped at her eyes with the palms of her hands. "Nazarov," she croaked.

"You mentioned the library?" Adi asked, voice wary. "Did something happen?"

And so Astrea told them. She told them about the things she'd written off: Nazarov visiting her in her dream, including how he'd fixated on Jin, and the shadows in Mattina's notebook and how the markings on the page had moved. She told them about Tomas's friend Lili and the professor they were supposed to meet with. And she told them everything Nazarov had said while she was in the palace. By the time she was finished, Jin's lips pressed together in a thin, worried line.

"Please, Jin," she whispered. "You have to believe me. It's really him."

"Of course I believe you," he said. "I just don't know how to make sense of it."

"What if what happened in Sezia wasn't a vision at all?" Adi asked. He'd come over to join them as Astrea told them everything, taking a seat in one of the plush armchairs while Jin still held Astrea in his lap on the floor. "What if that was Nazarov speaking to you then, too?"

What if Adi was right? What if the Sezia vision, this one at the library, and her dreams were all the void mages, somehow, getting into her mind?

"It didn't sound like him in Sezia," Astrea said, wiping at her wet cheeks. "Nazarov never visited me in my dreams until the other night."

"There have been more?" Adi asked.

Astrea nodded. "My whole life," she said. "They were always the same until recently, but . . . but Nazarov and those men on Solstice Night called me 'little Lightbringer.' And for a brief period when I was a child, I heard that nickname in my dreams."

For a stretch of her childhood, just after Saros had brought Astrea to Kalama, she'd had the same dream: a voice calling her that nickname, searching for her in the darkness. The dream had only continued for a short period, and then for many years, nothing. Until the night she got the emperor's letter. She told Adi and Jin that, too.

"I've never told anyone about that before," Astrea said. "I thought it was just . . . I don't know. Some strange coincidence?" She fisted her hair. "Skies, how could I be so naive? How could I not see this?"

"It's not like it's the world's most specific nickname," Adi hedged. That didn't make Astrea feel any better.

Jin sighed and said, "I think Adi's right. The void mages are sending you visions somehow, and it sounds like they have been for a long time."

"That's fucking ridiculous if it's true."

"And it probably cost him," Jin said. "It sounds like Nazarov couldn't maintain it for long. To project his voice and a vision like that over such a distance . . . Void or not, even a strong mage couldn't do that without a cost."

Adi nodded. "We probably won't be running into him again for a while."

"The dream and the library were only a few days apart," Astrea said. Would he come back tonight? How was she supposed to give him what he wanted if he wasn't really there?

"He could recover in that time," Jin said. "It would help to know where he is and what he's doing, though."

"Would the grand duchess know?" Adi asked. "Or Zephyrine, if we can somehow reach her?"

"I'll find out." Jin said it with such resolve that Astrea's heart ached. "Adi, can you go fetch the others? We all need to talk."

"Of course." Adi jumped to his feet as quickly as Astrea could blink.

"Tell them to meet us here in an hour."

Chapter 19

How did things change so quickly? Just that morning, Astrea had been on that very bed with Jin, doing some very fun things. Now, though, she was curled into him, and fat, silent tears ran down her cheeks. Although she was still terrified that Nazarov was coming, that he might already be there in Talmaris somehow, that wasn't why she was crying.

Jin rubbed big, slow circles on her back with one hand, the other stroking her hair. He hadn't asked her anything for the last ten minutes. He'd just brought her upstairs and set her in bed. He hadn't said anything at all, and for that, Astrea was grateful.

The relief and worry rolling off him tangled with something soft and warm she couldn't place. He wasn't angry. He wasn't disappointed. She had to focus on that. Slowly, Astrea unfurled her body and pushed up on her elbow.

Jin smiled down at her. "Hey."

She wiped at the last of her tears and murmured, "I'm sorry."

Jin's face fell as his eyebrows pulled together. "Why do you keep saying that?"

"This." She waved at the air between them. "Downstairs."

"There's no reason to be sorry."

She fiddled with the bedsheets, pinching the soft gray fabric between her thumb and index finger. "I don't want you to think I can't handle—"

"What—"

"I *can* handle it, I *was* handling it, but I just got so overwhelmed—"

"Az." Jin cut her off again, his finger tipping her chin up. "Look at me." She forced herself to look up, not at his mouth or his chin, but his eyes. "I know you can handle it, but you don't have to all on your own. Teams have to lean on each other."

"But—"

"No. There is no but. Nobody can do it alone, especially not something like this Paragon problem. Just look at me and the last eight years. I wasn't expected to do any of it alone. I couldn't have."

"But that was the military—"

"Az." Jin said her name so gently, it made Astrea want to cry again. "It doesn't matter if we're on the war front or dealing with whatever it is Nazarov is up to. You are part of this team. Nobody is going to be angry if you get upset or overwhelmed, and nobody expects you to figure it out by yourself."

"But I *want* to help—"

"Who said you aren't helping?" he asked. "I might have to knock some sense into them."

"No one."

"Ah." That stupid smirk of his returned. "So *you* told yourself that."

"Are you going to have to knock some sense into me?" she asked, trying to joke, trying to get his attention away from the conversation. She didn't want to talk about this anymore. It made her chest too tight.

"No, I would never do that." He scoffed. "But I might try to kiss it into you."

"Maybe it would help."

A low laugh rumbled from Jin as he helped her sit up. Only when she was copying his cross-legged pose did he ask, "Do you feel any better?"

"Not really." That spot on her back still ached, though it no longer felt like someone was jamming a sharp object into it. "I don't know why I react like that. I hate it."

Jin sighed as he took one of her hands in his. "Everyone responds differently to stress. I can't tell you why, but we do. Look at me when Ysabel told me about my mother. It's taken me a lot of practice to be able to calm down that soon. I don't want you to think you can't—"

"Lose control?"

"I don't think it's losing control, but sure," he said. "Do you have any ideas of what would help?"

The image of Kalama and Saros burning surged back into her mind, and Astrea forced herself to keep her eyes open. "It's hard when I can't tell what's real."

"Real?"

"When Nazarov . . ." She paused, the name making her throat tighten. Jin squeezed her hand. "When he . . . whatever that was . . . everything went dark before he could talk to me. I was sure it wasn't real, but then when he sent me back to the library, and I got to the house, and everything got so dark . . ."

Teal understanding sparked around Jin. "You thought it was him again?"

"Yes."

"I don't think that's unreasonable."

"Really?"

"Of course. We don't know anything about void magic. It probably feels like anything could be him, and you're the only one who's even got an inkling of this power he has."

Astrea blew out a shuddering breath. Jin *believed* her. He didn't just believe her. He understood her even when she didn't know how to put everything into words.

"Will you be alright if I leave?" Jin asked. "I need to go speak with Ysabel. Now."

"Shouldn't Ellie go with you?"

"I think Ellie will want me to go. Besides, they're not even back yet."

"Okay."

"You didn't answer my question. Will you be alright while I'm gone?"

"I'll be fine."

"Really?"

"Skies, you're annoying," Astrea muttered.

Jin just laughed, tangy amusement coating her tongue. Then he leaned forward and gave her a quick, gentle kiss. "I'll be back."

Then he was gone, disappearing into the hallway beyond. And even though Astrea was alone again, the same softness stretched and stretched toward her. She held onto it until finally, Jin was too far away for her magic to feel it anymore.

It was only after another half hour that Astrea finally worked up the courage to go back down to the parlor. She wouldn't have gone had she not been so thirsty.

Astrea didn't want to go downstairs. She didn't want to face Adi and see how he likely pitied her. She didn't want to leave the relative safety of her bedroom. After all, nobody had bothered her, and she'd heard Nicos calling after Eliana at least twenty minutes prior.

But she couldn't leave them with no information. Astrea wrung her hands together as she started on the last few steps to the first floor. There was a lot she needed to talk about with them.

"I don't care where Jin went." Eliana's voice drifted through the foyer, quiet but harsh. "I'm not just leaving her up there alone."

"Don't you think barging in is worse?" Cressida asked.

"Adi said we were meeting. If Jin isn't here, then who's supposed to fill us in? Adi himself isn't even here."

"I'm here, Ellie," Astrea said as she pushed the parlor door fully open.

Eliana flew into Astrea's arms in a blur of maroon fabric and minty relief, uninvited but not unwelcome. Astrea clung to her, a lifeline as the parlor walls seemed to close in around her again.

"What happened?" Cressida asked when Eliana finally pulled away. "I've never seen Adi so freaked out." Cressida pulled Astrea into a hug of her own, and Astrea almost stiffened. Cressida was one of her best friends, but the woman wasn't a hugger. But she, too, was a lifeline, and Astrea clung to her for just a moment.

"Can I get something to drink first?" Astrea asked.

"I made tea," Cressida said. "Or we have water."

"Water would be good."

As Cressida moved to the narrow credenza to their left, Eliana guided Astrea to the sofa. Cressida set a short glass etched with ornate designs on the coffee table, then pushed it toward Astrea. Two teacups painted with delicate purple flowers sat full but untouched.

"Drink." With a sigh, Cressida plopped down into the armchair closest to her. "Or talk. But for skies sake, what happened?"

Astrea took a sip of the cool water. The ice cubes clinked against the glass, and the cold water seemed to shock her mind. As exhausted as Astrea was, she needed to keep practicing creating her wall before she saw Lucian again. Putting it up while recounting everything seemed as good a time as any.

She breathed in, reaching for the limits of the energy she could sense around her body. As she pulled back, the energy's radius shrank until finally, it didn't extend more than half an arm's length from her. *Good enough.*

"I received a warning from Victor Nazarov." Astrea launched into the story as best she could. The library, the book, the dream, the conversation with Tomas, Nazarov, and everything she could force herself to tell them.

By the time Astrea was done, Cressida had her elbows on her knees, her head resting in her hands. "Fuck," she muttered. "Shit. If void mages can send visions . . . what does that mean for Stargazers?"

"I don't know," Astrea said. Stargazers' visions weren't always true to begin with, but with that kind of power . . . "I never really talked to my uncle about what his visions felt like. I know they aren't usually that long, though. He doesn't usually hear voices with them."

Eliana set her hand on top of Astrea's. Her skin was warm, and the red lacquer on her nails sparkled in the light. "I'm so sorry. I'm sorry my father invited this into our lives."

"It's not your fault, Ellie," Astrea said. "You have no reason to apologize." Besides, Emperor Aelius wasn't working with the Paragon. At least, it didn't look that way.

"Well, I'm still sorry," Eliana replied. "What a mess. Do you know when Nazarov is going to . . . contact you again?"

Astrea moved her water glass, watching the last of the ice dance as it continued to melt. "No."

"Do you know what he meant about my father?"

"No, he didn't say. Jin went to talk to Ysabel to see if he can learn—"

"I know. Adi mentioned something about increased security before he rushed off to find Jin."

Did Jin not understand that increased security would only solve part of the problem? They didn't know where Nazarov was in the real world. But he was in her mind. And Lucian's guards couldn't protect that. *She* couldn't protect that.

"Are you mad he went without you?" Astrea asked.

"No. This is an emergency."

Odd, to be sitting and drinking tea during an emergency, Astrea thought as Eliana finally reached for her teacup. But what else could they do? They were sitting ducks until Ysabel—or Zephyrine, if she ever got in contact with them—could give them more information about Nazarov.

The only good news was that Astrea's wall was holding both Eliana and Cressida's reactions at bay. Her control on it was starting to slip, but she held on as best she could.

"What do you think Nazarov wants?" Cressida finally asked. "Mattina's journal?"

Astrea nodded as Eliana said, "That has to be it."

"Where is it?" Cressida asked.

"Upstairs," Astrea said. "In my room."

Just the thought of Mattina's journal made Astrea's hands shake. She set her now-empty water glass down on the table and ran her hands through her hair. No matter what Jin said, she needed to pull herself together. This was not the time to lose it.

"Has Tomas sent over anything from the library yet?" Astrea asked. "He was going to send over a book and information about a professor I'm supposed to meet with tomorrow."

"Not that I know of, but I can check," Cressida said.

Tears started slipping down Astrea's cheeks again. She didn't know why. It was nice to be able to tell her friends, to let them help, even if it was by getting her a glass of water or finding a book. Her grip on her barrier finally slipped as Eliana pulled her into a hug and Cressida piled on from the other side. The parlor sofa wasn't big enough for the three of them to sit comfortably, but Astrea didn't care. She let their anxiety and relief mix with hers, welcoming the feeling of their energy and their arms around her.

"I'm sorry I'm a mess," Astrea said when they finally let her sit up straight. She wiped at her tears, her head aching from all the crying.

"You're not a mess," Eliana said.

"But we love you even if you are," Cressida added. "It's no worse than that time Ellie and Lady D—"

"Don't even think about it, Nikaphoros," Eliana quipped, and Astrea actually laughed.

"It would be nice if we had something happy to talk about for once." Cressida folded her arms and sighed wistfully. "I wonder what Ysabel is sending us for dinner tonight."

"Food?" Eliana asked. "*That's* the happy topic of conversation?"

"Beats talk of rebellions and void magic, don't you think?"

Astrea laughed again and leaned back into the sofa. "I actually have something different you might want to talk about."

"Oh?" Bright green curiosity flashed around Eliana.

Astrea wiped her palms on her skirt. Why was she so nervous to tell them this? They were her best friends. She told them pretty much everything, and they were going to find out anyway. It was certainly better than talking about the Paragon.

"I, uhm, last night," she started. "Well, skies, this is awkward."

"Oh." Cressida grinned and hopped off the sofa. "Oh, I *knew* it."

"What did you know?" Eliana asked, looking between Cressida and Astrea.

"You *didn't*, did you?" Cressida half whispered.

"Does someone want to fill me in?" Rusty annoyance flickered around Eliana. "This isn't about dinner again, is it?"

"No, it's not about dinner." Cressida pointed right at Astrea. A shit-eating grin spread over her face, joy and approval and humor wrapping around her willowy body in a kaleidoscope of color. "She slept with Jin. And that means you owe me, Ellie."

Eliana looked at Astrea, then Cressida, then back again. "You couldn't have waited another week?"

"What?" Heat coursed through Astrea's body, from her toes all the way to the tips of her ears.

"I thought it'd be another week at least before you two finally . . . you know. Yesterday's interruption had me so sure." Eliana's nose scrunched. "Spare me the details. And now I owe Cress, what, twenty lire?"

"You were placing *bets*?" Astrea squeaked. "You placed bets about my love life? That's all you have to say for yourselves right now? That's . . ."

"Funny?" Cressida offered.

"Invasive," Astrea corrected.

"Even if you've cost me money, it's about damn time." Eliana threw her arms around Astrea's shoulders, practically tackling her. The decorative pillows on the sofa stopped Astrea from fully tipping over.

"What's that supposed to mean?" Astrea asked, incredulous.

"Not *you*," she clarified. "My brother. He's had a thing for you since forever."

Astrea's cheeks burned, which only made Cressida's grin grow bigger. "Don't look so surprised, Az. Skies, the way he used to follow you around like a lost puppy . . ."

Surely Jin hadn't had a crush on her when they were younger, right? They'd always been friends, and he'd spent a good deal of time with her. Most of his free time, really. But Astrea had heard rumors as she walked the palace gardens, some of the aristocratic teens gossiping about who he'd danced with at dinners, who claimed to have kissed him, and even a couple who'd claimed to have taken a 'tumble' with him. Nothing Jin had ever done years ago had suggested he'd liked her as more than a friend.

"Am I interrupting?" As if on cue, Jin poked his head through the open parlor doorway.

"You're right on time." Eliana stood up and strolled toward him. "We have a lot to talk about, including what the consequences will be if you hurt my best friend."

Jin's questioning gaze turned from his sister to Astrea, his features softening. "I'll accept only the severest punishment if I do something so foolish, Ellie."

Astrea was sure she flushed the brightest of reds as Jin continued watching her. Eliana, though, was already pulling him out of the room.

"We need to talk about Ysabel first," Eliana said as they retreated into the foyer. "What's the plan? Tell me everything."

Astrea was glad to let them go discuss the implications of Jin's talk with Ysabel. They'd fill her in on whatever needed to be shared later. For now, though, Astrea half smiled when Cressida sat on the sofa again. She leaned against her best friend, exhaustion threatening to take hold.

Cressida wrapped an arm around Astrea's shoulders and asked, "You good?"

"I think I will be."

Chapter 20

"I assure you, Prince Varojin, that no void mage is going to get into this palace undetected," Lucian said. "I spent the entire afternoon yesterday briefing the palace guards and Talmaris's police leadership. They know what they're looking for."

Astrea's stomach tightened as she watched Lucian from across the guest house's dining room table. Morning sunlight filtered in through the windows, illuminating his perfectly crisp dark blue uniform. He was convinced; Astrea could see it in the set of his jaw. He was sure this was enough, but she wondered if it was actually too much. Should they really go shouting about the existence of void magic from the rooftops?

That voice in her dream before the dinner with Ysabel had suggested the void mages were tracking their movements. So did whatever happened with Nazarov. A vision? She still didn't know what to call it, but that didn't seem like the right word.

After Astrea had calmed down the day before, she'd sat with the others going over every detail she could remember from her different dreams and visions. They'd agreed on three things. The first was that there seemed to be two voices: an unknown man and Victor Nazarov. The second was that she wasn't having visions at all but rather that the void mages were somehow projecting themselves into her mind. Third was that the Paragon, whoever they were and whatever they wanted, seemed to have known about Astrea's magic for much longer than just this summer.

How? That was the question Astrea kept going back to. How did the void mages send her visions and dreams? And how did they know she was a Lightbringer?

Grand Duchess Ysabel hadn't been thrilled to learn that Jin and Eliana had chosen to hide Astrea's first 'vision' from her, nor had she been happy to learn that the Paragon were hunting Astrea. But the siblings claimed they would smooth it over with her in the coming days.

At least the commander is talking to us. He didn't seem happy, but their decision to hide things hadn't gotten them kicked out of Talmaris. That was something.

"Except we *don't* know what we're looking for, Commander." Jin leaned on the mahogany table, attention trained on Lucian. "What happened yesterday confirms we know just a fraction of what these people are capable of."

None of the rest of their group said anything as Jin and Lucian stared each other down. Adi shifted in his seat. Nicos glanced at Astrea. Eliana watched the commander, too, while Cressida simply stared at the steam curling up from her coffee cup.

"Prince Varojin." Lucian's voice tightened. "The grand duchess is working with her people in Kalama to locate this Nazarov fellow. We don't even know that he's on his way here. The only way we can increase security is to teach our guards what we *do* know."

"Nazarov isn't the only one," Astrea said. She wasn't sure Lucian heard her, but Jin's hand settled on her knee under the table. She'd explained it to her friends, but worry still bounced through the room. Astrea pulled that invisible wall back as much as she could.

"Well, of course he's not the only void mage," Lucian said. "We know there is at least one in Talmaris, and you mentioned that other man, the guard at the Helosian palace."

"Not him," Astrea said. She swallowed as Lucian's deep blue eyes settled on her. "I've been having dreams. I *thought* they were just dreams, anyway. And in one just a few nights ago, Nazarov seemed to be in our . . . my room even though I was asleep."

"Dreams?" Lucian leaned back into his creaky chair. "First visions, now dreams? You didn't think we needed to know this? You really thought it was a good idea to hide this from us?"

"I didn't think it was the void mages," Astrea muttered. "I thought I was just having bad dreams from the stress of it all."

"This isn't the first time this has happened," Jin said, "nor do I think it'll be the last. She's had several dreams that we think may have actually been these . . . well, visions isn't quite the right word. But we think they're connected."

"Victor Nazarov seems to be fixating on Astrea, Commander," Eliana said. "He might even be working with our father."

"All speculation for now. We will find Victor Nazarov one way or another, Your Imperial Highnesses. And you will all be safe here in Talmaris. I personally guarantee that."

How could Lucian be so sure of himself?

"If it would make you feel better," Lucian continued when their group stayed silent, "I will assign a guard to any of you if and when you leave the palace. I believe Tomas mentioned you had an appointment at the university?" His gaze flicked back to Astrea. "Something about a professor who might know more?"

Despite Astrea's sudden and dramatic exit from the library the day before, Tomas had still sent over more books as well as directions for their meeting with the professor. Was it really safe, though? Could they go?

"We do," Astrea said. "A little later this morning."

"The guard will drive you to this meeting, and he will stay by your side throughout. It will be an uneventful trip, I assure you."

"I'd like to go," Jin said.

"Prince Varojin—"

"I will not split my team up, Commander. Not anymore."

"Are we to have this argument every time we need to get something done, Your Highness?" Lucian asked. "You know where the grand duchess stands on this."

"And I know where I stand. We're not splitting up."

"The grand duchess is already upset that you kept this information from her, and your relationship is already fragile. Do you really want to further damage it?" Lucian asked. "I support what you and your sister are trying to do, Prince Varojin, but do I need to remind you that neither the grand duchess nor her council has made a formal decision about your little . . . rebellion?"

Jin's jaw tightened.

"Captain," Adi said, "we'll be alright. I'll go with her."

"Adi . . ." Jin huffed, almost as if he were trying to force his next words out. "You know we don't split up in these situations."

Though Jin was unreadable, anxiety and pain flared bright around Adi. Why didn't Jin want to split up? Astrea could understand their frustration, but they couldn't risk upsetting Ysabel or her council. It wasn't worth it.

"And you know that sometimes we have to," Adi countered. "Cress and I will go with her. We'll be alright, just like the other night."

Jin sighed, the heavy sound the only one in the room. "Fine," he said to Lucian. "But I want to meet this guard."

"Of course you will—" Lucian started, but Jin cut him off.

"Now." There was an edge to his voice Astrea had never heard.

The commander hesitated for just a moment, then he nodded. "Of course, Your Highness. Marko is right outside."

Jin stood. "Adi?"

"Right behind you."

As Lucian led Jin and Adi outside, Cressida muttered, "Well, I guess we should make sure we have what we need to meet this professor."

"I'll go get the books." Astrea got up and started upstairs as quickly as her legs would carry her. She didn't want to stick around to analyze Lucian's decisions. It was what it was; if he thought this was the best way to provide protection for the whole city, then they needed to trust him. Lucian knew his people. He knew his teams and what they were capable of.

As soon as she was in her bedroom, Astrea went to the wardrobe and pulled out her satchel. Mattina's notebook was tucked inside, as were the additional papers they'd found at the house. She took those out; the professor didn't need to see everything they had.

Shouldering her satchel, Astrea went back down to the foyer. Jin had his back to the stairs and was talking with a blond man. Adi and Cressida were there, and when Adi spotted Astrea, he waved.

She'd tried to apologize to him the night before. She still felt awful that she'd scared him so badly when she came back from the palace and panicked, but he wouldn't hear it. He'd said there was nothing to apologize for. And though Astrea had been afraid to see a myriad of things in Adi's aura—disgust, pity, annoyance—none of that had shown up. He'd even hugged her not once but twice.

As Astrea approached the loose circle, Jin shifted to make space for her. His hand, heavy and warm, found the small of her back.

"Marko," Jin said to the blond, "this is Astrea Sovna. Astrea, this is Marko Livante. He's the guard Lucian has assigned for today's outing."

Marko wasn't nearly as tall or broad as Adi and Jin, but Astrea was sure his slighter, smaller build meant nothing. Lucian wouldn't assign them a guard who couldn't help them fight off a void mage. A scar marred the apple of his right cheek, the mark noticeably paler than his sand-hued skin, and his wheat hair was styled in a half-up bun. His gray dress pants and white shirt made him look like any other man one might see on the streets of Talmaris. Marko couldn't have been more than a few years older than Jin and Adi.

"It's nice to meet you," Astrea said.

"A pleasure," Marko replied, his voice rougher than she expected. Just like most of the other Novarian guards, his emotions were locked tightly behind a wall. Even his gray eyes revealed nothing.

"Marko is a Tempest," Jin continued, "and well aware of what's going on. He'll be escorting you three to the university."

"Whenever you're ready, we can go," Marko said.

Jin nodded. "Just one moment, then they'll meet you outside."

"Of course, Your Imperial Highness." Marko inclined his head to Jin, then headed out the front door.

"When you're out there," Jin said to their trio, "be careful. I'm sure Marko is a powerful mage, but focus on each other if anything goes wrong. I want all of you back here in one piece."

Adi smiled at Cressida and Astrea. "You two ready?"

"Let's just get this over with," Cressida murmured.

Cressida started down the hallway to the front door, Adi on her heels. As Astrea hurried after them, Jin called, "And no punching anyone this time, please!"

Talmaris's university stretched out before Astrea, and it almost felt like home. The wide walkways, large green spaces, fountains, enormous trees, and brick buildings all reminded her of where she studied in Kalama.

She kept her magic wide open as Marko led them through the campus. The students and professors put off all kinds of energy: anxiety, excitement, boredom, frustration. There were no gaps other than the occasional wall like Jin's, which wasn't unexpected. The farther they got into the campus and the more emotion Astrea sensed, the calmer she felt.

It's going to be fine.

"Professor Shalysko's office is in the next building," Marko said over his shoulder as they passed another group of students. They all wore clothing similar to what Astrea, Adi, and Cressida had on: dark hues and pastels in a mix of fabrics, some with patterns and some solid colors.

"Do you know anything about him?" Adi asked.

"I've never met the professor," Marko said, "but Tomas would not have put you in contact if he could not help."

Adi simply rolled his eyes. "Right."

As they approached the next brick building, Marko opened one of the thick double doors and motioned for them to enter. The building's cool, light-filled interior was mostly empty. Behind the closed doors lining the hallway, Astrea's magic brushed against much of the same as before. Classrooms, she assumed.

They ascended a squeaky narrow staircase, then headed down two more quiet hallways lined with doors before Marko stopped. A plaque on the door read *Professor Kostas Shalysko*. Marko knocked, then stepped back. No answer came.

"How do things feel?" Marko asked.

Right. Of course Marko knew about her magic, and of course he knew she would be searching for voids. He had to know if he was serving as their guard.

"Fine," Astrea said. There were no voids here. There also wasn't anyone behind that door. "I don't think he's here, actually."

"Unfortunate considering you have an appointment," Marko muttered. He reached for the handle and turned it. It opened. When Marko pushed the door fully open, the room was empty of everything but the furniture, books, and small artifacts lining the walls. No professor.

"Should we just wait for him?" Cressida asked.

Adi brushed past Marko and stepped into the office. "I doubt he went far if he didn't lock his door."

"Waiting will be fine," Marko said. "Whatever you three decide to do in there is none of my business."

"You don't want to come in with us?" Adi asked.

"I have a dreadful lack of curiosity," Marko drawled. "I'll watch for the professor."

Did he *want* them to snoop around? Astrea didn't have to decide; Adi and Cressida were already moving into the office.

"Don't touch anything you shouldn't," Astrea whispered.

"Just looking around while we wait." Cressida examined a wall of diplomas in thick, mismatched frames. "Professor Shalysko sure has had plenty of time to study. Maybe he'll be able to help after all."

Adi perused the wall opposite Cressida. Several maps hung there, each decorated with different colored pins flagging sections of Novaria and the northern regions of Zaikud, Helosia, and Tornama.

"And he's well traveled," Adi murmured.

A colorful array of books and folios were organized in the bookshelves on the third wall. Miniature statues, pieces of jewelry, some kind of dagger, and even what appeared to be a small urn filled in some of the blank spaces on the shelves. The desk in the middle of the room—a solid, dark-stained wood piece—housed several stacks of paper and more books in neat piles.

Marko cleared his throat. "Professor Shalysko?"

Adi and Cressida both rejoined Astrea in the middle of the room.

"That's me," a nasal voice said from outside the office. A tall, gangly man appeared in the doorway, and gray confusion colored the air around him as he stopped short. He pushed his floppy brown hair out of his face. "Oh! Hello."

As Marko blocked the entrance with his arm, lavender surprise bubbled up around the professor. "Roll up your sleeves."

"Excuse me?" Kostas looked from Marko to Astrea, Adi, and Cressida.

Marko hadn't exactly been chatty on the car ride over, but he'd been well briefed if he knew to look for that tattoo. "Roll them up." His voice left no room for argument.

Kostas hastily yanked up the sleeves of his loose-fitting blazer and shirt for Marko to inspect. From Astrea's position, Kostas's pale complexion was clear. No sign of the Paragon tattoo, just a few dark freckles. With a nod, Marko dropped his arm and let the professor into his office.

"Professor Shalysko," Astrea said, "I'm Astrea. Tomas, from the palace library, set this meeting up . . ."

"Ah!" Kostas shuffled into the room and set a beat-up briefcase on his desk. "Am I late?"

"Just a bit," Marko muttered, and bright peach amusement flared around Adi.

"That's alright." Astrea followed Kostas as he sat down behind his desk. She made introductions for the rest of the team, then said, "We appreciate you meeting with us on such short notice."

"Tomas and Lili mentioned that you have some sort of unidentifiable language you need help with?" Kostas asked. "Can you tell me more about it?"

"I brought it with me." Astrea opened her satchel and pulled out Mattina's journal. She sucked in a short breath, then set the notebook in front of the professor. "Do you know what this is?"

Kostas examined the pages, then her, his sky blue eyes piercing. Curiosity and confusion twined around him in a blend of green and gray. "Where did you find this?"

"Southern Helosia."

"Helosia?" Kostas's thin eyebrows shot up. "What would this be doing in southern Helosia?"

"You recognize it?" Adi asked.

"I thought it was relegated just to the northern part of the continent," the professor replied. "I've found this language at several dig sites. Well." He chuckled. "Me and a few of my students. They often travel with me. I can't take all the credit."

Several dig sites? Just what was this language?

"Do you know what it says?" Cressida asked.

Kostas sighed. "Unfortunately, I do not. It is a . . . newer discovery of mine, just in the last few months actually. I've not yet been able to find any resources to begin translation work."

"Do you know how old these sites are?" Astrea asked, glancing at the maps on his wall.

"Oh, they date back to the Great Wars and earlier," Kostas said. "Some of them are much older."

"So around five hundred years old and older?" Astrea asked.

"Yes, give or take. Why do you ask?"

Five hundred years was one of the first constraints Emperor Aelius had put on Astrea and Jin's original project. Five hundred years of Novarian and Helosian history and mythology. A strange language found in southern Helosia and at Novarian archaeological digs from that same time period. That was not a coincidence.

So, Lord Mattina—and those other void mages, Astrea was sure—were connected back to the northern part of the continent. Very old parts of the continent. If they really were associated with this Paragon, just how long had the group been operating?

Astrea dropped into one of the wooden chairs in front of Kostas's desk. She wasn't sure if this was the right thing to do, but beating around the bush would do them no good. They didn't have the luxury of time. "Professor Shalysko, I need to ask you a question that stays between the people in this room only."

A nervous chuckle left Kostas as he looked up from the notebook. "What is going on?"

"I suggest you listen to her, Professor," Marko said. "This is at the grand duchess's order."

Kostas swallowed.

Astrea took a deep breath, then said, "I need to know if you've ever heard of something called the Paragon."

"The Paragon?" Kostas repeated. His narrow fingers drummed on the top of his desk as he muttered the name under his breath again. "I can't say I have."

"We think they're connected to this book and this language," Adi said.

"Have you ever come across references to strange, dark magic in your research?" Cressida asked. "Maybe they're not calling it the Paragon."

At that, Kostas's eyebrows furrowed and his aura lit up teal and green, a mix of understanding and curiosity. He stood and started for one of the bookshelves on the wall behind Astrea. Wind gusted through the room as Kostas froze in his tracks. Astrea turned, squinting against the harshness of wind and magic spinning out from Marko's palms.

"I am just getting a book," Kostas gritted out, orange fear pulsing around him. After a moment, Marko cut off his magic. "Skies," the professor muttered as he adjusted his blazer. "I am just getting a book!"

Marko said nothing, but wariness prickled Astrea's body.

Kostas retrieved a thick tome and brought it back to his desk. "Dark magic?" he asked as he began flipping through the pages.

"Yes," Astrea said.

The professor was silent for several moments as he scoured the text, but finally, he paused. He passed the book to Astrea. "Like this?"

The page was just a wall of text in Novarian describing some kind of battle. It was a vague reference at best, a single mention of 'dark fire' being controlled by a mage. Astrea's heart leaped.

"Maybe," Astrea told him. "Although this isn't exactly specific."

"It dates back to the early part of the Great Wars," Kostas said. "One of the sites where I saw the language is close to where this battle took place, actually."

"Is this what you were looking for, Miss Sovna?" Marko asked.

"It seems to be." It wasn't much, but a reference was a reference. It was more than they had.

"I think Professor Shalysko should come back to the palace with us," he said. "It's not safe for him to be aware of this investigation considering the . . . threat."

"Threat?" Kostas asked. "What threat?"

Astrea pressed her lips together. Marko was right. Besides, if the professor came back to the palace with them, Eliana, Jin, and Ysabel could decide what else the man needed to know. He was their best connection to the void right now. He was their best chance at answers.

"Do you have any family?" Marko asked.

"Not in the city," Kostas said. "My parents live out east."

"No partner or children?"

"None."

"Good. Please pack whatever you want to bring with you today, Professor. We will escort you back to the palace."

Kostas hesitated, then nodded. "I need to cancel my afternoon lectures. My students will be expecting me."

"Then cancel them," Marko said. "We need to return to the palace immediately."

Kostas started packing up a briefcase with several notebooks, then scrawled a note on a piece of paper. "You may keep the book with that reference," he said to Astrea as he handed her Mattina's journal. "I assume you will want to bring it with us."

"I'll take it," Adi offered. The book was thick, too large to fit inside Astrea's bag. She passed it to him, then slid Mattina's notebook back into her satchel.

"Are we ready?" Marko asked.

"Just let me drop this at my classroom," the professor said. "It's on the way out."

As Marko escorted them through the now-quiet building, Astrea's pulse raced. The Paragon.

They finally had a link to the Paragon.

The car rolled to a stop outside the palace's guard house. Nestled among a copse of oak trees and fragrant rose bushes, the gray brick building was set off to one side of the main palace. Astrea had been there just once before, the night they went to the void house and confirmed the Paragon were indeed in Talmaris.

She crawled out of the car after Adi, only to find Lucian standing below the guard house's front steps, arms crossed behind his back. Marko nudged Kostas toward him.

"And who is this?" Lucian asked.

"This is—" Marko started, but the professor cut him off.

"I am Professor Kostas Shalysko," he said as he straightened his blazer. "And who might you be?"

"Commander Lucian." He glanced at where Astrea, Adi, and Cressida stood to one side. "I assume there's a reason you've brought him here?"

"He's seen the language on several archaeological digs," Astrea said.

Adi held up the book Kostas had given them. "And may even have found a reference to void magic."

"I thought it best to bring him under protective custody until we straighten this out," Marko explained.

Lucian looked up at Kostas and frowned. "You're a professor of . . . ?"

"Archaeology," Kostas said, a mix of rusty annoyance and green curiosity flashing in the air. "What is going on, Commander? Your colleague here mentioned a threat before forcing me away from my office."

"We need to keep you here for the time being," Lucian said. "You'll be provided with whatever you need during your stay, of course. Marko will show you to your accommodations."

"Come this way, please, Professor Shalysko," Marko said. It was the most polite he'd been all morning.

With a final look at Lucian, Adi, Cressida, and Astrea, the professor nodded. "I assume we will speak more about this soon?"

"Yes, we will," Lucian said.

That seemed to satisfy the professor. He followed Marko into the guard house without another word.

"You're just whisking him off like that?" Cressida asked. "He has information, Commander."

"And we need to be careful, Cressida," Lucian replied with a sigh. "I know he comes at the recommendation of Tomas's friend, but I'd like to look into him more."

"But you could read him too, couldn't you?" Astrea asked. "He's not a void mage." On the entire drive back to the palace, the professor's emotions had been clear and strong: curiosity, confusion, anxiety.

"And he doesn't have the tattoo," Cressida said.

"That may be," Lucian said, "but that does not mean we know who this man is. We'll keep him in one of the rooms at the guard house. It's for everyone's safety that we do this."

"And how long is it going to take?" Astrea asked. They finally had a connection, and now the commander wanted to take it away. Well, not take it away, but he wanted to pause. It didn't feel like there was much of a difference. "We don't have forever."

"I think Lucian is right," Adi said. "Better to slow down for a moment and make sure we didn't miss anything."

"I'll have my people start checking into this Professor Shalysko right away," Lucian said. "By dinner tomorrow, we'll have our answers."

Astrea huffed. Lucian wanted a day and a half? She could see the logic, but still. More time spent waiting was more time Saros and the Nikaphoroses were stuck in Kalama with Emperor Aelius.

"And what are we supposed to do in the meantime?" Astrea asked. "We can't just sit around."

Lucian shrugged. "I'm sure you'll find a way to fill your time."

CHAPTER 21

Commander Lucian had been wrong. Astrea had no idea what to do with herself as they waited for him to finish checking into the professor's background. After leaving the guard house the day before, Astrea had trained some with Adi and Cressida, then spent the better part of the afternoon alone and trying not to think about everything. Eliana, Nicos, and Jin had been with the grand duchess all day and had, at least according to them, smoothed out the issue of hiding information. Never mind that they were still hiding the meteorite angle.

Ysabel's staff had just taken away their breakfast dishes, and Astrea had moved to the parlor with Cressida for the morning. Jin, Adi, and Nicos had gone down to the lake, though Eliana had disappeared just after breakfast.

Cressida flopped down on the sofa. Over the last few days, her emotions had been surprisingly steady, but now orange anxiety sparked around her.

"What's wrong?" Astrea walked to the window on the far side of the room and pulled back the heavy drapes. Sunlight filtered in, and outside, one of Lucian's guards patrolled by.

"Hate waiting," Cressida muttered. "And I hate having nothing to do."

"Why don't you go see what the boys are up to? You can keep up with them. Beats training with me."

In their training session with Adi the day before, he'd paired her and Cressida off for Astrea's practice. It was laughable to think Cressida would get anything out of that.

"I just don't feel like doing much of anything, I guess," Cressida said with a sigh.

"Maybe you'll feel like doing this," Eliana said as the parlor door swung open. She crossed the room in a few long strides and dropped a thick stack of paper on the coffee table.

"What is it?" Astrea asked.

"My preliminary plans for how I'd restructure the Helosian government. It could use a quick read before dinner with Ysabel in a few days. I want it to be somewhat coherent before talking to her and Crown Prince Veiko."

Astrea's eyebrows shot up as she moved toward the sitting area and plopped onto one of the chairs. That was what Nicos had been reviewing a few days earlier. "That sounds like something that needs more than a quick read, Ellie."

"Maybe." As she shrugged, the subtle sparkles in her scarlet blouse twinkled. "I feel like there are more important things to worry about right now."

Cressida pushed herself up to a sitting position. "That's far from the truth," she said. "All of this goes back to your father. Even if we figure out what the Paragon wants, it's for nothing if we don't get your father out of power."

"I know that's true, but the Paragon feels like the immediate threat." Eliana dropped into the vacant armchair next to Astrea and leaned forward on her knees. Orange anxiety spiked high around her. "I mean, we don't even know if anyone's going to really follow me into this rebellion."

Astrea reached for the papers. There were actually three reports, all bound individually. The neat, typed font had surely come from a typewriter. Who had helped her make three copies? Nicos? When had they found the time?

"They'll follow," Cressida said. "We were just talking to Lorenzi and a few others at your father's dinner. Some of the nobles are unhappy. A lot of the people back home are unhappy."

"That doesn't mean we'll win."

Astrea looked up from the copy she was flipping through. "We definitely won't if you think we won't. People are going to need you to be confident, Ellie."

"I think we can if I have enough support," she said. "It's going to come down to numbers, tech, and whatever my father is doing with void magic. We need . . . resources. Supporters. Everything."

"What about . . ." When Cressida hesitated, Eliana gave her a pointed look. She sighed. "This sounds awful, but what about something more covert? Then we might not need numbers."

"You mean like assassinating my father and Kaius?" Before Astrea could even react, Eliana continued, "While I don't love the idea of killing them, I don't think it would help. Kaius's supporters are entrenched. So are my father's. That could just set off a different chain of events. I'd look like a usurper, not like I was actually trying to do something for the greater good."

"Right, well . . . has Ysabel said if she's going to support you?" Cressida asked as she reached for another copy of Eliana's plans. "Will she give you anything?"

"Ysabel is more ready to support me than her council is. And unlike my father, she actually needs the support of at least four of the six council members if she's going to *do* anything. That's who I actually need to convince."

"Do they know of Jin's relation to Ysabel?" Cressida asked. "Would that sway them?"

"No, they don't, and no, I don't think it would help. They're concerned about how entangled their government might get in this and how it would impact civilians."

Astrea knew that was fair. Their little rebellion was not Novarian civilians' responsibility, even if it was probably in the entire continent's best interest to replace Emperor Aelius with Empress Eliana. The Novarians had a choice to make, and Astrea just hoped they could be convinced to formally support Eliana in some way. Maybe, at the upcoming dinner they had with some of Jin's Novarian family, they could at least win the support of the other royals.

"When did you have time to get through all of this?" Astrea asked as she flipped back to the first page of the report. From the headings she'd skimmed, it included everything from economic policy to bureaucratic reform to expanding the Senate's power to foreign relations. That was no small task. It was, at first glance, the plan for *after* the rebellion. The plan for what happened when Emperor Aelius was no more.

"Well." Eliana's smile was tight, her aura tinged magenta with embarrassment. "I may have started working on this back home."

"Ellie . . ." Cressida's voice trailed off. "You didn't tell us?"

"I didn't want you and Az to be in the crossfire if someone found out." She shrugged. "Nicos knew. I'm sorry I didn't tell you two."

"I may have run into Nicos the other day when he was reviewing this," Astrea said. Eliana cringed. "He's been helping you?"

"He has."

"Two rebels under one roof," Cressida mused. "Do you think your father ever suspected?"

"I'm not sure," Eliana said. "The last few months have just been so frustrating. I was doing it more as an exercise than plans, but now . . . well, I guess I was just prepared." She sighed, so unlike herself as she fidgeted with her skirt. "Will you two read through it for me?"

"Of course. I'll read it today," Astrea said. "But I trust you, whatever it is you want to do."

"Thanks." When Eliana looked up, those golden Auris eyes of hers sparkled. Sweet amusement coated Astrea's tongue, like someone had just dropped a dozen hard candies into her mouth. "Can you make Jin read it, too? Somehow, despite the fact that we're in the same location at the same time for the first time in years, I barely find a moment to talk with him alone. I wonder why that could be . . ."

"Don't even start," Astrea warned, but her voice lacked any edge. "I'll leave this room right now if you try to bring it up."

Yes, she'd told Eliana and Cressida about her relationship with Jin, but that didn't mean she wanted to get into any details, nor did she want to discuss the situation at length. She was just trying to enjoy her time with him instead of letting her mind throw her back into her anxieties.

"Fine," Cressida and Eliana said in unison.

"Or," Astrea continued, "we can talk about Nicos if you want."

Cressida sat up straighter as Eliana flopped back in the chair and covered her face with her hands. That magenta embarrassment was back, bright and pulsing.

Eliana groaned. "Do we have to?"

"We don't have to, but just know you aren't hiding anything from me," Astrea said. "From *me.*"

"Oh, skies!" Eliana cried. "The commander knows? I never even considered . . ."

"He probably doesn't *know,* but I assume he can see what I can."

The magenta shot higher. "Oh, skies, what if he told Ysabel?"

"You think he would?" Cressida asked. "He doesn't strike me as the type to gossip."

Astrea didn't love forcing the conversation on Eliana like this, but if her barrier was down, she could see everything playing out between them. And maybe talking about it now would help Eliana figure out what to do next. Maybe having both Astrea and Cressida there would make her more comfortable with it all.

"I don't think it's any of their business, but just . . . I don't know. Be aware of it when he's around," Astrea said.

Eliana didn't move a muscle, her face still covered by her hands as she curled up on the chair. "Skies, I've wanted to tell you both for months, but I've been so embarrassed."

"Why?" Cressida asked. "You know we like Nicos. I told you that the other night."

"I know, but I wasn't supposed to—" Eliana huffed. "It was supposed to be a one-time thing. One time, just after the spring equinox. Get it out of our systems. But now I need him, and I'm so afraid I'm going to lose him."

Astrea swallowed. "Ellie," she whispered, "I get it, but you've got to talk to him."

Eliana sat up with some effort. "I know."

Eliana Auris was many things. She was confident, loyal, funny, kind, and, yes, spoiled. She was also stubborn, and she didn't like asking for help. She didn't like accepting help. They were a lot alike in that way, Astrea realized.

"Let him support you," Astrea said. "He wants to be there for you. I mean, he fled Helosia with you. He's making traitorous plans with you. That means something."

"I think that means a lot," Cressida said.

Astrea took in her best friend: her round chin, straight nose, dark wavy hair, and the hint of red lipstick still on her lips. Dark circles under her eyes. Eliana's familiar, heavy stubbornness settled against Astrea's bones.

"And let us be there for you," Cressida added as she lifted up Eliana's reform plans. "We'll look at this, but talk to us, Ellie. Seems you've been keeping a lot to yourself."

"Just try to take care of yourself," Astrea said when Eliana remained quiet. "Please? Or at least let Nicos do it . . . if he hasn't already."

Eliana's eyes narrowed, then widened as Cressida snorted. That stubbornness faded as Eliana's aura lit up with peach amusement. "Did Astrea Sovna just make a sex joke?"

"A very bad one, yes."

Eliana laughed, the sound light and clear and so much more like her usual self. "I don't think I've ever heard you make one before."

"Well, there's a first time for everything," Astrea said, "especially when you need cheering up. Don't get used to it."

Astrea settled into her seat and flipped open Eliana's reform plans, but she couldn't focus on it. The colors in Eliana's aura calmed, only a faint sheen of magenta embarrassment and orange anxiety remaining. Eliana deserved to be happy, but she was stubborn. Astrea just hoped she would take her advice.

Though she'd been trying to get through the details of Eliana's plans for a reformed Helosian government all afternoon, Astrea's mind kept wandering.

The princess had laid out ideas for changes to the tribute system her father set up for the different noble houses—Eliana wanted to do away with it—ways they might streamline taxation, foreign policy—no more wars except when acting out of self-defense—and plans to enhance the Senate's power. Though Astrea hadn't managed to get into the details, she trusted Eliana's vision. She'd been criticizing her father's policies in private since they were teenagers.

Now, Astrea sat on the veranda with Jin, Nicos, and Adi. They'd taken up the small dining table there, shaded from the harsh late afternoon sun by the guest house and trees. Astrea held a few playing cards in her hand. Adi sat to her left; Jin and Nicos were across from them. They'd convinced her to try a card game, one she'd never heard of before. She barely understood the rules. Adi was the only reason their team was winning.

"Oh, this is good," Adi murmured as he slapped down a queen card in the fire suit. "This is very good for us, Az."

Astrea paused. He'd never called her that before. Only Cressida, Eliana, and Jin called her Az. But she didn't mind. She hadn't known Adi long, but it somehow felt like she'd known him her whole life. Across the table, Jin flashed her a quick smile.

"I'll trust your judgment on that," Astrea said. Following this game's quick turnaround times was difficult, especially when her mind kept drifting back to all the things they needed to do.

Nicos slapped down a king card in the water suit. Adi cursed and folded his hand. "Damnit, Masalis. I thought I had you again."

Nicos laughed as he began collecting everyone's cards. "Can't win 'em all, Kuwat."

As Nicos began reshuffling the deck, Astrea said, "Last hand? I need to get back to work."

"Dinner's in half an hour," Nicos said. "What can you possibly accomplish in half an hour?"

"Something, if I'm focused."

"Ellie's plans are solid. I've reviewed them a dozen times myself," he said.

"She just wants to be prepared." And Astrea wanted to help Eliana feel prepared, even if she had no doubt the plans were solid.

"She is." Warm pride radiated off Nicos. "I know she is."

The veranda's double doors squeaked as they opened. Commander Lucian stepped outside, his expression neutral and a folder clutched in one hand. Eliana and Cressida both exited right behind him.

"Sorry to interrupt," Lucian said. Jin straightened immediately. "My team looked into the professor." He lifted up the folder for them all to see. "I'll let you look at the details if you're interested, but he's clear."

"How thorough was this examination?" Jin asked. "It didn't take you long."

"We used the same process we use for all potential palace employees, Prince Varojin. It was very thorough."

"There wasn't anything unusual about him?" Eliana asked.

"No, unless you count the fact that several of his colleagues believe he's too chatty." When Eliana rolled her eyes, Lucian continued, "He's lived in Talmaris for years, and he grew up out east with his parents. He's been a professor at the university for quite some time, and his thesis was written on the Great Wars. It seems if anyone is up for helping us with this challenge, it would be Professor Shalysko."

"So, we can start investigating again?" Astrea asked.

"Yes. We'll have the professor at the library first thing in the morning to begin filling him in and figuring out our next steps."

Relief flooded Astrea's veins. *Finally.*

"I'll leave this with you," Lucian continued as he passed the folio to Jin. "Find me if you have any questions, Your Highnesses."

As soon as Lucian was gone, Nicos leaned back in his chair. "And just like that, we're back on track?"

"It would seem so," Jin said. He leafed through the folio, but his wall stayed heavy and strong. "If nobody else wants to read through this, I will tonight."

"Fine by me," Eliana said. "I'll read it at breakfast."

If anyone was going to be able to interpret Lucian's findings, it would be Jin or Eliana. Maybe Adi or Nicos. But Astrea? She didn't really care to read through it all if the experts thought it checked out. There was already enough for her to try sorting through without adding that to her list.

"I think I'm just going to take my dinner upstairs and keep working," Astrea said. "You know where to find me if you need me."

Eliana nodded, but Jin frowned. After bidding her friends goodbye, Astrea slipped back into the house and made her way to the second floor. She grabbed Eliana's plans off the desk, but the black cover of the *Myth and Magic* book caught her eye.

Tomorrow, she promised herself. *We'll get back to the investigation tomorrow.*

Chapter 22

By the time Astrea stepped out of the shower the next morning, the whole bathroom smelled of peony and honeysuckle. She'd woken up earlier than usual, which was already early, unable to sleep as her mind anticipated the work still to come. They needed to work with the professor to figure out what, exactly, Mattina's notebook said and how it was connected to this dark magic in the mountains.

After changing into a lacy white blouse and emerald green skirt, Astrea went back into the bedroom. Jin was finally awake, his back to her as he stood in front of the wardrobe. She'd been hoping to get some time alone with him, but letting him sleep had seemed like the better idea.

"I didn't wake you, did I?" Astrea asked.

"Not at all." He slipped on a dark blue dress shirt, then turned around as he began buttoning it. "Did you hear me come in last night? I tried not to wake you, but I had to clean up after Adi and I came back."

"No, I was out cold." Astrea had been so exhausted, in fact, that she couldn't remember if she'd had any dreams. "You were with Adi?"

"Training," Jin said as he finished buttoning his shirt. "My body still isn't used to being here, away from the war. I'm having a hard time sitting still for so long."

Astrea couldn't imagine that kind of change. To go from training and wars for eight years straight to putzing around a palace must've been almost disorienting. Even Astrea's disrupted routine was hard to cope with, and this wasn't all that different from her days working at the Great Library.

"Do you think it'll get easier?" she asked as she watched him tuck his shirt in. The muscles in his forearms flexed with the movement. How could such a simple thing make her stomach flip? She swallowed, then walked toward the desk. "Adjusting to all this, I mean."

"Well, I suppose it has to eventually. I think I'll always have to keep moving, though. It keeps me focused."

"Really?" Astrea asked as she opened her satchel. Mattina's notebook was still tucked inside. She may have walked around Kalama all the time, but that stamina did almost nothing for the time she spent with Adi and Lucian. "It just tires me out."

Jin laughed, the sound making Astrea's skin warm pleasantly. "That's why I like it. My mind doesn't have a chance to wander if I work my body that much."

"Doesn't seem to do that for me." She reached for the book Kostas had lent them next, frowning. It was definitely too big for her satchel. Just as she was about to set it down, Jin snatched it from her hand. "What are you doing?"

Jin moved her dark hair away from her shoulder, then pressed a kiss to the side of her neck. "Carrying your books for you."

"I can do that."

"Yes, but I want to do it."

It was a small thing, almost juvenile, as if they were on their way to school. Still, Astrea couldn't help but smile. "I'm a grown woman, you know."

"Oh, believe me, I know. But I don't think that means your partner can't carry a book for you."

"I suppose."

"And as for not tiring myself out enough," he continued, "I can think of a new routine to add in, if you want to help."

"Absolutely ridiculous," Astrea said with a laugh. "You're flirting with me right now?"

"Yes. There's always time for that before breakfast."

Again, his lips met the side of her neck, and Astrea leaned back into him. She didn't think she'd ever get tired of the feeling of his body so close to hers.

"You're going to be in trouble if you keep doing that." Astrea barely got the words out as Jin's desire and amusement washed over her in gentle waves. "We have important things to do today."

"You're right." With a sigh, Jin stepped to the side and reached for Astrea's hand. "You always were the responsible one of the two of us."

"Then let's get breakfast and get to work," Astrea said as she grabbed her satchel and pulled Jin toward the door. "Someone's got to keep us focused."

Their whole group had decided it was important to meet the professor and figure out what came next. But now, as everyone settled in around one of the large round tables in the palace library, Astrea wasn't so sure about being back in the space. She hadn't returned since the incident where Nazarov invaded her mind.

Astrea reached up and rolled the sapphire pendant of her necklace between her fingers. *What he showed you wasn't real,* she reminded herself, though that didn't ease the anxiety building in her bones. When Nicos gave her a puzzled look from across the table, she flashed a quick smile.

"I will be right back to escort Her Highness in," Lucian said.

"Ysabel's coming?" Eliana asked.

"Yes, Your Imperial Highness. She thought it best to speak with the professor herself and make it very clear what's expected of him." With that, Lucian headed out the door.

"Ysabel's quite hands on, isn't she?" Cressida asked once the library doors had clicked shut. "Don't think your father would ever attend a meeting like this."

"No, he'd just send Kaius in his place," Eliana muttered. "Speaking of, don't forget that we're meeting the rest of the grand ducal family in a couple days. If we can learn anything before then, it'd be ideal. I'd love something to present to Crown Prince Veiko and Princess Delfine. Anything to convince them to support our cause."

Jin had largely avoided the topic of his Novarian family, and Astrea didn't want to push him into talking about something that made him uncomfortable. Hopefully Veiko and Delfine would be as accommodating as their aunt.

"Two days isn't much time, Ellie," Jin said. "But we'll try."

Astrea wasn't sure what they'd be able to get done in two days, either. It would take some time to go through the different resources Tomas had, not to mention whatever evidence and theories Kostas had. He had so many artifacts and books back in his office on campus; surely some of them were connected to these ruins he'd found.

It wasn't long before Lucian and Grand Duchess Ysabel returned. As Ysabel exchanged pleasantries with them, Lucian disappeared up to the mezzanine, returning not long after with a confused Tomas in tow. Marko had impeccable timing, because just as Ysabel settled herself in a chair in the middle of the table, the library doors swung open. The blond guard escorted Professor Shalysko into the room and motioned for him to approach the table.

"Your Highness," Kostas said, lavender surprise flickering around his aura. "Highnesses," he corrected as he glanced at Eliana and Jin. "I apologize for my appearance. I did not realize I would be in the presence of royalty today."

His appearance seemed fine to Astrea. The professor wore a dark gray suit paired with a white shirt; he was certainly more dressed up than Jin. The only ones more dressed up than the professor were Ysabel, in a purple and black brocade dress, and Eliana, in a crimson dress she'd brought with her from Kalama.

"Professor Shalysko," Ysabel said. "It seems you might be able to help us with a problem."

"Indeed, Your Highness," Kostas said, his blue eyes flicking to Astrea for a moment. "These lovely young people have explained a small bit of what's going on. How may I be of service?"

"Please, have a seat," Ysabel said. "There is much to discuss."

It took nearly an hour for Ysabel, Lucian, Eliana, and Jin to explain the situation to the professor. He had plenty of questions, as Astrea expected he would. Tomas, too, had questions about the things Astrea had previously left out.

"Void mages exist? And are in Talmaris?" Kostas asked as he finally sat back in his chair. "I don't know that I can be of much help, Your Highnesses. I am not a mage."

"We aren't asking you to fight," Jin said. "We just need your help figuring out what's in that journal. You seem to be the only lead we have."

"And we expect your silence and undivided attention on the matter," Ysabel said. "That won't be a problem, will it, Professor Shalysko?"

"No problem at all, Your Highness." His eyebrows rose, then he grinned. "Perhaps we will make quite the discovery together. One for the history books, as they say."

"Excellent." Ysabel nodded. "Commander Lucian's team will continue providing security while you work on this project. You will be expected to remain at the palace at all times for your own safety. Should you need to go to your work or office, his team will escort you."

"I'll need to cancel the rest of my lectures for the week, Your Highness," he said. "I need to make a few calls."

"You may use the phone in my office," Tomas offered.

"I expect a report by the middle of next week," Ysabel said as she stood. "Thank you for your cooperation, Professor Shalysko."

"It's my honor, Your Highness. Anything for Novaria." As Lucian and Ysabel left the library, Kostas asked, "May I make those calls?"

"You may," Marko said. "Tomas's office is right upstairs." He looked at Jin. "We'll be back."

Tomas led the professor and guard up the spiral staircase, and much to Astrea's relief, the library was quiet again. Just the six of them.

"So," Cressida said as soon as Tomas's office door closed with a loud thud, "what do you think?"

"He's our only lead, right?" Nicos asked. "The sooner we can figure this out, the better. I don't like not knowing the specifics of what's going on at home."

"Hopefully Zephyrine will get in touch soon," Adi said. "She'll have news."

When Marko returned a few minutes later, he seemed bored. The professor and Tomas, though, were chatting like old friends.

"Lili never told me that story," Kostas said, peach amusement swirling around him. "She really did that while you two were in school?"

Tomas's boisterous laugh was cut off by Jin. "Gentlemen," he said, "it seems we have a ton of work to get through, and we're on a bit of a time crunch. What do we need to get started?"

"Of course, Your Imperial Highness." Tomas cleared his throat. "Yes, where to begin?"

Adi reached for the book from Kostas's office that Jin had set near the middle of the table. He opened it to the page referencing the dark magic, then slid it toward the librarian. "Our reference point," he said.

Tomas bent down and began scanning the page. He frowned, then his eyebrows rose as lavender surprise flickered around him. "In the Antare Mountains?" Tomas asked Kostas. "Near the Path of Ruin?"

"Sounds lovely," Nicos muttered.

"Simply a dangerous mountain pass," Kostas explained. "It's one of several locations where I have come across this mystery language. There's also a promising site in the Macadian Mountains. Do you have a map?"

"We can set one up, if someone is willing to help me?" Tomas half asked, half stated.

"Just tell me what you need me to do," Adi said.

"And Astrea," Tomas continued, "perhaps you and Cressida can begin pulling books about the Great Wars. Specifically from . . ." He flipped back a few pages before continuing, "Specifically covering the years 450 to 550."

"I'd like to look at mythology, too," Astrea said. "Perhaps specific stories that line up with where the professor has seen the language. I'm sure there's a connection there."

Tomas pointed across the room at one of the aisles that disappeared under the second-floor mezzanine. "Go check that aisle, the one between the bust of Grand Duchess Svenya and the fireplace. I'll find the Great Wars."

Astrea headed that way, and Cressida followed, her footsteps muffled by the thick rug underfoot. Astrea pulled her barrier tight around her; Tomas and Kostas were excited, so much so that Astrea couldn't focus on what she needed to be doing. She started scanning the shelves for anything related to Zaikudi, Novarian, Helosian, or Tornamian mythology. Those countries all bordered the mountains in the northern part of the continent. They'd all be worth looking at.

"Here," Astrea said as her fingers brushed a gold and green spine. It was a Zaikudi text by the looks of it, though Astrea couldn't speak the language. Jin and Eliana could read it. "Take this one." She pulled it out and handed it to Cressida, then moved down the row in search of anything else that alluded to Novaria, Helosia, or Tornama. By the time she was done, Cressida had a stack of a half dozen books cradled in her arms, another four in Astrea's.

"This is going to take forever," Cressida groaned.

"Look on the bright side," Astrea said as they emerged from the narrow aisle. "We're one step closer to figuring this mess out, and now we have all these people to help us."

"If you say so." Cressida said nothing else as she tottered back to the grouping of tables where their friends were setting up.

Astrea hoped what she said was true. It had to be.

It was time to find their answers.

The bulletin board Adi and Nicos had helped Tomas set up was bigger than any Astrea had seen before, and now it was covered in maps of Novaria and the northern parts of the continent. Tiny, colored pins marked the locations where Kostas had seen the void language in person.

There were three locations in particular where Kostas had found the language on ruins and artifacts, but he seemed to think two spots were their strongest links back to the Paragon. First were the ruins in the Antare Mountains on the eastern side of Novaria. That site not only had bits of the void language but was close to the location mentioned in the book referencing some kind of dark magic being used in battle. The second were a series of ruins in the Macadian Mountains, which had more examples of the language.

The only thing Astrea was sure of was that the Paragon was an ancient organization, not just a single person. If they'd been around since the Great Wars, they may have been around even earlier. They had yet to find any references to the Paragon specifically or any other mention of void magic. They'd sifted through over a dozen books already. There had to be information somewhere.

Eliana and Nicos had long since departed the library for Eliana to talk more with Ysabel about what was happening in Helosia and Corsyca. Cressida had stretched out on one of the sofas near the fireplace but had fallen asleep an hour before. Tomas was back in his office, and Marko and another guard had taken Kostas back to his quarters for the night. He'd promised to return in the morning with additional artifacts and notes from his office.

Adi, somehow, was wide awake and going through texts faster than Astrea. He *had* worked through an entire pot of coffee by himself, though.

"Hey." Jin's hand settled on Astrea's shoulder. "We should stop for the night."

"What time is it?" she asked.

"After midnight. Let's go to bed."

Astrea yawned. "I'm not tired."

"Well, I am," Jin said. "I'm exhausted. We can come back first thing in the morning."

"I should clean up before we go." Astrea turned back to the table where Adi was still reading. Books were scattered around, most of them already reviewed and useless. On the next table were the remnants of their dinner and coffee. Tomas had been opposed to them eating in the library, but Lucian had convinced the librarian to allow it this one time. "Tomas will hate that it's such a mess."

"Let the staff worry about that," Jin said. "And leave the books. We'll set things right tomorrow."

"I'm just going to bring this one with me," Adi said without looking up. "I'm nearing the end. I can finish it tonight."

"Bring the one I was reading, too," Astrea said. She'd been working her way through a Novarian mythology book for the last hour, and though she wouldn't tell Jin, fatigue hovered at the edges of her mind. She wasn't reading nearly as quickly as she wanted to.

Jin glanced down at her. "You cannot be serious."

"I just want to finish it."

He sighed but took the books from Adi. Astrea went to where Cressida was asleep on the couch and nudged her shoulder.

"Cress, wake up."

She jolted upright, a lightning bolt of anxiety zapping Astrea. "I'm awake. What's wrong?"

"Nothing's wrong. Let's get you to a proper bed."

They made their way back to the guest house, the first time Astrea had been back since leaving that morning. There were usually four guards stationed near the front doors, but even in the dark, Astrea could see more posted around the side of the house.

Cressida stumbled into her bedroom, calling a single "good night" over her shoulder as she disappeared into the darkness beyond. Jin passed Adi his book, then grabbed Astrea's hand and tugged her toward their room.

"You need to sleep," Jin said as he closed their door behind him.

"I just want to finish that one," Astrea said. "It won't take long."

"Az—"

"Ellie said we need to figure this out in just a couple days. Let me finish it."

"You can't kill yourself trying to find the answers. It won't be the end of the world if we need more time."

"It might be."

"Why are you assuming it'll be the end of the world?"

"Maybe your father wants that," Astrea said. "Maybe the Paragon do. I don't know. But you haven't seen what they've shown me, Jin." Just the thought of those visions and dreams made her want to march back to the library and not leave until she'd figured it out. "Whatever they want, it isn't good."

"I know I haven't, but that doesn't mean you need to—"

Astrea ground her teeth together. What did he not understand? The void mages had shown her Kalama burning. They'd shown her Saros, dead. They'd shown her the Helosian palace—Jin and Eliana's home—on fire. Cressida's home on fire. She had to do this. She had to figure it out before Nazarov came back. A few hours could make all the difference in the world.

"Give me the book, Jin."

He stared at her for a long moment, his jaw set in that Auris way. "No."

"Skies, you're stubborn," she muttered. She reached for the book, but he pulled his hand back. "Don't be childish."

"Half an hour," Jin said. "If you're not done in half an hour, you're coming to bed."

"This isn't a negotiation."

"Take it or leave it. That's the best I'm going to offer." He leaned toward her, his breath hot on her skin as he whispered, "Because I think you know I'm right. You just don't want to admit it."

Astrea glared at him, then snatched the book as he held it out to her. "I'll be downstairs."

Jin was right. Astrea knew that. But so was she. Any head start she could give herself for the morning would be worth it. Astrea marched downstairs and went to the parlor, turning on the table lamps before she settled on the floor in front of the coffee table. She laid out her notebook, then the book that actually held the stories she needed to finish going through. She flipped to the last page she'd been on.

It was a story about a princess who liked to spend time in the forest near her castle. Much to the king's dismay, she spent her time outside in the garden rather than entertaining suitors who traveled to court to win her affections. One day, she confessed to her father that she spent so much time in the garden because she was in love with the gardener. The king was upset by the news, so much so that he had the gardener imprisoned. The princess wept and wept and asked the stars for a way to rescue her beloved. She was granted magic to control the plants in the garden—a Greenkeeper—and defeat the prison guards. The princess rescued her gardener, and they ran away across the ocean to get married.

That certainly wasn't what Astrea needed to be reading about.

The next two stories in the book were similarly unhelpful. One was about a boy who learned to fireweave, and another was about a girl who became a Tidebacker. Each of those three stories pointed to the fact that people used to believe the stars granted worthy individuals their magic.

Astrea flipped to the next story, one called "The Mountain King and the Forest." It was about a king whose daughter was lost in the forest near their castle. He searched all day for her but couldn't find her, and when his knights suggested they continue their search in the morning, the king insisted they had to keep looking. As night began to fall, the shadows seemed to grow darker.

Astrea flipped the page, revealing a new illustration. A man stood in a dark forest, and among the shadows were a pair of bright red eyes.

Her chest felt like it was going to cave in on itself. Red eyes.

That was what she'd seen in her vision in Sezia. That was how Caliban's eyes had seemed to glow during their fight on the airfield.

Swallowing hard, Astrea continued the story. The king and his knights fought a so-called monster of darkness, and though some of them were mages, they could not defeat the monster. They managed to escape but not with the king's daughter. Only when the king returned with an army of mages the next day did they defeat the monster of darkness for good.

Astrea ran a clammy hand through her hair as she examined the final illustration. A shadowy form standing on the mountains in the distance, and in the foreground, the king, his daughter, and the army celebrating.

Was this it? Her clue about the void? Some covert reference to the Paragon? She laid her head down on the table and sucked in a breath, her eyes growing heavy. She needed to finish the book. There couldn't be more than twenty pages left, and maybe, just maybe, they'd have more answers.

Astrea just needed to finish reading.

Chapter 23

Astrea blinked. She was certainly no longer in the parlor. A soft pillow was under her head, and a warm blanket covered her body. Jin stared at her, eyelids half lowered.

"I was right," he whispered.

"I hate you." Sighing, Astrea rolled onto her back and tried to clear the sleep from her mind. "What time is it?"

"Early," he said. When she started to push up on her elbows, Jin shook his head. "Too early to go to the library. It's not even the seventh hour."

Tomas certainly wouldn't be there that early, nor would Kostas. But Astrea had notes she really needed to show everyone.

"Just lie here for a few more minutes," Jin said. "Then you can get up and do whatever it is I know you're already thinking about."

"I'm not thinking about anything."

Snaking an arm around her waist and pulling her closer, Jin kissed her neck. "Liar." He kissed her neck again. "Tell me what you're thinking about."

"How do you always know?"

"Because," he said before kissing her in the same spot for a third time, "you are *always* thinking about something. You've always been like that."

Astrea sucked in a breath when his lips met her skin for a fourth time. "You're going to have to stop doing that or I'm never getting out of this bed."

"Remind me why that's a problem?" he asked in that skies damn honeyed voice of his.

"We have void mages to find."

"Damn. I suppose it *is* your turn to be right." Jin sat up and ran a hand through his hair, detangling a few of his curls. "Fine. We'll do the responsible thing and get cleaned up, but let the record show I had other plans."

"Noted," Astrea said. Other plans sounded far better than more time in the library.

"Did you find anything last night?"

"I think so." As Astrea forced herself out of bed, she realized she was still in the clothes she'd been wearing the day before. She started for the wardrobe. "It's a story about a king who fought a 'monster of darkness' in the mountains," she said. "The illustrations showed a shadowy figure with red eyes."

"Like your vision in Sezia," Jin said.

"Yes. And Caliban's eyes had a reddish glow when we fought him in Kalama."

"I don't like that."

"Me either, but I think we're finally onto something." Astrea unbuttoned her blouse with one hand as she yanked the wardrobe doors open with the other. "I want to see if Adi found anything."

"Forget Adi for a moment," Jin hummed in her ear.

"What happened to being responsible?" she asked as Jin's hands slid around her waist again, his touch impossibly warm. What she wouldn't give to just ignore all their problems and stay right there.

"I'm just saying a proper good morning."

"You're ridiculous," Astrea retorted, but sweet amusement rolled off Jin as he pulled her closer still. Turning around and pushing up on her toes, Astrea pressed her lips to his. She kissed him long and deep until it elicited a low rumble from his chest. Only then did Astrea pull away. "Good morning."

"You're a wicked creature," he said as she turned back to the wardrobe. His hands dropped from her waist just before Astrea slipped her blouse off. "Truly wicked."

"Looks like it's your turn to be right," she sassed.

"Devious," Jin murmured. Astrea glanced back at him only to find him watching her carefully. Raspberry lust and peach amusement mingled around him and coated her tongue with tart, sugary sweetness. "If you need me, I'll be cleaning up in the bathroom."

Astrea smiled as she went back to her task. She changed into fresh underclothes, then slipped on the loose black and white gingham dress the Novarians had supplied. Jin traded places with her, going back out into the bedroom to change while she cleaned up and braided her hair.

When she started for the bedroom door, Jin grabbed her hand. "Whenever the professor ends the day today," he said, "so do we."

She didn't want to have this argument again. "But—"

"A few late nights are fine, but you need to rest. *We* need to. Alright?"

Astrea's eyebrows furrowed. "What do you mean by rest?"

"Believe it or not, I'm not just thinking about getting you back in bed." Despite her earlier playfulness, Astrea's cheeks heated. "There's plenty we need to be doing. Training, eating, sleeping, resting."

Eating, sleeping, and resting. The three things Saros hadn't done for months. It had frustrated Astrea for weeks before they'd fled Kalama. As desperate as she was for answers, she couldn't do that to herself. A couple hours to take care of herself that night wouldn't hurt.

"I suppose you're right."

Jin smirked. "I'm pretty sure it's three to one now, if we're keeping score."

"Two to three," Astrea shot back. "I was right that my book had something important."

"Fine, three to two. Now let's go figure out what this monster was."

Though nobody else had found anything referencing monsters of darkness or old mountain kings, Adi, Cressida, and Tomas all agreed with Astrea that it had to be a connection to the very void magic they were now trying to track down.

"Did you find anything, Adi?" Astrea asked as he settled into the empty chair across from her. Eliana and Nicos had still been asleep when Astrea had left the guest house, and though this was important, it wasn't something everyone needed to be present for. She could fill them both in later.

"Actually, I may have." He dropped a book on the table, its maroon cover worn with age. "A mention of a flagless army in the mountains during the Great Wars."

Cressida pulled out the chair to Astrea's right and sat down. "What's significant about that?"

"Wait, really?" Jin asked as he reached for the book.

"Strange indeed," Tomas said as he joined Adi and Jin. "Quite strange."

"Again," Cressida asked, "what's significant about that?"

"The factions during the Great Wars eventually formed the beginning of our current empires and continental powers. That, or the smaller territories were absorbed," Tomas said.

"To fly no flag during war is unusual," Jin explained. "That suggests a factionless group. In Corsyca . . ." He sighed. "Well, all three countries involved in that fight fly their flags. Literally over camps, of course, but they also stitch them onto uniforms. Our team is one of very few that don't officially attach themselves to a country, and that's by design."

Jin's covert team that took on some of the toughest missions. Flying no flag. "Could this army have been like your team, then?" Astrea asked. "Attached to a country but trying to stay unnoticed?"

"Oh, I doubt that," Tomas interjected. "During the Great Wars, even the smallest nations wanted to claim any possible victories for their own country. It was purely about gaining territory and power back then."

"It doesn't seem like the Paragon are loyal to any one country nowadays," Cressida said. "So they'd be considered flagless now, right?"

"And the book claims they were unusually strong mages," Adi continued. "Sounds familiar."

Familiar indeed. Victor Nazarov could project visions across—presumably—thousands of miles. And the other mage, the one who had given Astrea the vision in Sezia, may have also been far away. Caliban's magic had swallowed Astrea's light whole on that Kalamian airfield. Even if she didn't fully understand void magic, both Caliban and Nazarov were obviously powerful mages.

The palace staff had cleaned up all the trays of coffee and dinner food at some point, and now, a stout man with graying hair had arrived with fresh coffee. He started setting out cups for all of them, but Jin waved him off. The man bowed and murmured something about "Your Imperial Highness" before he hurried out of the room.

"Let me check for something," Tomas said as he straightened and pushed his glasses up his nose. "And for skies sake, do not spill that! These manuscripts are not easily replaceable."

As he waddled down one of the aisles, Cressida jumped up and headed for the tray.

"What part of the mountains was the flagless army from?" Astrea asked, taking a mug of steaming coffee when Cressida brought it over to her. "Does it say?"

"No, it doesn't." Adi's finger moved down one page and onto the next. "All it says is that in the year 480, a flagless army of strong mages participated in battles around the mountains. Then it moves on, something about a principality guarded by Earthmovers."

Mountains surrounded Novaria's eastern, western, and southern borders. Most of the southern border, anyway. It was too bad the text wasn't more specific.

"What genius wrote that?" Cressida asked. "No details? What kind of book is this?"

"Obviously someone who was trying to keep void magic out of the historical record," Astrea said. "They may have omitted everything else."

"Then why include that other part at all?"

"I don't know. Maybe it's a clue for themselves, like a reference point if they need to find something. Or an oversight as they tried to get rid of any evidence. Something they forgot to cut out." It wouldn't be the first time Astrea had seen an error in a book. She just had no idea what to think anymore.

Cressida sighed. "Yeah, maybe."

Tomas returned, muttering nonsensically to himself as he dropped three thick books onto the table next to Adi. "These texts," he said, "focus more on Old Novaria and less on the rest of the continent. Perhaps we can begin there for this morning."

"That's perfect," Astrea said, already reaching for one of the books. Adi took the second, then offered the third to Cressida.

That left Jin with nothing to read, but he was staring at those maps again, the ones of the northern part of the continent where the professor had marked certain areas from his research. "Tomas," Jin said without looking back.

"Yes, Your Imperial Highness?"

"Do you have any maps that focus in on these regions?" He pointed at three spots Kostas had marked off the day before. "Something with more detail?"

"Why don't we go upstairs to check?" Tomas offered. "If I don't have them, someone in the palace will. Perhaps in the war room."

As Jin and Tomas headed upstairs, Astrea took her book and notebook and settled on the floor near the fireplace. Something about sitting on the hard surface made it easier for her to focus. So close. They were so close. There had to be answers.

There was plenty of useless information in this book, just as there had been in the others. Side tangents about different generals and nobles, explanations of geography that didn't seem relevant, and even references to the Old Era, the time long, long before the Great Wars ever began.

Astrea fiddled with the end of her braid and looked up. Tomas had left the library a good half hour before, muttering something about 'the war room' as he disappeared into the hallway, and Jin had since gone back to staring at the maps. Where was the professor?

"Anything?" Cressida asked as Astrea walked past the sofa she was stretched out on.

"No," Astrea called over her shoulder. She headed for the coffee, long forgotten, and poured herself a second cup. It was barely warm. She downed the drink anyway. "You?"

With a sigh, Cressida mumbled, "No."

"Adi?"

"Maybe." He pushed his chair back and, without taking his eyes off the page, carried the book to where Astrea stood. "Doesn't that sound familiar?"

She followed to where his finger was pointing and started to read out loud. "It was during this campaign that Old Novarian armies first claimed to meet a flagless group with black-tipped flames." Astrea's heart jumped, but she continued, "The group stayed in the mountains, antagonizing fighters from both the east and west as they tried to pass."

"Well," Cressida drawled, "that sounds like void mages to me."

"Me too," Astrea said. Black-tipped flames. Void magic was more than that, but it was close. "Modern historians and archaeologists have found no evidence of this army or its mages," she read. "The claims of the Old Novarians remain unsubstantiated but highlight the complexities of the Great Wars."

"It would be really great if Kostas were here," Adi muttered. "Maybe the ruins are the evidence. Some kind of fort or settlement this army used as its base."

Astrea handed the book back to Adi. Armies from the east and west could be from Novaria and what was now the Zaikud Empire. It could also be the stretch of mountains separating Novaria and Tornama. Kostas had seen the language in both locations.

That was also similar to what that story had been about. A mountain king. So had the mountain king run into the void mage army? Was that really what the 'monster of darkness' was from that story? Who had led the void mages? Another monarch? Or had they had no leader at all?

"What are you thinking?" Jin asked as Astrea closed the distance between herself and the maps.

She stared up at the spots Kostas had marked off. Two of the sites were actually in the mountains: one site to the east, in the Antare Mountains, and one to the west, in the Macadian Mountains.

"Adi," Astrea said over her shoulder, "read the part about antagonizing other fighters again."

Pages rustled, then Adi said, "The group stayed in the mountains, antagonizing fighters from both the east and west as they tried to pass."

Just as Astrea pointed to the eastern site Kostas had flagged, Jin joined her and pointed to the one on the western side of Novaria.

"So which location did they operate from?" Cressida asked. Frustration scraped over Astrea's skin even as green curiosity fluttered around her friend.

"Kostas's book from yesterday referenced the Antare Mountains," Astrea said. "That old myth showed a king and a castle in the mountains. Maybe that's what the ruins actually are? Maybe that's the story your father wanted us to find from Novarian mythology?"

"It would be nice if the professor were here," Jin muttered. "You'd think he might know more about this."

"Where is he, anyway?" Adi asked.

"How kind of him to leave us to do this work alone," Cressida said. "He's really growing on me."

Adi shrugged. "Maybe he was too intimidated by the grand duchess's orders."

Until he'd left the library for the night, Kostas had been a mix of excitement, curiosity, and focus. He'd been enjoying the work and the research, which was really no surprise. It was connected to his academic work. In Astrea's experience, most professors lived for this kind of knowledge. Kostas hadn't seemed intimidated at all.

It was like the stars knew they were looking for the professor. The library doors opened as Lucian swept into the room. "Kostas's office was attacked," he announced as he strode toward them.

"Is he alright?" Astrea asked as concern jumped to life around Adi and Cressida. *Please, not another murder.*

"He is, apparently, incensed, but *he's* fine." Lucian sighed. "Astrea, Marko said there's something you need to see. Adi can join us."

"What is it?" Astrea asked.

"Marko did not say what it was, just that we should go down there. He refused to tell me."

"Adi, stay here," Jin said. "You and Cress can help Tomas get the new maps set up when he returns. Keep digging into this mountain connection. I'm going with Az."

"Prince Varojin—" Lucian started, but one look from Jin made the commander snap his jaw closed.

"I'm going. If Ysabel has an issue with it, let her take it up with me, alright?" Jin stepped behind Astrea, his warmth unmistakable but not unwelcome. As his hand settled on her shoulder, he repeated, "I'm going."

Lucian looked between Astrea and Jin, his emotions and expression unreadable. Finally, he nodded. "Very well. Let's not waste any more time."

The university's archaeology and history building was quiet. The classrooms on both sides of the hallway were empty. Empty, that was, except for a single form covered by a white sheet just inside a classroom doorway.

No. Not another murder, not here. Lucian had promised they'd be safe. Had promised the city would be safe.

Then the shouting started, and a torrent of rage, concern, and annoyance slammed into Astrea so hard she took half a step back. She didn't even look up at Lucian or Jin; she just sprinted toward Kostas's office.

Jin and Lucian both let out a string of curses as they followed her. Astrea ran up the stairs to the second floor, then followed two more corridors until she got to that familiar office door.

The closer she got, the more she could hear Kostas's incoherent rant. Rage pressed and pressed against her bones, suffocating. Astrea skidded to a stop just outside his office only to find Marko standing there.

"I think it's obvious what happened here, Professor," Marko said.

The entire office was trashed. Books were scattered on the floor, pages torn to shreds and the rest burned black. The maps and diplomas that once decorated Kostas's office walls covered the floor, the glass front of their frames shattered. Fragments of artifacts—old tablets, jewelry, and miniature statues Astrea had seen just a couple days before—lay scattered among it all, destroyed beyond recognition. It was all gone.

And painted on the top of the professor's desk was the mark of the Paragon. Two concentric circles and a four-point star.

"What the skies happened?" Lucian asked, his voice sharp.

"You haven't seen the worst part yet," Marko said, motioning for them to go into the office. "Look at what's painted above the door."

Astrea pushed past Jin and stepped into the office. Slowly, she turned to look at the spot above the door, just like Marko said. There, in the same white paint used to paint the Paragon symbol on the desk, were just four words.

Give us the Lightbringer.

Jin cursed, and Astrea closed her eyes.

Why? Why did they want her? Why were they doing *this,* murdering people, just to get to her? She was nobody.

"I assume that is about you, Miss Sovna," Marko said.

Lucian stepped into the room, another string of curses falling from his lips as he examined that same wall. "Who was on duty with you this morning?" he snapped at Marko.

"Cari," Marko said. "I sent her to look around the campus for any of these voids you mentioned."

"Fine. Go find her. The police will be here soon, and I want this place watched round the clock. When you're done, come back to the palace."

"That's it?" Kostas snapped, his aura bursting red with rage. "No apology? This is my life's work! Gone! Destroyed! You did not tell me this would happen."

Astrea swallowed, turning to survey the rest of the office again. Broken glass crunched under her shoes. If the void mages already knew Kostas was working with them . . . had they followed Astrea? Was it Nazarov? Was he here in Talmaris?

"Because we didn't think it would," Lucian fired back. "Do not blame this on us. This is not our doing."

Jin's hand squeezed Astrea's shoulder. She looked back at him, but his gaze was fixed on the professor now. "We need to go back to the palace," Jin said. "I don't think it's safe here."

"But—" Kostas started.

"Professor, that is an order," Lucian snapped. "Follow us downstairs to the car or I will ensure you regret far more than losing some books."

Rage flared bright and hot around Kostas again, but he nodded and followed Lucian out the door. Jin's hand rested on the small of Astrea's back as he ushered her out of the office. She took one last look at the room, her stomach twisting.

Was any place in Talmaris safe?

Chapter 24

Give us the Lightbringer. Those four words played over and over in Astrea's mind all the way from the university to the palace. Now, as they walked back toward the library, Astrea's steps slowed. Was she endangering all these people simply by being there on the palace compound? Was she endangering Talmaris by being there?

Jin stopped next to her. Except for one of the guards stationed near the junction a few dozen feet away, the hallway was empty.

"Astrea? Prince Varojin?" Lucian called, turning to look at them as he herded Kostas into the library. The professor's rage and frustration had quieted. Astrea knew she should've tried pulling her senses in; Lucian would be able to see she wasn't practicing. But she didn't care.

"We'll be right there," Jin said, and Lucian nodded before disappearing inside.

Before Jin could get a word in, Astrea asked, "Why do they want me?"

"I don't know."

"Why would they do that to his office? Why would they kill . . ."

"I don't know, Az."

"It's my fault," she whispered, gaze trained on the buttons climbing up the front of Jin's dark shirt. "It's my fault, just like what happened in Kalama and to that man when we went to that house with Lucian . . . I shouldn't have gone to the university. I should be—"

"None of that is your fault." Jin's hands settled on her shoulders. "I promise, even if just Adi and Cress had gone, the Paragon would've still figured out we were working with the professor. They obviously have far more resources than we thought."

"Was it Nazarov? Is this what he meant when he said he'd see me soon?"

"Hey." Jin's pointer finger brushed Astrea's chin, tilting her head up until she looked at him. His wall was solid. "Those are all fair questions, but focusing on them right now won't help. What's in front of us?"

Astrea swallowed. "Kostas's research and Mattina's journal."

"Let's focus on those, alright? Complete the mission."

"Alright." *Complete the mission.* She could do that.

Jin brushed some of her hair away from her face. "Really?"

"I'll *try.*"

"Good." He pressed a quick kiss to the top of her head. "Shall we go see what else Kostas can tell us?"

Astrea led the way back into the library, her magic aching as the full force of Kostas's reignited, wild emotions pulsed through the room. She pulled her barrier closer to her body, tighter until she couldn't pull it in anymore. Lucian glanced at her and nodded.

"I've filled everyone in about what happened at the university, Your Imperial Highness," Lucian said as Jin and Astrea joined everyone near the tables and maps.

Cressida and Adi both looked toward Astrea, but she shook her head. They could talk later.

"I'm sorry about your work, Kostas," Jin said, "but we may have found something to make up for it. There may be an opportunity here for you to solve a bigger mystery."

Kostas peered up at Jin first, then Astrea, then the board and maps behind them. "What is this?" he snapped.

Astrea sucked in a deep breath. "We found a reference to a flagless army from the Great Wars," she said, then explained how they thought it might correlate to the void magic referenced in the mountains and the myth she'd found. They showed Kostas the text Adi had found next. "Before we left Kalama, someone who was familiar with these topics told us a book we were looking for contained both accounts of the Great Wars and old myths. We think they're connected, that some important history is being disguised as just a story."

Though Astrea kept her senses under tight control, the tension in Kostas's body loosened. His shoulders relaxed as they reviewed the meager evidence they'd found.

"It would make sense," Kostas said as he ran his hand over one of the maps. "Your theory about mythology and history, I mean. The ruins in this part of the country are old, very old."

That was all well and good, but it did not bring them any closer to reading the void's language or give them an understanding of the void's power. It did not bring them any closer to understanding why the Paragon were hunting Astrea.

"Is that where we need to go, then?" Adi asked. "To these ruins?"

"Perhaps." Kostas slowly faced the group, his shoulders tight. "Perhaps it would be worth our while to revisit these places. My notes are gone, but there is surely more I did not discover on my first and only visit. It can take many visits over many years to truly understand a site's lost knowledge."

"You think it would help us?" Jin asked.

"I don't think it would hurt, Your Imperial Highness," Kostas said. "I certainly have nothing left to lose by making such a trip. I can only hope there is more information yet to be uncovered there. Perhaps even some . . . translations of this language."

"What do you think?" Jin asked Astrea. "Would it help?"

She hesitated. Everything in Helosia had pointed them to Novaria, and everything in Novaria was pointing them to these ruins now. *Complete the mission.* "It's our only lead," she finally said. "We should go. It might tell us something."

"Then we'll go," he said. "East would be toward the actual void magic reference, right?"

Cressida nodded. "That's what's in the book."

Just as Adi started to speak, Lucian cleared his throat. "As much as I understand your eagerness to chase down this lead, I think you're all missing something very obvious here."

Awareness prickled Astrea's skin as Lucian's midnight blue eyes settled on her face. "And what is that?" she managed to ask.

Lucian crossed his arms over his chest. "The Paragon are interested in you, Astrea. And while I would not suggest we give you over to them, your presence is luring them out from wherever they're hiding."

"You're not using her as bait," Jin snapped as he took half a step forward. "Have you lost your skies damned mind? You've seen what they're doing to their victims. You want to put Astrea in that position?"

"They want Astrea for something," Lucian said. "They will not kill her."

"So just because they don't want to kill her means this is a good idea?"

"It's not up to you, Prince Varojin. It's up to Astrea."

It was like a Tempest had sucked the air out of the library. Astrea's grasp on her barrier fell. The full force of Cressida's anger and Adi's concern nearly knocked her over. Even Kostas was surprised, lavender taking over the hot rage still pulsing faintly around him.

"You cannot be serious," Cressida said. "You haven't even fought one of them, Commander! None of you Novarians have. You wouldn't suggest it if you'd seen what they can do."

"I've seen eight corpses covered in void magic, Miss Nikaphoros," Lucian seethed. "You think I don't know what the void mages are capable of? They're in my city just as much as they were in yours."

"That doesn't mean we—" Adi started, but Lucian cut him off.

"I'm not suggesting we set you out in the open unprotected, Astrea." Lucian's posture stiffened. The badges pinned over his heart caught the library chandelier's light. "We would remain in control of the situation. We would set a trap for them in Talmaris, and the full force of my security team would be behind us."

"You said the university would be safe," Astrea mumbled.

Lucian cocked one eyebrow.

"And what about the mountains?" she asked, though the question sounded silly. Lucian's gaze flicked to where Jin still hovered right behind her. "It seems like a good way to gather more information."

"And capturing one of these Paragon sycophants is also a good way to gather information," Lucian said. "We can do that with your help."

Lucian really thought using her as bait was a good idea? Of course, trying to find the Paragon made sense. They'd made it plenty clear that they would do what they had to do to find Astrea, and she hated that. But putting herself in their path? In Talmaris, where there were civilians who could get hurt, too?

She supposed they could try to clear their trap of civilians, but wouldn't that make the whole setup easy for the Paragon to spot?

"No." Astrea shook her head. "No, I won't do that. Finding them is important, but it seems too dangerous for everyone involved. There's no way you can guarantee the safety of that many people."

"We've kept you safe thus far." Lucian frowned. "You doubt us?"

"We're behind palace walls," Jin said. "We've barely left the palace. That's different, and you know it."

"If you don't want to do this, Astrea, I can't make you." Lucian shook his head. "But I think it's a foolish, foolish mistake not to try."

"I'm willing to go to the mountains," Astrea said, "and I'm willing to help in other ways, but I'm not comfortable with what you're asking, Commander."

Lucian sighed, a heavy, exaggerated sound. His wall was still up, the only one she couldn't read in the room now. Even Jin's warring anxiety and relief pressed against Astrea, strangely comforting.

"Fine," Lucian finally said. "We'll begin making preparations to travel to the mountain locations the professor has identified. We'll just have to get our information another way."

"Thank you," Astrea said.

"I'm not doing it for you." The hard edge to Lucian's voice was unmistakable. "I need to keep my people safe. If this is the only way you all will help us get answers, then so be it."

Guilt pierced Astrea's gut. Yes, people would be put in danger if she agreed to Lucian's plan, but they would be in danger regardless. Maybe the best thing she could do for the civilians here was to get to the mountains and stay there.

Chapter 25

A warm bed in a cool room was the best feeling in the world. Astrea curled into the blankets; both her mind and eyes ached. After getting Lucian to agree to the mountain excursion, she'd spent the better part of the afternoon balancing two tasks: looking for that elusive connection between the Great Wars and the old myths, and working with Tomas and Kostas to pull additional books for their group to go through. Once Kostas had calmed down, he'd been helpful and had assisted her and Tomas in narrowing things down greatly.

The commander had also suggested they continue their lightbringing lessons the next day. Astrea didn't love the idea of spending time with Lucian when he seemed to be angry with her, but she needed *someone* to train her. She'd just have to deal with him.

Now, she clutched one of Jin's old letters in her hands. She hadn't touched them in a few days, her mind too raw from everything that had happened with the vision, Nazarov, and the professor's office. But there was still so much she didn't know about Jin's past, and it seemed like a good distraction from everything else.

Astrea had already read about the time he was home for the winter solstice festival four years prior. He'd wanted to see her, apparently, and wanted to say hello, but couldn't make himself. Skies, she wished he had sought her out. She'd still been in university then, though in those days, she also spent almost all her free time at the Nikaphoros home. Maybe she wouldn't even have been at the palace; she couldn't remember.

She'd just started on a letter about some nonsense Adi and Jin got up to at Fort Avalon when the bedroom door opened. Sweat soaked Jin's entire body, no doubt due to whatever exercises he and Adi had just finished. He winced as he leaned down to untie his boots.

"What happened?" Astrea asked.

"Nothing." Jin straightened and pulled off his shirt with a grunt. "Just pushed myself too hard."

Setting his old letter down, Astrea slipped out of bed. She padded toward him, her bare feet barely making a sound on the floor. "Do you want me to—"

"There's no need," he said, his smile gentle as he grabbed her waist and pulled her closer. Her entire body pressed into his bare—and incredibly clammy—skin. "Sore muscles hardly require healing."

"Fine." Sweat beaded on the end of his nose, then dropped onto Astrea's cheek. She pushed away from him. "Gross."

"Oh no," Jin said in that honeyed voice, "this beautiful, wonderful woman is sweaty now, too? If only there was some way we could both clean ourselves up."

"You're ridiculous," she retorted as she fought a smile.

Another drop of moisture landed on Astrea's cheek. "Shower with me."

"Just for that, I don't think I will."

"Oh, you're no fun." Jin took half a step back. "Fine. I'll be quick," he said, his voice returning to the calm, natural one. "It's been too long of a day."

Every day they were gone somehow seemed like five days running together. Just that morning, they'd found Kostas's office to be destroyed.

The message demanding the Novarians turn Astrea over to the Paragon. How had that been just hours before?

"I'll come to bed when I'm done." As Jin pulled off the rest of his clothes, he dropped them in a pile near the bathroom door. "Don't wait up for me if you don't want to."

Soon, his body was on display, the umpteenth time Astrea had seen it since they got to Talmaris. They were so different that way. Not just Jin's lack of modesty but how different their bodies were. Where Jin's was hard and muscular planes, Astrea's was mountains and valleys of soft curves. And Jin did not seem to mind. In fact, he seemed to revel in it if their recent nights and early mornings were any indication.

Astrea followed Jin into the bathroom only once he was in the shower. She washed her face at the sink, then went back to the bedroom and changed from her nightgown into one of Jin's clean shirts. In the only two romantic relationships she'd had during her university years, she'd never had sleepovers. But sharing this space—and clothes, she supposed—with Jin just felt right. Waking up next to him every morning felt right, as did falling asleep with him every night.

Admitting that was almost scary. Part of her was worried she was just clinging to the one good thing she had right now. But it was also more than that. There was something easy and natural about being with Jin. She felt safe with him. Understood. Like she could just be herself. And that *was* good. Very few people in the world made her feel that way, regardless of conspiracies and wars.

As she crawled back into bed, Astrea picked up the discarded letter again. Adi had joined Jin's team three years earlier to take the place of the teammate Jin lost during the Delian-Helosian War. Jin had written about how hard it was to process what had happened, especially knowing how Adi had to feel being sent in as a replacement. Jin had been in that position once, had been sent in as the replacement Fireweaver when the one before him died.

She couldn't imagine. Jin had been through so much in eight years, and she still had to read about everything he'd seen during the lead-up to the Corsycan War. How had he not broken down? Astrea could barely hold it together lately.

Jin's shower was quick; he'd returned in less than fifteen minutes. Now, as he walked back into their bedroom in nothing more than a towel, Astrea set the letters on the bedside table and burrowed into the blankets.

Being with Jin felt right, yes, but sitting there in a luxurious bedroom with everything else going on felt so wrong. What would Saros think? What would he have to say about the Paragon's message? And what would he have to say about Astrea preparing to go to the mountains?

The mattress dipped as Jin crawled into bed next to her, clothing thankfully back on. He pulled her toward the middle of the bed and ran a hand through her hair. "Am I being too clingy?" he asked. "You usually avoided close quarters when we were younger."

While that was true, they'd also sometimes lain in similar positions. Not in bed but on the floor, either in front of the fireplace in Jin or Eliana's rooms. They never quite cuddled like this but rather stretched out side by side while they talked. That was one of the few situations where Astrea appreciated someone being close; having physical space usually helped her gain some peace from the constant sensory input of her magic.

Astrea sank down and rested her head on Jin's shoulder. "I'll tell you if I need space."

She didn't know how long they sat like that, him playing with her hair and holding her close, before he whispered, "You know we're not going to give you to them, right?"

"You think Ysabel wouldn't hand me over if it meant they left her city alone?"

The thought had lingered at the back of Astrea's mind all day. Lucian had promised they wouldn't just *give* Astrea to the Paragon. But Ysabel had agreed to work with them because she wanted the Paragon out of her city. If it came to that, what would stop the grand duchess from simply giving in to the Paragon's demands?

"I wouldn't let her even if she fucking tried."

"But—"

"No buts." Jin shifted so he faced her, but Astrea kept her gaze trained on the dusting of hair on his bare chest. "How far did you get in the letters?"

The letters? That was what he wanted to talk about?

"I was reading about Adi joining your team."

A ghost of a smile crossed Jin's face. "I'll spare you the need to read one of them that's coming up," he said. "The Delian-Zaikudi War in Posan was one of Adi's first missions with us."

"Adi mentioned it to me."

Surprise whispered over Astrea's skin. "When?"

"In Sezia. He didn't tell me much, just that you were doing reconnaissance and—his words, not mine—that he fucked up." Adi had also told Astrea that they'd destroyed the Zaikudi camp by themselves and staged it to look like the Delians did it. But she kept that to herself.

"Adi didn't fuck up. Our teammate Dorin did. The four of us were there in Posan in the dead of winter, trying to locate Zaikudi camps. We weren't supposed to engage, just figure out what they were capable of doing.

"I was in charge of the mission. Adi was frustrated at how the mission was going, which wasn't *bad,* but it wasn't productive. And Dorin, well." Jin sighed. "Something in him changed after Lando died. When

I wasn't around, he told Adi to take a walk. A snowstorm had moved in, and we weren't exactly supposed to be there. Helosians weren't supposed to be there."

Astrea swallowed.

"We had very few rules as a team. Number one, leave no teammate behind. Number two, leave no witnesses."

"I know," she whispered. "Adi told me that, too."

"Of course he did." Jin sighed again. "I broke our third, unofficial rule, which was to stick together if we could. I went to find Adi on my own, but by the time I did, a Zaikudi patrol had already found him and were dragging him back to their camp. None of this was part of the plan. We weren't supposed to split up."

Stick to the plan. That was what Jin had warned Adi to do in Sezia. *We aren't supposed to split up.* That was what Jin had been worried about the day before, all the days before, whenever Lucian and Ysabel weren't letting him leave the palace.

Everything made a lot more sense.

"I grabbed the rest of the team. Our new plan was to sneak in, grab Adi, and get out. We couldn't leave him. But I think the Zaikudi knew we were there all along."

"Why?"

"By the time we fought our way to get Adi, we found the camp's leader holding him. The man knew who I was somehow. He knew all about what I'd been doing during the Delian-Helosian War."

"I thought your involvement on your team was a secret," Astrea said. Jin's team was not something the general public seemed to know about, and Emperor Aelius certainly hadn't announced Jin's wartime movements.

"It was supposed to be. The leader was a Tempest. He threatened Ellie and my niece, saying he'd tell his people in Kalama to leave them alone if I went with him."

"Was he bluffing?"

"I don't know. But when I refused, he started pulling the air from Adi's lungs to try to force my cooperation."

Jin started tracing small, smooth circles between her shoulder blades, something she'd noticed he did often. He would draw them anywhere: her arms, her hands, her knees, and now her shoulders.

"Dorin was the only other one who had seen what my fireweaving could really do that day when we lost Lando," he continued. "And even though I swore I'd never do that again, I did. And even though I hate that power, I'm glad I did it."

Adi had told Astrea that 'they' destroyed the entire Zaikudi camp. *They*. Not Jin. Not Jin setting his fireweaving off like a bomb. She said nothing as steely pain blossomed around him.

"As it turned out, the camp was home to a large group of non-mage soldiers, so they had a lot of weapons caches there. My fireweaving triggered a series of explosions around the camp. The whole place was just . . ."

"Adi told me," she whispered. "Not the details, but he alluded to it."

Jin pressed a kiss to the top of her head, then pulled away enough to look down at her. "What I'm trying to get at is that when I tell you that nobody—not Ysabel or Lucian or any other skies damned person in this city—is going to hand you over to the Paragon, I mean it. If they try, I'll send them to the stars myself."

"Because of rule number one?"

"Well." The corners of his mouth twitched up. "Adi and I stand by that rule, but because it's you. Nobody's going to take you from us. From me."

That power he hated so much . . . "I can't ask you to do that, Jin."

"You're not asking. I'm not even offering. I'm telling you that I would not hesitate, whether I need to do it tomorrow or a year from now." Astrea grabbed his hand. Whether it was to steady him or herself, she wasn't sure. "I know Saros isn't here," he continued, "nor are Sarsali and Balthazar, but we're your family, too. I feel confident saying no one else in this house would hesitate to tell Ysabel to fuck off."

Astrea's eyes burned. She'd always considered Cressida her family—they were practically sisters after all these years—and thought of Eliana as family, too. But Adi and Nicos? She didn't know them as well. And yet, her mind whispered to her that yes, she wouldn't hesitate to tell Ysabel to fuck off if their positions were switched, if the Paragon were after one of them. They were a team now. Maybe not a family but certainly a team.

And Jin. That purple reverence vibrated around his body again. How could he be so confident in that when he'd been gone for so long? But the colors dancing around him didn't die. They didn't fade. They were bright, strong, true. And then her mind whispered that yes, she would do the same for him, too. Of course she would.

"Jin . . ."

He leaned down and kissed her, but that was it. It was chaste, gentle. It left Astrea wanting so much more.

"I'm afraid," Jin said, "that I pushed myself a little too hard with Adi and Nicos. Now I can't do all the things I very much want to do with you."

"You really won't let me heal you?" Astrea pushed up to her elbows, scanning the parts of his body visible above the blankets. No bruises, scratches, or swelling. Just that old, knotted scar on the front of his left shoulder. "What happened here?" she asked, running her fingers over it.

"Oh, that? Six or seven months ago, we were on a mission in Corsyca, and I got shot. There and my torso. That didn't scar as bad, though."

"You got *shot*? By whom?" Even as she touched his shoulder again, the only thing she could feel in the room was fatigue. It surrounded her, all-consuming and threatening to drag her under.

"Some Delian Metalli."

"And yet you're sitting here acting like it's nothing."

He smiled at her. "Because I'm fine. Lie down." When she huffed, Jin chuckled. "I'm *fine*, just tired. And I'm going to murder Adi for goading me into that last match. Now I've missed dessert."

"Dessert?" Astrea asked. "I don't think—" She stopped as peach flashed around Jin's head and sugar coated her tongue. "Oh, skies. How original."

"What, I'm not allowed to tease my partner with a dirty joke?"

Partner. Astrea tried not to get stuck on that word. *Partner.* He'd used the term before. She knew it was true, that they were partners in every sense now, but hearing him say it felt so good.

"I don't think that was a joke as much as it was bad innuendo," she said.

Jin hummed as he rolled over and pulled Astrea closer. "Well, maybe I'm just going to have to keep practicing."

Astrea shoved into his shoulder, and he laughed deep and clear. "Go to sleep," she muttered as she rolled over and switched the bedside lamp off. "All that training's gone to your head."

Jin draped an arm over her waist and pressed a kiss to the back of her head. Astrea's heart danced. She leaned back into his warmth and let those strong, clear emotions wash over her magic until they started to fade and Jin's breathing began to slow. Only then did Astrea finally sink deeper into the bed and close her eyes, hoping she didn't dream of Corsycan shootouts or angry void mages.

CHAPTER 26

"Astrea?" Lucian called. "Astrea!" Fingers snapped in front of Astrea's face, and she blinked. Blue eyes met hers, Lucian's impatient scowl directed right at her.

"Sorry," Astrea murmured.

"You're distracted."

"I won't let it happen again." Astrea pushed her shoulders back.

They were in the palace infirmary, a well-lit room with dark wood floors, a simple white ceiling, and multiple cots covered in plain gray sheets. Except for the two of them, the room was empty.

As she'd feared, Lucian was upset with her after refusing to go along with his plans. She'd hoped that the new day might put him in a better mood, but he'd been cold since they arrived at the infirmary ten minutes before. Dinner with the grand duchess and Jin's cousins was later that night, but first, Astrea was due for another lesson.

"As I was saying," Lucian continued, "just as we use our emotions as fuel when we fight, we use them as fuel when we heal. The good and the bad—both can help us when we need them."

"Alright." Astrea wasn't sure what else to say. She'd never considered it that much, but as she thought back to how she'd healed Eliana on Solstice Night, Astrea had been a mix of calm and panic, fear and desperation, and she'd still managed to pull on so much healing energy.

"At least try to pay attention, will you?" Lucian asked.

"I *am* paying attention," Astrea protested. "But I don't think this is where I need to focus my time."

Lucian's eyebrows rose. "You want to quit training?"

"What? No, of course not!" What made Lucian think that? "I'm already a strong healer. That's the easiest part of my magic for me to use. The part that feels natural."

"And so you think you don't need to practice?" he challenged.

Fiery hot frustration boiled in Astrea's veins. "I'm *thinking* our training sessions would be better spent working on something I'm not already decent at. Besides, nobody's around." She gestured to the empty room. "What am I supposed to do in here?"

Lucian huffed and ran a hand through his hair. He wasn't wearing his usual commander of the guard uniform, nor was his hair in its usual neat bun. Instead, it hung loose around his shoulders, and he was wearing something like Adi and Jin wore when they trained: tight pants, loose shirt, and combat boots.

"Fine," he said. "You don't want this lesson? We'll work on something else today."

Astrea fiddled with the end of her braid. "I would appreciate it."

"Come with me."

The commander left no room for argument or question. He simply turned and strode toward the infirmary's exit. Astrea hurried after him, following him down several narrower corridors. This part of the palace, though still beautiful, wasn't nearly as extravagant as the main portions.

After several more turns, Lucian pushed open a door. Bright afternoon sun temporarily blinded Astrea, and she shaded her eyes with her hand as they headed into the gardens. Gravel crunched under Astrea's boots, the sound grating on her nerves. Though she couldn't read Lucian with her magic, his quick pace and sharp posture only made her grit her teeth.

When they made it to their usual spot by the lake, Lucian stopped and said, "Let's begin with you telling me what has made you so distracted."

He couldn't be that dense, could he? Surely the commander knew what had her distracted. He'd been there the day before at the library. He'd seen Kostas's office. He'd been there when they'd decided they needed to go to the mountains.

"I'm frustrated," she said. "Confused."

"Why?"

"Every time we seem to get closer to the void, it's like something pushes us back. We still don't know who can translate the language for us. We still don't know why Nazarov and the Paragon are looking for me. I hate not having answers. Sometimes this all feels pointless."

"Frustration," Lucian said. "Fear. Shame. Your shield is down. Have you been practicing?"

"I've been busy," she snapped.

"Ah, and anger." The commander smiled. It wasn't nice. "You're going to make this lesson easy."

"What lesson?"

"We've already discussed emotional energy as fuel. Emotions are just one more type of energy, correct?" he asked, and Astrea nodded. "Summon your light."

Astrea pulled on the energy swirling in her body. A miniature white star formed over her palm, growing as she pushed her frustration into it. She'd always been able to summon and dismiss light, but doing it this way was far easier. Simpler. It no longer felt like trying to push a boulder uphill or smother a campfire with a tea towel.

"Make it bigger."

"We went over this already."

"Make it bigger, Astrea."

With a huff, Astrea pushed more energy into her light. It swirled around her hands.

"Very good." Lucian nodded. "Even if you refuse to act when you should to help this city, you catch on quick."

Astrea's jaw tightened. If Lucian wanted to be upset with her, he could be. She would not risk death just for his poorly devised plan.

"So if controlling my light is this easy," Astrea said, "what else do I need to know?"

"There's nothing easy about a fight," the commander said as he stared out over the sparkling lake. "But seeing as your aim is still . . . subpar . . . I have a way you can make it easier."

"How?" She would do anything to make this easier. She needed one skies damned thing to be easy.

"Lightbringers can do more than summon light, Astrea. We are healers, and we are empaths, but we can also inflict great damage."

Lucian's voice was calm, but he didn't look at her. She wasn't sure, but he seemed to be watching all five of her friends as they jogged around the lake. When had they come outside?

"The easiest way to take down an enemy," Lucian continued, "is to take control of your opponent's emotional energy. Harness the energy they produce—the energy *you* produce—and use it to attack them from the inside out."

Astrea would do *almost* anything to make this easier. "That sounds . . ."

"Efficient?" When Lucian looked down at her, his gaze was cold. Astrea shrugged. "Why does this trouble you so much?"

"I just . . ."

"This is war, Astrea. You think that void mage would hesitate?"

When Astrea blanched, Lucian smiled that nasty smile again. This was a side of him she hadn't seen before. Lucian was straightforward, yes, but this was cold and calculating. But of course he would be this way. He wouldn't be the captain of Ysabel's guard if he weren't.

"The threat is coming whether you want it to or not."

"I understand what's at stake."

"Do you?" he challenged. "There is no room for hesitation in battle. If your opponent has left their emotions open, use that to your advantage."

"Isn't that painful, though?"

He scoffed. "And being struck by a fireball? That's not painful?"

A burn from a Fireweaver would heal. Being knocked out by an Earthmover's rock was temporary. The same could be said for every other branch of magic. But using someone's emotions against them? That seemed particularly cruel.

"Perhaps we need a demonstration," Lucian snapped, "so that you can understand the efficacy of this technique."

Pain exploded in Astrea's chest. She staggered back several steps, her mind aching and body seizing. Cold terror overtook her at first, but hot anger soon bled in, a disorienting mix. The air around her pulsed as a thousand tiny needles stabbed into her flesh. She couldn't breathe. All she could do was collapse onto the soft grass.

"Now you see how this can bring an opponent to their knees in a matter of seconds," Lucian said as he stared down at her. Her chest burned in the same spot it had when Nazarov had shown her that vision, burning all the way through to her back. "Now try it on me."

The pain died just as suddenly as it had come on. Astrea let out a sputtering cough as air surged back into her lungs. Reaching up, she wiped away the tears streaming down her cheeks.

"No," she croaked.

"Excuse me?" Lucian's eyebrows shot up. "No?"

"I won't do that to someone else."

Just as Astrea finally started pushing herself back to her feet, pain exploded in her chest again. She collapsed back to the ground, barely managing to catch herself before she fell flat on her face. Why was Lucian doing this? He'd been kind, if a bit aloof, since they'd arrived in Talmaris. This was not the commander she knew.

"Look at me," Lucian ordered.

Astrea forced herself to look up. His emotions were completely open to her now, bright in the early afternoon sun. Light green focus surrounded him, as did rusty annoyance, red anger, and vermilion pride.

"Reach for my energy," Lucian said, "and hold on to it. Then feed me whatever it is that's bothering you."

"I . . . can't . . ." Astrea gritted out.

Pain warped her mind. She couldn't focus.

She didn't want to do this.

She didn't want to be training right now, and she certainly didn't want to make Lucian feel this kind of pain, even if he was a skies damned scumbag.

"Yes, you can." Lucian widened his stance, like he expected to go down at any moment. When pain flared hotter in her whole body, Astrea cried out. She might actually be sick. "Attack back, Astrea. Or are you weaker than I thought?"

Astrea sucked in a breath. She was not weak.

"I doubt you could hurt me even if you wanted to," Lucian goaded. "Maybe that's why you're so scared to let the Paragon find you."

"No—"

"So unprepared and untrained. You know you won't be able to handle them, just like you can't handle the rest of this. No wonder Varojin coddles you—"

Astrea's hand snapped out, reaching for the energy dancing in the air around him. She squeezed her fist closed, watching the annoyance and concern through her tears. *Fuck you.* Astrea pulled her hand back toward her body.

There were plenty of things that made Astrea upset. Emperor Aelius. The fact that any of this was happening. The weak Novarian coffee she was stuck drinking. The nasty, horribly true things Lucian was saying to her. She pushed those things toward him—into him—and watched the rust and red and green in the air around Lucian flare.

Even as he stumbled, Lucian smiled. The pain in Astrea's bones loosened.

Magic burned in Astrea's veins as she pushed more toward him. Saros lying to her. Saros deciding to stay in Kalama. Sarsali and Balthazar staying behind, too, and leaving Cressida to do this without their support. The Paragon for destroying all of that research her friends could've used.

Lucian fell to his knees, bright teal approval overtaking his aura. "Very good," he said through gritted teeth. "Now let it go."

Astrea pushed to her feet, fists still clenched tight as she held onto Lucian's energy and forced her own pain toward him. She fed him her rage, her shame, her fear, until he began coughing. Until orange fear jumped to life in his aura. Only then did Astrea drop her fists.

The magic in her body began to settle as she thought of Cressida and Eliana teasing her the night before about the way Jin looked at her. Astrea and Cressida teasing Eliana about the very same thing regarding Nicos. Sarsali and Balthazar calling Astrea their daughter before she'd had to flee the country. Her whole family and how much she missed them.

That anger and rage she'd forced onto Lucian felt awful. So had his words. But attacking him back like that wasn't who Astrea was. It wasn't who she wanted to be, no matter how many terrible things the commander said to her.

"Very good," Lucian said as he shoved to his feet. He coughed again, then pulled at the collar of his shirt. "Very good, Astrea." He smiled that nasty smile again. "You're stronger than I gave you credit for, and as I said, a quick study."

"What the fuck was that?" Astrea hissed. "Why didn't I know it was possible to do that?"

"You didn't get much training. There's much you don't know."

"Bullshit," she spat, chest heaving. "I may not have had practice, but I think I'd know if I could do something like that." Lucian watched her, those midnight blue eyes unyielding. She tried to focus on the white-knuckle hold she had on her magical barrier. Was he going to say *anything*? "Well?"

"The world has forgotten much of what mages are truly capable of," he said. "It has forgotten their true power, and Lightbringers aren't the only ones who draw on their emotional energy to influence their magic."

"So you're telling me my friends have been doing something similar the whole time and just forgot to mention it?"

"No, I'm saying the opposite!" Lucian half yelled. "People have strayed from magic's true nature and its possibilities. They're focused on their wars and sports matches and on who can move the biggest rock or summon the largest flame. They do all of that without thinking about where their power comes from. Lightbringers just harness that energy in a different way. We have the strongest connection to it."

"And if people have forgotten about this," Astrea said, trying and failing to steady her voice, "how do *you* know?"

"You think I'm hiding something?"

"You *were* hiding something! You . . . you attacked me!"

This was not going how Astrea planned, not at all. She had started to trust Lucian—trusted his judgment, trusted him with her magic—and now he was attacking her?

"Astrea." Lucian sighed and pinched the bridge of his nose. He sighed again. "Astrea, there are some things that have been kept secret for a reason. Do you think advertising that Lightbringers have this ability is wise?"

No, of course she didn't. That would be a nightmare in the hands of someone like Emperor Aelius. "I don't understand how it's been kept a secret, then. And why would you tell me? You barely know me."

"If a group realizes it's for their own benefit to keep some things to themselves, don't you think they would do that?" Lucian asked quietly. "Is it so different than your uncle having you hide your magic for so many years?"

"This isn't about Saros."

"It was merely one example. The Paragon are another, are they not? They've kept void magic a secret for . . . well, it seems like for a very long time. Hopefully we'll have those answers soon."

Astrea barely swallowed the lump building in her throat. Was it really as simple as Lucian claimed? That Lightbringers either didn't know they could do this or, if they did know, never told others?

"Are we done?" Astrea snapped.

"Yes."

Adi approached from their left, the rest of her friends just behind him. "There she is!" he called. "Lightbringer extraordinaire!"

"Hey, Adi," Astrea said, offering him a small smile. It was the best she could muster, the ghost pain of Lucian's attack still pulsing through her body. Or maybe that was the echo of the pain she'd inflicted on the commander; she couldn't tell.

"Is she ours for the taking, Commander?" Adi asked.

"She is all yours," Lucian said. He nodded at Astrea. "Consider what we discussed today. I'll see you at dinner."

As Lucian started back toward the palace, Astrea let her shoulders drop. This was too much. She had a dozen more questions for the commander, but she needed space from him.

"Four laps, then we'll get started," Adi said as he pointed to the lakeside path. "I want to see some energy!"

The others started on their laps, and Astrea was about to join them when Jin grabbed her hand. "What did you and Lucian talk about?" he asked.

"Nothing."

"Az."

"What?" She couldn't bring herself to look up at Jin, instead focusing on her boots and the vibrant green grass under them. She didn't want him to see that side of her. The fact that she'd turned on Lucian so quickly made her sick to her stomach. And what was it even for? It would do no good against the void mages; they released no emotional energy to manipulate. When Jin said nothing, Astrea muttered, "We talked about my magic."

"That's it?"

"That's it."

He watched her for another long moment before he finally said, "Alright. Come on. Adi will kick my ass if I don't keep up with him."

Astrea started jogging after Jin, but as she ran, she glanced over her shoulder. Lucian was at the top of the hill that led back up to the palace, his arms crossed as he watched them. She pushed away the shame boiling in her veins and forced herself to go faster. She had to catch up to her friends.

Chapter 27

Astrea's flat shoes barely made a sound on the smooth palace floors as she hurried after Jin, Cressida, and the rest of her friends. The skirt of her dress swished along the tiles. Lucian's pace was almost punishing considering they were on their way to a dinner party rather than an emergency meeting.

What was the commander's problem? She could understand him being upset that she didn't agree with his plan to trap the Paragon, but saying those nasty things to her? Had he simply been trying to force her to retaliate? Or did he know they were actually true and not just a taunt? Astrea didn't want them to be true, which was why she was now determined to keep training with Adi as much as she could. It would take years to get to her friend's skill level, and that meant she had to practice as much as she could.

The only good thing was that Astrea's chest had stopped hurting. She'd checked it with her magic after finishing up her training with Adi. There'd been no swelling, no tears she could find, and no increased blood flow to the area. And still, it had ached for several hours after the incident.

Focus, Astrea scolded herself as Lucian turned down a long corridor.

They all needed to make a good impression tonight. It was the first time any of them were meeting Ysabel's heirs, Crown Prince Veiko and Princess Delfine. Before leaving the guest house, Eliana had also informed them that both heirs' wives would be present, as would Veiko's two young children. These were the people they needed to sway to support their cause so they, in turn, could help Ysabel sway her council.

No pressure. They passed under a glass dome ceiling colored by the magenta and orange sunset. Hopefully they could pull it off and convince Ysabel's heirs that they were more than a tiny group trying to overthrow the continent's most powerful leader. Astrea had no idea how to do that, but she'd try.

At least they were dressed for the part. As they approached a set of double doors, Astrea smoothed the front of her plum-colored dress. Its neckline was decidedly more modest than the last gown she wore to one of Ysabel's dinners, and it paired nicely with her sapphire necklace. Ysabel's staff had delivered it to the guest house just an hour before, along with new outfits for everyone else, too. Jin was in all black while Eliana wore scarlet. Nicos's dark gray suit was somber, as was Adi's blue one. Cressida, at least, looked livelier in her wide-legged topaz pants and coordinating blouse.

Lucian opened the doors without hesitation or pretense, revealing an opulent dining room larger than the one they'd joined Ysabel in days earlier. Thick Tornamian carpets covered the dark hardwood floors, and paintings and tapestries accented the sage green walls. A long table that could seat a dozen took up the middle of the room. On the far side of the space was a gold-trimmed fireplace. Astrea's shoulders tightened just before Jin's hand found its usual place on her lower back.

"You good?" he whispered.

"I'm fine."

It was the second time she'd lied to him in just a few hours. After training, he'd tried asking about Lucian and their lesson again, and she'd managed to avoid giving him the truth. Could she tell Jin about it? They'd promised not to hide things from each other—from any of their friends—but this seemed like it might just make Jin angry. And him being angry just before this crucial meeting was bad for their future plans.

"Alright, well . . ." He trailed off, then said, "Let's just try to make the most of this, shall we?"

"Sure."

Ysabel stood in front of the fireplace with four adults and two small children. Astrea couldn't read any of them; she had her barrier pulled tightly around herself, so much so that it was suffocating her. Commander Lucian's stiff posture and refusal to look her in the eye told her it was the right choice, though.

"Excellent," Ysabel said as she approached alone, "you're here. Are you ready to meet the family?"

Jin's shoulders tensed. He'd always hated such formalities when he was younger, too, though back in those days, Astrea only heard stories from him and Eliana. The palace dinner party back in Kalama had been Astrea's first time *really* seeing Jin at the Helosian court.

Astrea brushed her hand against his, and he captured it, squeezing it once.

"Lead the way," Jin said to Ysabel, though he didn't drop Astrea's hand. Instead, he tugged her along with him as Eliana followed the grand duchess.

"You want me to meet them now?" Astrea whispered as quietly as she could. She had assumed he and Eliana would speak to the royals first.

"You don't have to," Jin said. "But I'm just . . ."

Nervous. He was nervous. Astrea didn't need her magic to know that was true in her bones. Anyone would be nervous to meet the family they didn't know they had, especially under such dire conditions. They weren't just here for a friendly chat.

"Let's go." Maybe she couldn't convince the grand duchess to support a tiny bunch of rebels, but she could support Jin in that moment. And Lucian be damned; Astrea was going to try to gauge Jin's family's mood.

Ysabel watched them carefully as they approached, and to Astrea's surprise, her walls were down. Nothing but cool curiosity drifted off Ysabel and the adult cousins. The children, though, radiated boredom. *Poor things.* Astrea couldn't imagine trying to sit through an affair like this at such a young age. She didn't even want to sit through it at twenty-four.

"Well," Ysabel said in Novarian, a small smile tugging at her mouth, "Princess Eliana, Prince Varojin, these are my niece and nephew."

The resemblance between the man, one of the women, and Ysabel was obvious: white skin and piercing purple eyes. But where Ysabel's hair was nearly black like Astrea's, the other two had hair similar to Jin's: a deep, warm chestnut with a soft curl.

Ysabel nodded toward the woman with the purple eyes and her bronze-skinned companion. "Princess Delfine and her wife, Katerina." She nodded next to the purple-eyed man and the blonde. "And Crown Prince Veiko and his wife, Letizia."

"It's wonderful to finally meet you," Eliana said. Despite her years studying under Saros, she'd never been able to master the way Novarian vowels were pronounced. Southern Helosians tended to stress their syllables.

"Yes," Jin said, that mask of his from his father's imperial court noticeably missing. He sounded almost unsure, but his accent was less pronounced than Eliana's. "I'm sure our familial connection was just as much as a surprise to you as it was to me. I appreciate you all being so welcoming."

As the royals exchanged pleasantries, Astrea didn't know if she should cut in. She also didn't know if holding onto Jin's hand was appropriate, but he hadn't dropped it. Surely *that* wouldn't give the Novarian royals reason to dismiss their rebellion, right? Veiko, Letizia, and Katerina offered polite smiles to Astrea, but Delfine finally grinned, revealing perfectly straight teeth.

"Varojin," she said, her voice light and airy, "my aunt has told us some about you, but I must admit, I'm so curious about my cousin from the south. She did not mention you were married. Are you going to introduce your wife?"

Heat crawled up Astrea's neck, engulfing her face and ears. *Married? Wife?* What gave Princess Delfine that idea?

"I'm so sorry," Jin said, a breath of a laugh leaving him. Whether he was apologizing to Astrea or the others, she wasn't sure. "Not married, but perhaps someday she'll make an honest man out of me."

At that, bright peach amusement and—*oh, skies*—teal approval flashed around Eliana. Astrea didn't know whether she was going to kill Jin or just let her foolish little heart skip a dozen beats at the mere suggestion. She pulled her magic back toward herself with great effort; Lucian didn't need to see this. But she was tired, and it stopped once it was about three feet away from her being.

"This is Astrea Sovna," Jin continued. "My partner and a key player in this situation my friends and I have discovered in Helosia, actually."

"Oh." Delfine chuckled. "Well, it is a pleasure to meet you, Miss Sovna, despite the circumstances. Perhaps someday we will have a reason to celebrate, yes?"

"The pleasure is mine, Your Highness." Astrea smiled, but she didn't dare address Delfine's comment either way.

"And who are these two?" Eliana asked as she smiled down at the two children.

"Ah, the most important introductions of the night," said Veiko, his expression softening. He was several inches shorter and several years older than Jin. "These are my children, Princess Helena and Prince Leo. Children, say hello."

Helena, the older of the two, must have been around age five. She stared up at Jin, her purple eyes bright. Other than her eye color, she had her mother's delicate nose, blonde hair, and warm white skin. The little boy, Leo, couldn't have been older than three, and he was his mother's twin, right down to the wide green eyes.

"It's a pleasure to meet you, Princess Eliana and Prince Varojin and Miss Sovna," Helena said sweetly.

Jin squatted down in front of her. "It's nice to meet you, Helena," he said as he extended his hand to her. Helena shook it as best she could. "How about you just call me Jin? That's what all my friends call me."

Helena smiled shyly and nodded.

"And you can call me Ellie," Eliana said.

Helena smiled again despite her fingers nervously playing with the fabric of her frilly pink dress. Leo's face was half hidden in his mother's blue skirt, but he kept glancing up at Astrea.

"They begged and begged to come tonight," Letizia said with a laugh, "and now I'm afraid they're being shy."

"Oh, that's alright," Jin said as he stood. "Our eldest brother has two girls. They've never been fond of these kinds of things."

"And I must admit, I prefer a more relaxed environment myself. Delfine is the much better party guest." Veiko glanced at Astrea, then back to Jin and Eliana before finally looking at Ysabel. "Perhaps we can skip the formalities. After all, Varojin, we're family. And Eliana, we're family in a way as well."

"Yes, of course," Ysabel said. "Let's introduce you to the rest of our new Helosian friends."

As Ysabel and the others started toward the middle of the dining room, Jin laced his fingers through Astrea's. His wall was strong, but his features had relaxed some in the last few minutes. Astrea had just started to ask Jin how he was feeling when something—someone—tugged at her skirt. Bright purple eyes stared up at her, green ones not far behind.

"Are you a princess?" Helena asked. "You have pretty hair like a princess, like Aunt Katerina."

The corners of Astrea's mouth twitched. Katerina indeed had beautiful hair; she'd styled her dark, tight curls with a few simple gold clips. If that were the only requirement to be royalty, Cressida would also fall into that category. So would many people in the world.

Astrea pulled her hand from Jin's and squatted down in front of the young princess. "No, I'm a librarian," she said. "Do you like books?" Helena nodded vehemently. "That's my job. I help people find books they want to read."

"Can you help *me* find books?"

"I would love to, Princess Helena." Astrea couldn't say no to that earnest face and question. She'd always loved books and used to beg Saros to take her to the bookshops in Kalama whenever he had days off. And when she'd still worked at the Great Library, she'd sometimes helped patrons' children find novels or other fun things to read while they waited for their parents to be done.

Helena smiled shyly again as Leo inched forward. Behind them, Letizia had turned around and started back across the room.

"I like stories," Leo said, so quietly Astrea almost didn't hear him.

"You know," Jin said as he joined Astrea on the floor, "I like stories too, Leo. Do you have a favorite?"

His lips pursed. "I don't know."

"You do too," Helena drawled. "You said it's 'The Little Warrior.'" She looked back at Astrea. "Leo *always* says he doesn't know."

As the little boy's eyes welled up with tears, Astrea reached for his hand. "Oh, that's alright, Leo," Astrea said. Then she smiled at Helena.

"It's alright if we don't always have the answer. And it's alright if we change our minds, too."

Helena's nose scrunched up like she was seriously considering what Astrea had just said. Letizia finally reached them, and she knelt behind her two children immediately.

"My sweets," she said, "how about you go upstairs and have some more time to play before bed?" That broke Leo out of his despair. Golden joy exploded around him, and his brilliant smile could've blinded Astrea. "Say goodbye to Prince Varojin and Miss Sovna."

Both children waved before being led off by their mother, and Astrea waved back.

"I suppose we should join my cousins," Jin said as he helped Astrea stand. "Let's get the rest of this over with."

"It's not so bad. Helena and Leo were sweet," Astrea said as they walked toward where the others were talking. Both Veiko and Letizia had left the dining room with their children in tow.

"They liked you," Jin said.

"They liked you, too."

"Yes, but the woman with the pretty hair and books is far more interesting than me," he said. "Not that I can blame them."

Astrea's belly curled as Jin rubbed his thumb over the top of her hand and the faintest hint of lust and desire reached out to her. Not shielding herself was almost worth it, especially when that sweet approval coated her tongue and warmth like sunshine spread over her skin.

"Hopefully Ysabel's ready to start dinner," Jin said. "I'd really like to get out of here."

"And you say I'm impatient."

Jin started to speak, then cut himself off as they finally rounded the dining table. Lucian was watching them intently. Why was the commander so interested? He certainly seemed to disapprove of their relationship

. . . at least to some extent. Even Ysabel hadn't been all that interested when Jin had called Astrea his partner; there hadn't even been a hint of surprise in her aura. Astrea supposed that was some kind of approval from the grand duchess.

Lucian said nothing to them, and instead, Jin and Astrea joined Eliana and Delfine.

"My cousin," Delfine said. "You're a Fireweaver, yes?"

"I am."

"I find mages so interesting." Delfine pursed her lips. "Ever since I was a little girl. I always wanted to be a mage."

"Does it not run in the family?" Jin asked. "My mother wasn't either."

"Not as strongly as we would like," Delfine said with a sigh. "Though there have been a few. Leo's been showing signs of being an Earthmover, from his mother's side." She smiled at Astrea. "And Commander Lucian tells me you're a Lightbringer."

"I am, Your Highness," Astrea said.

"We've had a few of those in the family tree too. Perhaps"—she looked between Astrea and Jin, one eyebrow raised—"there will be more in the future."

Eliana brought her wine glass to her mouth, and though Astrea pulled her senses in tighter, she was sure peach amusement was dancing around her friend.

Jin simply smiled as he said, "Maybe Helena will surprise you all. You never know with these things. There's still time for her magic to manifest."

They spent the next half hour covering all sorts of topics with Jin's family: everyone's experiences in Kalama, a bit of Jin's military history, where Astrea had lived in Novaria when she was a child, and even some about Katerina and Delfine's lives, too.

It wasn't long before Ysabel called everyone to be seated. Veiko and Letizia had returned sans children just in time to join them for the meal. Once everyone was seated—Helosians on one side of the table and Novarians on the other—the staff came and went with multiple courses, and conversation stayed on the lightest of topics. To be expected, Astrea supposed, when Ysabel and her family were still hiding Jin's true heritage and the void problem. How much did Veiko, Delfine, and their wives know about *that*, anyway?

Astrea didn't have much spare energy to think about it. Whenever she wasn't focused on holding her magic tight against her body, she was avoiding Lucian's irritated gaze and Delfine's intensely personal questions.

At last, when dessert and coffee finally arrived, Ysabel dismissed her staff and Lucian followed them to lock the dining room door. That couldn't be good. Astrea tried to focus on the four-layer chocolate cake in front of her, but she couldn't make herself take more than a couple bites of the rich dessert.

"Well," Ysabel said from her seat at the head of the table. "Now that we're alone, I'd like to invite any questions about the . . . situation . . . now that you've all gotten to know each other more. Of course, I expect the knowledge of Jin's parentage to stay within this circle."

"Do you know why your mother hid the truth from you?" Delfine asked.

"Straight to the point, Del," Katerina murmured, her wide nose wrinkling. Delfine's wife had been quiet through most of the dinner, though Astrea had learned she was originally from an aristocratic family in the Taipoli Islands. Other than that, she hadn't been able to gather much about the woman.

"I think it's a fair question," Delfine said as she set her fork down on her plate. "I like Varojin and his sister, but Caliste hid this from the whole family. *You* hid this from the whole family, Aunt Ysabel. Why?"

"Caliste was my cousin," Ysabel said simply. "She seemed distressed by her situation in Kalama. I thought I was helping her by doing as she requested."

Astrea couldn't blame the grand duchess for that, though it pained her to think that Jin's mother was in a bad situation in Kalama. What would that have been like, being the emperor's mistress and bearing his child while also keeping such a big secret?

"I truly don't know why my mother did that," Jin said. "I wish I did. I might even have more questions than you, Delfine."

"And you believe your father doesn't know?" Delfine asked.

"We don't believe he does. If our father knew he had that kind of connection back to Novaria living under his roof . . ."

"He would exploit it," Eliana cut in. "Our father is nothing if not exploitative, just to name one of his many awful qualities."

Veiko's eyebrows rose, but a sly smile pulled at Delfine's mouth. "Well," she said, "it seems I have even more reason to like you two. You're straight to the point too, Eliana. You truly plan to dethrone your father?"

"I do," Eliana said. "He's done enough damage to Helosia and its neighbors. They've all done enough damage to each other. We're long past due for a change."

Delfine lifted her long-stemmed wine glass in a one-woman toast, then took a healthy sip. Veiko, however, didn't look as convinced. His eyebrows knitted together.

"My aunt says you have plans to transition from your father's policies to your own," Veiko said. "Would you be willing to share them with us in more detail? While replacing your father on the Helosian throne would be a benefit to the continent long-term, a rebellion risks destabilizing all of Helosia's neighbors in the short-term."

All of Helosia's neighbors, meaning all the other countries on the continent. Helosia shared borders with Delia, Zaikud, Novaria, and Tornama. Would the other nations stay out of Helosia's internal issues? Astrea doubted the Delians and Zaikudi would.

"I'm aware of those risks," Eliana replied. "Just as I'm aware of civil unrest in both Delia and Zaikud. But I think our father staying in power risks further destabilizing the continent, especially considering what we've learned about void magic."

Astrea watched Jin's cousins carefully, though none of them appeared fazed by Eliana's mention of void magic. Of course they'd been briefed; they were Ysabel's heirs, after all. To keep them in the dark would be a mistake.

"I'm inclined to agree," Veiko said. "With the right plans and strategies in place, and with the right external support, you may be able to avoid drawing out the internal Helosian war."

Civil war. Astrea had known, of course, that there would be war in Helosia, at least to some degree. Not everyone would support Eliana's claims; plenty of civilians and nobles alike backed Kaius. But hearing it spoken about so distantly, so impersonally, didn't sit right with Astrea. Lots of innocent people would get hurt. Many innocent people would also be hurt by void magic and were already being hurt by the Corsycan War.

"While I do think opening dialogue with our father might be important"—Eliana leaned around Nicos to look down the table at Jin—"I think we must consider targeted strikes and only expand fighting if absolutely necessary. I don't wish to hurt my people."

"Perhaps we can review your plans with you in the coming days, Eliana," Ysabel said. "Before we make a formal recommendation to the council."

Eliana nodded. "I would be happy to go over them with all of you in depth."

"And perhaps, we can soon have another dinner together with the council," Ysabel said. "Something informal, just like tonight. I believe if they get to know you both, they will see why I want to support your efforts."

Informal? If gowns and three-piece suits, overflowing floral arrangements, and hand-painted and crystal dishware were what Ysabel considered informal, Astrea would hate to see what she considered formal.

"Will you be back from your travels soon, Varojin?" Letizia asked. The woman had the softest voice, almost like wind whispering through the trees. "Ysabel says you are to travel to the mountains?"

The airship would be ready for them by the next evening. They would leave late in the day, arrive in the mountains by the morning, hike to the site, investigate, and then return to Talmaris. Without Kostas's full research team, Astrea wasn't sure that such a short time would give them what they needed. But going with a small team would be safer; fewer people would be put in danger. Hopefully they found something useful.

"We'll be back," Jin said. "We're leaving tomorrow night and won't be gone for too long."

"Excellent." Ysabel smiled. "I'll get started on those plans in the morning. Now please, finish your dessert in peace. Enough talk of war and magic. Skies knows there will be enough of that in the coming weeks."

As the rest of the table continued discussing lighter topics—Veiko's interest in art, Delfine's interest in gardening, Cressida's work with her father, Adi and Nicos's hobbies—Jin leaned toward Astrea.

"What do you say we get out of here?" he whispered in Helosian.

Ysabel had made her exit about fifteen minutes before, escorted by Marko—though where he'd come from, Astrea didn't know. The others were still absorbed in conversation and that decadent chocolate cake.

"Can we?" she asked.

"We can do anything we want."

Getting out of there sounded much better than staying, especially if Delfine's questions started up again. The woman was relentless, meddling more than Eliana and Cressida did. That was the difference, though. Eliana and Cressida could tease, but they knew when to stop. Delfine didn't.

"Then let's go."

Jin stood first, then offered Astrea his hand. Lucian stood with them, and Astrea forced back a sigh. What did he want? Could he not just leave them alone?

"Do you need to be escorted somewhere, Your Highness?" he asked.

"No, thank you," Jin said. "Veiko, Letizia, Delfine, Katerina, it was lovely to meet all of you. But considering we're traveling tomorrow, Astrea wanted to review some final notes with me again before the trip."

Notes? *That* was his excuse? That was the most convincing thing he could come up with?

"We didn't mean to keep you," Katerina said.

Delfine, however, smirked. It wasn't a disapproving look. It was pure amusement.

"No, no, that's alright." That honeyed voice and smile of Jin's were back. "In fact, I hope my sister and friends will stay. They deserve a break."

"We do still have wine to get through," Delfine said, her mouth pulling up slyly. "Please stay, Eliana and friends."

Glancing down the table, Astrea caught Eliana's eye. She smiled, and Eliana smiled back, but it was the same amused look Delfine had given them.

"I've never been one to say no to good wine or cake," Eliana said. "We would love to stay."

CHAPTER 28

As soon as Jin closed their bedroom door, Astrea let her shoulders drop and her magic spread as wide as it wanted to go. It didn't stretch all that far from her body, instead creating a roomy radius around her. She could breathe again. Feel again.

"You didn't really want to go over notes, did you?" Astrea asked. She didn't have to. Raspberry lust danced around Jin in a mesmerizing pattern, brightening the dark room.

"Not unless you want to," he said as he shrugged off his suit jacket.

"Well, it probably wouldn't hurt . . ." As Jin's face fell, his aura wavering, Astrea giggled. Skies, it felt so good to laugh. She felt like she hardly did it anymore. They used to laugh all the time, all those years ago. "I wish you could see what I do."

"You . . ."

"Of course I don't want to look at notes right now." All they'd been doing was looking at notes. One night off wasn't going to stop them from finding answers.

"Unbelievable," he murmured as tart lust and sweet amusement filled her mouth. Jin prowled closer, the corners of his lips quirking up. "Then what would you rather be doing?"

"Oh, all sorts of things."

As Jin reached her, he grabbed her by the waist and pulled her into his body. Astrea's heart hammered in her throat, unignorable but pleasant. "Let's be specific."

Astrea wiggled out of his grasp and turned toward their bedroom door. "I suppose I could change and go for a run," she said. "You and Adi seem to love doing that."

"Not happening. What else?"

"Surely there's reading to do."

"We've been reading for days. Try again."

With a smile, Astrea spun toward him. She was just inches from their door, hands clasped behind her back. "We could play a game."

Jin stepped closer, his hands already undoing the buttons on his waistcoat and shirt. "A game?" He stopped right in front of her, so close she could feel his body heat. "You want to play a game right now?"

"Don't you?"

"I really, really don't."

"Picky." Peach amusement flared around him, and warmth washed over her. "What do you want to be doing, then?"

"You're very lucky right now, Az."

"And why's that?"

"Because." Jin pushed in closer until her back pressed against the wall just next to the door. Raspberry lust clung to his limbs. That striking, deep purple reverence twined with it, as did more peach. It was so beautiful, this sunset made just for her. "As much as I want to fuck you against this wall, I'm going to be a gentleman and fuck you on that bed instead."

Astrea's insides burned, molten and churning. No one had ever spoken to her like that. Every time she and Jin had been together since that first night, he'd been so gentle. Attentive. This, though. This was different. And she liked it.

She peered up at him. "Maybe I want you to fuck me against the wall."

Jin wasted no time. He stooped, kissing her neck, her jaw, her lips. He tasted like that white wine they'd had at dinner, light but lush. "Is that really what you want?"

"There's a first time for everything."

His fingers tangled in the hair at the nape of her neck as he kissed her hard and deep. Astrea opened her mouth to him, moaning as he took her lower lip between his teeth. Every inch of her ignited.

"My dress," she said as she pulled away. "Help me get it off." Astrea couldn't reach the little buttons holding the back of her gown together, but she desperately wanted to feel his hands on her skin.

Jin pulled her away from the wall and started working on the buttons. As he worked, Astrea kissed his neck and jaw, her fingers running through those loose, messy curls. They'd grown out a bit in the last couple weeks. It suited him.

He groaned. "I can't do this quickly if you're going to distract me."

Astrea turned so he could access the back of her dress. As soon as the buttons were unhooked, Jin slid the bodice's straps off her shoulders and pushed the gown off her hips. His hands roamed her torso, her breasts, the base of her throat.

"Bed," he breathed into her ear. "Now."

"What happened to the wall?" she asked, missing his warmth as soon as he pulled away.

"Bed," he repeated.

"Bossy," Astrea sassed. Sweet approval washed over her again and again, almost like she'd eaten a spoonful of sugar.

Still, she climbed into bed and wiggled out of her bloomers as she watched him undress. Jin didn't even watch where he was throwing his discarded clothes; his eyes were glued to her.

"Now," he said as he climbed on top of her, "isn't this better than a wall?" His fingers trailed down her sternum, then the soft hill and slope of her belly. Astrea shivered. "Now I can touch you properly." His hand continued descending, past the dusting of hair between her thighs and right to her clit.

Astrea trembled with anticipation. His forehead dropped to hers, those fingers moving in slow, gentle circles. When she let out a breathy gasp, he smirked.

"I love making you make that noise."

Heat flushed Astrea's face, but Jin didn't seem to notice. Instead, his fingers circled several more times before they dipped down into her.

What was it about being with Jin that made her unable to think straight? Maybe it was the energy dancing around her—lust, joy, pride, determination—or maybe it was her own desire. Skies, she wanted him. She wanted him so badly. Astrea reveled in it. She let it all wash over her again and again.

But she also didn't want to be selfish. Jin was attentive, so much so that Astrea could barely focus. Reaching between them, she wrapped her hand around his erection. She'd barely done anything, had barely moved her hand, but Jin sucked in a breath before nipping at her neck. Emboldened, she stroked him once, twice, a third time.

"Do that again," he whispered. When she did, he sucked in another sharp breath. "Shit."

Jin pulled his fingers out of her as he backed up and stepped off the bed. Then he hooked his arms under her knees and pulled her down the silky sheets toward the edge of the mattress.

"I don't think I can wait," he practically pleaded. "Ready?"

"Yes." She didn't want to wait anymore, either. She didn't need to.

Still standing, Jin stroked himself twice before pushing into her. It was a welcome stretch, a relief. Astrea wrapped her legs tight around his waist, and when she pulled him closer, he groaned out another swear.

Competing lust and warmth settled in her bones, drowning out the rest of the world. All of her senses homed in on those feelings and the way Jin pounded into her. She couldn't think, could barely breathe, and it was the best feeling in the world.

One second he was standing over her, kissing her, and the next she was being flipped onto her front. Jin nudged her legs apart with his knees. "Good?" he asked.

"Yes," Astrea breathed, burying her face in the sheets and spreading her legs as she pushed up on her forearms.

He tugged her hips up, then buried himself deep inside her. Astrea moaned into the mattress, trying to stifle herself despite the empty house. But Jin was making that very difficult as he plunged in and out of her, one hand on her hips and the other finding hers as her fingers twisted the sheets. Sparks danced through Astrea's lower belly and up toward her lungs. She wanted to scream or moan or *something*, but all that came out were the tiniest gasps as she pushed her hips higher.

As Jin pulled out of her, he nudged her onto her back. Astrea rolled over all the way and settled back among the pillows. She tried to steady her breathing as she brushed hair away from her face.

"You good?" he whispered. When she nodded, Jin leaned toward her, erection brushing her belly, and murmured, "I need to hear you say it."

"I'm good."

"Do you want to keep going?" That purple reverence danced around him, weaving its way between the gold joy and raspberry lust flaring higher. The colors were so bright she almost had to look away, but she didn't.

Astrea threaded her fingers through his hair and kissed him. She never wanted it to end. Just as he pulled away and sucked in a breath, Astrea whispered, "Of course I do. Do you?"

"Az," Jin said against her throat, "I don't want anything else right now."

He slid into her again, gentler and slower this time. Then he sat up, hands gripping her thighs and pushing her hips back. Astrea didn't know how, but Jin hit the right spot again and again and again. And when he reached for her clit again, Astrea pushed his hand away.

"Don't stop." She barely got the words out. He held her in place, continuing to slam into her as she touched herself with one hand and grabbed his shoulder with the other.

Astrea's eyes closed. The lust and desire swirling around her. The feeling of Jin's skin on hers. The way her body tightened more and more as Jin's thrusts grew sloppier by the second.

She cried out. Trembles rolled through Astrea's body again and again as her release came, as Jin seemed to spill inside her forever. His entire body shook as he pressed his forehead against hers. When he finally pulled out, Jin rolled to the side and tucked his head into the empty spot beside hers.

He kissed her shoulder. "Still good?" he asked as he draped one arm over her waist.

"Very good."

He kissed her shoulder again, his fingers brushing against her hair as Astrea tried to catch her breath. Even Jin blew out a heavy sigh as they both settled into the pillows. His emotions still pressed into her, far less intense than before. It was comforting, really, to feel him both with her magic and his body against hers.

Somewhere in the back of her mind, Astrea figured she should clean up, but she was weak in the best way. She didn't think she could move even if she actually wanted to. Jin didn't move, either, other than to play with the ends of her hair.

"Did Delfine upset you at dinner?" Jin asked after a few minutes. "I didn't realize she would be so nosy. I thought I'd left the busybody family member behind in Kalama."

Astrea stared up at the canopy hanging over the bed. He wanted to talk about that now? Delfine's questions had been straightforward—unusual, at least in Kalamian social circles. Even Ysabel had not asked questions like that. Astrea had been more embarrassed than upset. But what did she tell Jin? That her stomach had flipped when he'd implied this might be serious?

She could see that plainly at times—his colors were so bright, so strong—and yes, he'd told her he wanted to really try at their relationship. That it wasn't just one night. But hearing him say it at dinner, in front of cousins he barely knew and in front of their friends, was different.

"Hey." Jin pushed up on his elbow, leaning over to cup her face with his free hand. His thumb stroked her cheek, gentle. Reassuring, even as his anxiety pressed painfully into her chest. "Did *I* upset you?"

"No! Skies, no." She smiled. "I was just surprised."

"Surprised by her question or my answer?"

Astrea watched him for a moment. That purple and gold sheen still surrounding him. The gentleness in his eyes. The way his eyebrows pulled together almost imperceptibly, just like they did when he was worried. "Both."

Orange anxiety joined the other colors still dancing in the air. "Surprised in a good way or a bad way?"

"In a good way."

They had only been reunited for a little more than a month, and it wasn't like they were exactly able to do all the normal things courting couples did. Relationships moved quickly in Kalama, but how could Jin be so confident after such a short time? After so many years apart and with so many unknowns?

"I didn't mean to put pressure on this or us," he said gently. "I hope you know that."

"I know." And she did. Jin was not impulsive, but he'd always been honest. Almost always.

As he settled back down next to her, Astrea tried to focus on anything other than her erratic pulse. She didn't want to put pressure on them, either.

She didn't even know if there was anything to put pressure on in the long run. What were the rules for princes? In Helosia? In Novaria? Astrea wanted to ask, but she wasn't sure she wanted to know the answer. *Maybe I just need to enjoy whatever time we have together.* The thought made her heart hurt, because if she was honest with herself, she'd found her mind wandering through the possibilities, what kind of life they might live together for years to come. She pushed it all far into the back of her mind.

"You should get some rest," Jin said. "You'll need it if you want to be ready for what comes later."

"What's later?" When a ridiculously proud smile lit up his face, Astrea groaned. "I thought it was important."

"Oh, but it is important." He kissed her shoulder. "Seeing how many times I can make you climax in a day is essential work."

Laughing, Astrea reached to the side and grabbed one of the pillows. She brought it over to drop on his head, but he wrestled it from her with no effort at all.

Jin tossed it to the side as he climbed back on top of her and said, "Shall we get back to it?"

Something unpleasant pounded through the very core of Astrea's bones. She blinked against the dim morning light.

"Jin!" someone yelled. She knew that voice, but her sleepy mind didn't want to work.

Astrea nudged Jin's shoulder, and he groaned. She nudged him again when Adi yelled for a second time.

"What?" Jin yelled back, his voice croaking. He fell back into the pillows and reached for Astrea. His hands were so warm against her bare skin.

"It's the general!" Adi called through the door. "She's made contact. Hurry up!"

Jin sighed as he pressed his body against Astrea's. "Remind me why I don't just quit everything and move both of us to an island very, very far away."

"Sounds nice," Astrea mumbled as she curled into him.

He kissed her neck before rolling away. "I'll be back."

Jin moved through the room quietly, though when the wardrobe doors slammed shut, he whispered a quick apology. The bedroom door opened and closed with a soft click.

They were supposed to be leaving for the mountains later that day. Astrea was also supposed to meet Adi for a little more training; the clock said she still had half an hour before she needed to be ready. She'd meant to wake up earlier, but Jin had been serious about his work the night before. Her bones felt like jelly now. Astrea buried her face in the pillows as she tried not to replay every wonderful moment in her mind's eye.

And then it hit her.

The *general* had made contact? That had to be Zephyrine Kanakos. Scrambling out of bed, Astrea searched in the low light for something to put on. Jin's black dress shirt from the night before was still on the floor, and she slipped it on before turning on the bedside lamp.

If Zephyrine had made contact, that could be a good or bad thing. Was she on her way? Or did she have news from Kalama?

Astrea searched the floor for her bloomers and tugged them on, then set about picking up the rest of their discarded clothes from the night before. She knew she needed to wait to hear what Zephyrine had to say, but Astrea's mind immediately jumped through the possibilities. The war had started. Sarsali and Balthazar had been arrested. Saros had been thrown in jail or executed. The Helosians were heading for Talmaris.

Stop it, she warned herself as she went to the bathroom. There was no point guessing when she'd find out in a few minutes. Astrea had just finished brushing her teeth and braiding her hair when Jin returned.

"Zephyrine will reach Talmaris late tomorrow afternoon." He paused, his gaze flicking up and down her body. She was still wearing his shirt, and sweet approval rolled over her. "We'll leave for the ruins once she's in the city. I convinced Lucian to delay the trip until she's here."

"Is that wise?" Astrea asked. "To delay it, I mean."

"The rest of my team is with her. I'd like them to be around."

"You think we'll need them? Should we be bringing more Novarians?"

"Need them at the ruins? I doubt it, but I don't want to leave Ellie with just Nicos. I'll have them stay with her, and we can continue on as planned."

"Well." Astrea looked to where their packed suitcases sat near the wardrobe. "Now what?"

"Adi said he'll be waiting for you by the lake."

Astrea went to the wardrobe and pulled out a pair of her sporting clothes. She liked spending time with Adi, but Astrea also hated the thought of running first thing in the morning. Maybe she could convince Adi to skip that part just this one time.

"Are you and the others joining us this morning?" Astrea asked as she adjusted her pants.

"I'd planned on it after I talk with Ellie," Jin said.

Pulling on her boots next, Astrea hurried over to where Jin stood. She kissed him on the cheek, but Jin caught her by her hand and pulled her back to him. Her core tightened as he kissed her properly, the way he'd kissed her the night before.

"See you soon," he said. "Tell Adi not to be too hard on you today."

"No wonder Varojin coddles you." Lucian's words jumped to the front of her mind unbidden. Had Jin told Adi not to push her at all? Was that why her progress felt so slow? Adi had assured her every day that she was improving, that training took a long time. She swallowed hard.

"Oh, it's alright if he makes me work." Astrea took one step backward, then another. "It's better, in fact."

Gray confusion spiked high around Jin's body. "Az—" he started, but she forced a smile.

"Tell Ellie I said good morning!" Astrea called a bit too cheerfully over her shoulder. She hurried to the door and slammed it shut behind her. She had a lot of work to do, and she didn't need anyone to take it easy on her.

CHAPTER 29

The sunrise colored the sky a muted mix of lavender, pink, and deep blue. A handful of wispy clouds drifted overhead. It was an especially chilly morning, one of the coolest since they'd arrived in Talmaris. Astrea shivered as she headed toward the lake.

She'd expected to see Adi waiting in his usual spot near a large hydrangea bush next to the path he seemed to enjoy running around. Instead, a shorter, pale figure stood in his place.

What did Commander Lucian want? He'd seen her; there was no turning back. Astrea pulled her barrier in as tightly around her body as she could and started down the hill.

"Good morning," Lucian said as she neared. His voice was calm, almost light. Friendly. Friendlier than he'd been in days.

"Hello." It was as polite as Astrea could force herself to be. She was used to walking on eggshells around people with far more power than her—magically and politically—and though Astrea knew she needed Lucian to teach her, she was angry with him. Angry with herself.

Lucian rolled his eyes. "Don't tell me you're still upset about what happened."

In some ways, Lucian reminded Astrea of her uncle. They were nearly the same height and shared similarly dark hair. But unlike Saros, Lucian was almost too ready to engage. Obviously he had sought her out; there was no way this was a coincidence.

And Astrea was just like Saros in that she did not want to engage even though she probably should. "I just wasn't expecting to see you," she said. "I'm waiting for Adi."

"I see." Lucian pressed his lips together and huffed. "I thought we would continue our training since we'll be delaying our trip. It gives us practically two more days."

"Is that wise?" The question left Astrea before she could think twice about it.

"There's much you still need to learn. I wouldn't be a good teacher if I didn't ensure you're armed with the things you need to know."

Astrea crossed her arms. "You taught me plenty yesterday."

"I knew it," Lucian muttered.

Adi crested the hill leading back to the guest house, Cressida right by his side. They both waved, and Astrea waved back. She'd never been so happy to see her friends, not even when Cressida rescued her from that awkward meeting with Jin at the Whiskey Dream.

"Didn't realize you'd be out here, Commander," Adi said. "Will you be joining us?"

"No, he won't," Astrea said quickly. Cressida raised an eyebrow.

"Unfortunately, Adi, I have some things to take care of thanks to the delay in our schedule." Then, Lucian said to Astrea, "Perhaps tomorrow we'll continue our lessons." He brushed past her and headed for the palace looming in the distance.

"I feel like I missed something," Cressida said. "What were you two talking about?"

"Nothing, he's just cranky today." The lie came too easily. "Are you two alright with the delay in the trip?"

Cressida frowned, and Astrea shook her head. She knew that frown. Cressida was about to argue.

"It'll be good to have Zephyrine here," Adi said. "And the rest of the team, too. I'm just relieved they're getting out of Helosia."

"Hopefully they come bearing news of what's happening at home," Cressida said. "Like, real news, not whatever the newspapers are reporting."

"News or no news, we're wasting sunlight," Adi said. "Five laps today."

"Wasting sunlight?" Cressida rolled her eyes. "It's not even the seventh bell."

"Exactly. So let's go."

"You can get started," Cressida said. "I need to ask Az something." When Adi started to protest, Cressida added, "Unless you want our friendship to get to a new level very quickly, Adi, I recommend you let us have a moment. I'm not keen on bodily function chat with you just yet."

"At least walk while you talk, alright?" With that, Adi started off at a brisk jog away from them.

Walking sounded just fine to Astrea. She headed in the same direction as Adi. "If it's really something ailing you, just tell me now," Astrea said as Cressida joined her. "And if it's not, just tell me now anyway."

"At least now I know you're cranky, too," Cressida said. "What gives? You seemed to be in a great mood last night when you left dinner."

"Were Jin's cousins upset that we left?"

"Delfine and Veiko? No, I don't think they cared. They were really interested in what Ellie had to say. But Lucian definitely seemed put off."

Astrea groaned. While it was great news that Delfine and Veiko had been so engaged with Eliana, the information about the commander just left Astrea feeling empty.

"Did anyone else seem to notice Lucian's mood?" she asked.

"I don't think so." Cressida paused, the only sound filling the silence that of a few birds singing their morning songs. "What's really going on, Az?"

Although Astrea didn't really want to think about how awful the day before had felt, she needed to tell her friends. And starting with Cressida seemed manageable enough. "Yesterday, I had a lightbringing lesson with Lucian."

"Yes, I remember."

The breeze made Astrea shiver again. "Did you know that Lightbringers can use someone's emotional energy to hurt them?"

Silence stretched on between them as they walked. Cressida shoved her hands into her pockets, eventually asking, "What do you mean?"

"You know how Lightbringers can see and feel emotions? Well, apparently we can also use that energy to hurt others."

"Really?" Astrea still had her barrier wrapped tightly around herself, but she was sure if she didn't, lavender surprise would be bubbling up around Cressida. "You're serious?"

"Lucian thinks that's the best way for me to defend myself, but I can't do that to someone, Cress. I just can't."

"Why not?"

"Because it felt awful when he did it to me. And it felt worse when I attacked him back. I didn't want to, but he kept saying all these awful things about how weak and scared I was for not agreeing to be bait for his plan, and how Jin—" Astrea's voice cracked on the last word. "It really hurt, Cress. For hours after. Lucian didn't even warn me he was going to do it."

"Lucian did what to you?" That low, cold voice did not belong to Cressida.

Both women stopped walking. Astrea peeked over her shoulder. Jin was behind them, arms folded tightly over his chest. Where had he come from? How long had he been behind them? That was one of the disadvantages of having her barrier up; Astrea couldn't sense other people coming. How had neither she nor Cressida heard him?

Astrea loosened her barrier, and both Jin and Cressida's red-hot anger flooded the otherwise peaceful morning. "Jin—" she started, but Cressida cut her off.

"That asshole attacked her during what was supposed to be a lesson!" Cressida yelled.

"Lucian just—"

"Mage teachers are always supposed to walk you through what's going to happen and what they're doing. Always." Cressida's voice softened as she added, "Don't make excuses for him, Az. Just don't."

Maybe Astrea was making an excuse, but that didn't change the fact that Commander Lucian was her best bet for learning more about her magic. Magic she needed if she was going to help stop the Paragon and Emperor Aelius.

Jin sucked in a heavy breath and clenched his jaw. Astrea could've sworn his eyes burned in the early morning sun peeking through the thick trees. "Someone please remind me that killing the commander is probably incredibly bad for diplomacy."

"Want some help?" Cressida muttered.

"You two aren't killing anyone." Astrea sighed. "Can we please just forget this?"

Heavy footsteps sounded behind Jin, and he stepped aside just in time for Adi to stop near them. His eyebrows furrowed. "What are you three doing just standing here? Laps, remember?"

Cressida waved her hand dismissively. "We've got bigger issues than running laps."

Oh skies. Astrea tilted her head back to look at the sunrise. More confusion was moving their way; Eliana and Nicos weren't far behind Adi.

She wanted to disappear. Astrea hadn't meant for them all to find out like this. Talking to Cressida first, then Jin, would've been manageable.

"Please," Astrea whispered. "Please don't make a big deal out of this. Besides, you two beat each other up all the time," she said, nodding to Jin and Adi.

That furrow between Adi's eyebrows deepened. "I'm sorry, what?"

"Lucian attacked her without warning," Jin said. "A lesson is not a sparring match, Az."

"He *what*?" That shrill question came from Eliana. Heat singed Astrea's skin as crimson rage jumped into the air. "When I see Ysabel, I'm going to—"

"Please, Ellie, don't," Astrea said. "Don't tell Ysabel. I need him to teach me if I'm going to help the rest of you. I don't want him to lose his job."

"He's not going to lose his job," Jin said. "But he knows better. He knows that's unacceptable behavior."

Could her friends not just drop this? Heat burned her from all directions, proof of their anger.

"What happened?" Eliana asked.

Sucking in a deep breath, Astrea explained, again, what Lucian had taught her about taking control of other people's energy and using it against them. She explained how it hurt and where it hurt the most, and Jin kept glancing at her sternum.

"And you attacked him back?" Nicos asked. When she nodded, teal approval spiked around him. "Good for you."

"He wanted me to," Astrea said. "He kept taunting me and trying to force me to attack back. I just wanted him to stop saying . . ."

"Stop saying what?" Eliana asked.

Astrea looked down at her boots as she said, "He said I was weak, that I couldn't hurt him even if I wanted to and that was why I wouldn't go along with his plan to be bait." She watched Jin through her eyelashes. His jaw muscle tightened. "He was just trying to provoke me."

A few morning songbirds began to sing in a nearby tree, the only sound aside from the lapping of water at the lake's edge. Though Astrea didn't want to lose her chance to learn lightbringing, if she was honest with herself, the fact that her friends were so upset made her feel a little more sane. Just minutes earlier, Lucian had acted like it was ridiculous for her to be upset about the whole thing.

"Was I wrong to refuse to go along with his plan?" she asked. "Should we have set a trap?"

Their jumbled responses made Astrea cringe, but even among the noise, their answer was clear: they backed her decision.

"I'm glad you refused," Nicos said. "Lucian was going to get someone killed if we went along with it. Too many variables and unknowns right now."

"Then why did he propose it? He doesn't seem like the reckless type," Astrea muttered.

"Because he's as desperate for answers as we are," Eliana said.

Silence settled over them. Astrea focused on the sound of the lake lapping against the shore. The wind rustling the stems of the weeping willows. The ducks quacking nearby. Yes, Lucian was desperate. They all were. Scrambling for *anything*. But still . . .

"Will you do it to me?" Jin asked. "Will you show me what Lucian did to you?"

"What?" she asked, horror prickling her scalp. "What? No, I'm not going to—"

"Az," he said gently, "I've never heard of a Lightbringer having that ability. I need to know what this is we're dealing with."

"What?" she asked again.

"Nor have I," Adi said, and Nicos and Eliana echoed their agreement.

Lucian had claimed very few in the world knew about this. Astrea hadn't been so confident about that, but if anyone else would know about it, she would've expected Jin and Adi, two elite Helosian soldiers, to have that information. Even Nicos probably would've given his position protecting Eliana. And if Emperor Aelius had known, surely he would be sending Lightbringers into war with that ability in mind. She could only imagine how useful that would be on the battlefield.

It was just like what Jin had told her about Posan. He'd set his fireweaving off like a bomb twice while at war, a power that no other Fireweaver seemed capable of. None that he'd met, anyway. Perhaps this really was better kept a secret.

"It doesn't bother you that Lucian knows some hidden Lightbringer ability?" Astrea asked.

"Sure it does," Jin said, his voice almost sad.

"He said all of you use your emotions as fuel for your magic. Is that true, too?"

"Oh, we definitely use it as Fireweavers," Nicos said.

Eliana nodded. "And Sparkcasters."

"Maybe I do a bit," Cressida said. "I've never really thought about it."

"I do," Adi said. "The opposite of those three, though." He motioned to Nicos, Eliana, and Jin. "I need to feel in control. Grounded. Giving in to what I'm feeling doesn't help. Maybe that's just from all my time at Fort Ironwing, though."

"Remember what I told you about Delia and Posan?" Jin asked. "That's the key for me. Letting all of that inner turmoil come to the surface. I still have to control it, but that energy helps me generate that power."

Astrea sucked in a shuddering breath as Eliana asked, "Delia and Posan?"

"I'll tell you later, Ellie, I promise," Jin said. "But right now, I'm more concerned with how this actually works. Will you show me, Az? Please?"

"I don't want to hurt you," Astrea whispered.

Astrea couldn't do that to Jin, could she? It had been so painful. But as orange anxiety vibrated around him, Astrea knew she had to. Knowing that this ability could be used against most of them without any notice was terrifying. What if they made Commander Lucian mad and he decided to retaliate?

"Alright," Astrea finally said. "But on the condition that you let me ease the pain after."

"You're not—" Jin started, but she shook her head.

"I am. That's the only way I'll agree to this."

"Fine, but I don't like it."

Cressida, Adi, Eliana, and Nicos moved to one side of the lakeside path as Jin and Astrea moved onto the soft grass. Doing this with an audience was somehow worse than just attacking Jin, but Astrea tried to shake off the feeling.

"I need you to remain open," Astrea told Jin. "No walls. I only know how to do it if you let your energy out. Whatever you were feeling about Lucian before, think about that."

Jin's shoulders heaved as he sucked in a breath. The faint rage that had stayed around him flared bright, as did anxiety and concern. The crimson, orange, and dark green pulsed around him in a steady rhythm.

"Ready?"

Jin nodded.

Astrea wasn't sure *she* was ready, but she latched onto her own fear before reaching for Jin's energy. She closed her fists, then pulled back, just as she had with Lucian. But she couldn't force her energy toward him.

"I trust you." Jin's voice strained with the words. Discomfort bloomed in her chest, just a whisper of what he was surely already feeling. "Do it, Az."

The sooner she started, the sooner this would be over. Astrea pushed her fears of hurting him and of her magic toward him. He grunted and stumbled back a step. She pushed her fear of the Paragon, and her silent rage at Lucian, right into Jin's body. As soon as his knees hit the grass, Astrea dropped her fists and thought of everything good she could: how gentle he'd been with Helena and Leo, how good it had felt to hear him say he was serious about their relationship, how nice it was to wake up with his body curled around hers. And then Astrea ran to his side.

"Well," Jin said, his hand splayed across his sternum, "that definitely fucking hurts."

"I'm sorry," she whispered, already tugging on her magic as she laid a hand on his back. She pushed the healing energy into him, and that ghostly pain emanating from him doubled in her body. Jin gently pulled her hand away. "You said I could heal you," Astrea protested.

"And you took the edge off." He smiled at her as they stood, but it wasn't convincing. "I promise."

She would not do that to Jin again, not even if he asked. Astrea wasn't sure she could do that to anyone. It had felt awful attacking Lucian despite his taunts.

"How do we protect ourselves from this?" Adi asked.

"My barrier protects me from it," Astrea said, then explained what she'd been working on with Lucian. "You all need barriers, too."

"We're not Lightbringers, though," Eliana said. "I definitely can't feel how far out my emotions are going."

"Jin, you're hard to read most of the time," Astrea said. He nodded. She'd told him, weeks before, that he often seemed to be surrounded by a wall. "How?"

"I'm not trying to make myself hard to read. I just try to keep myself calm and controlled," he said, as if it were truly that simple.

Astrea glanced at the rest of their friends, whose confusion, curiosity, and anxiety were bright. "Even if it is some rare Lightbringer talent, I don't like the idea that someone could turn it on you all."

Adi smiled. "Sounds like it's time for a lesson."

"I'm supposed to meet Ysabel this morning to discuss some of my plans," Eliana said. "Can it wait?"

"After lunch," Jin said. "We'll meet after lunch, and Az is going to teach us whatever she can."

Chapter 30

"No, not like that," Astrea said. "I can still see your emotions."

Rusty annoyance flashed in the guest house's parlor as Eliana clenched her fists in her lap. "What do you mean you can still see them? I'm pulling them in, like you and Jin said!"

After what happened by the lake, Astrea had insisted on still training with Adi. She hadn't been able to focus, though, as her mind just ran in circles around the issue with Lucian and her questions about General Kanakos. Eventually, they'd returned to the guest house, and not long after, Eliana had returned from her meeting with the grand duchess.

Now, Astrea stood with Jin in front of the parlor's fireplace, the others all perched on the soft armchairs and sofa. Teaching her friends to rein in their emotions was not going smoothly. Astrea had again explained what Lucian taught her about creating her own barrier, though as she'd anticipated, that hadn't helped her friends much.

"Focus on making the emotions smaller, Ellie," Jin said. "Contain them. Imagine them as a ball that you make smaller and smaller."

"Easy for *you*," she muttered, more of that rust spiking in the air. But finally, Eliana's aura shrank back toward her body. The color dimmed.

"Better," Astrea said. "Imagine surrounding yourself with a wall or a shield."

"This is hard." Eliana flopped into the sofa, her colors exploding to full brightness again.

"Don't you like hard things, Ellie?" Cressida quipped, then squealed as Eliana chucked a decorative pillow at her head. Amusement tickled Astrea's nose.

"Well, keep practicing. You almost had it." Astrea watched Adi's aura dim and waver before exploding back out again. Nicos was the only one having more than marginal success.

"How do you do this all the time?" Cressida asked. "I don't like it. It's uncomfortable."

"I know it is. Keep practicing." Astrea had been making the same complaints to Lucian just days ago, and though it was still difficult for Astrea to keep a tight grip on her energy all the time, it was getting easier.

"Are we sure it's necessary?" Eliana asked. "I mean, if nobody knows this Lightbringer secret except for a few people in the world, surely we'll be alright."

"Do you really want Lucian knowing all of your business?" Astrea asked, her gaze flicking to Nicos, then back to Eliana. "Besides the obvious potential danger." Eliana huffed as her aura first expanded with magenta embarrassment, then shrank and dimmed again. "Better, Ellie. Keep working on it."

"And you say I'm ruthless in training," Adi quipped. "We've been at this for half an hour already!"

"Which should be nothing for you, Adi," Jin said. "Zephyrine would hate to know you've gotten soft."

"Yeah, whatever," he muttered.

As the others continued practicing, Jin uncrossed his arms and reached for Astrea's hand. "Can we talk for a moment?" he asked quietly. "It'll be quick."

"Sure." Astrea led the way to the closed parlor door, then called over her shoulder, "Keep going. Don't forget I'll be able to tell if you give up!"

All four of their friends groaned, and Adi yelled something about her being "worse than Zephyrine" before she and Jin stepped into the foyer.

Jin closed the door behind him. Even from the middle of the foyer, Astrea could feel the ebb and flow of everyone's energy in the parlor. Their frustration was like sandpaper against her skin.

"You could've told me about Lucian," Jin said when he joined her. "There I was, carrying on and flirting with you like nothing had happened. I feel like an ass for not knowing."

"You're not an ass. And I *was* going to tell you . . . I just wanted to forget it happened for a few hours first."

"Fuck, I hate this." He sucked in a heavy, almost defeated breath as he ran his hand through his hair. "Just when I thought we were getting somewhere with the Novarians, one of them has to have their head up their ass. You'd think the commander of—"

"Wait," Astrea said. Just at the edge of her magic, something changed. A heavy wall pressed against her, but it wasn't from any of the four in the parlor. "I think he's coming."

A moment later, the front doors swung open. Lucian strode in, Marko by his side. Astrea pulled her magic back, back, back toward herself as Jin faced the Novarians.

"Good, you're here." Lucian sized up Astrea, then Jin. "Where's your sister, Prince Varojin? There are things we need to discuss."

Jin was silent for a long moment, then asked, "What's this about?"

"The Paragon have struck again."

"What?" Astrea whispered. But . . . she hadn't left the palace. They hadn't gone anywhere.

Behind Lucian, Marko shifted from one foot to the other.

"Let's just discuss this as a group, shall we?" Lucian suggested.

Jin guided Astrea in front of him as they walked toward the parlor door. Just as she opened it, Eliana yelled, "You should've warned me that controlling—" The words died on Eliana's tongue as Lucian strode in behind Jin. "Oh, Commander. Hello."

"Let me get straight to it," Lucian said. "Your Imperial Highnesses, there has been another murder. Two victims this time, both with void magic found on their bodies. Both near a hotel in downtown Talmaris. Obviously nobody from your group was there this time, and there was no note demanding we turn Astrea over. We don't yet know the purpose of these murders, but they appear to have happened last night."

Astrea's stomach sank. If she'd agreed to be bait for Lucian, maybe this wouldn't have happened. Maybe they would've already had answers. *Or maybe you'd have learned nothing at all,* her mind argued.

"Thank you for coming all the way here to tell us," Eliana said, her voice surprisingly flat. "Is there anything you need from us while you investigate?"

"No, my team will be handling it while we're in the mountains," Lucian said. "I just thought it was important that you were made aware." He glanced at Astrea. "You're trying to teach them to hide their emotions away?"

"I—" Her first instinct was to deny it, but Astrea lifted her chin. "I thought it was important."

Cressida shifted in her seat, and Eliana's jaw tightened. *Please don't say anything,* she thought at them.

"I see." Lucian surveyed their group, then nodded. "I assume you've told them."

"Of course I did. It seemed like poor judgment to leave them vulnerable."

"Wise, considering the circumstances. We aren't the only two in the world who know how to do this." Lucian crossed his arms behind his back. "I'm sure the lot of you think poorly of me, and Astrea, I owe you an apology in particular. I should not have handled that lesson the way I did."

Even a couple months prior, Astrea would've accepted Lucian's threadbare apology and tried to move on. She still wanted to. But she pushed against the instinct. Why was Lucian apologizing now when just that morning, he'd been irritated by her hurt feelings? Had Eliana said something to the grand duchess? Or could he sense her friends' distrust now? Astrea wanted to let her magic expand, but she couldn't make herself.

"No, you shouldn't have," Jin finally said. "I spent more than a year getting nasty trainers out of one of our programs back home. What you did crossed a line."

"And unfortunately, I cannot uncross it," Lucian said.

"Can we speak outside, Commander?" Astrea asked. She didn't need Jin stepping up for her, nor did she want an audience for this.

Lucian said nothing as he returned to the foyer. Astrea followed him and pulled the door closed behind her.

He regarded her, his expression neutral and impossible to interpret. Was he annoyed? Angry with her again? Angry with her *still*, especially considering the two new murder victims?

"What is it, Astrea?" The words, while direct, held no malice.

Astrea's heart thundered all the way up her throat and into her ears. "You were wrong to do that to me with no warning."

"I know. I apologized just a moment ago, didn't I?"

"You said you owe me an apology. That's not an actual apology."

Lucian let out a long, slow sigh. "Splitting hairs, isn't it?"

Astrea swallowed. "No."

Pushing his shoulders back, Lucian said, "I'm sorry, Astrea. I was in the wrong. I still think it's something you needed to learn, but I will not be so forward again. We'll go at your pace."

That wasn't exactly the world's best apology, but when Lucian offered her a small, tight smile, she nodded. She had a feeling it was the best she'd get from him. "Alright. Thank you."

"Is there anything else?"

"Actually, there is." She'd been pondering the question for the last day and still didn't have an answer. "How would that even help us fight the void mages? I told you they're hollow, like there's no energy to pull from. Doesn't that exercise become useless?"

"We'll find a way."

How? It wasn't like they knew any friendly void mages they could practice with.

"When we're back from the mountains?" she asked.

"Alright," he said. "It's best to focus on what comes next. We can discuss this more when we've returned."

"Do you need to tell Eliana anything else?"

"No. I'll see you tomorrow for the flight."

As Lucian called for Marko and led the younger guard out of the house, Astrea rubbed her hand over her face. Two more murders. Lucian changing his tune so quickly. Still no answers.

Tomorrow, she promised herself. Tomorrow, she would be on her way to the ruins. On her way to answers.

Astrea pushed her shoulders back and returned to the parlor. Her friends watched her, wary. "Well," she said, "what are you doing? You're supposed to be practicing."

Chapter 31

The day had finally arrived. General Zephyrine Kanakos was set to land at a military base outside the city within the hour. Jin, Adi, and Lucian were already at the fort overseeing final preparations, and Marko was set to escort Astrea, Cressida, and the professor there.

With the delay in their original plan, that meant they'd be heading west instead of east so they could make it back in time for the dinner with the Grand Novarian Council. East, toward the Antare Mountains, would've been in the direction of the actual void reference they'd found, but Astrea was still excited to go west. Professor Shalysko had found the void language at ruins there, too.

Now, Astrea crouched on her bedroom floor in front of the wardrobe, sifting through the few pieces of evidence they actually had about the Paragon. There, with Mattina's notebook, the sheets they'd taken from the void house, and the folios detailing the various murders, was Saros's note. Astrea hadn't touched it since that night they landed in Talmaris.

I'm trying, Uncle, she thought as she unfolded the note and reread his messy scrawl. *I'm trying to find answers just like you asked me to.* Astrea still wished she knew what visions he'd had of her. Maybe Zephyrine would have news from home. Something. Anything.

After setting the note back down, Astrea gathered the rest of what she needed: Mattina's notebook, so she could compare the text against the sample at the ruins, and the mythology book referencing the monster in the mountains. She wasn't sure if it would help, but it was worth reading over one more time before they landed. Then she stuffed everything into the canvas knapsack Jin had left her. Its dark gray material and leather straps made it look almost identical to the one he kept his military gear in. In fact, it looked just like the one he'd taken from their borrowed airship the night they landed in Talmaris nearly a fortnight prior.

Everything else was already packed and waiting downstairs. With the knapsack slung over her shoulder, Astrea smoothed the front of her dress and left behind the bedroom that had come to feel like the only safe place in the world.

A voice echoed up the stairs as Astrea descended. Kostas stood in the middle of the foyer, chatting about skies knew what. Enthusiasm danced over Astrea's skin, light and electric. Marko, stoic as ever, simply watched.

"Ah, Astrea!" Kostas called as she descended the last few stairs. "Wonderful! Are you ready to go?"

"Ready." Astrea shifted the bag on her shoulder.

"Have you ever been out to the Macadian Mountains?" Kostas asked. "It's a beautiful place, truly beautiful. I think you're going to really appreciate the site—"

"Professor," Marko said, the word sounding more like an order than something friendly, "would you go check that the driver is waiting out front? Then I'll begin bringing the bags out."

"Oh." Kostas glanced at Astrea, then Marko. "Of course." The professor hurried off without so much as a single word, and for just a moment, brilliant mint sparkled around Marko.

"You're relieved," Astrea said before she could think better of it. Marko just chuckled and shook his head.

"Just wait until you spend the next few days with him. You'll see why."

Astrea hadn't seen much of Marko since that incident at Kostas's office. In fact, they'd exchanged little more than a few polite pleasantries and information about the Paragon.

"What makes you say that?" she asked.

"Babysitting is not how I planned to spend my week. The professor is . . ."

"Eccentric?" Astrea offered.

"Annoying," Marko corrected. "Incredibly annoying. He doesn't shut up."

Astrea's laugh echoed through the foyer. That was Marko's concern? That the professor was annoying? "He can't be that bad."

"Prepare yourself," Marko muttered as they went into the parlor. "Tonight's flight will be trying."

Cressida, Eliana, and Nicos were there, orange anxiety radiating off the former two. Astrea's suitcase and a few other bags sat piled near the door.

"Are you ready to go?" Eliana asked from her spot near the windows on the far side of the room. She crossed her arms over her abdomen, her shoulders tight and expression grim.

"Ready as we'll ever be," Cressida said. "Don't look so nervous, Ellie."

"I'm not nervous."

"Marko," Nicos said, already crossing the room and heading for the door, "would you care to help me load the car?"

The two men gathered up the bags in silence. Astrea adjusted the knapsack still hanging from her back. She preferred her satchel, but bringing it on a mountainous hike didn't seem prudent. Once both Marko and Nicos were gone, Eliana sighed.

"You two do what you need to do, alright?" she said. "Don't worry about insulting Lucian or even the professor. Do whatever it is you need to do to get those answers. Jin will back you up."

Insulting Lucian was low on Astrea's list of priorities. He may have apologized for the incident during that lesson, but she didn't want to provoke him any more than she had the last few days.

"We'll do what we need to do," Cressida said, then smirked. "Tell you what. We'll even bring you a souvenir."

"And what could you find for me in the mountains, Cress?"

"A very large rock."

A small smile pulled at Eliana's mouth. "Just what I've always wanted."

"We'll find something about the Paragon, Ellie," Astrea said, though she knew she couldn't make that promise. "Just focus on what your father's up to and keeping the grand duchess on our side."

"That I can do." Eliana nodded. "Let's get you to that fort, shall we?"

The three women exited the parlor in silence. Outside, the first stars twinkled overhead, a few rogue clouds drifting through the deep blue sky. It wasn't all that different from the night they'd first arrived.

Astrea was just about to take a step forward when an arm slung around her shoulders, yanking her to one side. Her head nearly bumped into Cressida's as they both collapsed into Eliana's hug.

"Wow, Ellie," Cressida said with a laugh. "We'll miss you too."

"I just feel like I haven't done that enough these last few weeks," Eliana whispered. Astrea squeezed her shoulders. "See you in a few days."

"Bye, Ellie," Astrea said. "Try not to drive Nicos too mad."

Eliana stuck her tongue out. "I make no promises."

As they wrapped up their goodbyes to Eliana and Nicos, Astrea's heart grew heavier. Leaving Eliana and Nicos behind, while the logical choice, felt wrong. They didn't always get to see each other every day back home, but this felt different. They'd fled the country together, and now they were splitting up. But it was temporary—just a few days—and Eliana had work of her own to continue.

A black car with dark tinted windows idled on the drive. It had three doors: one for the driver, two for the back rows. Kostas was already climbing into the vehicle's back row.

"It will take about an hour to get to the fort," Marko said. He inclined his head, a silent request for Astrea and Cressida to join the professor. They both got in, claiming the middle row for themselves. Marko joined Kostas in back.

"I must say," Kostas started as the driver—one of Lucian's many guards—pulled away from the house, "expeditions such as this have always been . . . more for my own curiosity. This one feels important."

"It is," Astrea said. The professor had been so upset when his research was lost, but now, his emotions were high, giddy, bright in the darkness of the car. She supposed that was better than dealing with a sulking professor for the next few days.

"It will not be fun, Professor," Marko drawled. "This is strictly business. In and out. We stay no longer than we need to."

"I know, I know." Kostas huffed. "You have already told me that, Marko."

Astrea tried to hide her smile as Marko stifled a groan. "Let's just sit quietly for the next while," he suggested. "Get some rest while you can. It's never easy sleeping on an airship."

Astrea settled into her seat next to Cressida, watching out the window as the palace's guest house faded from view. Strictly business. It was time to complete the mission.

Fort Gambit was little more than a shadowy, towering thing in the growing darkness. Two tall gas lamps flickered outside the main gate, but Astrea couldn't make out anything more than a few feet outside the car.

As the driver spoke to a guard on duty, the tall, iron-studded gates swung open, and the car rolled inside.

Despite Marko's suggestion for quiet on the ride to the airfield, Kostas had been anything but. He'd talked about his past travels, detailing trips from Zaikud to Tornama and the northern reaches of Novaria. Now, though, even he was quiet as he marveled out the window.

Astrea had never been to a military base before. Inside the gate was a paved road curving through the dim expanse. Flames danced in more tall gas lamps lining the road. She could barely make out a series of buildings to her left, and far beyond was a small airfield. Several airships sat dark and quiet, but one in particular had all kinds of activity around it. Astrea shifted on the uncomfortable bench seat. That had to be Zephyrine's ship.

The car had barely stopped when Marko opened his door. Astrea had kept her magic pulled tightly to herself on the drive, unwilling to both listen to the professor and feel his range of emotions for that entire time. Now she spread her magic out, and the world came alive around her. Cressida's wavering anxiety, bright orange and rough. Kostas's golden joy. Marko's steady wall.

"Let's hurry," Marko said as he opened Astrea's door. "It looks like everyone's already waiting for us."

Astrea climbed out of the car. The gray airship looming before them was actually no bigger than the one they'd flown up in from Helosia. The lights in the main cabin illuminated the row of windows. Inside, several people moved around, and a tall, backlit form emerged from the open door. A mix of marigold excitement and mint relief blossomed against the dark night.

"Hey!" Adi called as he got to the bottom of the stairs. "You made it!"

"Expecting something else?" Cressida asked.

"Nah." Adi brushed past both Cressida and Astrea and headed for the trunk, where Marko was unloading their bags. "Let's get going. Gotta introduce you to the team and get Civan and Lennor out of here."

"Civan and Lennor?" Cressida asked.

"The twins," Adi said, as if that explained everything in the world. Astrea knew Jin and Adi operated as a team of four under their normal circumstances. Those had to be their other two teammates.

Astrea followed the others into the bright airship. Windows lined one side of the main cabin while several doors lined the other. A narrow metal staircase in the far back corner led to the second floor. A glass wall separated the pilot's area at the front of the ship. A long, wide table took up the middle of the cabin, and along the wall with the windows was a sleek row of padded benches. It was . . . utilitarian.

Near the pilot's area was a shorter, dark-haired man Astrea had never seen before. He chatted with Jin, whose back was to the main cabin door. But as soon as the group's footsteps started echoing through the ship, Jin turned. As soon as he saw Astrea, he smiled, and his shoulders loosened.

"Zephyrine!" Jin shouted. "Civan, Lennor! Come out here."

One of the doors on the far wall creaked open, revealing a short woman around Astrea's age. Her warm tan skin nearly glowed in the cabin's light, and her dark brown hair was tied into two braids. A lithe man strode out behind her, identical in looks right down to their small, pale blue eyes and flat noses. Then, a tall woman clambered down the stairs, her all-black outfit reminiscent of the ones Jin and Adi wore. Her white hair was a stunning contrast to both her cool brown skin and her clothes. Lucian followed her downstairs.

"Introductions before we begin," Jin said, "but let's make them quick. We need to get going. General Zephyrine Kanakos."

Astrea remembered Zephyrine Kanakos from Solstice Night. She'd only caught a glimpse of the woman then, but her gray eyes and stark white hair were just as striking now. Despite her hair, the retired general couldn't have been more than fifteen years older than Jin. That put her close to Saros's age.

"And Civan and Lennor Rusas," he said, nodding to the other two strangers. The twins were built more like dancers than soldiers, their bodies lean. Civan wasn't much taller than his sister. Then Jin motioned to the pale, dark-haired man still loitering near the pilot's area. "And that is Damian, our pilot."

Jin went down the line next, introducing Marko, Kostas, Astrea, and Cressida. While Damian, Civan, and Zephyrine were hard to read like Jin, Lennor was completely open. Green curiosity sparkled around her, and her smile widened when Jin introduced Cressida.

"If there are no more introductions," Lucian said, "I believe it would be best if Civan and Lennor were to head to the palace. We should take off soon if we want to stick to our schedule."

Something shifted around Lennor and Adi, a sheen of orange anxiety vibrating around the two of them. They'd already been separated for weeks; that had to be hard enough without splitting up again immediately after reuniting. But Jin wanted his team to guard Eliana, and it made Astrea feel better knowing people Jin trusted with his life would be there to protect her best friend.

"Of course," Jin said.

"The rest of you can go ahead and get settled upstairs," Zephyrine said. "We'll take off as soon as Jin's ready."

As the twins scooped up their bags and headed for the door, Lennor peered over her shoulder. Her gaze lingered on Cressida for one heartbeat, two, and then she headed into the night.

"Know her?" Astrea asked, glancing over to find Cressida smiling.

"No," she said, "but I sure wish I did."

"Come on." Astrea looped her arm through Cressida's. "There'll be plenty of time to chat with her when we get back."

"I'm holding you to it," Cressida murmured as they headed for the stairs. "You and Ellie can't be the only two getting action around here."

Astrea's entire face heated as she got to the top of the stairs and turned right. The second level was just like their original airship, too. She headed two doors down to an open one and found Jin's luggage inside. Despite Zephyrine's presence—and Lucian's ever-watchful eye—Astrea assumed they'd be sharing. She hoped Jin would still be open to that.

"How about you go to your own room and mind your business?" Astrea quipped. "Or you might hear some things you don't want to."

Cressida laughed, her amusement bright and clear against the dark metal walls. "Hard pass. I'll be in here"—she pointed to the room across from Astrea's—"if you need me."

Astrea closed the door behind her, then dropped down onto the bed. The mattress was hard, at least compared to what she'd gotten used to in Talmaris. It was just for a few days, but she was going to miss that bed. *Listen to me*, she thought. *I've become spoiled.* She let out a harsh breath. Despite her joke to Cressida, Astrea was not in the mood for anything other than a good night's sleep. She was going to need it if they were finally going to do this.

CHAPTER 32

Takeoff had been quiet, far smoother than the day they fled Kalama. Instead of flying into storm clouds, their airship passed through the easy, star-filled sky.

It had been nearly an hour since takeoff, and Astrea had just been sitting in her room, staring at the strange language in Mattina's journal and trying to breathe as her mind revisited everything she still had to do. *Progress*, she reminded herself. Everything was progress.

The door squeaked open, and Jin poked his head inside. "Az?" He pushed farther into the room, extra luggage in tow.

"Oh, sorry." Astrea scrambled up to take one of the bags from him, but he waved her off. She'd become so fixated on the book again that she'd forgotten about her luggage.

"That's alright." Jin set their bags down, then smiled at her. "Lucian and Kostas have already gone to bed for the night."

"Good." No overly talkative professor and no cranky commander to deal with.

"Want to come downstairs? Zephyrine's got some news to share. I thought you'd prefer to hear it from her firsthand."

Astrea forced herself not to sprint down to the main cabin. Instead, she took her time descending the narrow metal stairs. Instead of the pilot's dark hair, it was a blond who now controlled the ship. Marko?

Astrea shook her head as she followed Jin to where Cressida, Adi, and Zephyrine were seated.

It was unfortunate the airship was so utilitarian; she missed the soft sofas of the ship they'd flown up in. Instead, Jin sprawled out on one of the benches set under the windows. When Astrea sat next to him, he draped his arm around her shoulders. With no Lucian, Jin certainly wasn't being shy. Astrea leaned into his side.

"So," Zephyrine said, "first things first. Apelo and his family are at their estate in the north, and Noemi is settled just north of Kalama. The Nikaphoroses are alright, and so is Saros."

"Oh, thank fuck," Cressida whispered as minty relief exploded over Astrea's tongue.

Astrea's breath hitched. Safe. They were safe. Her family was safe. Hot tears pricked her eyes. That was good. That was the best news Astrea could hope for, really. Yes, Grand Duchess Ysabel's people had said the same, but hearing it from a Kalamian Jin trusted meant even more.

"The emperor doesn't suspect Saros?" Astrea asked. She assumed Zephyrine knew about her magic by now, so she said, "He isn't mad that my uncle and I lied for years?"

Zephyrine raised an eyebrow. "He's attending council meetings, and I saw him going to the observatory, so either the emperor is unaware or simply doesn't care. As long as your families all keep their heads down, suspicions around them have blown over."

"What makes you say that?" Adi asked.

"Aelius was looking into your families, of course, but I think he realized it was a dead end. He's shifted his attention fully to the Badlands, though he sent a team to Sezia a few days after you fled."

"I don't like that he's fixated on the Badlands," Jin said. Astrea didn't like it, either, even if it wasn't a surprise. "For his excursion, right? I assume it's for more meteorite."

Sighing, Zephyrine settled back against the hard bench and crossed her arms. "Aelius is not giving the council much information about the excursion or expenses. Much of the military is getting antsy now that your father has paused their paychecks to chase this . . . space rock he's so interested in."

"He's already got the meteorite in Kalama, though." Adi glanced at Cressida. "Weren't you working with it?"

Cressida shrugged. "I was, but he must think there's something more out there."

"Your father has mobilized some of the military in the city as well," Zephyrine continued. "He's trying to keep the order, but rumors are spreading that Eliana fled the country. Civilians are worried about her; there's a lot of support there."

"But does that translate to an actual rebellion?" Jin asked. "Are the numbers there?"

"That remains to be seen, but people are working on it. I don't think it will take long for the military to turn if they go without pay for more than a few months. At least half the council is against this move. That's good for your sister."

Good for Eliana. Bad for everyone else. It was reassuring, at least, that Eliana had quite a bit of support back home, both in the government and outside of it.

"Does he know we're in Talmaris?" Jin asked. "Not hearing from him at all has me—"

"Honestly, Jin, I'm not sure," Zephyrine said. "He's spinning the story about the fight at the palace and airfield, part of his attempt to quell the rumors about your sister."

"Spinning it how?"

"He's been trying to convince the council that he sent you and Eliana away due to threats made against your lives, though he won't tell them where. As for the airfield, he said it was a rogue attack by the Delians, an attempt to further their war efforts."

"And they believe him?" Jin asked.

"As I said, the council and people are split on other issues. This isn't any different."

"I still don't trust that he hasn't reached out to us in some way," Jin muttered.

Zephyrine's lips pressed into a thin line. "Nor do I. I'd assume he at least knows you're here, though I can't even hazard a guess as to why he's left you alone. Let's just make the most of the time we have before he comes knocking."

"How'd you get out of Kalama, anyway?" Adi asked.

"It wasn't easy," Zephyrine said. "I told them I was going to look for Anjou's ship, though if they realize I made a stop to get Lennor and Civan, the council and emperor will obviously know that's not what I'm doing."

"Is his ship actually missing?" Adi asked.

"My husband is a shipping magnate," Zephyrine said to Cressida and Astrea.

Cressida sat up straighter. "Wait, Anjou . . . as in Anjou Lazzaro? *The* shipping magnate?"

"Yes."

"My father does a lot of business with him," Cressida said. "I'm sorry, I didn't realize you were married."

"It's a recent marriage," Zephyrine said simply. Astrea glanced at the general's ring fingers; both were empty. "Anjou does a lot of business with everyone. And yes, his ship is missing. Nobody's heard from him since a few days after you all fled Helosia."

"That's awful," Cressida said.

But as Astrea watched Zephyrine, no sadness bloomed around her. Though the general was hard to read, Astrea didn't miss the faint sheen of green curiosity surrounding her now. Did the general not like her own husband? Some couples in Kalama, especially the wealthier ones, simply got together for convenience or other benefits.

"While I don't love that he's missing," Zephyrine said, "he can take care of himself. It might even be for the best that he's out of the country considering what's going on."

When Jin said, "Hopefully he turns up soon," Zephyrine simply nodded.

"Did my uncle mention anything else?" Astrea asked. It was probably pointless to ask, but still, she added, "Anything about visions he's had?"

"No, he did not." Zephyrine sighed. "He didn't know the truth of where I was going, either. I thought that was for the best. We only interacted in council meetings."

"Whatever my father's found in the Badlands must be important if he's willing to push the rebels and the council so far, and if it's possibly even driving him to ignore me and Ellie," Jin said. "I just wish I knew what it was."

A throat cleared behind them. "Apologies, Your Imperial Highness," Kostas said. He took a few tentative steps toward them. "I was coming downstairs in search of something to drink, and I overheard you mention the Badlands?"

Jin's arm, still draped around Astrea's shoulders, tightened. "Yes, we were just catching up on some news from home."

"Ah. I've always wanted to visit the Badlands. Helosia has quite the array of natural wonders . . . so many places I'd love to visit, really."

"The kitchen's right this way, Mister Shalysko," Zephyrine said as she stood. "I'd be happy to show you."

Zephyrine shepherded the professor toward a door on the right side of the cabin. Only when the door shut behind them did Adi speak.

"The Badlands, huh?" he asked. "Do you think it's another meteorite?"

"I don't think there's any good way for us to find out right now," Jin said. "Let's just focus on the question we can try to solve, alright? Focus on the Paragon. Once we know more about them and void magic, we can figure out how it links back to my father."

Focus on the Paragon. Astrea could do that. Zephyrine said Saros was safe, that Sarsali and Balthazar were safe. For now, anyway. And they were so much closer to finding an answer about the Paragon. If she could just learn something at the ruins, maybe she'd finally be able to figure out how to save her family and Helosia.

Strong, warm arms pulled Astrea backward just as she startled awake. The ship pitched to the right, then leveled out again.

"Turbulence," Jin rasped. "Just turbulence. Go back to sleep."

Astrea shuddered, then rolled over and pressed her face to Jin's chest. Going back to sleep was the last thing she wanted to do. She hadn't slept well, plagued by dreams of Helosia on fire or the airship crashing. They weren't her usual nightmares, and Nazarov hadn't shown up either, but they weren't pleasant.

"What time is it?" she whispered.

"Early. Maybe six." He pulled her closer.

"Did you sleep?"

"Hardly."

"When will we get there?"

"A couple hours probably." Jin settled against the pillows with a heavy sigh. "Go back to sleep."

"Can't." Astrea tried to blink away the last remnants of sleep. The thin, hard airship mattress was definitely not made for comfortable travel. "Gonna get up."

Jin groaned and tightened his hold on her. "I woke up early every day for eight years . . . can't we just stay here for a while?"

"Once my mind is awake, it's awake."

"I love your mind," he whispered, "but it also wakes up far too early." He pressed a kiss to the side of her mouth. "I'll be down in an hour."

Astrea forced herself out of bed. She scrubbed at her face, then stumbled to the claustrophobic attached bathroom. After washing up, Astrea found a clean set of clothes despite the darkness. She almost summoned her light, but Jin seemed to be asleep, and she didn't want to wake him.

Once dressed, Astrea slipped into the hallway and closed the door behind her. Even the corridor was dark, so Astrea summoned a pinprick of light above her hand—just enough that she could see where she was going.

The entire ship seemed to be asleep save for two presences downstairs. One seemed bored, but the other was like Jin, nothing more than a heavy wall that she could sense. Astrea tried to keep her steps down the metallic stairs quiet but was sure she failed. She let her light fade away to nothing but a sprinkle of stardust when she reached the main cabin.

"Ah, Astrea," came Zephyrine's airy voice from the door near the kitchen. "You're up early."

Damian was flying again. Outside the windows, only darkness and the occasional star were visible. A hint of sun had started to creep up behind what looked like the outlines of mountains.

"Good morning, General . . . Lady . . ."

"Just Zephyrine." She smiled and held the kitchen door open. "Coffee?"

Astrea followed Zephyrine into the narrow galley kitchen. A white ceramic coffee pot sat on one of the otherwise empty counters. A pour-over brewer was tucked into the small sink in the far corner of the kitchen. Zephyrine poured a mug of coffee for Astrea, then slid over a basket of sugar cubes.

"No cream," Zephyrine said, "but you don't need it. I brought the good stuff."

Skies, it smelled heavenly. Novarian coffee was fine, but the bold, smooth Kalamian coffee was, in Astrea's opinion, far better. And Zephyrine delivered on the promise; it was delicious.

"Thank you," Astrea said. "Jin should be down soon."

Zephyrine nodded, then headed for the kitchen door. "Come, I have something for you. Now's as good a time as any."

Sucking in a deep breath, Astrea grabbed her coffee and followed the general. What could Zephyrine possibly have to give her? It obviously wasn't anything from Saros, nor from the Nikaphoroses.

Zephyrine circled the large table in the middle of the cabin so that her back was to the windows. Several maps were spread out there, and two stacks of black fabric sat at one end of the table.

Motioning to the one on Astrea's right, Zephyrine smiled. "That's for you."

"What is it?" Astrea set her mug down and reached for the bundle of cloth. Thick cotton was on the bottom—pants? A shirt?—but the top item was leather. Realization washed over Astrea as she lifted it.

"You can thank Jin for this," Zephyrine said. "He asked me to get sets for you, Cressida, Eliana, and her guard before I left the city. The twins took the other two sets with them."

Gear. Gear like what Jin and Adi had worn that night in Sezia. She hadn't seen them in it since then. Astrea fingered the heavy leather. An array of buckles, straps, and laces covered it.

"If Eliana's truly set on overthrowing her father, we're going to war," Zephyrine said when Astrea still remained quiet. "I'm sure that's not what you want to hear, but it's the truth. I can't foresee a future in which Emperor Aelius and Prince Kaius abdicate peacefully."

Astrea knew they were going to war eventually; she just didn't see how she'd be able to help. She wasn't keen on using Lucian's little Lightbringer trick. She *could* serve as a healer, though. And she would. Ironic, considering what Saros had put her through to avoid that very fate.

Setting the armor back on top of her stack, Astrea nodded. "Thank you for getting it. I'm sure it wasn't easy to do on short notice."

"No trouble for a friend of Jin's."

"You two seem close," Astrea said. In all the letters of Jin's she'd read, Astrea had come to the conclusion that without Zephyrine Kanakos as his commanding officer, Jin probably wouldn't have survived the last eight years. She'd helped guide him through battle, loss, and near-death.

"Don't tell him I told you this," Zephyrine said, her voice lowering, "but I've always had a soft spot for him. Reminds me of my younger brother."

"You have a brother?" Astrea asked.

"I did."

"I'm sorry."

"Don't be. Can't change the past, and it was many years ago." Zephyrine's wall let nothing through. "Though I'm glad to see Jin is trying to correct his mistakes."

Did Zephyrine know about that? *All* of that?

"Oh, well—" Astrea started, but Zephyrine's light chuckle cut her off.

"I tried several times over the years to talk some sense into him. Seems he finally took my advice. Good, too, seeing how I'm usually right and all." She winked, and Astrea actually smiled.

"Thanks for the coffee." Astrea didn't know what else to say, and she certainly didn't want to dive into all that history with Zephyrine. As the general had said, the past was the past, and Astrea and Jin had agreed to move forward together. *Partners.* Astrea tucked the bundles of cloth and leather under one arm, then picked up her mug. "I should take this upstairs."

"More coffee will be here when you want it," Zephyrine said. "We should get to the landing site in, oh, maybe two hours. Do me a favor and make sure Adi's awake? I'll check in with Commander Lucian."

"Sure."

Astrea hurried back upstairs, not bothering to be quiet as she headed for both Adi and Cressida's doors. Neither seemed keen on waking up, but with promises of coffee, both agreed to be downstairs within the hour. After dropping Cressida's gear off at the end of her bed, Astrea slipped back into her and Jin's room only to find him standing and stretching.

"Zephyrine wants us down there soon," she said. "Couldn't sleep?"

"No." He eyed the bundle in the crook of her arm. "Zephyrine gave you the gear?"

"And coffee," Astrea said. He lifted the mug from her hand and brought it to his mouth, taking a quick sip. She dropped the gear onto the bed and glared at him. "Hey! That's mine."

"Is there such a thing as yours and mine?" He hummed, then took another sip. "Or is it just ours now?"

"When it comes to coffee, get your own."

Jin laughed, the sound low and warm, as he passed the mug back to her. "I suppose that's fair."

Astrea rounded the side of the bed and flicked on one of the sconces mounted next to it. Then she set her coffee down on the narrow metal table set up in the corner.

Jin straightened the blankets on the bed, then looked down at the gear. The buckles shone faintly in the lamplight. "I'd like you to wear that for the next few days," he said.

"Oh, come on. I know I can't wear a dress, but this?" She grabbed the chest piece and shook it once, the buckles clinking.

"It's just temporary." When she sighed, Jin added, "Please?"

Astrea sighed again. She'd trusted him about everything else up to that point. If he thought she needed to wear it, she'd wear it. "I need help putting it on."

He smirked. "I thought you might."

As Jin moved around their narrow room and bathroom, Astrea changed into the thick black pants and shirt first, then pulled her boots on. It was almost like any other morning when they got dressed for training. In a few minutes, Jin was dressed the same as her.

"Alright," Astrea said as she finished securing her braid with a blue ribbon. "How do I put the rest on?"

Jin loosened a few buckles and strings. "Arms up."

She lifted her arms, adjusting her posture as Jin guided the chest piece over her head. Once it was on, he fiddled with the buckles and strings again, and the armor tightened around her torso. It wasn't as uncomfortable as she'd expected, though the weight of it was unfamiliar. Then Jin strapped a belt around her waist and attached a dagger enclosed in a sheath.

"Oh, now *this* is just ridiculous," she mumbled.

"Get used to it," he said as he stood back and examined her. "We're going to war. This is the new normal."

"We're going to ruins in search of information," she corrected. "Today isn't a war. And I don't even know how to use this thing."

"Today may not be, but it's just a matter of time until we're back in Helosia. And we'll teach you to use it when we get back to Talmaris."

"Do you think it'll actually be a war?" Astrea asked. "Full-blown, like what Prince Veiko warned against?"

"Hard to say, honestly. I certainly hope not, and Zephyrine will help us narrow our focus even more than I can. I'd really rather not wage war on our own people if we can help it."

Astrea nodded.

"The good news," Jin said as he closed the space between them and wrapped his arms around her waist, "is that you look very cute."

"Just ridiculous," she said again before Jin kissed her. She drank in that familiar warmth gliding over her skin. "Am I officially set for the mission, Captain?"

A wry smile pulled at his mouth. "Captain? You haven't called me that in weeks."

"I'm just teasing."

"I think I might actually like it."

Astrea rolled her eyes. "Oh, here we go."

"Pack whatever else you need in your knapsack, and leave room for a sleeping bag. Then come on downstairs. I'm going to check in with Zephyrine." Jin kissed her once, twice more, before smiling. "And get my own coffee, I suppose."

"Good." Astrea circled the bed, picking up her mug and taking a sip. "See you downstairs."

As Jin left their room, Astrea grabbed her knapsack, checking that both the mythology book and Mattina's notebook were tucked safely inside. They were. She had everything she needed, so Astrea headed for the hallway, ready to join her team.

CHAPTER 33

Though Astrea imagined many things for their visit to the ruins, she never would have thought a Helosian army general would be instructing her to jump out of an airship and onto the side of a mountain.

"It's simple," Zephyrine said as the group stood in a loose circle near the airship's door. "I'll go first. Marko will follow. Then you'll all jump out one by one, and our air will ensure you make a safe landing. Damian will take the ship to a safe landing site, then be back to pick us up in two days."

Zephyrine Kanakos may have been a powerful Tempest, and Jin may have trusted her with his life, but Astrea did not like the sound of this. On her right side, pale orange anxiety wavered around Cressida's body, and Kostas's aura was a mirror image. Everyone else, however, seemed comfortable with the idea.

"Stand back while I open the door," Zephyrine instructed. Once everyone but Marko had moved toward the opposite side of the cabin, Zephyrine spun the wheel that sealed the door. Locks tumbled free, then she opened it. Cold air blasted into the cabin as Zephyrine smiled over her shoulder. "See you out there."

And then she jumped.

Marko followed.

Astrea's entire body tensed. She couldn't see where they went from her angle, but she was sure they must've made it safely to the ground because Lucian strode toward the door.

"Professor, would you like to go first?" he asked.

"Well." With a shaky hand, Kostas adjusted the straps of his knapsack. "Alright."

"First you make us wear armor," Cressida said to Jin, "and now you want us to jump out of an airship. Unbelievable."

"Oh, come on, Cress," he said with a laugh. "Adi and I have done this dozens of times. It's perfectly safe."

"Safe," she echoed. "Right. Safe. You must be out of your skies damned mind, Auris."

As Kostas, then Lucian, disappeared into the clear blue morning, Astrea swallowed hard. Jumping out of an airship. She could do that, right? She'd gotten on the back of Jin's motorcycle. She'd punched someone in Talmaris. She'd learned new things about her magic. How hard could this be?

"I'll go first if it makes you feel better," Jin said.

Astrea and Cressida both followed Jin to the door. The airship barely drifted along the edge of the mountain as Damian, the pilot, held their position. Below, both Marko and Zephyrine were waiting, hands outstretched. Kostas and Lucian had moved away from the mountain's edge and stood safely behind the Tempests. Jin flashed a quick smile over his shoulder, then jumped. Invisible air caught him, controlled by the two Tempests to guide and slow his fall. He landed with the grace of a cat, like it was the easiest thing in the world.

"You next, Sovna," Cressida said. "Then you can heal me if I break my nose."

"Gee, thanks."

"You'll be alright," Adi said. "Zephyrine and Marko won't let you fall."

If the two Tempests failed, it was a long, long way down the side of the mountain to the valley below.

She shoved down the last of her reservations, checked that her knapsack was secure on her back, then jumped into the early morning light. Wind slapped at her face. Her braid whipped around behind her. She couldn't breathe. She was falling too fast.

But then she slowed, that invisible magic guiding her forward and onto the solid ground below. She stumbled as she landed. Strong arms grabbed for her, and Jin hauled her several feet away from the edge.

"See?" he asked. "Not so bad."

Astrea smoothed back her braid, then adjusted the heavy pack on her back. "I'm deducting all points from the times you were right before this," she said. It may not have been the worst thing, but Astrea didn't want to jump out of an airship again anytime in the near future.

"I don't think you're allowed to do that."

"Too bad," she muttered, earning her a bemused grin.

Astrea turned just in time to see Cressida jump from the ship. She yelped as the Tempests' air caught her, then let out a string of nasty curses as she landed. Astrea and Jin both tugged her away from the edge just as Adi leaped out of the ship. Like Jin, he landed with practiced ease before strolling to the group.

"And we're all in one piece!" Adi declared, arms stretched out to either side of himself as if to show he was indeed unharmed. High up in the air, the open door was pulled closed by Damian, and then the ship started off to the northwest. "Shall we get started, Professor?"

Kostas's determination pushed against Astrea's senses, warm and strong. "Indeed, let us go. This way, this way. It's not too far of a walk from here."

Astrea settled her knapsack on her shoulders again, then followed the professor south toward a dense thicket. On the other side would be the ruins.

Western Novaria was beautiful. All around them, pines and evergreens stood proud and tall, and colorful rhododendrons dotted the otherwise green and brown forest. While up in the ship, Astrea had been able to see the stretch of the northern Macadian Mountains far into the distance and all the tiny, glittering lakes. She couldn't see the water now, but through the breaks in the trees, she could still make out the mountains that surrounded them. There wasn't a single cloud in the pale morning sky.

Despite the weight of the leather chest piece Jin had insisted she wear, Astrea was actually glad to have it on. The mountain air was far cooler than even Talmaris's weather, and she was sure that without the extra layer, she'd be even colder than she already was.

Marigold excitement and red determination spiked high around the professor. As the trees began thinning, he called, "Not much farther!"

"Adi," Jin said as Kostas started forward on his own, "you and Marko take the west side. I'll take the east. Lucian and Zephyrine, take the south."

"South it is," the general replied as she started after the professor.

"And you two," Jin said to Cressida and Astrea, "be mindful, please. Make sure the professor doesn't wander too far in his"—Kostas let out a joyful yelp—"enthusiasm."

The closer they got to the edge of the forest, the windier it became. A gust tugged at the strands of hair Astrea hadn't been able to capture in her braid, but nothing could distract her from the ruins rising up before her.

They weren't like anything Astrea had seen before. Even in pictures and textbooks, she hadn't seen something so ancient. Crumbling archways and columns marked what Astrea assumed was once a building. Wide, shallow stairs led to more stone flooring on the ground, ferns and a few weeds growing through the cracks. Beyond that was more of the same: half-standing walls, collapsed roofs, fallen columns, pedestals with the remnants of what had to be statues. All the gray stone was wind-battered and fading.

As she walked toward the shallow stairs, Astrea turned in a circle. Cressida was just a few paces ahead of her. To the east was clear, providing a panoramic view of the mountains. To the south, west, and north were more of those towering pines and evergreens, some of which had started encroaching on the ruins themselves.

One thing was for sure. Astrea sensed nothing other than their group. There were no voids. No other people. They were alone.

"Excellent!" Kostas sucked in a deep breath, then surveyed the area behind him. "Nothing like the mountains. It's as beautiful as I remember."

Over the next few minutes, the rest of the group began returning to the center of the ruins. It wasn't long before they were all gathered in a loose circle around where Kostas had started spreading out other objects he'd pulled from his knapsack: a collapsible shovel, what looked almost like a sextant, a magnifying glass, and delicate brushes and blades.

"So," Jin said, "where do we begin, Professor?"

Kostas held up his toolkit and grinned, his electric excitement pulsing marigold in the air. "I'm so glad you asked, Your Imperial Highness. Let's get started."

For the first couple hours that morning, they helped the professor lay out a low line of rope to form a grid, which he then copied onto some hand-drawn map he'd pulled out of his pack. It was a part of the site he hadn't examined thoroughly yet, he'd explained, complete with additional diagrams and a map of the ruins in one of his various notebooks. Kostas was more organized than Astrea had anticipated.

When Cressida had asked if it was necessary to create such a system for just a couple days' worth of research, Kostas had said, "True scholars treat sites with respect and order. Only scoundrels and thieves approach this without some kind of system."

Astrea really didn't care about Kostas's sense of right and wrong when it came to old void mage ruins, nor did she care about the few artifacts Cressida and Adi had found with their magic. Anonymous bronze statuettes, old arrowheads, and remnants of beads didn't tell them anything about the Paragon's motives. What she cared about was the void language and what it might mean.

"Professor," Astrea said, glancing over at where Kostas had spread out his maps and diagrams on the wide, flat remains of a column, "can you show me the void language? I know we need to look at the entire site, but I'd really like to compare it to my sample."

"Ah, yes!" Kostas straightened and adjusted the sleeves of his tan jacket. "Prince Varojin! Could you please come here?"

As Jin wandered over, Astrea looked to where Marko strode back and forth near the edge of the forest. He, Lucian, and Zephyrine had spent the last couple hours splitting their time between patrolling the outskirts of the site and assisting with the research preparations when they could. Astrea kept her senses open, trying to monitor for the void as she followed Kostas's directions.

"Now that we're settled, we can split up," Kostas said. "While Adi and Cressida work here, we can go look at this language. It's in one of the buildings to the south."

They circled through the ruins as Kostas showed them the open space near the middle of the first 'building.' Farther south was a more intact structure. Crumbling statues stood near what could've been an entrance to something, and the remains of an old well rose up to Astrea's right. She couldn't be sure, but one section even seemed like it may have been the remains of a tower. Nature had reclaimed whatever humans had once built there.

"Based on the short time I've spent here," Kostas said as they continued on, "I believe this was a temple at some point." He motioned for them to rejoin him near the foot of the ruins.

"I thought you said these were from the Great Wars," Astrea said as she gazed up at a crumbling archway. "These look older."

The more time Astrea had to inspect the stones, the more obvious it became that though they'd once been closer to white, weather and mildew had grayed them over the centuries. A few ferns had even managed to grow through some of the cracks.

"Perhaps they are," Kostas said. "There were many magnificent civilizations before the Great Wars. And so much knowledge we lost thanks to that destruction."

"That book said an army roamed the mountains," Astrea said as she followed Kostas through what might've been a doorway centuries earlier. The breeze gusted, pulling at the extra fabric of her shirt that stuck out from the sides of her armor. "Could this be where they had a fort rather than a temple?"

"Perhaps it was a fort *and* a temple. In its current state, it is impossible to know."

They passed several broken pillars, the pieces scattered on the ground near a set of shallow stairs. They moved deeper into another building, or what was left of it. Sections of the roof were missing, as were parts of the walls. Sunlight barely filtered in, wind whistling as it forced its way through the many cracks and crevices of the ruins.

"Ah, it's right where I remembered it to be." Kostas stopped in front of a damaged bust. It was nearly taller than Astrea and placed up on a low pedestal. "I'm glad to see it's undisturbed."

"Who is it?" Jin asked.

Something about its face seemed familiar. The square jaw, the long hair. The crown. Its nose was broken off, but still . . . Where had Astrea seen that face before?

"An ancient king, I believe," Kostas said.

"Like the king from that story Astrea found?" Jin asked. "Or maybe the leader of the void mage army the history books talked about?"

"I can't say for sure," Kostas said. "I did not spend as much time in this section as I wanted to during my last visit. We were only able to stay for a couple weeks before we had to return to the university."

Summoning faint light over one palm, Astrea leaned closer to the statue. She ran her fingers over the ancient rock, the stone so smooth and carefully carved. There, on the statue's thick base, were letters nearly worn away by time and the elements. In fact, Astrea couldn't see them unless she angled her light just right.

"Tytas Ramkas," she read aloud. His name was spelled out in not just the continental alphabet but also in those strange, looping letters of the void language. Astrea looked up at the statue's face again. *The bust Raela purchased for the Great Library*. That was where she had seen it. The bust the government had agreed to purchase despite cutting funding to the library. Raela had said it was from the northeastern part of the continent, though. "I've seen this before," she said, turning toward Kostas and Jin.

Lavender surprise flickered around the professor for just a moment. "I thought you'd never been here."

"I haven't." She looked at Jin. "Did Raela ever show you what she purchased for the library?"

"No," he said. "Why?"

"It was a bust exactly like this, only smaller," Astrea said, and Jin frowned. "Raela didn't know who it was, just that it was from the north-eastern part of the empire. I think Theo convinced her to buy it."

Kostas huffed. "Curious."

"Does anyone else know about this place?" Astrea asked.

"I'm sure someone does," the professor replied. "My students have been here, of course. As far as Helosians or anyone else who would know about it, I can't be sure."

"Raela and I thought it was some long-forgotten king," Astrea murmured.

So was there some kind of . . . void kingdom here? An ancient Paragon-controlled territory? Had people worshipped this man, Tytas Ramkas? Celebrated him?

"Why would Theo sell a Paragon-linked statue to your father's government?" Astrea asked Jin.

"Some kind of test?" Jin frowned. "You said it was unmarked, right? Maybe he wanted to see how much my father already knew about the Paragon or if it would make him start sniffing around."

Kostas hummed. "Antiquities such as this often fetch a high price . . . although I do not believe they should be sold off like that. Could this Theo have had some financial incentive?"

"Perhaps both," Jin said. "Test the government—if he realized my father was starting to learn about void magic—and gain extra funds."

Too many questions, but Astrea could bring this information back to Tomas. He might be able to find more about an old kingdom in this part of the continent or some ancient ruler with that name. Something to connect him back to the void and the flagless army.

"There is more, of course," the professor said, waving at a part of a wall just in front of him. It looked like there were indentations in it, but Astrea couldn't quite tell. "The language is all over these buildings."

As Kostas moved to one side of the room, Astrea stepped toward the wall behind the statue, Jin right by her side. Though the stone had been damaged by time and the elements, she could make out the pattern.

"Jin," she said. "The notebook, it's in my bag."

He moved behind her and opened her knapsack, then pulled out the notebook. He flipped it to a random page and held it up next to the wall. The swirls and loops were identical to the language in Mattina's notebook.

"This is amazing," Astrea said. "This is just . . . wow. I've never seen anything like this in my life."

"I don't understand how we're supposed to translate a language with no connection to another language we know," Jin said after a long moment. "How is this supposed to help us?"

"We'll find a solution, Your Imperial Highness," Kostas said. "We will find one."

CHAPTER 34

Each discovery Adi and Cressida made—golden bracelets, more arrow-heads with the void language inscribed on them, pieces of broken pottery—thrilled Kostas, though Astrea wasn't sure how it helped solve their Paragon problem. All these ruins proved was that there had, in fact, been a void group there a long time ago.

Astrea was beginning to think Kostas's theory about this being both some kind of fort and temple might've been correct. What remained of the architecture—wide columns at even spacing, the statues large and small—suggested a temple. If she tried, Astrea could even imagine some of the Kalamian government buildings that had been repurposed from temples from long, long ago. Is that what the Paragon—or whoever the ancient void mages had been—did here?

And Jin's earlier question circled her mind endlessly. How *would* they translate the void language without anything to compare it to? They'd need to find someone who spoke the language, though that person would likely be a member of the Paragon. They could find a linguist to try to build the language from scratch, but they'd still need *some* translation to use as the building blocks. And Tytas Ramkas's name in two languages—Novarian and void—was a start, but surely they'd need more. Besides, that process could take months. Or longer. They didn't have that kind of time.

368

Jin approached, a thermos in hand. Though the mountains weren't cold—it was still summer, after all—there was a particular chill in the air. He sat down next to her on the wide stairs, then opened the thermos and poured steaming coffee into the lid-turned-cup.

"Here," he said as he offered it to her.

Astrea sipped the coffee, inhaling the strong, earthy scent. It was just what she needed. "Could the answers be out east?" she asked as Cressida joined them and set a half-broken ceramic vase on the fern-covered stairs. A couple dozen feet away, Kostas pointed at a spot in the grid and said something to Adi. "This isn't getting us anywhere."

"At least we have proof they were here," Cressida said.

Astrea turned and stared at the ruins behind them. She'd spent the entire morning and better part of the early afternoon examining the worn indentations of the stone to no avail.

"Though part of me feels like this is just Kostas using us to replace what the Paragon destroyed in his office," Cressida continued as she lowered her voice. "Any other situation? This might be fun, digging around up here. But right now? I agree. It's a waste of time."

Was that what this was? Kostas's attempt at replacing what the Paragon stole from him without really trying to solve the mystery?

"I don't think he'd purposefully waste our time," Jin said slowly. "I think it's just going to be impossible to figure out the language without a cipher. We knew this was likely to happen."

After draining the last of the coffee from her cup, Astrea handed it back to Jin. He screwed it onto the thermos. "I guess I'll keep trying to figure something out," Astrea said.

"Good luck," Cressida said as Astrea scooped up her knapsack. Jin stood, too. "I'll let you know if I find anything relevant out here."

"And I'm going to check with Zephyrine," Jin said. "I'll come join you shortly, Az."

Astrea headed south again. As she picked her way through broken chunks of stone and the thick brush growing at the site, Marko waved at her. She waved back. Though she still didn't know much about Marko, he'd been right about the professor. Kostas had continued chatting about everything under the stars when he had the chance: Kalamian coffee, Astrea and Cressida's lives back home, stories from his travels. The more comfortable he got around them, the more he talked. And the more he talked, the more Astrea just wished he'd be quiet.

As Astrea entered the building, she looked again at the bust of Tytas Ramkas and shook her head. *I'll figure you out later.* She summoned her light, her body aching with the effort. Was Lucian's magic so sensitive after pushing his empathic senses out for hours on end?

She settled down on the hard ground to look at the words near the bottom of the wall. Though she could not read the void language, Astrea hoped there might be some kind of pattern she could find, or a letter from one of the other languages she could speak. Neither option would replace a cipher, but any additional information could be useful.

Astrea moved from left to right, top to bottom, throughout the room. She even examined the outside walls of the structure, but some of the flora and fauna of the area had grown too thick for her to get through on her own.

When the sun started sinking lower in the sky, Astrea finally went back inside. There would be no use, she was convinced, in continuing to search the walls for answers that simply weren't there. But where did that leave her?

"Astrea!" Kostas called. Electricity buzzed along her skin. "Come over here!"

Astrea moved through the collapsing building to its northern entrance. The professor's marigold excitement was unmissable against the graying stone. She skirted around a series of broken pieces of roof until, finally, she was near the eastern edge of the ruins.

"Did you find something?" Astrea asked.

"Indeed I did!" In front of Kostas was a pedestal, though whatever statue had rested on it was long gone. He stepped to one side, then motioned for her to look. "It's right here, on the back. Look at the inscription."

Astrea stooped to get a better look. There, in Helosian of all things, were just a few words. They were so small she almost couldn't read them. "Balance will be restored," she read aloud.

Balance. That was what Victor Nazarov had been shouting about back in Kalama during their fight in the garden. Something about the sun and the moon and the Paragon restoring balance. Astrea swallowed.

"I know it is not exactly a cipher for this peculiar language," Kostas said, "but it is something, is it not?"

"It is."

And it was. Confirmation of Nazarov's odd words, sure, but it also gave Astrea another idea. She headed back for the southernmost building, ignoring Kostas's calls.

Astrea hurried to Tytas's mostly intact statue. She circled it, focusing her light on the pedestal. There, etched on its back edge, were more words, so small and worn she almost couldn't make them out. In *all* the continental languages, too.

"The world must be reborn from chaos and destruction," she whispered as she read the Helosian, then Novarian, then Tornamian. The Zaikudi and Delian words were foreign to her, as were the void letters, but she was sure they said the same.

A shiver ran down Astrea's spine. Balance. Chaos. Destruction. Was that what the Paragon wanted? But why would they cover these walls in a language no one could read yet put these other languages on statues?

And what did any of that have to do with Astrea herself? Did they think she would help them in their mission? Or know someone who could, maybe thanks to her imperial connections?

"Did you find something?" Kostas asked from where he loitered near the northern entrance.

She reread the inscription out loud for him, then asked, "What does it mean?"

"Perhaps it is some ancient creed of this Paragon," he said.

"An ancient creed for an ancient void cult." She sighed. At least this information might help in their research back at the palace.

"Cult . . ." Kostas trailed off. "You think they're a cult?"

Astrea shrugged. "A secret language, organizing underground, strange symbols and tattoos. I don't know what else to call them."

"A cult implies worship."

"You thought this might be a temple, right?" Astrea offered as she traced the letters with her finger. "Whatever they are, this isn't good."

"In my study of civilizations and history, I've come to find that many groups believe their creed to be true, even when others may not support it," Kostas said, and Astrea raised an eyebrow. Didn't every group think that? "Perhaps these Paragon are simply trying to . . . survive."

"They destroyed your research and have been murdering people, Professor. Is that survival?"

"I cannot speak for them." Green curiosity wavered around him for half a heartbeat before disappearing. "I'm simply sharing what I've learned over the years. Try thinking their way. Try to understand why they may hold up these ideas. Just think about the Great Wars and all the chaos and destruction that time brought."

In her reading at the palace over the last couple weeks, Astrea had ignored a lot of details that had nothing to do with void magic. But some things still stuck out to her. The dozens of smaller countries that made up the continent back then. The various groups fighting for over a century as they tried to consolidate power for themselves.

The fact that void magic apparently disappeared sometime during or after those wars, not just from society but from the history books, too.

"I think they want revenge," Astrea whispered.

"Come again?" Kostas asked.

"Void magic is gone from the record of the wars, so obviously the void mages who lived here didn't win," Astrea said. "They want to restore balance to magic. And destruction . . . Maybe they want revenge after going into hiding for so long. Maybe they want to bring void magic back to the public stage."

Kostas smiled down at her. "An intriguing theory. Perhaps we can focus on that tomorrow, yes? I believe the general mentioned something about dinner being soon."

"I'll join you in a few moments," Astrea said as she pulled her notebook out. She wanted to copy down this new translation they had. "Go on without me."

As Kostas wandered off toward their camp, Astrea let out a harsh breath. Even if her theory proved true, what did any of that have to do with her? *The world must be reborn through chaos and destruction.*

She just hoped they could figure out the rest of the Paragon's plans before any of that came to pass.

Back home, after a long day, Astrea would normally take a shower, change into her favorite pajamas, eat her favorite dinner, and go to bed early. But that would not be the case after her long day at the ruins.

She stared at the ground where Jin had laid out two sleeping bags side by side. Around them, the others were doing the same. Cressida was less than pleased if her aura was anything to judge. Zephyrine and Adi seemed perfectly fine. Marko seemed indifferent, but Lucian, too, was not thrilled at the prospect of sleeping on the ground. Professor Shalysko was a different story entirely, marigold excitement clinging to him.

They'd already had dinner—what Zephyrine called dinner. Dried meat, cheese, and crackers. Astrea would've preferred one of Cressida's pasta dishes, but there would be no such thing, just as there would be no soft bed to curl up in. As they'd eaten, they'd discussed what they'd found, and everyone had agreed that the words inscribed on the statues had to be connected to the Paragon. Their search would begin again in the morning and conclude by mid-afternoon to give them time to get back to the palace before their dinner with the Novarian Grand Council.

Stars twinkled overhead, a brilliant band of purple, blue, and white cutting through the night sky. Astrea wandered a few dozen feet away from the camp to get a view unobstructed by the trees. She'd always been able to see the same band in Kalama, but it hadn't been so brilliant. So bright.

"It's beautiful, isn't it?" Jin asked, his voice soft as he joined her.

"It's not like this back home," she said.

"Every time I went on those hikes with Zephyrine, I saw it. And every time, I wished you were there so I could show you. I knew you'd like it."

Astrea breathed in. The stars practically called to her, energy vibrating just underneath her skin. "Saros always told me I was drawn to the stars because of this." She summoned her light, letting it dance around her fingers in a soft, gentle flow. "I don't know that I ever really believed him."

"And now?" Jin asked.

"It certainly feels different. Maybe it's just in my mind."

"Let's get that mind of yours to bed," Jin said. "Lucian and Zephyrine are taking first watch, then you and I will take over for them."

"Let me see if I understand this correctly," Astrea said as she dismissed her magic and followed him back toward camp. "First you make me wear this"—she tugged at her armor—"then you make me jump out of an airship, and now you're making me sleep on the ground?"

"It's just camping," he said, but delicate amusement tickled Astrea's nose.

"Camping's always better when we have chocolate," Adi said as Astrea dropped onto her sleeping bag. Jin's was between them, and Cressida was on Astrea's other side.

The campfire behind them flickered, and Jin waved his hand at it. The flames calmed, burning low and steady in the night.

"What?" Cressida asked as she buttoned herself into her sleeping bag. "What chocolate?"

Astrea tugged at her armor, and Jin had to help her take it off. She doubted she'd be able to sleep with it on.

"Ellie used to send him chocolate every couple of months," Adi said. "It became a bit of a tradition on our training expeditions for him to bring that chocolate. We've spent a lot of nights just like this."

"Except they're usually far colder," Jin said.

Though Astrea knew about the hikes Zephyrine made the team go on, thanks to Jin's letters, she hadn't realized chocolate was involved. "So not only have you made me jump out of airships and sleep on the ground, but you didn't even bring chocolate to compensate for it?" Astrea asked. "That doesn't seem right."

"Have you ever been camping?" Adi asked.

"Camping?" Cressida scoffed. "For me, camping is anything less than a luxurious hotel."

"Didn't peg you for the type," Adi said, a mix of peach amusement and green curiosity tangling around him.

"Yes, well, when your father is an engineering tycoon, you get accustomed to a certain lifestyle." Cressida burrowed into her sleeping bag and muttered, "And this is *not* that lifestyle."

"What about you, Az?" Adi asked. "Are you a fan of the great outdoors?"

"I like Cressida's mother's garden, but I don't think I'm a fan of this." Astrea motioned to the hard ground littered with pine cones and rubble.

Adi frowned. "You two are no fun."

As Zephyrine and Lucian headed away from the camp, Jin dimmed the campfire until it barely put off any light or heat. The mountain air was crisp, the breeze chilly. Astrea was just glad she had a sleeping bag at all, even if the ground *was* uncomfortable.

"How proper are we being tonight?" Jin murmured, so low Astrea was sure only she could hear.

"What?" What could they possibly do that was improper with all these people around?

"How close are you comfortable getting?"

"Oh." Astrea would've climbed into Jin's sleeping bag with him just to get warm, but that seemed both impossible and improper, especially with the way Lucian glared in their direction. "Close is good," she murmured before wiggling closer to him.

"It's very cute when you do that," he whispered.

"Pretty sure you've said that to me before too, Captain," Adi said from behind Jin. "Get some new lines, for skies sake."

Astrea couldn't help it. As soon as the first giggle escaped her, she couldn't stop the rest. Cressida began laughing, too.

"You're insufferable, Jin," Cressida wheezed. "Truly. I think I liked it better when you were gone."

"Is it true?" Jin asked with a laugh. "Am I insufferable?"

"Maybe," Astrea said.

"All four of you are!" Marko called from somewhere behind Adi. Thankfully, the professor seemed to be asleep.

"Don't be jealous, Marko!" Adi called. "There's plenty of room over here if you want to come snuggle with us!"

"Not happening!" Marko called back.

"But I like cuddling!"

"Go to sleep, Adi!" Marko called again. But the tiniest, faintest hint of curiosity sparked somewhere behind Astrea, whispering over her skin as her friends laughed.

Thinking back on her sleepovers with Cressida as a child, Astrea smiled. Balthazar, Sarsali, and Saros used to beg them to go quiet down and go to sleep. What would their family say if they were there with them, too?

As she considered it, Astrea took in that brilliant band of starlight and smiled again. Someday, she'd take her family here. It might require a luxury airship to get Balthazar and Cressida this far from civilization, but she was sure Sarsali and Saros would love it.

Someday, when the Paragon were no longer a threat and when Emperor Aelius had been removed from power, Astrea would get them all together. Someday might be far away, but she clung to that idea even as sleep took hold.

Oh, little Lightbringer.

Astrea knew that voice. She knew it, and she forced her eyes open before the familiar command could order her to look. The campfire light had died, replaced just by the thick blanket of stars above. Behind her was Jin's heavy body, his arm draped over her waist. On her other side was Cressida, curled up in her own sleeping bag.

Astrea couldn't move more than her eyes. She tracked the shadows flitting across the quiet campsite. She couldn't see Marko or Lucian. They were supposed to be on watch for the rest of the night. Where were they?

So good to see you, Miss Sovna, the voice said. *And you even brought friends here to our sacred ground. How nice.*

Victor Nazarov morphed into existence from nothing but shadow. Inky darkness dripped from his hands as he crouched in front of Astrea. He touched the tip of her nose, his fingers unnaturally cold. She wanted to scream, to tell everyone to wake up, but she couldn't move.

Tell me, Miss Sovna, have you figured out what the Paragon are after? he asked, voice light. Amused, even. Shadows crept up his face, much as they had crawled up the men on Solstice Night.

Though her mouth didn't move, Astrea managed to ask, *Why don't you just tell me and stop playing games?*

I thought it was obvious, Victor said. *Chaos. Destruction. Balance.*

Those were the words carved into the statue, but they didn't explain what they wanted with Astrea. And as Victor began strolling around the campsite, Astrea had the feeling he wasn't going to tell her even if she asked.

Still, she replied, *That doesn't mean anything. What do you want with me?*

Victor's only response was a chuckle. He crouched down near Cressida next, those same shadows dripping from his hands as he smoothed several curls away from her face. Finally, Marko and Lucian came back into view, not more than a couple dozen paces from where Astrea lay frozen. She silently begged them to move, begged her body to start working.

See you soon, little Lightbringer, Nazarov cooed just before his body morphed into shadows again.

Astrea squeezed her eyes shut, then opened them again as she flailed in her sleeping bag, trying to get the buttons open. Marko and Lucian were *right* there, so close. She had to tell them. She opened her mouth to shout, but Jin's voice snagged her attention.

"Az?" he asked, the word heavy with sleep as he brushed her arm with his hand. "What's wrong?"

Footsteps crunched across the grass and rocks, and dark green concern flashed nearby. She didn't have to look up to know Lucian had come over.

"Nazarov," Astrea choked out. "He was just here. He was here, I swear. You didn't feel him?"

The commander frowned, his thick eyebrows drawing together. "I sensed nothing out of the ordinary."

Astrea deflated, flopping back onto the hard ground and digging her fingers into her hair. She stared up at the stars high above, searching for any constellations between the towering trees. She couldn't get herself to focus, though.

How was that possible? If Nazarov was invading her dreams, how was he able to project exactly her surroundings back at her? It was not the first time he'd done it. Did that mean he was nearby? She pushed her magic out until it hurt, but they were alone. No voids. No other emotions or walls or anything. It was just the eight of them.

"They know where we are," Astrea said. "I mean, I think they know. He showed me this exact campsite. He was here. Somehow."

Now, Cressida and Adi had started to stir, too. Marko and Zephyrine moved closer, cool wariness drifting off them and across Astrea's exposed skin.

"We should pack up camp and send up the flares for Damian," Zephyrine said. She started tugging her armor on with practiced ease. "Stay alert until he gets here."

Adi and Jin got up immediately. As Astrea sat up, she watched Marko circle the camp and stir the professor. Next to her, Cressida yawned.

Within just a few minutes, Jin had lit a flare, which crackled high above their camp in a brilliant explosion of red. Zephyrine assured Astrea it wouldn't take long for Damian to arrive with the ship. Within another ten minutes, the sleeping bags had been returned to everyone's packs, the professor had double-checked that he had the artifacts collected, and Zephyrine had pulled some kind of coffee contraption from her bag. Astrea finally had a small thermos lid filled with the hot coffee, and she clutched it tightly as she sat in front of the low fire.

"Why won't they just tell us what they want, Cress?" Astrea asked when Cressida dropped onto the ground next to her. "Why are they just taunting us? What could it possibly get them?"

"I don't know."

"He said they want chaos, destruction, and balance, but he wouldn't tell me what they want with *me*." Astrea brought the makeshift mug to her lips. "Are they just trying to confuse us?"

"If it wasn't for what happened on Solstice Night, I'd say yes," Cressida said.

A throat cleared just as Kostas squatted down next to Cressida. "These Paragon are after you, Miss Sovna, right? That's what the mess at my office was about, and now this dream?"

"Yup," Astrea muttered.

"Perhaps they feel they need you for something. Maybe they think you can help them," he said.

"Why would they think that?" Astrea asked. "I don't know anything about them. I can't read their language."

Kostas shrugged one shoulder. "They must have a reason for seeking you out like this. Surely there is something special about you."

"I'm just a Lightbringer."

"A balance to their void, right?" he suggested.

"Then why not Commander Lucian? Or one of the thousands of other celestial mages out there?"

"Yes, well." Kostas flashed a tired smile her way. "Perhaps it's something to think about further."

As the night sky shifted from impossible darkness to deep blue—the first sign dawn was approaching—Astrea stared out over the mountains and valley below. She'd tried to come up with anything to answer Kostas's question. She didn't mean it in a disparaging way; there was simply nothing remarkable about her. She was a Lightbringer. She was of common birth and had next to no power. She had powerful friends, yes, but even if the Paragon were going after her to manipulate her friends, it would still be easier to simply go after the others directly. She had no significant fortune. She wasn't even a historian; it wasn't like she was an expert in lost Paragon history or anything.

So why her? Why track her down? Why not just tell her what they wanted?

Chapter 35

The flight back to Grand Duchess Ysabel's palace had been far less relaxing than the flight to the ruins. Though they'd managed to get away from the ruins before the morning sun even broke the horizon, before Nazarov or anyone else had shown up, Astrea hadn't been able to sit still. After the shortest, coldest shower of her life to get off the dust and sweat from her time in the ruins, she'd pored over the notes she'd taken, then pored over the scraps of evidence they had.

Chaos. Destruction. Balance. Those words had to mean something. *The world must be reborn through chaos and destruction.* She must've been right when she'd told Jin she thought the Paragon wanted to end the world. She had to have been. The visions. Those words. But why? Was it really for revenge after they lost the wars? To restore balance to magic? How could destruction do that? Her notes couldn't tell her those answers.

And she still didn't have an answer by the time they were following Lucian through the palace halls. Adi, Zephyrine, and Cressida had all gone back to the guest house, but Kostas and Marko trailed behind Astrea and Jin. Deeper and deeper they went, down corridors Astrea didn't recognize, until Lucian finally stopped at an arched doorway. The walnut door was closed, and a mountain was carved into the wood just above Astrea's eye level. Lucian knocked once, then opened the door and ushered everyone inside.

It had to be Ysabel's office. The large space was ornately decorated, a thick Tornamian rug taking up most of the floor and heavy wooden bookcases lining two of the four walls. Ysabel sat at a desk in the middle of the room, and off to one side was a round table that could seat eight. Also seated in front of Ysabel's desk in two plush, royal blue armchairs were Eliana and Nicos.

"You're back," Ysabel said as she stood. She pressed her lips into a thin line.

Lucian closed the door behind Kostas, the last to enter. "I thought you might like an update from Miss Sovna in person."

Me? Astrea glanced from Ysabel to Eliana. Her friend's expression was tight, but she smiled. Dark half-moons had made a home under Eliana's usually bright eyes.

"Victor Nazarov came to me in a dream or vision again," Astrea started. That seemed like the easiest place to begin. "He still won't tell me what he wants, but he's definitely fixated on me."

After sitting at Ysabel's insistence, Astrea told the grand duchess and Eliana everything she could. Chaos, destruction, and balance. How those words had been not just carved into the ruins but whispered to her by Nazarov. Lucian confirmed Astrea's claim that neither of them had been able to feel Nazarov's presence, and he explained that he hadn't wanted to take a chance by staying in the mountains when Nazarov may have been nearby.

"You don't have *any* other information on Nazarov?" Jin asked. "Your people haven't been able to find even a clue as to where he may be?"

"All I know is that they don't think he's in Aelius's custody anymore," the grand duchess said. Her gaze flicked to Kostas, who had started shuffling through his bag. "What were you able to find at the ruins, Professor?"

"Oh!" He pushed his glasses up his nose and flashed a half smile as he set a miniature bronze statue on the table. "Unfortunately, with the trip being understandably cut short, I wasn't able to find what I was looking for, Your Highness."

"And that was . . . ?" Ysabel prompted as Kostas continued pulling objects out of his bag. When he set out several of the arrowheads marked with the void language, a broken piece of pottery, and his notebook, Ysabel simply arched an eyebrow.

"Information, of course," Kostas said. "Miss Sovna and I were unable to crack this void language, though we found a few translated words and were able to identify the bust of whom appeared to be some ancient ruler, Tytas Ramkas."

"Tytas Ramkas?" Ysabel echoed.

"You do not recognize the name, Your Highness?" Kostas asked, and Ysabel shook her head.

"You think he's an ancient ruler?" It was the first question Eliana had asked, the first time she'd even spoken a word.

"Theo brought a similar statue to the Great Library back home," Jin said dryly. "Astrea said it was delivered just before the solstice celebrations."

Eliana chewed on her lower lip, her fatigue pressing heavily against Astrea's skin. "Wonderful," she muttered.

"Would Tomas know who this Tytas Ramkas is?" Lucian asked.

"Perhaps," Ysabel said. "It's worth taking the information to him regardless. And besides that, Lucian, you need to speak with Mariya. She's had another vision."

"Of the Paragon?" Astrea swallowed hard.

"Indeed," the grand duchess said. "She saw the Paragon's symbol on an office building downtown. I've already sent Vernie to investigate, but perhaps it would be best if you joined them and their team on site."

"When did she have the vision?" Lucian asked.

"While you were on your way back to the palace, very early this morning."

Astrea's stomach sank. She could only imagine what that meant. More notes demanding the Novarians hand Astrea over to the Paragon? Perhaps another murder, like the ones the day before they left for the mountains? Maybe something else entirely just to throw their investigation into more chaos?

Chaos. Destruction. Balance. Was that part of what Nazarov meant? Was he simply trying to be confusing on purpose to follow some ancient creed? But what would that possibly accomplish?

"I will speak to Mariya and then join Vernie and their team," Lucian said. "Marko, stay with Her Highness today." Without another word, the commander slipped out of Ysabel's office and shut the door with nothing more than a soft click.

"Professor," Ysabel said, "perhaps Marko can escort you to the library and you can get a head start on that conversation with Tomas. I need to speak with Miss Sovna and Prince Varojin about another matter."

The professor didn't seem fazed by the suggestion, instead packing up his belongings with a few quick farewells. Rusty annoyance, however, colored the air around Marko as he herded Kostas toward the door. Only when they were gone did Ysabel speak again.

"We still have our dinner tomorrow with my council," she said. "I know Nazarov's reappearance has shifted your focus, Varojin, but this meeting must go well. Veiko and I are prepared to vouch for your sister, but all of you must be focused on this meeting."

"Politics are Eliana's strength, not mine," Jin said. When Ysabel pinned him with a look, he added, "But I know how to stay on task. Don't worry about dinner."

"Good." Ysabel nodded. "Alright, off to Tomas. Please tell him I said to drop everything to begin studying this Ramkas figure."

As soon as they were outside of Ysabel's office, Jin pulled Astrea off to one side of the hallway. Nicos and Eliana followed, the four of them huddled in the empty space. Astrea let her magic spread out wide, but the only other people she sensed nearby were Ysabel and a guard far down the hall.

"I'm going to talk with my team about the Nazarov problem," Jin said, his voice low.

"I really don't think Ysabel knows any more about him than we do, Jin," Eliana said. "Truly. I've spent the most time with her, and I don't think she's lying about that."

"Nor do I," Jin said. "But that doesn't change the fact that her priorities lie elsewhere. And while I understand her desire to focus on politics over the next couple days, I don't like that Nazarov keeps finding Az."

"Do you think there's a way we can prevent it?" Astrea asked.

"I wish I knew." He smiled at her, but it was sad. "Zephyrine usually has good ideas. Maybe she's thought of something."

Something. Anything would be worth trying if it could keep Victor Nazarov out of Astrea's mind.

"Ellie, Nicos," Astrea said, "do you have time to come to the library with me? Or can you send Cress over, Jin? I don't want to be stuck with the professor if Nazarov does . . . whatever it is he does again."

"We'll go," Eliana said quickly.

Jin walked with them to the library, which Astrea was glad for, as the other three seemed to actually know this part of the palace. As they stopped outside the wide library doors, Jin stooped to place a quick kiss on Astrea's cheek. And then he was gone without another word.

Eliana looped her arm through Astrea's and tugged her toward the door Nicos held open. Kostas and Tomas had set up at a table near the fireplace on the far end of the room.

"Ah, Astrea! Your Imperial Highness!" Tomas called as Eliana half dragged Astrea toward their table. "You're just in time. The professor was filling me in on everything that happened in the mountains and everything you found."

Up close, Astrea spotted those same artifacts from before spread out on the table, as were several others and Kostas's notes. Astrea's fingers twitched. Cressida had taken Astrea's pack back to the guest house, but she wished she had it now. That's where her notes were.

"Tell me, have you ever heard of this Tytas Ramkas?" Eliana asked as she dropped into one of the empty chairs at the table. "Apparently he's a figure of interest back home as well."

"A figure of interest," Tomas mused. "Unfortunately, Your Imperial Highness, there are too many of those throughout history for me to know them all by name." He chuckled, and peach amusement tangled in the air around both him and Kostas. Astrea's brows furrowed; it wasn't exactly a funny joke. "But surely there is information on this man somewhere in Talmaris. Now we simply have to track it down."

"In Talmaris?" Eliana asked. "Not here, in your library?"

"Perhaps here," Tomas said, "or perhaps at the university's collection. Or one of the museums, or even in the palace or city archives."

The palace. The university. City archives. There were too many places to sort through in a timely fashion.

"Would any of your colleagues know that name, Kostas?" Astrea asked. "Surely there's a faster way to find this information."

"These things take time," the professor replied almost sorrowfully. "Imagine all that we could discover if we had a faster way to find such things. Alas, we do not." He paused, then added, "It would, of course, go more quickly if we had more people to help us."

"Cressida can help us," Astrea said. "And Adi."

"Two additional pairs of eyes, while helpful, will not make that much of a difference," Kostas said. "Your Imperial Highness, perhaps . . . well." He let out an uneasy chuckle. "Perhaps, if you're not too busy yourself, you and your guard could help us. I don't mean to be forward, but . . ."

"Of course I'll help," Eliana said. "Just tell me where we're starting."

Astrea pinched the bridge of her nose. That was not wise with the dinner right around the corner; Eliana needed to focus on swaying the council. But red determination spiked around her in quick, rapid pulses. Of course Eliana wanted to do this. It was something to tie the Paragon to Emperor Aelius, a real link. They had to chase this down no matter what.

As promised, Eliana had stayed with Astrea at the library for the rest of the day. They'd worked with Tomas and Kostas to begin sifting through all sorts of books that might reference that ancient ruler. Cressida had joined them, too. They hadn't found anything before dinner, but they had made good progress and figured out a plan for the next day.

Now, Astrea watched on as her friends chatted with Jin's team. They'd settled in the parlor after dinner with their dessert, some tart Astrea didn't love. Cressida's were better. And it wasn't that she didn't want to get to know Lennor, Civan, and even Zephyrine, but Astrea found the conversation difficult to keep up with, especially after a long day of travel and study.

"There's no way you don't have more to say than that, Civan," Lennor said, peach amusement bright and light around her. She looked up from her spot on the floor near the fireplace to where her twin hovered near the windows. "Not when Adi just called you out."

From what Astrea had gathered in the last hour, the twins had settled in around Eliana in the couple of days they'd been at the guest house. Perhaps it was Eliana's insistence on not being called by her title, or perhaps it was that the twins were used to Jin's casual ways. She didn't think it mattered either way.

"I have nothing to say," Civan mumbled. "Adi knows where I stand on the issue."

"The *issue*?" Eliana asked. "I thought this was a long-held dispute over chocolate?"

"Serious business," Adi called from his spot on the floor. Cressida, sprawled out next to him, laughed. "Just like the ongoing competition your brother and I have over who's won more spars."

Astrea imagined that, in a different time and place, they might have nights like this as friendship began to grow. No wars. No Paragon. No royalty, even. Just eight young adults—and Zephyrine—bonding over silly, friendly rivalries and food.

"And you know that I've got a clear edge over you," Jin said from his spot next to Astrea. "Don't expect it to change any time soon."

Despite his arm draped over the back of the sofa and one leg propped on the other, Astrea didn't miss the tightness in Jin's voice. Before dinner, he'd told her that neither Zephyrine nor the rest of the team had any idea how to track down Nazarov. Their best bet was to have Lightbringers searching for voids in the city and palace, which Commander Lucian had already organized. It was a first step, at least.

"That sounds like a challenge if I've ever heard one." Cressida grinned at Lennor. "Are they always like this?"

"Competitive, you mean?" Lennor nodded. "Always."

"We're not competitive," Adi and Jin said at the same time.

Lennor gestured to the room. "My point exactly."

"Adi and Jin may be competitive, but they know each other almost better than they know themselves sometimes," Zephyrine said. "You two have been like that since the beginning. I'm glad it worked out that way, because admittedly, I wasn't sure it would."

"Why?" Eliana asked. "Because Jin's stubborn?"

"Not as stubborn as you, Ellie," Jin retorted, and she stuck her tongue out.

"Not because of Jin or Adi, actually." Zephyrine smiled, a sad, gentle expression. "Because I wasn't sure the old team could handle losing one of their own, let alone having another much younger teammate brought on. But Adi proved them wrong just like Jin did."

"Aw, Zephyrine," Adi said, something ticklish and gentle skittering along Astrea's skin. He rubbed the back of his neck. Was Adi *shy*? "Not like you to say so many nice things at once."

"She's getting soft in her old age," Jin quipped.

"Old age?" Zephyrine scoffed as she settled back in her armchair. "Don't make me bring out the nickname."

"Nickname?" Eliana and Lennor asked in unison.

Jin groaned. "Not this."

"Yes, this." Zephyrine flicked a lock of white hair over her shoulder. "We called him 'kid' for years. Because he *was* a kid. Still is sometimes."

Despite every worry poking at the back of Astrea's mind, she smiled. Jin would hate that nickname. And the way he groaned now, she knew he still hated it.

"What's worse," she asked, "that or Your Imperial Highness?"

He peered down at her. "Now that's just not fair."

"You have to choose," Cressida said. "Which is worse?"

"My imperial title will always be worse." There was no malice to Jin's words, just his simple truth. "Do we really have nothing better to discuss tonight?"

"Not unless you want to revisit all the things we already know we have to worry about," Eliana said. "Which I don't particularly care to do. We can worry about them again in the morning."

Astrea couldn't simply shut off her worries, and she doubted Eliana actually could, either. There was too much at stake, too many unknowns. But worrying about everything all night wouldn't actually get Astrea closer to her answers. Maybe she could try to enjoy herself and the company of friends old and new.

Chapter 36

Trying to get work done in a very limited amount of time always set Astrea on edge. It was even worse when she had to keep stopping to answer questions and look at what others were doing.

"I think this is the direction we need to be moving," Kostas called out from the table he'd taken up for himself in the library.

Though Eliana had assisted the day before, Ysabel and Veiko wanted one last meeting with her, Jin, and Zephyrine before the dinner happening later that day. But Adi, Cressida, and the twins had joined Astrea in the library as they searched for information about Tytas Ramkas.

"What direction?" Tomas asked as he scrambled down the stairs leading up to his office. He'd been doing that all morning, going up and down, up and down, as he thought of other books and returned to his catalog.

Astrea dug her fingers into her hair. Even with her barrier pulled tightly around her body, every noise made her muscles tighten. Extra assistance was great, but it was so distracting. So grating on her fried nerves. She'd barely slept, afraid that Nazarov was going to show up in her dreams again.

"Astrea, you mentioned something about a Fireweaver king and Novarian queen yesterday, right?" Kostas asked.

"Yes, Professor."

"I think I've found it, and I think it's exactly what we need. Come look."

Astrea's joints cracked and protested as she pushed out of her seat. She hadn't moved for a couple hours. Cressida, who'd been sharing her table, stayed seated. Adi and the twins, who were all sharing another table, didn't move either.

"Where is it?" Astrea asked, trying to tamp down her annoyance. Kostas was just trying to help. And he *was* helping.

"Right here, look." He pointed to a page on the left, then its partner on the right. "And there's more after this, too."

Blinking to try to clear her head, Astrea took the book from the professor. "Beginning in the year 450, clans of warriors living in the Macadian Mountains joined the wars," she read. "The Novarians needed to pass through the mountains to fight off an aggressive Fireweaver king, who continually tried to push north. They clashed with these flagless warriors, who were said to also target the Fireweaver's army."

"That sure sounds like them," Adi said. "Based on the other reference we found."

Astrea pinched the bridge of her nose and squeezed her eyes shut. "It certainly fits."

"You're not pleased?" Kostas asked.

"I'm just tired, Professor." Tired didn't even begin to describe how she felt. How drained she was. But it was the only explanation she could really offer.

"I can keep reading, if you'd like to take a break."

"I'm fine," she said quickly. She needed to do this. "May I take this?"

Kostas let out a soft chuckle. "You don't need my permission."

Astrea took the book to the sofa near the fireplace. But instead of sitting on the furniture, she plopped on the hard wood floor. The rug was the only cushion.

Astrea continued reading silently, trying to block out everyone's murmurs as they went back to their own texts.

Apparently, after several years of back-and-forth fighting with the flagless mountain warriors, the Novarian queen went to the Fireweaver king with an offer. She'd wanted to work together to take out the mountain group, then sign a truce with the king. The two monarchs joined forces, and when they defeated the mountain group, the Fireweaver turned on the queen and took over part of the Macadian Mountains for himself.

There was no mention of dark fire, though the passage did say the flagless army was very strong despite its small size. There was no mention of Tytas Ramkas. But Emperor Aelius had asked Astrea and Jin to look into a battle between a Fireweaver king and Novarian queen. He'd said it was the start of the Helosian Empire. This passage, while lacking particular details, fit what she knew of that story and what she knew of the Paragon from that time period. It fit with the other account about a flagless group antagonizing two other armies.

It had to be them. It had to be the beginnings of the Paragon . . . or some version of them. It was likely Tytas Ramkas and his group. And if not him, his descendants or ancestors.

Astrea flipped through a few more pages. The chapter was small, buried within a section of the book about battles on the northern part of the continent. It mostly detailed the heavy losses the mountain group, the Fireweaver king, and the Novarian queen had all suffered in those few battles.

Perhaps those bad losses had forced the void mages to retreat into the mountains to regroup, or ultimately driven them to hide away from the rest of the world.

And maybe that was where the myth about the mountain king came from. If clans of void mages lived in the Macadian Mountains long ago, perhaps it was about a leader of another clan or one of the many small countries from centuries before. The monster of darkness from that story could've been one of the void mage clans.

A gentle hand on Astrea's shoulder made her jump out of her skin. Cressida crouched next to her. "Anything?" she asked.

"It's got to be them," Astrea said. "It all fits together, even if some of the specifics aren't there."

"That's good, then." Cressida gestured down at the book. "Why don't you take a break? You look exhausted."

"I'm fine."

"C'mon, Az. We all need a break. Lennor and Adi wanted to take a walk anyway. We've been locked in here for hours."

"And we have one measly chapter to show for it."

"Well, let Tomas and Kostas keep searching. We have a dinner to get ready for."

Astrea's jaw tightened. "But—"

"You're doing it again," Cressida said. "You're fixating. This isn't good for you."

"We need answers, Cress. The council might even want information tonight."

"You think they're going to care about some old dead guy and his mountain army?" Cressida asked. "They're going to be concerned about Ellie's plans and what the emperor is up to. Take a break. We can come back to this tomorrow."

"But—"

"Do I need to get Jin in here? Because I will."

Why did Cressida care so much anyway? Astrea didn't need more than an hour to get ready. She could keep working. She could go to Tomas's catalog—if he'd finally let her touch it—and find something else about the northern battles. Or call someone at the university and ask for a meeting first thing in the morning.

But Cressida's stony expression deterred her from arguing anymore. It was the same one Sarsali had given both of them over the years.

"Fine," Astrea muttered.

When Cressida offered her a hand to help her off the ground, Astrea took it. She brought the book back to Kostas, and after asking him and Tomas both to narrow down their search even more, finally left the library.

Astrea smoothed the front of her dress, a black, glittery garment with a flowing skirt. The grand duchess's tailors had made it and sent it over that morning, along with outfits for the rest of their Helosian group. It was as formal as what Astrea had worn to the emperor's dinner weeks before, and it was still far outside her comfort zone. And the skies damned *seams*. She huffed. The seams on the right side of the dress kept rubbing against her hip and torso, painful despite the soft fabric.

It was going to be a long night.

She finished fiddling with her hair, letting it drape over her shoulders in long, loose waves, then clasped on the necklace Jin had first gifted her weeks before. The small teardrop sapphire winked in the light as she turned in the mirror. The seam of her bodice rubbed her side again, and Astrea sucked in a deep breath. *It's fine*, she told herself. *It's fine*. She was just going to have to find a way to ignore it. She was going to have to find a way to get through the night.

She returned to the bedroom, where Jin was buttoning up his shirt. His outfit matched hers, an all-black, three-piece suit. Even his shirt was black. Somber. Was that Ysabel's point? To look incredibly serious for the council?

"You look beautiful," Jin said as Astrea stalked toward the desk.

"Thanks." Her voice came out tighter than she wanted. Jin was just being polite. Honest, probably, too.

Silence for one heartbeat, two. Fabric rustled, and a hanger clinked against the wardrobe doors. Astrea flinched.

"Is everything alright?" Jin asked.

"Everything's fine." Astrea picked up the tube of lipstick Eliana had given her a few hours before. Astrea hated wearing lipstick; she found something about it too dry and chalky. But she needed to look the part, didn't she?

"I think I've known you long enough to know something's wrong, Az," Jin said gently.

She clutched the lipstick tube tighter in her hand. "I just don't like dressing up."

"You don't like the dress?"

"It's not . . . it's not about the dress," she huffed, her back still to him. "It's uncomfortable, and I already feel so out of place. Why am I even going to this dinner? I won't be able to convince the council of anything. I should be working."

"You're going because you're part of the team, and the council wants to talk to all of us. They want to know more about Ellie's plans, but they also want to hear about your experience with void magic."

"Right," she muttered.

"I'm serious," he said. "As for the dress, do you want me to talk to Ysabel? Get her people to make you something for another night? I'm sure this isn't our last meeting like this."

Do you want me to talk to Ysabel? Jin's words ran through Astrea's mind in circles, joining Commander Lucian's. *No wonder Varojin cod-*

dles you. Cressida's. *You're fixating. This isn't good for you. Do I need to get Jin in here?* She clutched the lipstick tube so tightly she was afraid she'd break it, so Astrea slammed it back on the desk.

"Az?" Jin's surprise whispered over her skin, almost painful as that seam rubbed her side again. "What's wrong?"

What was wrong? What was *wrong*? Everything was wrong. Everything since the start of summer crashed into her, almost out of nowhere. One day. She just wanted one day where things didn't overwhelm her and she found the information she needed. Was one day so much to ask?

"Poor little Lightbringer, right?" Astrea snapped as she turned around. "Astrea can't fight. Astrea's bad with magic. Astrea's got some void mage stalking her. Astrea's overwhelmed. Can't handle uncomfortable dresses or dinner parties."

Rage and shame and regret burned through her all at once, especially as Jin just stood there, eyebrows furrowed and suit jacket in hand.

"I've been handling this Lightbringer shit my entire life. And I may not always keep it together, and it may seem ridiculous, but you couldn't even handle feeling like this for twenty minutes, alright? You don't know how hard it is, feeling every single thing the entire *world* does for twenty-four years and having to pretend you don't feel any of it at all. But I've been managing just fine, and I don't need you stepping in now."

Jin swallowed, the furrow between his eyebrows deepening. "I didn't say you *needed* me to step in. I was just offering—"

"Well don't offer, okay?"

With a sigh, Jin tossed his suit jacket onto their neatly made bed. "What has gotten into you?" he asked. "You've been in a terrible mood since you woke up."

"Am I not allowed to be in a bad mood?"

"Of course you're allowed to be in a bad mood or any kind of mood, but I'd really like to know what's wrong."

"What's wrong?" Astrea asked with a tight half laugh. "Everything's wrong, Jin! Everything!"

"Az—"

"I was supposed to come here to find answers so I could save Saros and the Nikaphoroses and Helosia, but I'm standing here in this ridiculous, painfully uncomfortable dress, and you're looking at me like I've lost my skies damned mind, and nobody even believes in my ability to do any of this!"

"Who doesn't believe in you?"

"Everyone!"

"Who, Az?" he pressed.

"Adi, Cress, Ellie, Nicos, you—"

Jin's jaw tightened. "You think I don't believe in you?"

"Lucian doesn't believe in me," Astrea said, a nonanswer. "The person who's trying to teach me doesn't even think I can do this. He said you coddle me, and he's right. You coddle me because *you* don't believe I can handle any of this, either."

"When have I ever said any of that?" Jin snapped. "You're putting words in my mouth, and that's not fair."

"I—"

"And I'll get to Lucian's bullshit in a moment," he continued. Astrea huffed and crossed her arms. "When have *any* of our friends said that to you? Have they actually said that to you?"

None of them needed to say it. It was only becoming more obvious. How they checked in even more after the Paragon had painted those words in the professor's office. How Cressida had forced her out of the library earlier. *This isn't good for you.* How Adi wasn't pushing her harder in training. *No wonder Varojin coddles you.* How Jin checked in with her every night. *Do you want me to talk to Ysabel?* How Saros had never let Astrea venture outside Kalama or do anything that might be a risk because of one single vision. How Jin hadn't even let her walk around Kalama by herself after what happened on Solstice Night.

Some tiny, distant part of Astrea knew this wasn't logical. It wasn't rational. Some of those moments and restrictions had very likely saved her life. Some of them were very likely just her friends being worried about her. Her friends caring about her. That didn't change the shame pulsing through her again and again. The anger. The confusion.

Astrea shouldered past Jin. He said her name, but she ignored him. Instead, she grabbed her satchel, then yanked her lavender dress off its hanger. She reached for an extra handful of underclothes, too, before stalking to the settee in front of the fireplace.

Jin sighed. "What are you doing?"

"I just need some space."

"Space?"

"After dinner. I know this meeting is important for Ellie, so I'll be there. I'm just going to sleep in Cress's room for a couple nights."

"You don't *have* to come to this dinner if you don't feel up to it or even want to. It won't be the end of the world or the end of the mission. You can talk to the council in the morning."

"And this is exactly what I'm talking about." Astrea folded up a pair of bloomers and shoved them into her bag. "Little Lightbringer can't even make it to one skies damned dinner. Shocking!"

The floor barely creaked as Jin moved, then stopped. "Az," he whispered, her name little more than a plea. "Come on. I'm sorry, I didn't mean—"

"No." She forced her eyes to stay open as she faced him, hoping the air would dry her tears. She couldn't cry now. Not in front of Jin, and certainly not before going to meet Ysabel's council. "I just need a couple days to get my head straight. I'm fine."

Jin deflated. He'd just started to say something when a knock echoed through the room.

"You two ready?" Cressida yelled. "We need to leave."

"Two minutes, Cress!" Jin yelled back. Then his gaze shifted back to Astrea as he whispered, "Az, please don't—"

"We need to go," she said, swallowing hard. "Get your jacket."

As much as Astrea's heart ached, she forced herself to turn around and go to the door. She opened it just enough to slip outside, then pulled Cressida down the hall.

Cressida glanced over her shoulder. "Where's Jin?"

"Can I stay in your room tonight?" Astrea asked instead of answering.

Green confusion danced in the air. "Sure . . . but why?"

"I need some space."

"Well . . . sure," Cressida said. "Stay with me however long you need."

Chapter 37

Astrea never imagined herself as the type to attend diplomatic dinners with heads of state—aside from the rare event with Eliana over the years—and yet this was her third such meal with Grand Duchess Ysabel in a mere couple weeks.

Unlike the first two dining rooms Astrea had seen in the Novarian palace, this one was clearly meant for political affairs. The table alone could seat twenty-five, perfect for the large group filtering into the room. That was to say nothing of the ornate midnight blue wallpaper, tapestries and gold-framed art on the walls, dark wood floors, and crystalline dishware.

Next to her, Jin was stiff. Still, he led her to their seats as if nothing was wrong between them. Astrea didn't know why she'd snapped at him like that. That wasn't her. That wasn't how she wanted to behave. He'd been right. She'd put words in his mouth, and that wasn't fair. After dinner. She would apologize to him right after dinner.

Cressida and Adi sat to Astrea's left, Nicos and Eliana to Jin's right. The rest of the Helosian group was there, too, though Astrea didn't pay much attention to their exact seating arrangements. Across the table were six people Astrea didn't recognize—Ysabel's council, presumably. Princess Delfine and Crown Prince Veiko were also there, their wives at their sides. Even Lucian was present.

Focus, Az. She needed to focus. Tonight was about Eliana. About Helosia. Sucking in a deep breath, Astrea settled back into her chair. She was even more exhausted after that outburst than she had been earlier in the day.

Dinner started with the fanfare expected by nobility. Palace staff made a show of pouring wine into crystal goblets and setting ornate platters of food on the table. As they did so, Astrea tried to study the six members of the Novarian Grand Council. They were a mix of open and closed. Four of them were easy for Astrea to read, their curiosity, frustration, and calm all mixing together. The other two were closed off just like Commander Lucian and the grand duchess herself. Of course, Astrea had no good way to actually tell Eliana or Jin what she saw in that moment, but they could always debrief after dinner.

"So," Grand Duchess Ysabel said as the serving staff exited the room. The first course had been laid out, some kind of steaming broth in wide, shallow bowls. "Council, you obviously know Princess Eliana, Prince Varojin, and Nicos Masalis, but I don't believe you've yet met our other Helosian guests."

She went down the line of the table introducing Astrea, Cressida, Adi, Zephyrine, Lennor, and Civan, then moved on to the six Novarian council members. Astrea heard the councillors' names, but none of them stuck in her mind.

"We've been speaking more, Your Imperial Highnesses," said one, a thin woman with lavender eyes, red hair, and sun-kissed skin. "My fellow council members and I are in agreement on one thing. We are not keen on getting the Novarian people involved in a Helosian issue."

"Councillor Makivna—" Eliana started, only for a different councillor—a man with skin, hair, and eyes so light he looked like he could be made of snow—to raise his hand.

"I know you hoped for a different outcome, Your Imperial Highness," he said. "We think you would be a good fit for the Helosian throne, but it is not our place to get involved in another country's affairs."

"Councillor Reis," Zephyrine said, "with all due respect, this is far more than Helosia's issue. Has Her Imperial Highness not explained what her father is up to?"

"With *all due respect*, general," said a woman with dark corkscrew curls, terra cotta skin, and light brown eyes. Her gaze flicked from Zephyrine to Eliana and back again. "I don't believe any of your party truly understand what it is the Helosian emperor is up to."

"Sinni, please," Grand Duchess Ysabel said. "We've been over this at length. Emperor Aelius is after void magic. You know what these Paragon can do with it. The Helosians cannot be allowed to have it."

"Should he not be allowed to have it," said a bald, brawny man with umber skin, his baritone voice ringing out over the clinking of spoons, "or should the rest of us prepare to take control of such magic as well?" His bright green eyes surveyed the Helosian side of the table.

Flickers of lavender surprise danced around the room, though no such reaction came from the council. They all remained calm, as if this idea was something they had all discussed. Both Jin and Cressida shifted in their seats. Astrea's stomach tightened.

"I don't think you understand what this magic can do," Jin said. "I don't think any of you understand what it can do. The devastation my father will wreak with it under his control."

"And that is why we must also gain control of it, Your Imperial Highness." The councillor who spoke smoothed the ends of her long, dark hair, then sighed. "This is a distasteful topic for dinner, Ysabel. Must we discuss it now?"

To Astrea's surprise, the grand duchess simply nodded. "You're right. We should continue discussing this after dinner."

After dinner? If they could not convince the Novarians now—if Eliana, Jin, and the Novarian royal family had not convinced them over the last couple of weeks—would they ever?

The rest of the meal's courses passed with painful small talk and some of the richest, most delicious food Astrea had ever had in her life. Wine-braised meat with mushrooms, roasted vegetables, thick dark bread, fried potato dumplings, crispy roasted chicken, and more. And her mind was even more frayed than it had been before dinner. Every clink of utensils against dishware and every smack of someone's lips made Astrea cringe and want to scream.

By the time staff finally cleared away the last of the dinner plates and brought in dessert, the Novarian councillors all seemed to be in better spirits. Though two were still unreadable, the four Astrea could glean emotions from had grown calmer.

Jin hadn't relaxed at all through dinner, nor had Astrea. He'd participated in conversation only when directly addressed. Once they'd finally steered the conversation away from Helosian politics, a tenuous calm had settled over the opulent dining room. Astrea wasn't convinced it would last, not when Eliana, Zephyrine, and Ysabel seemed keen on pushing the issue. Worse was that Crown Prince Veiko didn't appear to be ready to fight the council. He'd stayed silent through a good part of the meal, though his wife Letizia kept several of the council members laughing.

Astrea poked her fork into the decadent chocolate trifle topped with raspberries and strawberries. Any other day, she might devour that trifle. But not now. Not when they were on the precipice of failure once again. Eliana and Ysabel had to find a way. If not to convince the council tonight, to at least keep the door open for negotiations.

"Council." Lucian cleared his throat. "Now that dinner is over, perhaps we can revisit the topic you're all so keen on avoiding." Before any of them could respond, he continued, "I would like to point out that Emperor Aelius has been positioning himself as hostile to Novaria for years, just as his father before him did. He already has at least one void mage in his service, and you've seen the recent reports from Corsyca. Even if we pursued bringing some under our jurisdiction, we are already behind."

"Hostile?" The bald councillor scoffed. "What about the summit this autumn, Commander? Did you forget about that? We haven't had issues with the Helosians in over two decades since Her Highness first worked out a trade agreement with them. If Emperor Aelius is not keen on starting a war with *us*, then why disturb the peace?"

"I don't think the summit was ever meant to truly be friendly, Councillor Tarsaya," Jin said. "Miss Sovna and I uncovered void magic while preparing for that very event, and it was all at my father's direction. I've told you this."

Councillor Tarsaya waved one thick hand and picked up his wine glass with the other. "What, he *wanted* you to discover this secret he's been keeping?" he asked, then took a long sip of his wine. "Was he going to bring us to Kalama just to have his void mages assassinate us?"

"Maybe," Jin said. "I wouldn't rule anything out at this point. In fact, I'm surprised you would still consider attending given what we've told you about the void mage at the palace and what's been happening in Kalama."

"Your Highnesses," Sinni said as she gazed around the table, "Your Imperial Highnesses. I recognize that while you all may be keen on stopping Emperor Aelius, we need more information about his plans before we willingly sign the Novarian public up for such a cause. It will not be an easy task, taking down the Helosian government."

"We've told you everything we already know, Councillor," Eliana said. To Astrea's surprise, Eliana had been unreadable to her magic for most of the dinner. "We need time and resources to gather more information."

"A rebellion with no resources is not much of a rebellion at all," said Councillor Tarsaya with a shake of his head.

"Which is why we must help them, Reimo," Ysabel said to him. "I do not understand why you are all being so resistant when just last week, we seemed to be coming to some kind of middle ground on this issue."

"We have yet to hear from General Kanakos." The councillor who spoke—Jules, Astrea thought someone had called them—had a soft voice that almost matched Letizia's. Their deep blue eyes searched the table, a soft blush spreading over their pale cheeks. "Perhaps she has insights she can share with us to help us reach a different conclusion."

It wasn't exactly what Astrea had hoped for, but at least Jules was open to hearing more. That had to be a good sign, as was Ysabel's insistence that there was more to be done.

"I'm available whenever you'd like to discuss the support we do have back home as well as the resources I'm able to provide, Councillor," Zephyrine said. "As early as right after this dinner if you want to get the conversation started."

Councillor Jules smiled. "While I appreciate your enthusiasm, General, tomorrow would be better. Your Highnesses?" Veiko, Delfine, and Ysabel all nodded their agreement. When Councillor Jules looked across the table toward Jin and Eliana, they both agreed, too. "Then it is settled," they said. "We will meet tomorrow."

Though Councillor Tarsaya's aura flared with bright, rusty annoyance, Astrea would take that meeting if it was all they could secure tonight. At least one councillor was keeping an open mind about the situation. Even Councillor Sinni, though more reluctant, seemed to at least be open to getting more information before making a final decision.

Next to her, Jin relaxed slightly. She wanted to reach for his hand under the table, to reassure him everything would work out. That the two of them could talk later. But she couldn't make her hand move. Not when he'd barely look at her. He didn't even look up from the espresso the staff had brought in with dessert.

The group finished their dessert with more heavy, tense small talk. Astrea didn't see the point. Why not simply call an end to the dinner and let everyone get on with their nights? There was no progress to be made before the next meeting in the morning. They could not change the councillors' minds in just one night.

Ysabel had just opened her mouth to speak when a loud boom, boom, boom echoed through the dining room, distant but unmissable even over the noise of the dinner. The very foundation of the palace rocked and rumbled, almost like an earthquake. Jin, Adi, Lucian, and the twins were on their feet in less than a second, Zephyrine and Nicos not far behind.

"What is going on?" demanded Reimo.

"Stay here, Your Highnesses," Lucian said, already tossing his napkin on the table and heading for the door.

Though Jin remained frozen at the table, his eyes tracked Lucian, Astrea assumed, based on the footsteps and closing door. Then Jin turned to her, the first time he'd truly looked at her in more than two hours.

"Can you feel anything?" he asked her.

Astrea pushed her magic out wider as the dining room doors slammed open. Lucian crashed into the room with all the grace of a wild animal.

"Your Highnesses, we need to get you out of here," he said as he closed the doors. "Marko and Vernie have reported—"

Another boom echoed through the palace. An explosion. It had to be, based on the way the palace rocked again. Even the plates and glasses on the table clinked and shook. And there it was. That unmistakable power, that strange static. That cold, wrong emptiness.

"It's the Paragon," Astrea said.

As the council members began to protest, Lucian whistled loudly. "Save your complaints and accusations for later," he ordered. "If you care about your lives, leave. Now." He pointed to a narrow door tucked away in the back of the dining room, one Astrea had noticed staff exiting and entering through earlier in the night.

Chair legs scraped against the wood floor, barely audible over the next explosion that rocked the palace. The Novarian Grand Council didn't utter another word as Prince Veiko ushered them toward the rear exit. All walls were gone now except for Lucian's, Jin's, and Zephyrine's. Panic, fear, and confusion all surged through the room, suffocating and overwhelming. That strange rise in power kept pushing against Astrea, preceding crashes and shouts in the hallway outside the dining room.

"Lennor, Civan," Jin said, "go with them. Coordinate with Lucian's people. We'll be right behind you." The twins asked no questions; they followed the Novarians out the back door. "Nicos—" Jin started, only for Eliana to cut him off.

"We can't leave, Jin," she said as she threw her napkin down on the table. "We know how to fight them."

"What happened on that airfield back home doesn't count as fighting them," Jin said.

Astrea gripped the edge of the table as an impossible number of voids surged forth in her awareness. Cold. Cold and hollow and wrong. "Go, Ellie." There had to be at least a dozen, all of them moving closer. "There are too many."

"Come, Eliana," Grand Duchess Ysabel said. Astrea hadn't realized she was still there, but she was loitering halfway between the rear exit and the table. The rest of the Novarians had disappeared. "It will be safer if you come with me. My people can handle this."

Eliana's chest heaved. "But—"

"Part of being a leader is knowing when to step in and when to retreat," Ysabel said. "Be wise, Eliana. Now is not the time to sacrifice yourself, not when there is so much you haven't even started doing yet."

Astrea was sure Eliana was going to refuse, but she finally nodded. With one last look over her shoulder, Eliana headed for the back door, Nicos right behind her like a shield. Part of Astrea thought Eliana may have had a point—they were the only people in the palace who knew even a fraction of what the void mages were capable of—but Ysabel also had a point. Helosia needed Eliana.

"Cress, Az, get out of here," Jin ordered. "Help evacuate any civilians on this floor."

"But—" Astrea started. One look from Jin made her cut herself off. Going up against the Paragon was not Astrea's idea of a good night, but there were civilians here. Veiko's children were somewhere in the palace. The whole grand ducal family was. Maybe she could help in her own way. Guide people away from the voids.

Something crashed outside the dining room as Jin shoved Cressida and Astrea toward the rear door. Cressida dipped out of his reach. She flung one hand out. Metal groaned as the doors budged open, then shut again as the hinges screeched. Cold pressed into the very core of Astrea's being.

The doors exploded open, wood splintering and cracking. A wall of flame shot up in front of Jin, extending the length of the room. A wall of shimmering starlight followed. Lucian's arms pushed out as he widened his stance. Even beyond the fire and light and broken doors, the Paragon were impossible to miss.

Like Jin's team, the dozen figures flooding into the room wore dark uniforms, but all comparisons stopped there. Masks like the ones Astrea had seen all those weeks ago in Sezia covered their faces, a variety of colors. Some black trimmed with white, others red trimmed with black, blue, and more. Expressionless. While many were those cold voids, a few had wildly flaring emotions. Anticipation, excitement, anxiety—it all pummeled Astrea, and she dragged her magic back toward herself.

"Go," Jin pleaded over his shoulder. "We'll be right behind you."

Jin knew what he was doing. Adi and Lucian knew what they were doing. Jin and Adi had taken out camps with double, triple the number of soldiers during the war. If anyone was going to take on that room and survive, it was them.

"Be careful!" Astrea yelled to them as Cressida pulled her toward the back exit.

They ran into a long, narrow hallway. Unlike the rest of the palace, the space was simple stone and sparsely decorated. Servant and staff halls, Astrea was sure, though they were empty now. A few doors lined the wall to their right. Astrea and Cressida sprinted past those.

"End of the hall," Astrea said. "There's a corner." That had to be where Eliana, Nicos, and the others had all gone.

"Can you feel where they are?" Cressida called back to Astrea.

Astrea let her magic spread out again, pushing and pushing until it was painfully distant from her body. There was too much she could feel—the voids, the warring emotions, even pain from somewhere behind her. They'd just reached the end of the hall. Cressida was turning right to follow the next corridor, but Astrea stopped. Pain pulsed in her left shoulder, her chest, her ribs.

"Someone's hurt." Astrea pivoted, already starting back the way they'd come. What if it was Jin? Or Adi? Even Lucian—worse if it was Lucian. Jin and Adi needed him to track those voids. "I have to—"

Cressida yanked Astrea back so hard they both stumbled into the wall behind them. "Now is not the time to play hero, Az. They'll be fine."

As Astrea pushed off the wall, the hairs on her arms prickled. "It's—"

Stone and flame and smoke exploded through the corridor as the very floor underneath Astrea shook. She bumped into Cressida, whose arms were stretched out to either side of her. Her muscles trembled, and as the dust began to clear, Astrea could see why. Sections of the walls had started to collapse in, and Cressida's magic was the only thing keeping them both from being crushed by rock. It was nothing short of a miracle the ceiling hadn't started to cave in, too.

Astrea racked her brain. Light would do nothing now. It could do nothing for the strain on Cressida's magic, and it couldn't do anything to prevent the walls from caving in around them.

"Need to go back," Cressida gritted out. "On the count of three, run. I'll let this go."

"You'll be crushed!"

"Did you forget I'm a much faster runner than you? I'll be right behind you," Cressida said. "One, two—"

That electric cold pulsed in the air. Astrea reached for Cressida. Some invisible force pushed Astrea back. Her back slammed into the portion of the still-standing wall behind her, all breath leaving her body.

Astrea screamed, unable to move as pain seared through her. Her vision clouded over, black dots turning everything nearly indistinguishable. Ghost pain flared in her shoulders, legs, head. Astrea was sure she heard Cressida cry out somewhere nearby, but the ringing in her ears drowned out the rest of the world.

She tried pushing up on her elbows, but a boot connected with Astrea's chest and forced her back down. Her head slammed into the hard floor. As her vision finally cleared, it wasn't a masked intruder whose face she saw. Lord Victor Nazarov smiled down at her.

"Hello, little Lightbringer."

No. Not him, not here. Astrea didn't have time to consider it beyond that. When Nazarov grabbed Astrea's wrists and hauled her upright, she pulled back. Their first meeting at the Whiskey Dream flashed in her mind. She summoned her light, trying to press it to his exposed arms. Victor wrenched both of her arms so hard, Astrea's magic faltered.

"Now, now," he cooed. "That's not very nice when I'm about to take you on holiday, is it? We can do this the easy way or the hard way."

How could this get any harder? The Paragon had already attacked the palace, had attacked all of her friends. Astrea pushed up on her toes, trying to get eyes on Cressida. There she was, flat on her back and surrounded by broken stones.

"Cress—!" The rest of Astrea's words died on her tongue, cut off by her scream. Hot and cold fire burned her wrists where Nazarov still held her.

He sneered, "Easy or hard way, little Lightbringer. Your choice."

Trying to focus with Cressida's ghost pain, her own void fire burns, and the smoke filling the hall was nearly impossible. Still, Astrea pulled on the energy buzzing just under her skin again, letting it flare bright and hot and right into Nazarov's arms.

He hissed and pulled back. Astrea rammed her knee straight into his crotch, then shoved past him and ran toward Cressida. Dropping to her knees, Astrea ignored the pain of rough stone digging into her flesh.

"Think my leg's broken," Cressida barely whispered. "Head hurts."

Astrea took in as much of her best friend and the collapsed wall as she could. Large stones still pinned her leg to the ground, but there weren't many. "Just get the last few off, Cress. You can do it. I'll heal you."

Cressida groaned. "Can't."

"Yes, you can!" Maybe that wasn't fair; Astrea could barely think straight as ghost pain pulsed through her body. But Cressida had to try. Astrea couldn't just leave her there with Nazarov. "You can do anything."

"Go, Az," Cressida said, "find Nicos and—"

Nazarov yanked Astrea backward, his hand gripping her hair so tightly Astrea thought it might simply rip from her scalp. And in the same moment, panic swept over Astrea's skin, bright and hot.

"Get away from them!" Jin roared.

"Oh, the leader will be *so* pleased," Nazarov said, voice so low Astrea barely heard him.

He wrapped one arm around Astrea's waist. His other snapped out, grabbing Jin's wrist as soon as he was near them. Then they were all sucked forward.

Darkness surged around them, all-consuming. Wind howled and whipped as the shadows caved in. That same panic pushed against Astrea again and again even though she couldn't see anything but darkness.

Then Astrea's feet met hard ground, and around them, a battle raged on. Guards fighting mask-clad figures. Smoke billowing up from the palace's entrance to her right. And was that . . . it looked like Kostas Shalysko, a knife protruding from his gut and shadows covering—

Darkness surged around Astrea again as she was pulled forward. The vortex around her was disorienting, impossible. It was like moving through the void itself.

She met hard ground again, this time stumbling and falling onto her burned hands. She cried out, both in surprise and in pain, as she rolled to her knees.

"Az, run!" Jin shouted from somewhere behind her.

Astrea tried to look around, to ignore the shadows that seemed to still press in around her vision. Tall buildings rose up next to them. In the distance, shouting. Somewhere beyond a copse of trees, the roar of engines. And behind her, Jin advancing on Nazarov as fire burned over his hands.

"Go, Az! Run! Find Adi!"

Find Adi? How the fuck was she supposed to find Adi? She needed to get back to Cressida, too, to help her. But Astrea couldn't let Jin fight Nazarov alone.

"Go!" Jin yelled again.

That strange static prickled all over Astrea's body. She ran, not away from Jin but toward him. He might yell at her later for not following orders, but she didn't care. She'd almost reached them. She pulled on her light, welcoming its familiar warmth as it danced around her hands.

Fifty feet, maybe less, separated them.

She could make it.

Sharp pain stabbed between her shoulders, darkness crowding her vision as she stumbled to the ground. *Not so fast, Miss Sovna,* an unfamiliar, feminine voice purred.

Astrea couldn't see anything. Something—someone—slammed into her from the side. Rocks scraped Astrea's exposed arms and back, but still, she couldn't see.

And then that vortex returned, pulling her body through the void. The last thing she heard was Jin calling her name.

CHAPTER 38

When Astrea's body crashed into solid ground again, she could've thrown up. Between that strange mode of travel, the heavy Novarian food in her stomach, and her aching body, Astrea was surprised she didn't simply vomit until she was a shell of herself.

Someone yanked her up to her knees. Before Astrea's vision could even clear those strange shadows, rough fabric was tied around her eyes. Neither Jin's panic nor his wall was in Astrea's magical awareness. Somewhere nearby, there was the rush of anticipation, rough irritation, and . . . something she couldn't quite place. And there was also void. So much of that cold, empty feeling where there should've been something.

Astrea blinked, but her eyelashes just brushed against the fabric. Panic surged through her. She needed to find a way back to Cressida. She needed to find a way to get to Jin and Adi. And where was Eliana? Had she and Nicos made it out? Astrea couldn't just sit there and—

Rough, calloused hands grabbed Astrea's shoulders and forced her to her feet. She stumbled as the room swayed.

"Told you not to jump so much with her," someone muttered, a deep voice. "Where's the other one?"

"Victor couldn't get them both." A quieter voice, still harsh. Feminine. The same one that had talked to Astrea before they moved through the shadows. The floor creaked. "I had to step in. At least I got one."

Was Jin still at the palace? And where was Nazarov?

"Do not be so rough with her," a third voice, this one soft and feminine, said.

Those calloused hands dug into Astrea's arms. "The One wants to see you, Lightbringer."

"What?" Astrea managed.

"The One wants to see you," the deep voice repeated, as if that was going to explain everything. "Let's go."

Before Astrea could ask anything else, someone shoved her forward as another grabbed her by the elbow and half dragged her. Floorboards creaked as they walked. A thud came from somewhere above them. And all around her, that void pressed in, in, in.

After several turned corners and opening doors, the person dragging Astrea finally dropped her elbow. They grabbed one of Astrea's wrists, right next to the burn from Nazarov. Astrea tried to swallow her pain, but vomit still crept up her throat. She swallowed again. The person guided her hand to what felt like the back of a chair.

"Sit down," they ordered.

Resisting seemed pointless. Astrea fumbled her way into the chair.

"The One will be in shortly," the rough voice said. "Ninette, take her blindfold off."

One set of footsteps moved away while another moved closer. A door closed, then gentle fingers removed the fabric from around Astrea's eyes. She blinked furiously, trying to adjust to the room's dim candlelight. She was in some kind of office, the walls and furniture made of heavy, expensive-looking wood. A few built-in bookshelves on the wall behind the desk were mostly bare except for a few books. There wasn't even a window in the room.

When a small figure moved into Astrea's peripheral, she jumped. The other woman wore a mask much like the ones the palace attackers had. The obsidian material covered her entire face, silver paint marking the sides and holes for her eyes. Blue peered out at Astrea, bright and almost kind. Green curiosity bubbled around the stranger.

"Hello." The woman smoothed a pale hand over the front of her dark gray shirt. Her voice was the same soft one as before. "I am Ninette, and I am here to serve the moon. Do you need anything?"

Astrea stared at her. Did she . . . need anything? Did she *need* anything? Of course she did. She needed to leave. But Astrea doubted that was what the woman was offering. So, she asked, "Where am I?"

"You are with the Paragon." It sounded like Ninette smiled. "Would you like some water?"

"No." Astrea didn't want anything these people might offer her. She needed to find a way out.

"Very well." Ninette nodded. "The One will be with you shortly."

Though Ninette moved somewhere behind Astrea, she didn't leave the room. Ceramic and glass clinked. Ninette even began humming to herself.

Astrea's pulse thundered through her body so violently she thought it might crack the chair she sat in. Was this where the Paragon would have taken her if she'd left Kalama with them all those weeks ago? Where were they? Still in Talmaris? Maybe. Unlikely. Why would they keep her in the city?

And the more she dropped into her magic and tried to sense the people around her, the more her heart raced. She and Ninette were hardly the only people nearby. Faint as they were, she could feel multiple voids and emotions, just like at the palace. An unexpected mix given who had taken her. Just how many Paragon were there?

The door opened with a low groan. As a tall, lithe man swept past her, the air grew frigid. His complexion was almost as pale as Astrea's, his long hair the same near-black. Unlike Ninette and the other Paragon Astrea had seen, this man wore a bright white mask edged by obsidian, and he was pure void.

If it weren't for the mask, he might seem like any other man she'd seen on the streets of Talmaris. His dark, fitted suit was more appropriate for a business meeting than . . . whatever this was. The stranger sat on the other side of the desk, opposite Astrea.

"Miss Sovna," he said in smooth Helosian. She knew that voice. It wasn't the one from her recent run-ins with Nazarov in her mind, but from earlier dreams. The one who had first called her little Lightbringer years earlier. "I apologize for the . . . unorthodox methods used to get us in the same room."

She said nothing. Astrea didn't need her lightbringing to know this man wasn't sorry. His voice held no hint of emotion, no shred of regret.

"I'm simply glad that after all these years, we're finally able to chat," he continued. "Ninette, please, bring our guest something to drink."

Astrea almost laughed. Guest? She was hardly the Paragon's guest.

"Why did you take me?" she asked. "Where's Jin? And who are you?"

"I am who they call The One," the man said. "Your princeling used some . . . unorthodox methods of his own. He won't be joining us today."

Had Jin killed Nazarov? Or simply escaped? Would he try to find her?

"And as for *taking* you, you are our guest, Miss Sovna, and an important one at that."

Ninette approached, then set two teacups and saucers on the desk. Would this man, The One, take his mask off to drink? Astrea didn't plan on taking anything from these people, that was for sure.

"If I'm so important, why would you attack the palace?" Astrea asked. Behind her, soft footsteps scuffed across the floor, then the door opened and closed. Ninette's wariness drifted farther and farther away from the office. "And hurt people? Why not just tell me why you wanted to talk and have a normal conversation?"

The One chuckled, a deep, low sound. "Always the inquisitive one, little Lightbringer." As he said the nickname, it sounded almost affectionate. Astrea tried not to shiver. "I've been waiting for this moment for a very, very long time. You truly don't know why?"

"No," Astrea muttered. "I don't know."

"Let me ask some of my questions," The One said. "Then I'll answer yours."

She nodded. Maybe, if she tried to play along, he'd let her go. Maybe she could convince him they had the wrong girl.

"What can the sun do?"

"I'm . . . I'm sorry?" Astrea asked. "The sun?" He motioned with two bony fingers for her to continue. "Like, the sun in the sky?"

"Oh, Astrea," he scoffed. "I know you're not a foolish girl. Just tell me what the sun can do, then I'll answer one of your questions."

Even with the mask blocking his face, Astrea got the sense that this man was not interested in a basic astronomy chat. But what did he mean, the sun?

His eyes narrowed. They were like ice, the palest of blues. "Kostas truly didn't get that far in his lessons with you? I was hoping my Advocate was wrong about that."

Astrea swallowed thickly. "What?"

"I knew the process was going very slowly, but to think you didn't even *touch* on the subject is simply shameful."

"Professor Shalysko?" Astrea barely whispered the name. "No, he—"

"He was not a very good teacher, it seems," The One muttered. "Don't know how he managed to hold down that job at the university all these years."

"But he—" Astrea tried again. Commander Lucian had checked into the professor. They'd found no connection to anything out of the ordinary. "But you destroyed everything in his office."

The One simply shrugged. "Some things—some people—are worth sacrificing."

Professor Kostas Shalysko. She'd thought the attack on his office, the pure outrage he'd felt and shown, had been about Lucian's team not keeping his things safe. He'd even blamed Lucian specifically, hadn't he?

"Why would he still work with you after you did that to him? Why would he keep trying to teach me?"

"He knew his mission."

What did that mean? Astrea tried recalling more of what Kostas had said to her, if he'd let anything slip. But nothing stuck out to her, not with the fear and pain clouding her head.

"Are the Novarians involved?" she asked.

"No."

Astrea didn't know if she believed him or not. "Not even Tomas?" He was the one who'd sent them to Kostas's office in the first place.

"No. As I said, I've been waiting for this moment for a long time, Astrea," The One said. "After your uncle took you to Helosia, my attention turned elsewhere. You were so young, and there were other things I needed to tend to."

Astrea swallowed.

"After you ran away from us at that ridiculous festival, I decided to try something a little different. Education," The One said. The dark paint around the edges of his mask glinted as he tilted his head. "Theo didn't have the courage to nail you and the princeling down, but once you arrived in Talmaris and showed up at that university, well, imagine my delight."

"Why take so much time? Why not just tell me what you wanted me to know?"

"After we managed to keep ourselves and our history hidden away from the world?" The One scoffed. "Little Lightbringer, come, you of all people must know that sometimes, hiding is a path to survival. Fourteen years, right?"

"I don't—" Astrea clutched the side of her head, digging her fingers into her hair. Skies, her head hurt. She'd hit it too hard on the floor at the palace.

"The professor couldn't lead you to the answers too quickly without exposing who he was," The One continued. "And I was hoping, with time and discoveries and proof, you would see reason. See the history and the truth and stop resisting. Come to your own conclusions and see the true path. My plans are nothing that couldn't have waited a few more months if that was what it took, but . . ."

Then why do any of it? Why destroy Kostas's office? Why give Kostas such a short timeframe to teach her?

Chaos. Destruction. Balance.

"Balance must be restored soon." He didn't move a muscle as he said, "The continent has been out of balance since before the Great Wars, when the monarchs began conquering their neighbors and imposing their rules on others. A Stargazer from long ago predicted that the sun and moon were to come together, and when they did, balance would return."

Balance will be restored. Was that what the inscription at the ruins had referred to, this ancient Stargazer's vision?

"The sun and moon come together all the time," Astrea said. "The moon often rises during the day, and even eclipses aren't—"

"Not the real sun and moon," he snapped. "What do you think *you* are?"

Astrea almost laughed until Ninette's voice replayed in her head. *"My job is to serve the moon."*

"That's why you've been looking for me?" she asked. "Because that's what you think I am?"

"It's what I know you are, little Lightbringer," The One said. "And what do you think that princeling of yours is?"

This man could not be serious, could he? If she weren't terrified, Astrea might actually laugh. It was ridiculous. The moon and sun? She and Jin were just two people. Visions were never set in stone. That was why stargazing magic was so fickle; people's choices could change the future at any moment.

"As I said, I've been waiting for this for a long time," The One said. "A very, very long time. But it seems my earlier setbacks were not for nothing. Because not only are you here now, but you and your princeling running away from Kalama have set in motion the very thing I've been working toward for so long."

Astrea swallowed past the bile rising in her throat again. Though she was sure she knew the answer, she asked, "And what is that?"

"Why, the civil war in Helosia. It's only a matter of time until that country tears itself apart. Just look at what's happened in Delia over the years. I think my work there speaks for itself."

The Kingdom of Delia hadn't had a stable government in nearly two decades. Different members of the royal house had been infighting for years over who was the true heir, and there had been several military coups in that time, too. It was part of why the emperor launched the Delian-Helosian War in the first place years earlier; he'd been trying to take advantage of the unrest.

"That was the Paragon?" Astrea asked.

"Indeed it was."

"But civil war is not balance. It's chaos."

"Are they that different? Are the wars these monarchs and empires fight against each other really that different?"

Astrea didn't know how to answer. Besides, what she thought didn't matter. Even with the void pulsing around him, she knew The One believed what he was saying. The conviction in his voice was clear and strong.

"We are destined to work together, Astrea." The One leaned back in his chair and steepled his fingers in front of his mask. "We both want Emperor Aelius out of power. We both want to see his reign end. Neither of us want him to control the void. I could have what I want, and you could have what you want."

Astrea fidgeted in her chair. "What do you know about what I want?"

"You could go home, and you would no longer have to hide who you are. Is that not worth everything?"

It wouldn't be like that with Eliana in power. Eliana wanted to end the wars. She wanted to decentralize some of the imperial government's power and phase out tribute payments. Those were only the beginnings of her plans. Eliana had plans to change so many things once they stopped her father.

The One clicked his tongue. "Surely you recognize that his daughter taking the throne will not mean change. Not in Helosia, and not on the rest of the continent, either."

Could he read her mind? "It would," Astrea forced herself to say. "Eliana is different."

"A daughter of war." The One gestured vaguely to the room. "A descendant of despots. Do you really think she'd want to give any of that up once she has it? Surely you aren't *that* naive."

"And you think chaos wouldn't create a different kind of power vacuum?"

The One chuckled, a dark sound. "Chaos balances itself out in the end. That Helosian Empire would be too fractured for just one power to rise. The powers that try to fill the vacuum would eventually reach a stalemate. Chaos is the natural balance, and it *will* return to this continent."

This man wanted to tear Helosia apart. Not just Helosia. The continent. Sure, Helosia had its problems—plenty of them—but that scale of war would be unimaginable. She couldn't even fathom the number of casualties that would bring, what kind of people would try to step in to claim power for themselves. People like Prince Kaius. People like The One.

"You are meant to help me restore balance, Astrea," he continued. "You are meant to help me restore balance not just to the world, but to magic. Void magic has been hidden for far too long."

Astrea simply stared at that expressionless mask of his. Balance. Chaos. Destruction.

"I'm just one person," she whispered. "I don't even have control over my own lightbringing. How am I supposed to help you?"

"You're teachable."

Again, she stared at him. Even if she believed this man—and she didn't—Astrea wouldn't help him. She couldn't. Not if he wanted to destroy nations. Not if he thought destruction would bring that balance. She would not help him do something that would hurt so many innocent people who would simply be caught in the middle of it all. The visions this man had sent her—Helosia on fire, Kalama on fire, everything consumed by shadows—flashed through her mind. Civil war in Helosia wasn't ideal, but the chaos the Paragon wanted to unleash would be different. So much worse.

"I cannot let you stop what has already been set in motion." The One sighed. "And I must say, I'm surprised you don't want to help. You know the consequences of the emperor having more power."

This was more information than she knew what to do with. She just hoped she could remember it all long enough to actually do something with it. To find a way to get back to Jin and her friends, to tell them.

"At least tell me where the book and journal are," The One said.

Theo Kadis's book? Mattina's journal? They'd known the Paragon wanted Theo's book, but what could the journal say that The One would want it back? She wasn't willing to find out.

"Theo Kadis's book?" she asked instead, her whole body tensing. The One nodded. "We thought you might've already had it—"

The One's voice held lethal promise as he said, "Tell me where they are."

"I don't know."

He slammed one hand on the desk so hard Astrea thought the wood might crack. She flinched. The One folded his arms over his chest. His suit jacket barely wrinkled. "If you will not help me now, Astrea, I cannot help you when Tovan returns."

"Who?"

"I know you can sense the other people with us here. Those here with us today are a mere fraction of our true numbers," The One said. "Though some of them are new recruits, most of them have been waiting for this for generations. A chance to fulfill their duty and restore balance. We supersede nations and borders, and whether you help us willingly or not, we will bring this continent to its knees. We are everywhere, and we will no longer be ignored."

Astrea swallowed. *Generations* of Paragon members? She and her friends had thought the Paragon, or some related group, went back centuries. Were these the descendants of those powerful mages from the mountains during the Great Wars? Was this man—The One—possibly even a descendant of that ancient king, Tytas Ramkas?

"I won't help you," Astrea whispered. "I won't help you hurt that many people."

"Death and destruction are the natural ways of the world," The One said. "They bring rebirth. Something better."

"I won't help you," Astrea said again even as her own cold fear bloomed in her heart. "I can't help you."

"A shame that you lack such open-mindedness, Miss Sovna. Really. I would've expected more from you." When she said nothing, The One let out a heavy sigh. "Fine." The word was frozen. Harsh. "Then I will transform you into someone who will. I will break you down day by day, week by week, until those friends of yours cannot recognize you or the work you do for the Paragon."

Ice flooded Astrea's limbs as she asked, "Where are my friends? Where did you bring me?"

"Where they are and where you are does not matter, little Lightbringer," The One sneered. The door opened, a confusing mix of heavy frustration and giddy anticipation pressing into Astrea's bones. "Tovan."

Astrea's pulse doubled, tripled, as she chanced a look over her shoulder. A man not much taller than her but with thick, corded muscles stalked closer. Not one inch of his skin was exposed. Like Ninette, he wore an obsidian mask that matched his clothes. Unlike Ninette, his mask was trimmed in red. Amber eyes peered out. In one gloved hand, he held a silver syringe. It caught one of the candles' flames, glinting with promises Astrea didn't like.

"Last chance, Astrea," The One said.

Astrea couldn't do it. Whatever fate awaited her at the hands of this Tovan and the Paragon, she would not help them. She would not help them destroy countries. She would not help them kill thousands and thousands of people. That was the only outcome to the Paragon getting what they wanted. Destruction. Death. Chaos. Rebirthing the world. There were many things wrong with the powers that controlled the continent, but Astrea would not help the Paragon.

"Fine." The One nodded, and Astrea steeled herself. "I suppose we're doing this the hard way."

Tovan approached from her right and lifted the syringe.

"Last chance," The One said to Astrea. She tensed. "Do it, Tovan."

Tovan rammed the syringe into Astrea's thigh, right through the skirts of her dress. Pain exploded through her. As he lowered the plunger, fire pulsed under her skin. It took everything in her not to cry out.

And as Astrea looked up at The One again, she swore his mask smiled a predator's smile as he said, "See you soon, little Lightbringer."

The world around her faded away, and everything went dark.

CHAPTER 39

"Little Lightbringer," a familiar voice called. "Open your eyes."

She didn't want to. She'd been through this before, this same taunt.

"I told you to open them."

Something peeled her eyelids back, forcing Astrea to look. It was the Novarian palace, nothing left but smoke and ash and bodies. She'd seen this image before.

"You should've just come with us weeks ago. This is your fault."

She wanted to cry, but her eyes were dry, so dry. Even her mouth was dry. Dusty. She needed to cough, but she couldn't do that either. She couldn't move, couldn't look away from the bodies of her friends caught among the wreckage.

"Why?" she asked, voice cracking. "Why did you do that?"

"Because when little Lightbringers misbehave, they must accept the consequences."

Fire burned over Astrea's skin, hot and cold all at once, consuming every part of her. She screamed and screamed as the image of the palace gave way to darkness again. All she could see were shadows, and all she could hear was that voice.

"There are far worse things I can show you, little Lightbringer. You'd better answer my questions next time."

Astrea's mind lurched forward through the darkness, fire burning her again. She wanted to scream, but she couldn't. She couldn't do anything at all.

"Wake up, Miss Sovna," a soft voice said.

Astrea blinked furiously. Her head ached. Her entire body ached. Rolling over, Astrea vomited into a bucket placed on the floor. She retched until her head pounded.

"I told him that would be too high of a dose," that soft voice said. Ninette. That was her name, wasn't it? "I brought you some water, and there's food if you're hungry."

Astrea lifted her head as she pushed the bucket away. That fair-skinned woman was watching her, expression unreadable behind her mask. Yes, Ninette. That was her name.

"What dose was too high?" Astrea croaked as she looked around the room. The walls were dark, stony. So was the floor, though a threadbare rug covered the middle of the room. This was not The One's office. She was on a hard, narrow bed fit for a child, not a grown woman. Astrea tried to sit up straight, but the room spun around her. "What did you give me?"

Ninette's lavender surprise flickered in the room's low light. "You don't remember?" she asked. "I told you this last time."

"Last time?" Astrea echoed, the words almost catching in her throat.

Yes, there had been a last time. This was not the first time she had woken up like this. Vomiting. Confused. On this hard, tiny bed. But she couldn't remember what was being given to her. Couldn't remember how long it had been since she'd last been awake.

"It is blue lotus and something to make you sleep," Ninette said softly. "Tovan has been giving you too much. The One will not be pleased by this disobedience."

Astrea collapsed back onto the cot. She was tempted to close her eyes, but closing them just brought back visions of the Novarian and Helosian palaces, dead bodies, and worse.

Chaos. Destruction. That was what the Paragon wanted, and that was what The One was showing her. Endlessly.

Wherever she was, Astrea was freezing. Her gown from the council dinner did little to keep her warm. Her limbs trembled. There was no blanket on her cot, just a folded set of white clothes at the foot of the bed.

"Those are for you to change into," Ninette said. "The One thought you would be more comfortable."

"I'm not wearing them," Astrea muttered.

What did the Paragon care about her comfort? They were drugging her. Had kidnapped her. Astrea's head pounded in time with her heart, her thoughts fracturing with each breath she took. Blue lotus. They were giving her blue lotus. Why?

"He wants you to wear them," Ninette said, orange anxiety dancing around her. When Astrea made no move to reach for the cloth, Ninette said, "He will be angry if you do not wear them, and he is already angry."

If The One was already angry, wearing the clothes offered to her would not make a difference.

"You do not want to make him angry," Ninette said again. "Please. It is my job to serve the moon. Let me help you."

"If you want to help me, tell them to stop drugging me," Astrea croaked as another wave of nausea hit her.

"They will not listen to me. It would be easier if you just answered his questions and do as he asks."

Astrea's eyes fluttered closed. Her arms. She needed to check her arms for burns, where they'd been burning her in the dreams. She touched her forearms. The skin was smooth on one arm, nothing there except for the handful of freckles that had accumulated thanks to the Kalamian sunshine. On the other arm was where Nazarov had burned her back at the palace. Astrea couldn't bring herself to summon her light. Couldn't even find that energy in herself.

"It is not real," Ninette said softly. "Whatever you feel in the dreams is not real."

"How does he do it?"

"It is called dreamwalking." Behind Ninette, the lock on the thick mahogany door tumbled free. "Please," she whispered, "just change into the clothes."

Tovan stalked into the room and slammed the door shut behind him. Astrea flinched, the cot underneath her creaking with the movement.

"Why hasn't she changed?" he snapped at Ninette. The red edges of his mask glinted in the low light.

"I have tried to convince the moon to—"

"Do what Ninette tells you," Tovan barked at Astrea. Though his mask remained neutral, rusty annoyance and crimson anger burst to life around him.

Not void, Astrea realized. Remembered. The room tilted as she moved her head too quickly. Not everyone here was void. Her mind felt slow, like she couldn't quite think straight.

Tovan prowled closer. Astrea pushed herself back into the corner as far as she could, her magic barely surging forward even as she pulled and pulled on it. Light built around her hands, low and pathetic. Little good it would do her, anyway. Tovan smacked her. Her cheek stung. He smacked her again.

"Tovan—" Ninette started forward, but he waved her off.

"Don't bother," he muttered as he produced a syringe. "It's time for her next dose anyway."

"Please." Astrea pushed back farther into the corner, but she had nowhere to go. Cold stone scraped her back. "I don't know what to tell him. I don't have the answers he wants. I'm not who you think I am."

Ninette simply shook her head as Tovan plunged the needle into Astrea's thigh. She closed her eyes as her muscles began to burn. She just had to find a way to convince them.

"Is that what you want to happen to your princeling?"

She was back on the mountain, but the bodies weren't on the ground. Her friends were fighting, overrun by void mages.

"Don't hurt them," she begged. "Please."

Her friends backed into a tight circle, an earthen wall surrounding them. The void mages opened fire, and those inky black flames swallowed the earth, then her friends, whole. The image receded as darkness took over again.

"I'm getting tired of your games, little Lightbringer," The One snapped. "Tell me what I want to know."

Something new flickered to life. Saros. Her uncle. He leaned over a long table, explaining something to Emperor Aelius. The image was hazy, impossible to focus on.

"He's working with the emperor now," The One said. "To find you."

The image was silent, but when Saros's mouth moved, it was clear what he was saying. Astrea. Lightbringer. No. Saros wouldn't do that to her.

"He's saving himself," the voice said. "You can do the same. Tell us where the book is. Give me the journal."

"No."

The image changed as flames began to burn her again. Astrea felt tears as they formed and fell, but she couldn't stop watching the image play out before her. Cressida, kneeling on the ground, a blade in her gut. Jin laid out next to her, blood pouring from his throat. Eliana, motionless.

"Wrong answer, little Lightbringer."

"Why won't you just tell him what he wants to know?" That voice was soft. Different.

Astrea's body shook violently as she vomited over the side of the bed. She'd never felt so sick in her life.

"Well," that voice said with a sigh, "at least you got it in the bucket this time."

Astrea slumped back against something hard as the world spun and spun around her at dizzying speed. Two blank faces peered down at her.

"You have to stop crying," the soft voice said. "He doesn't like it when you cry."

"Stop talking to her like she can hear you," a harder, different voice snapped.

"Maybe she could answer if you were giving her the proper dose."

"Maybe it's to shut her up. I can hear her screaming all the way down the hall."

"It is not working, Tovan. The One will be angry with you."

"Just move so I can give her the next round."

"My patience is wearing thin, little Lightbringer," The One growled. "If you're trying to protect them, that time has passed. Answer my questions, and all of this will end."

"I can't!" Why did he not understand? Astrea didn't have the answers. She'd failed for weeks on end. "I swear, I don't know anything."

"You're more resilient than I gave you credit for."

The darkness receded, revealing an image of gravestones. Lucian. Zephyrine. Marko.

"You have caused this."

Jin. Eliana. Cressida. Nicos. Adi.

"I didn't do anything," she whispered.

"And that is exactly the problem, little Lightbringer."

Astrea woke with a start, as if she had been held underwater for too long and desperately needed air. She was cold. So cold. The narrow bed under her creaked as she shivered.

Astrea forced herself to look to her right despite how it made her head swim. Ninette. The woman with the mask. She perched on the edge of a nearby chair, a rickety wooden thing. The ceiling lights, though dim, hurt Astrea's eyes.

"You must change into the new clothes even if you do not want them," Ninette said gently. "Please. I will help you get up, and then you can use the washroom and change."

Anything. Astrea would try anything to get them to stop with the dreams. Despite her trembling limbs, Astrea forced herself to stand up. Ninette showed her where there was a small bathroom in the back corner of the room, hidden behind the wall Astrea's cot was pushed up against. It had a porcelain toilet and sink, though there was no mirror. It felt like she'd been in here before, but Astrea couldn't remember.

Every joint in Astrea's body throbbed as she moved around the narrow space. It was barely wide enough for her to stand next to the toilet, but after relieving herself, she did as Ninette instructed. She managed to get out of the dress she'd worn to Ysabel's dinner, and she managed to slip into the clothes provided by the Paragon. Soft white fabric draped off her body, barely warmer than her dress had been. The sleeves were trimmed with black stitching and only reached halfway to her elbows, leaving her arms cold. The pants skimmed her ankles, and Astrea kept on the flat black shoes she'd worn to the dinner. She tucked her sapphire necklace under the neckline of her shirt.

When Astrea cracked the bathroom door open, Ninette was right outside. She took Astrea's dress from her arms and ushered her back into the room. The rug covering the middle of the space looked like it had once been decorated with purple and white flowers, though now it was mostly gray. In the far corner of the room was a small table.

"Right this way." Ninette ushered Astrea toward the thick door on the far side of the room. "We must not keep The One waiting."

"Where are we going?" Astrea asked as Ninette opened the door and pushed her into an impossible darkness beyond. Once Ninette closed the door and blocked out the dim lights, Astrea couldn't see anything, not even her hand when she held it in front of her face.

"The One wants to speak with you," Ninette said from next to Astrea. Then her cold hand touched Astrea's arm, gentle. "This way, please. We must hurry."

Astrea didn't have the energy to consider the darkness pressing in around her, suffocating as it was. Her head swam as they walked. How much of the drug were they giving her? Did The One really think that drugging her was going to make her give him answers? Or did he just want to keep her sedated and weak?

Astrea didn't know how long they walked. It could've been minutes or hours. The earth underneath her, though obviously solid rock, felt like it moved. Astrea didn't know how Ninette was able to navigate the dark turns and corners without any light, but soon, the Paragon woman stopped in her tracks.

"There are stairs here," she said. "Be careful."

Careful, Astrea thought ruefully. *Right.*

Astrea tried to count the stairs as they walked up, but she lost track after the first dozen. Eventually, they stopped again, and Ninette dropped Astrea's arm. A door opened, and candlelight flooded the small foyer ahead of them. The ornate decor was made of dark wood. The painting of a family of three—father, mother, daughter—hung on one wall. Who were they? Something about the mother and daughter—warm brown hair, cool complexion—was familiar, but Astrea couldn't place it.

Ninette steered Astrea through the foyer and down a corridor. A few Paragon members milled about. They wore the same masks as Ninette, some in different colors but always trimmed with black or white. And like Astrea, they all wore loose shirts and trousers. Instead of being white like hers, theirs were black.

Worst of all, they all watched Astrea as she was forced down several short hallways. Many of them were void, but many were not, and those who were not didn't contain their emotions at all. Curiosity, disgust, pleasure, and a myriad of other emotions assaulted Astrea's magic, sliding across her skin and vision with unbearable intensity. She tried to shut it down, but control was impossible, slippery like she was trying to grab a bar of wet soap in the shower.

She barely even noticed when they reached a door and Ninette herded her inside a room. It was the same office as before.

"Please, have a seat," Ninette said as she gently guided Astrea to the same chair as last time. "The One will be with you shortly," she said before leaving the room.

Astrea took in the small, sparsely decorated space. Alone. Alone and out of her cell. She swayed as she shoved to her feet. Steadying herself with the edge of the desk, Astrea sucked in a deep breath.

She needed to find something. A way out. Information. A weapon. Anything. She circled around his desk and found several drawers. One was locked. But with each other one she pulled open, she found nothing.

Behind her were those mostly empty bookshelves. She lunged for them and the few books tucked on a middle shelf. She scanned the spines. No titles. Astrea grabbed the first one—a small, red volume—and opened it.

It wasn't even a real book. The inside pages had been hollowed out. And in their place? Nothing.

Astrea wanted to scream, but she grabbed the next book. Blue cover, same hollowed-out inside. The third book was green and empty, too.

That drawer. She needed to get into that locked drawer. Trying to escape into those hallways was not an option. Not with so many Paragon still nearby. Not with her head so fuzzy from the blue lotus.

But Astrea didn't even have a chance to examine The One's desk. Heavy footsteps sounded outside, and a void crept closer, closer, closer. Astrea scrambled back toward her chair just as the door opened. She was only halfway to it when The One stepped into the room.

"And what were you doing, little Lightbringer?" he asked as he closed the door behind him. His gaze flicked to the hollowed-out books Astrea hadn't bothered to set back in their proper spots.

"Stretching my legs," she lied. "How long have I been here?"

"Always with the questions despite not answering mine, I see," The One muttered. "Five days."

"Five days?" Astrea asked as she sank back into her seat. She'd been with the Paragon for five days? Between the dreamwalking—that was what Ninette had called it, right?—and the drugs, everything was just a blur.

The One sighed. "Perhaps I've been going about this all wrong."

"I told you a thousand times," Astrea muttered as she stared at her hands folded in her lap, "that I don't know what you want and I won't help."

"At least look at me when you speak with such disrespect."

Astrea considered not looking up at all, but the edge in The One's voice promised more terrible visions if she didn't obey. She forced her gaze up. He looked the same: that white mask, the dark suit, the hardness in his eyes.

"If you would simply work with me, then all of this could change," The One said, his voice almost gentle. Kind. Astrea squeezed her eyes shut. "We will give you a better room to stay in. Hot coffee. That is one of your favorites, right? At least tell me where Theo's book is, and I'll have Ninette make the preparations."

"I can't give you answers I don't have," Astrea pleaded. She contemplated lying, but she was sure that when he eventually realized she had lied, everything would get worse. "Why won't you believe me?"

"Because you're trying to play me for a fool. Stretching your legs? Really?"

Something in the air changed, making the hair on Astrea's arms and neck prickle. Then Victor Nazarov appeared in a puff of shadow. He smiled at Astrea, his face not covered by a mask. Those copper eyes she'd first seen at the Whiskey Dream so many weeks ago flashed with something unreadable.

"Hello, little Lightbringer," he snarled. "I hear you're causing trouble."

An ache settled deep in Astrea's chest. "I'm not."

"Oh, but you are," he said as he strolled around The One's desk. A dark, barely healed red wound covered his forearm, a mix between a burn and a gash. "That little princeling of yours is causing trouble, too. Would you like to see?"

Jin? They didn't have him, did they?

"Show her, Advocate Nazarov," The One snapped.

Astrea steeled herself, but instead of Jin being dragged through the door, familiar pain scratched between her shoulder blades. Her vision went dark as her body seemed to move forward. Astrea gripped the edges of her chair, a tether until her vision cleared again.

When it did, it wasn't a palace on fire or the graves of her friends that she saw. Construction crews working to rebuild a portion of one wall of the Novarian palace. Adi and Nicos laughing about something. Eliana speaking with Ysabel. Cressida watching on from a distance with a sad, puffy face, like she'd been crying.

And Jin. Jin was a different story entirely. He wrapped his arm around the waist of a petite brunette. The woman giggled when he leaned down to whisper something to her. Worst of all was when he kissed her, his fingers threading through her hair.

It wasn't real. Couldn't be real. None of what The One had shown her was real.

"Troublesome, isn't it?" The One said from somewhere nearby. "The only one who seems to care is the Metalli. She begged your friends to keep searching for you, and yet . . ."

"No," Astrea choked out. "I know these are just visions. It's not real."

"True that we can provide false images," The One said coolly, "but we can also provide the truth. They often linger in the darkness, those truths we do not want to look at too closely. Like your princeling. Your friends."

"No," Astrea said again, even as she watched the scene. Cressida turned away from it all, tears streaming down her cheeks.

Jin had promised. He'd promised he wouldn't leave Astrea behind. Adi had said they didn't leave anyone behind. They were supposed to be a team. Partners.

You fought with him, some tiny, distant part of her mind whispered. Her chin trembled. *You yelled at him. You never apologized. What did you expect?*

"Is that really who you want to call your lover?" Nazarov practically purred into her ear. "He didn't even wait a week before replacing you."

"They're not your friends, little Lightbringer," The One said. "Friends help each other, right? So help us, and we'll help you."

Astrea wanted to close her eyes, but it would do nothing against the vision. Even if it were true, even if her friends had abandoned her, she would not help the Paragon.

"I can't," Astrea said. "I can't help you."

"Can't or won't?" The One asked.

"Can't," she insisted, although both were true. "I can't."

A hand clamped around Astrea's forearm. Pain seared across her flesh. She cried out as her vision went dark, the images of her friends receding. When the office came back into view, Nazarov smiled down at her and pulled his hand away from her arm.

The One may not have actually hurt Astrea with the dreamwalking, but this was no dream. Her skin puckered and bled.

No. Anger and pain and energy pulsed through her. Astrea shot a quick, bright ball of light into Nazarov's face as she pushed out of her chair. He stumbled back, barely avoiding the attack, and sneered. Astrea staggered away from both men.

The door. Could she make it to the door? She pulled on her light again, faint as it was.

"Told you she was a little bitch," Nazarov growled as he stalked forward.

As he reached for Astrea, she punched straight out, just like Adi had taught her. But her body was so weak; even that made her wheeze. Nazarov blocked her blow, then grabbed her forearm and yanked her down so fast she fell to her knees.

"Pathetic," he muttered before cracking a punch across her temple. The world spun around Astrea as her whole head pounded in time with her heart. "Why do you always insist on doing things the hard way, Miss Sovna?"

"Enough, Advocate," The One said.

Nazarov crouched in front of her and pulled on her hair, leaning forward as he whispered, "You should've accepted my offer weeks ago."

When she said nothing, Nazarov yanked on her hair again. Astrea cried out, unable to stop herself.

"I said enough, Advocate!" The One barked. "You will not hurt her. You will not touch her again after this. Is that understood?"

With a huff, Nazarov let her go. Astrea steadied herself just in time to see The One stand up from behind his desk and open a drawer. When he reached inside and produced a silver syringe, Astrea tried to scramble away from Nazarov, but he grabbed her elbow and held her tight.

"Just hold her still," The One said as he rounded the desk.

"Please," Astrea whispered as he approached. "Don't."

"Should've remembered your manners sooner, little Lightbringer," The One hissed before jamming the needle into Astrea's thigh.

She didn't even try to fight the darkness as it rushed forward.

Chapter 40

The One never seemed to run out of things to show Astrea. The Novarian palace. Kalama. The Great Library. All of her friends and family. The emperor. Even Jin's little cousins. He never ran out of questions, either.

The new routine was obvious to Astrea even in the brief periods of lucidity. Whenever she woke, either Ninette was there or she woke up in total darkness and Ninette came in later. Astrea would stumble around, half-high, to use that ridiculously tiny toilet if needed or to take water from Ninette. Not long after, Tovan would show up and dose her again, and the cycle would repeat.

When Astrea woke next, it wasn't Ninette's masked face watching her from across the room. Victor Nazarov sat on Ninette's usual chair, one leg crossed over the other. Astrea's vision tilted and bent, but even so, she could make out the nobleman and his giddy, maskless face.

Her stomach sank. She tried to push herself up, but her wrists were bound in front of her by thick rope. At some point, Ninette had cleaned and bandaged Astrea's burns. She would've healed them herself, but when she'd first woken up after firing her light at Nazarov, Astrea had found her wrists tied. The rope pressed painfully into her bandages now.

Foolish, she chided herself. *You were foolish, like always.*

"You're not very cooperative, little Lightbringer," Victor said. He made no move to stand. "You're tougher than I expected."

"I don't know what you want me to say," she croaked. "I'm not the moon. I can't help you. I don't have answers."

Nazarov clicked his tongue. "I know you're the moon."

"Why do you think that?" Her voice cracked as she asked, "Why?"

"So the Stargazer said," Nazarov replied, as if that explained it all. "And I think you do have answers."

"I've already told your boss that I don't know where his book is. You asked me if I'd found it while we were in Kalama, like you knew I hadn't found it."

He shrugged. "Maybe you've found it since."

"We haven't found anything."

"Then tell me about the rebellion. What is Eliana planning?"

The rebellion? They'd never discussed plans to go home, not really. All she knew was what Eliana wanted to do once she actually got the throne. "I don't—"

With a heavy sigh, Nazarov shoved to his feet. "Let me guess. You don't know about the book. You don't know about the rebellion. You don't know about the emperor's plans. Do you know about *anything*, Astrea, or are you utterly useless?"

Useless. The one thing she didn't want to be. But as Nazarov said it, Astrea knew it was true.

"Yes," she said. Pleaded. "I'm useless. I've been trying to tell you that."

"What of the princeling's magic? Surely he's told you about that."

That, Astrea knew. But she wouldn't tell. Jin's strength as a mage, his ability to create those impossible explosions, would be a boon to what the Paragon wanted. They could never know about that. When she said nothing, Nazarov shook his head.

"Why are you protecting him when he's left you here with us?" Nazarov stalked closer. "When he allowed you to be taken that day at the palace?"

"He didn't—"

Nazarov crossed the distance between them. In one quick, sharp move, he slapped her. Astrea's face stung. Her head ached and pulsed, disorienting.

"He doesn't care about you," Nazarov snarled as he hauled her off the bed.

Pain bloomed between her shoulders. Her vision went dark, quickly replaced by the Novarian palace. Jin with a blonde. Cressida bawling. Jin with a redhead. Eliana speaking with Ysabel and Veiko. Jin with a brunette. Adi laughing with Nicos. Jin with two of the women from before, both of them putting their hands all over him.

"Stop," Astrea begged.

"I'm doing you a favor, little Lightbringer," Nazarov whispered, his voice so close to Astrea's ear. His hand barely dipped under the neckline of her shirt. Her necklace. He grabbed her necklace, then pulled on it, hard. The clasp snapped, and then that familiar, cool metal was gone. "The Metalli is the only one who gives a fuck anymore. Stop protecting the rest of them."

No. Astrea refused to believe that. Even if she and Jin had argued, she refused to believe—

"It's been two weeks and they haven't even bothered to look for you."

"No," Astrea said. "No, you're lying. I have no reason to believe you."

Nazarov shoved her forward, and the vision cleared from her mind. As she looked over her shoulder again, void flames roared to life over Nazarov's hand. The hair on her arms prickled just before Tovan and a thin, dark-haired woman appeared behind Nazarov. The woman seemed strangely familiar, but she was pure void.

"Tovan, Solana. Good," Nazarov said. "So nice of you to join us."

"Finally," Tovan muttered. "Better make it quick, boss. The One's expecting her to get another dose soon."

"What is it Ninette always says?" Solana's voice went up an octave as she said, "The One will not be pleased."

Nazarov snorted. "Just hold her down."

"Wait—" Astrea started, but Tovan kicked her in the ribs.

Astrea wheezed as she doubled over, her bound hands making it impossible for her to catch herself. She tried pushing to her knees. One of Tovan's thick hands grabbed Astrea by the ankle, dragging her backward. The rough stone floor scraped Astrea's belly as her shirt rode partway up her abdomen. Solana circled to Astrea's front and held her arms down against the cold floor.

"If you would stop protecting them," Nazarov said, "you could start protecting yourself, Astrea. We don't want to hurt you."

Astrea swallowed a scream as Solana's void fire licked her arms and hands.

"If you would just do your duty and help us, all of this could be avoided," he said. When Solana burned her again and still Astrea didn't scream, he huffed. "This is getting boring, isn't it?"

"We wouldn't want to bore our guest," Tovan agreed.

Though Solana wore the same mask as Tovan—obsidian etched with red—Astrea was sure she smiled as she said, "That would make us bad hosts, and we don't want to be bad hosts."

Astrea struggled against the two Paragon, but they held her down like she weighed no more than a feather. Tovan's giddy anticipation pressed against Astrea, unwelcome and foreign. Something cold pierced Astrea's back. As sharp metal sliced her skin, she broke. Something between a sob and a scream tore from her throat.

"Do you want to tell me what you know now?" Nazarov asked.

"I don't know anything!" Astrea cried.

"Wrong answer."

The knife met her skin again, just below the first gash. An animalistic cry escaped Astrea as she writhed on the floor. Away. She had to get away. She kicked out, but Tovan and Solana pushed down on her limbs even harder.

"Still not jogging your memory?" Nazarov asked, voice laced with false sincerity. Sickening golden joy flashed somewhere to Astrea's right, but she could barely see through the tears. "At least tell me what Varojin can do."

As the knife tip pressed into a spot higher on Astrea's back, she choked out, "He's a very strong mage." That was true, wasn't it?

"You think we didn't know *that*? Try again."

She couldn't tell them. She couldn't tell them about Jin's ability. It would just make them want him more. And deep down, Astrea knew that even if she told them everything they wanted to know, the Paragon would not let her go. They would not stop.

"That's all I've ever seen him do. He was gone for years. I've barely even seen him fireweave in Talmaris." All true, yet not what Nazarov surely wanted to hear. "He wasn't even training me, it was all—"

The knife pressed into her back a third time, slow and cold as it tore through flesh and muscle. Astrea's entire back pulsed in time with her heart. Warm blood seeped down the sides of her torso. If she'd eaten anything, she would've thrown up on the spot. But all she could do was lie on the ground and will herself not to cry more.

"Solana," Nazarov barked. With just her name, Nazarov must've sent some kind of command. The weight bearing down on Astrea's throbbing arms lifted, then Solana disappeared in a puff of shadow.

"Maybe a little time down there will serve our guest well," Tovan said as he let go of Astrea's legs.

"I agree. The One's gone soft. Useless, really." Nazarov crouched in front of Astrea and flicked the end of her nose. "If you're smart, you'll stop protecting them and start helping me. Otherwise you're going to have much bigger problems than you do now, little Lightbringer. Trust me."

And then he was gone, nothing but tendrils of darkness left in his wake. Astrea didn't dare move to look at Tovan. A boot collided with her ribs again, delivering a heavy crack. She wheezed, every breath shuddering.

"Ninette will deal with you whenever she returns," Tovan muttered. "Worthless."

As his footsteps retreated and the door opened, then closed, Astrea waited. The lights flickered off. It was only when she was bathed in darkness and she could no longer feel Tovan's giddiness that Astrea finally let herself cry.

Ninette had come back twice more that Astrea could remember. The first time, she'd been horrified to find Astrea facedown on the floor, bleeding, and had said The One would not be pleased to find out what Nazarov had done. Astrea had thought the woman might finally do something to truly help her, but instead, Ninette had just implored Astrea to provide the information the Paragon wanted. To fulfill her duties.

The second time, Astrea had convinced Ninette to remove the rope on her hands for a few minutes, just so Astrea could go to the bathroom more easily. Ninette had agreed, and once Astrea had been alone in the tiny washroom, she'd managed to pull on just enough of her healing magic to lessen the sting of the bandaged burns on her arms. She hadn't been able to do anything for her back or ribs, though. Ninette had seemed none the wiser.

Now, Astrea curled in on herself, shivering as goose bumps prickled her skin. Everything hurt. Everything ached. Every breath felt like someone was stabbing her again and again.

She didn't know how long she'd been awake, but neither Ninette nor Tovan had returned. Solana and Nazarov were nowhere in sight. Astrea wasn't even sure how long had passed since that last encounter with Nazarov or her last lucid conversation with The One. She squeezed her eyes shut, blocking out the darkness of her cell. The One had invaded her dreams again with more questions about Jin, about Mattina's journal, whispers of balance and power and comfort if only she would help the Paragon.

None of it mattered. Astrea didn't want balance or power. She just wanted to go home.

Maybe her friends weren't coming for her. Jin had promised he wouldn't let Ysabel hand Astrea over to the Paragon. He'd promised he wouldn't let them have her. And yet here she was. And it had been weeks.

It could've even been longer than two weeks now. It was impossible to tell the passage of time here in the dark. Everything blurred together.

She curled in on herself even tighter despite the pain in her back and ribs. Her teeth chattered. What if that scene The One had shown her at the Novarian palace was actually true? Had her friends moved on? Convinced the Novarian council to aid Eliana's rebellion? That was probably for the best anyway. If the Paragon wanted Astrea and Jin and had to wait to continue their plans until they had both of them, maybe it was for the best that Jin had left her here. Maybe it was best that he'd abandoned her.

Hot tears burned behind her eyelids as she reached for the necklace that was no longer there. Jin had left her here just as he'd left her in Kalama all those years ago. He'd promised he wouldn't. Had she really been foolish enough to believe him? Had she really been foolish enough to think their time together meant something? That he could really want to be with her after all these years and all that had happened?

Leave no one behind. That rule applied to his team, not her. This was her fault. None of this would be happening if it weren't for her. Of course they had left her here. She hadn't been smart enough to figure this out, hadn't been strong enough to fight off the Paragon. What would be the point in saving her?

A sob broke free from Astrea's chest, her entire body shaking as she stopped trying to hold her tears back. Her cries echoed through the room, crashing over Astrea again and again in humiliating waves.

She would always be a weak little Lightbringer, just as the Paragon called her. She wasn't worth rescuing. She was useless, just like the Paragon said.

Astrea couldn't scream anymore if she wanted to. She didn't know how long she'd been in this room.

Sometimes they gave her a break from the visions, from the flames that burned her in her dreams, but it was never for long. Eventually, Tovan always came back with another syringe, always came back with more blue lotus. The One kept coming back into her mind as she slept, trying to pull information from her that she simply didn't have to give.

Astrea would die there, she was sure of it. Nobody was coming to save her, and she couldn't save herself. She was too weak. She'd failed, just as she'd failed that very first night behind the museum in Kalama. The One had shown her that scene, too, among many others.

Astrea couldn't even cry anymore. All she could do was lie on her cot and stare up at the ceiling until Tovan came back with her next dose.

Eventually, though, nature called. She didn't want to get up, but pissing herself didn't seem like a good option. Forcing herself to stand, Astrea first braced herself against the wall as the dizziness receded. Then she forced the tiniest bit of light to dance over her hand, the effort draining what little energy she had. Astrea used the sad excuse of a bathroom, then stumbled back toward her cot.

Her body burned with every breath. She needed to heal herself. Had to find a way despite her bound hands and uncooperative magic.

She lay back down on the cot, then tried moving her hands toward her abdomen. The rope dug into her wrists, but Astrea pushed past the discomfort until the sides of her hands touched her torso. Would that be enough?

Astrea searched deep inside her being for that spark of light. That energy. Just like before, it didn't want to come to the surface, was small and weak. Like her.

Please, Astrea begged herself. *Just a little bit.*

With another sharp, painful inhale, she managed to coax her light forward. It was faint, a mere fraction of what it usually was. But as she willed it into her torso, willed it to find the thing that needed healing, a fraction of relief rushed through her. A broken rib, mirror healing and mirror pain warring.

The relief stopped almost immediately, replaced by a dull ache.

That couldn't be all she had to give, could it? That couldn't be all the magic she had in her.

A knock echoed through the darkness, followed by Ninette's muffled voice. "Astrea! May I come in? Are you awake?"

"Yes!" Astrea called back, her voice hoarse as she forced her arms to relax away from her torso.

The overhead lights flickered on, and the door unlocked. Astrea squinted at the sudden brightness.

"I have brought you some water," Ninette said. "Tovan will return soon."

Astrea almost considered asking Ninette if she would untie her wrists again. She'd seemed sad and concerned the last few times she visited Astrea. But no, Astrea didn't think Ninette would do that. There was no way she'd risk upsetting The One, and in the last bout of dreamwalking, he'd been irate.

Instead, Astrea let Ninette put a cup to her lips, then drank when she tipped it back. The water was cold at least and soothed her sore throat.

"How are you feeling?" Ninette asked as she returned to her tray in the far corner of the room.

"Fine," Astrea lied. What else could she say?

"I wanted to bring you new bandages and supplies to clean the burns on your arms," Ninette said gently, "but The One would not allow me. I am sorry."

Of course he wouldn't allow her. It was probably for the best, though, since Astrea had managed to heal the worst of that damage some time ago. Ninette would know, and then she would probably tell The One.

"Thank you for trying."

"Have you considered more of what he has told you?" Ninette asked as she brought a refilled cup to Astrea.

Astrea took another drink when offered. "About how chaos is the way to restore balance?"

"Yes. It was what our forebears did," Ninette said, "and it is what we must do, too."

"I see," Astrea murmured. Jin and Cressida had always said Astrea was a terrible liar, but Ninette didn't seem to pick up on it. "I think I'm beginning to understand."

Mint relief blossomed around Ninette, and it sounded like she smiled as she said, "Oh, I'm so pleased to hear that. I have been hoping you would come around."

"It's just a lot to take in," Astrea said, watching as Ninette returned to her tray again. "It's very different from the way I'm used to thinking."

"It's different from the way most people think. Chaos scares people, but it should not. It is the natural order."

The One had mentioned something like that during Astrea's last lucid chat with him. She still disagreed, but keeping Ninette talking seemed like a good idea.

"Is that what the Paragon have always believed?"

Ninette finally abandoned her tray, instead moving to sit on that rickety chair opposite Astrea's bed. "Yes," she said as she sat, "even in the time of King Ramkas, the first One."

King Ramkas, the first One. Astrea had been right about Tytas Ramkas, then. "Is that what you've always called your leader? The One?"

"Yes, it is," Ninette said. "Dreamwalkers have always been our kings." She sighed. "But not all accept our message. Some have wandered from the true path."

The true path? Could that be why Caliban, Emperor Aelius's guard, was at the Helosian palace? How many of these wandering void mages might there be?

"That's unfortunate," Astrea said. Her voice sounded flat, but she hoped it came across as exhaustion to Ninette. "That must be difficult."

"Oh, it is." Ninette nodded. "I appreciate your concern, though I am not surprised. You are the moon, after all."

"What does that mean?" Astrea asked, trying to hide the desperation she felt. "Everyone keeps saying that's who I am, but I don't understand."

"The prophecy. You are the moon." When Astrea just stared at her, Ninette huffed. "The sun and moon balance each other. The moon is inquisitive and sensitive, ever present. The sun is strong and bright, unyielding. Together, with the Paragon, you will bring balance to the continent."

That didn't really explain why Astrea and Jin were being forced into these roles. Lots of people were inquisitive and sensitive, strong and bright. Lots of people had all those qualities. So what, their magic? A celestial mage and fire mage? Thousands of people across the continent shared their same abilities, controlled the same elements.

"I see," Astrea said quietly, even though she felt no closer to a true answer.

"The One will be so pleased to know you're taking his ideas into consideration. He's always said you are a smart girl, Astrea, and I've always believed him. Though he is stern, he is a wise leader."

Astrea had no plans to actually help The One. She had no plans to do anything to help the Paragon. The One had said he would break her down day by day until she was a tool for him to use. Astrea was so tired of fighting back against the visions, but she could not let that happen.

Maybe it had already happened. Maybe they had already broken her. But she would not let them keep her.

Maybe she was a fool for ever thinking she could outwit the Paragon. Maybe she had failed time and time again when it came to finding answers on her own. But now . . . now she had information. Information The One had given her during their very first conversation. Information from Ninette about this true path. About dreamwalking. She tried to commit the details she could remember to her fuzzy memory: the fact that generations of Paragon had seemingly lived here, that they wanted to bring chaos and destruction, that they believed in some old Stargazer's vision.

Astrea stared up at the ceiling, straining to pick out any details in the dark stone as she listened to the sounds of Ninette moving around the room again. Yes, she needed to try to leave, but her body and mind were so tired.

Even if Jin had abandoned her, Cressida wouldn't. But Cressida couldn't spend forever looking for Astrea, nor could she look alone. She certainly couldn't look for weeks. Eventually, Cressida would've had to assume she was gone. Did Cressida blame herself? Astrea hoped not.

Snap out of it, Astrea scolded herself. But even in her head, her voice sounded flat. Tired.

Even if her friends had abandoned her, Astrea finally had some under-standing of what the Paragon wanted. And she could do something the Paragon didn't know about.

Astrea had hated when Lucian turned those emotions on her. She had hated it. But he had been right. She hated that, too.

The One was void; she couldn't attack him that way. So was Nazarov. But Ninette was not void. Tovan was not void. Some of the other Paragon there weren't void, either, though most were. Astrea's magic had been able to tell her that much.

She had to try. Astrea couldn't sit in this cell and rot. Skies forbid one of those visions of her friends were right, whether the ones of them at the palace or the ones of their graves . . . she still had to try. There were still people in Helosia who needed help. Saros, Sarsali, Balthazar, Raela, and countless others.

Next time they come, Astrea promised herself. *Next time Ninette and Tovan come, I will leave.*

Astrea's body ached, but the hunger she'd felt for so long had faded. Her head still pounded, but she was sure that it was caused by the near-constant injections of blue lotus. Her magic, weak as it was, would have to be enough. Astrea was getting out of there, even if it killed her.

The Paragon could not have her.

Chapter 41

Knowing she needed to find her way out and actually doing so were two very different things. Astrea tried to ignore the oppressive shadows pushing in around her and the itchiness growing on her thighs as she waited for Ninette's return.

Her plan was simple. Astrea needed to make Ninette upset, and then she would attack. Tovan would be easy; he was irritated every time he returned to her cell. She would attack them, and then she would lock them in the room, turn off the lights, and run. Then she just had to find a way out of the darkness that waited for her beyond her cell door.

With trembling hands, Astrea began braiding her hair. The problem with this plan was that she had to use her magic. Astrea could barely summon her light. Would she be able to use this trick Lucian had taught her? She'd only done it twice before, and she hadn't been drugged for weeks back then.

I have to try, she told herself. *Just try*. Trying and failing would be better than not trying at all.

Astrea had no idea how much time passed, but finally, a familiar knock sounded on the door. Then Ninette's muffled voice called out, asking for permission to enter.

"I'm awake!" Astrea called back.

After a few more seconds, the lights flickered on. Ninette appeared with her usual tray and carafe of water. "I thought you might be thirsty," she said as she closed the door behind her.

"I am, thank you," Astrea said, forcing a smile. Her skin felt tight as it stretched. Astrea couldn't remember the last time she'd smiled, even if it was a fake one. That night long ago with her friends at the palace, most likely. "Ninette, I know you're supposed to follow orders, but could you take off the rope just for a while? It's so itchy." When Ninette hesitated, Astrea said, "Please? Just for a few minutes."

"Well . . ." Ninette trailed off, but when Astrea forced another smile, she sighed. "I'm sorry, Astrea. I cannot."

"Not even if it's what would serve me?"

"The One says you do not know what will serve you best. He must make the decisions for now."

Astrea tried not to deflate, but could she even do this with her hands bound? "What if we just loosen them so I can use the toilet?" she tried. Ninette hesitated again, so Astrea added, "It's just . . . difficult . . . when I'm bound like this."

Ninette set the tray down on the small table in the far corner of the cell, then nodded. "Yes, I suppose it would be. Alright. Come here."

Astrea stood as carefully as she could, her legs shaking as she approached the woman. Though Astrea was average height, Ninette was short, almost shorter than Eliana. She made quick work of the bindings on Astrea's wrists, only loosening them enough that Astrea could at least get full range of motion. If she tried, she could probably get them off, but she'd have to wait until Ninette was restrained.

"Thank you," Astrea whispered earnestly. "I'll be right back."

How Astrea was going to make Ninette angry, she didn't know. She slipped into the bathroom and closed the door behind her. There was nothing but a toilet and pedestal sink. Rust stains near the knobs and handles hinted at their neglect. Could she break something? She didn't have the strength to break porcelain. Maybe she could pretend to fall? *No, that would just concern her.* She needed to make Ninette angry. Annoyed. Something.

When Astrea went back into the cell, Ninette was in her chair. The tray she'd placed on the table in the far corner had that glass carafe on it.

"Let me just get you some—" Ninette started, but Astrea cut her off.

"May I do it? I . . . miss doing things for myself. It feels good to move around."

Ninette turned, regarding her from behind that mask, then nodded. "Alright."

Astrea took slow, measured steps to the table. The top was covered in old carvings, a few smiling faces and letters. Had the last person to be locked here carved those? Surely Astrea wasn't the first the Paragon had held. Why else would they have this underground cell?

She picked up the carafe with both hands. The movement was awkward with the rope still tying her arms together. Her hands shook. Water splashed out of the cup and onto the table as she tried to pour. Astrea didn't have to fake that; she was so tired that even a simple pitcher felt like it weighed a thousand pounds. She did have to force herself to drop it to the ground, though. It shattered on impact, a dozen shards of glass laying among the puddle of water at her feet.

"I'm so sorry," Astrea said with a gasp.

"Oh my." Though Ninette's voice was calm, rusty annoyance flickered around her. "No trouble," she continued as she lowered to her hands and knees. "I'll just clean this up."

Astrea's magic strained her body and mind as she begged it to move. It responded, slow at first but growing stronger as her pulse quickened. She reached for the annoyance arching toward her, closing her fists and grabbing hold of the emotion. Her palms itched. She poured her energy into it just as Lucian had taught her. Just as she'd done to him that day at the palace. She poured in the pain she felt every time The One burned her with his void fire in her dreams. How she'd felt when Tovan, Solana, and Nazarov had beaten her.

Ninette choked as her gaze slid to Astrea's. White terror and icy shock bubbled around the woman, and Astrea grabbed those, too. She pushed and pulled the energy flowing between them, mixing her fear with Ninette's. Astrea's body shook. Her lungs tightened. And finally, Ninette's eyes rolled back in her head, and she slumped over.

Astrea pulled her magic back quickly and knelt on the ground. Ninette was still breathing, but Astrea doubted she'd wake up anytime soon.

Nausea and shame surged up her throat as she stared down at Ninette. This woman had been complicit in drugging her and keeping her locked up, so why did Astrea feel so bad?

She pushed the thought away. Compassion and guilt would get her nowhere with these people. Not when she needed to leave.

It took some maneuvering, but Astrea got the rope off one wrist. Good enough. With great effort, she dragged Ninette's unconscious form back into the tiny washroom. The gashes on Astrea's back cracked and stung. She closed the door. Her breaths came in shallow gasps as she dragged Ninette's chair back to the bathroom and jammed it under the door's handle. Then Astrea stumbled back to her cot and dropped down onto the hard mattress.

It wouldn't be long before she had to do that all over again. Tovan always came soon after Ninette did. Part of Astrea wanted to leave then, to run while she had the opportunity, but Adi and Jin's words echoed in her mind. *Always stick to the plan.* Yes, she would do that. Once she got Tovan in here, she could lock them both inside. There were still plenty of Paragon—especially void mages—for Astrea to deal with. If locking

Ninette and Tovan in here for a while bought her more time and a couple less Paragon to fight, that would be worth the effort.

It wasn't long before Tovan showed up. "Ninette," he grumbled as he walked in and closed the door behind him. "You know you aren't supposed to—"

Astrea grabbed for the rust red annoyance flickering around him. The same terror and shock burst up as with Ninette, but so did something else: rage. Astrea reached out for that bright crimson and forced it back into him with all her strength. She forced her anger toward him, too. Anger at him, at The One, at Nazarov, at herself. That rage burned through her, setting her on fire. The syringe in Tovan's right hand clattered to the ground as he sank to his knees, nothing but the sounds of his choking filling the room.

He glared at her. Astrea clenched her fists tighter as her magic faltered. Her limbs trembled. *Please,* she begged herself. *Finish it. You have to.* What if she didn't? What if she failed now, too?

No. She would not.

Tovan's eyelids fluttered closed. He slumped to the ground, unconscious. Chest heaving, Astrea stared down at the man for a moment, then grabbed the syringe from the floor. She jammed it into Tovan's thigh and pushed the plunger down, just as he'd done to her so many times. That'd slow him down.

She needed to leave. Skies, Astrea was exhausted, but she needed to leave. *What else do I have to do?* She looked at Tovan again. He wore the same monochromatic outfit as Ninette, but it was more like armor than the soft, draping fabric of Ninette's clothing. Astrea hadn't noticed before, but a dagger was attached to his belt. She pulled it out of its sheath, the thing smaller and heavier than she expected. She cut the rest of the rope off her wrist.

Still holding the dagger in one hand, Astrea crept toward her cell door. She cracked it open and peered outside. It was dark, so impossibly dark in the hallway. Astrea pushed her awareness out as much as she could, running into nothing nearby but the unconscious Paragon members behind her. Still, Astrea knew the rest of the Paragon were around somewhere. She was just going to have to deal with them.

Astrea slipped into the hallway, then locked the cell door behind her. It was a massive metal padlock, but neither Ninette nor Tovan was a Metalli as far as Astrea could tell. Hopefully it would hold them.

The darkness was so thick. Impenetrable. Unnatural. She felt along the wall—cold and filled with small dips and bumps—near the door until she found the light switch. She flicked it off. Ninette and Tovan could suffer in that darkness just like she had. Just like she was now.

Which way had Ninette escorted Astrea when they went to visit The One's office? She couldn't remember. Left or right? She tried to recall that day, but there was nothing in her mind. All she remembered was walking for a long time before eventually stopping at the bottom of the stairs.

She needed to just pick a direction. The One would be trying to enter her mind soon, and he didn't need her to be asleep to dreamwalk. The visions he and Nazarov had put in Astrea's mind while she was awake were proof enough. But would he be able to tell she was awake? That the blue lotus was wearing off and that she hadn't received a new dose?

Doesn't matter, she told herself. *Just go left. Get moving.*

Astrea started that way, one hand trailing the wall next to her and the other hand clutching the dagger. Summoning her light here would be too much of a risk, even if it was empty and silent. No other energy came into her awareness, almost like it was just her in the entire place. Could that be possible? Had the rest of the Paragon left? She tried to feel for any other presences or doors just in case there were other prisoners. It crossed her mind that her friends might be nearby, but then why would The One bother drugging her and locking her up for weeks? If he had Jin, The One wouldn't wait to enact his plans.

Her hand trailing the wall suddenly met empty air. Astrea reached out with her other hand, only to find air to her right, too. Was it some kind of junction? A corner? Astrea stepped back to where the wall had last been, then felt around its edge. Yes, it was some kind of turn into another hallway. She followed.

Wandering in pitch darkness was the last thing Astrea wanted to be doing. She could barely catch her breath, though whether that was from fear or the exertion of so much movement after so long, Astrea wasn't sure. It didn't matter. Even if The One didn't dreamwalk to her, surely he would know something was wrong when Tovan and Ninette didn't return to their other stations.

Astrea's breath started coming faster, but she forced it to slow. She couldn't lose it. Not now. She had not come this far to fall apart now. *It's like the hedge maze at home*, she told herself. It was just darker. Impossible to see. Usually filled with people who believed she was half the key to their delusions. But she could do this. She had to.

After walking another twenty paces, Astrea's fingers met air again. She rounded another corner. Another twenty paces and awareness exploded through her, harsh and grating. Something stabbed between her shoulders as the world spun.

Little Lightbringer, The One growled in her mind. *Where did you go?*

The darkness spun and spun around her. Astrea stumbled as she continued forward. She just had to keep going. That was her only plan now: run. She pushed her legs faster, nearly slamming into a wall but managing to turn right and keep going.

I see what you did to Ninette and Tovan, The One whispered.

Her vision blurred, an image of the burning Kalamian palace taking over the darkness. She kept running.

Impressive. Imagine what we could do together. What we could do with the Sunreaper. The Sunreaper and Souleater, with the Paragon at last.

Sunreaper? Souleater? *Doesn't matter,* Astrea told herself. Up ahead, her magic skimmed the edges of that impossible coldness. Void mages. She couldn't tell how far away they were—maybe several hundred feet? Astrea went back the way she'd come, willing her legs to go faster. She couldn't fight them all on her own.

There is no place for you to go that we cannot find you, The One hissed. *Darkness is our domain.*

An image of Talmaris burning flashed in Astrea's mind. She stumbled again. *Not real,* she reminded herself. *Not real.* Nazarov had shown her many things that weren't real. Neither was this. It couldn't be.

She gripped the dagger tighter until its hilt dug into her hand. Astrea focused on the pain of it pressing into her palm. The pain in her torn back. The pain in her arms and thighs and ribs. The pain was real.

I cannot let you leave, little Lightbringer.

Fuzziness crowded the edges of her vision. It wasn't void magic; she was simply too tired. Too weak. Still, Astrea pushed her magic out again, wider, until it physically hurt. More distant voids were heading her way.

At the next junction, Astrea turned right. For all she knew, she was going in circles. She pushed herself faster, and she was sure she was going to vomit. Days without food, days with drugs being pumped into her system—maybe she was a fool for thinking she could do this. Still, she pushed on.

I cannot let you leave, The One said again. This time, an image of Saros, much younger than he was now. No gray in his hair or worry lines around his eyes. A familiar lake with mountains in the distance. A familiar laugh, one she hadn't heard in years. *Just like I could not let your mother leave.*

Astrea stopped dead in her tracks. Her mother? What did The One know about her mother?

Even Saros did not know the truth, The One whispered. *Roxana had to be taken out.*

What do you mean? Astrea didn't know if he could hear her, but she couldn't stop the thought replaying in her mind. *What do you mean?*

"Found you." Copper flashed in front of her, a strong hand grabbing her wrist as cold fire burned through her bandages and down to her skin. "Really thought you could get away?" Nazarov asked.

Astrea swung out with her right hand. She stabbed the dagger into the first flesh she came in contact with. Nazarov roared as he dropped her other arm.

"You stupid little bitch," he hissed. Metal clattered on the stone floor.

Astrea shoved past him and ran.

Her breath came hard and fast as she sprinted through the dark. Nazarov grabbed her braid and yanked her back. Astrea screamed as she tumbled into him. Nazarov went down with her, and Astrea kicked and scratched and punched as he tried to hold her down. She was too close. She was too close to escaping. He would not take her back to that cell while she still had breath in her body.

Astrea pulled on her magic again, pleading with it as it resisted. She fed it her fear, the panic surging up her throat, the pain flooding her body. That energy deep within her rushed forward. Astrea shot a ball of light into what she thought was Nazarov's face. He grunted but didn't drop her.

"Why are you fighting us?" he growled, more of that cold fire burning her flesh. "You are meant to serve the Paragon."

Darkness swirled around them, Astrea's stomach flipping over itself as he transported her. Wherever they landed was just as dark, but they didn't stay long. They jumped again and again and again until Astrea couldn't tell right from left anymore.

The next time they landed, Astrea shot another tiny ball of hot white light at Nazarov. He hissed, then jumped them again. Shadows swirled around them. When they crashed and landed, the light nearly blinded Astrea. It was no longer stone underneath her feet but wood. She blinked, trying to take in her surroundings. There. That familiar painting of a family of three: father, mother, daughter. Nazarov had taken her upstairs into the foyer, just like Ninette had.

When Nazarov's angry, twisted expression appeared in Astrea's line of sight, she kicked out at him. He grabbed her leg, then they jumped through shadows again.

They landed. Astrea's head thunked against the wood floor so hard that stars swirled in her vision.

"What are you doing, Advocate?" The One shouted. "I told you to stay away from her!"

"You really thought that would hold her?" Nazarov asked. "You saw what she did to Ninette and Tovan."

Astrea rolled over and pushed to her elbows, trying to hold in the sputtering cough building in her throat.

"She cannot do that to us," The One hissed. "Do not allow the others to go near her."

"There's no point!" Nazarov yelled as he crossed the room. Astrea didn't move. "We have what we need to draw the Sunreaper out."

"You think I don't know that?"

"You certainly aren't taking any action! Just like you didn't take any action when Kostas was wasting his time at the ruins! Just like you haven't taken action for years!"

"Contrary to what you believe, Advocate, you're not the one in charge here. I am your king."

Nazarov chuckled, a dark, sinister sound. "You are no *king*."

Astrea snuck a glance over her shoulder. The two men stood toe to toe behind The One's desk, one masked and one unmasked. Nazarov wasn't as tall as The One, but he didn't back down as he shouted about unkept promises and plans and prophecies. Astrea glanced to the door, her heart pounding in her ears.

There was no other option. If she stayed in this room, they were going to take her back to that cell. Back to that darkness. At least here, she had a chance. One chance.

Astrea pushed to her feet, but Nazarov and The One continued shouting at each other. Something about Helosia and the civil war and their plans. She didn't care. Astrea reached for the door handle just as a surprised shout and sickening squelch made her flinch. She yanked the door open just as ghost pain flooded her body. It burned the way it had burned that woman behind the museum in Kalama, all-consuming fire.

Astrea didn't turn around to see whose body thumped against the floor.

She ran.

Chapter 42

Astrea sprinted down the hallway. There was a single door a dozen feet away. She would go there, and she would deal with the voids on the other side.

Ten more feet.

"Little Lightbringer!"

Five more feet.

"I thought I told you not to run."

One more foot.

Nazarov appeared just in front of the door. Astrea couldn't stop in time and slammed into him. He grabbed her shoulders and shoved her so hard she stumbled and hit the floor.

"It's too bad I need you," he said, "otherwise I'd kill you now."

When Nazarov stooped to reach for her, she shot light into his face. It hit its mark, leaving angry red burns right on his jaw. Nazarov snarled.

"Hasn't anyone told you that stabbing and burning people isn't very nice?" He grabbed her arm, and they jumped through the shadows again. Astrea yelped as they landed in darkness. "Perhaps you need to relearn your manners while you're our guest."

Nazarov shoved her back against a wall, the breath leaving Astrea's lungs as she smacked into cold stone.

"My boss never did understand how to get things done," he said as Astrea sank to the ground. "But I'm in charge now. We'll get the Sunreaper soon, and then soon, I'll be done with both of you."

Was this really how it was going to end? Astrea had gotten so close, or at least, she thought she was close. So, so close. But wasn't that how all of this had been? She always came close to finding an answer, only for the rug to be pulled out from under her, only for there to be a thousand more questions she couldn't answer. Only for her to fail again and again and again.

Maybe that was her fate, to fail. She wasn't going to solve the void problem. She wasn't going to stop Emperor Aelius. She was going to die right there in that impenetrable darkness.

"*I'll* be done?" a voice called through the dark. It sounded like Tovan. "Cutting out Solana and me already? That wasn't the deal."

"Shut your mouth," Nazarov spat from somewhere ahead of Astrea. "Where's Solana, anyway?"

"Fuck if I know."

Nazarov sighed. "Just help me take her back to her cell."

Back pressed against the wall, Astrea curled in on herself. She couldn't go back to that cell. She couldn't take any more blue lotus. She couldn't take any more of that void fire burning her from the inside out. She didn't care what the alternative was. Nazarov could kill her if it came down to it. Because the Paragon could not have her. They would not keep her there.

"Come on, little Lightbringer," Nazarov murmured, his words so gentle now. Fabric rustled. A hand brushed her shoulder. "We won't hurt you anymore. I'm sorry. Just come with us."

Astrea squeezed her eyes shut and tucked her head down against her arms.

"Oh, come on, Astrea," Nazarov snapped as he burned her shoulder. She swallowed a scream. "Just do as you're told. You've already made this so hard on yourself, stubborn little bitch."

No. They could not have her. She shifted as she pulled on the last trickle of light she had in her body.

"Good," Nazarov said, almost gently. Kindly. "Good. Come, we'll have Ninette prepare you a better room and a hot bath. Then we can talk about this."

Astrea sucked in a breath and forced herself to slide her hand into his. Then she pulled on that light, forcing it up. A brilliant glow lit up the space around them.

It fizzled out almost immediately.

Nazarov dropped her hand. Then something sharp stabbed through the front of Astrea's shoulder. She screamed as one of them twisted a knife deeper under her skin and the other yanked her hair.

"You're lucky we need you alive, little Lightbringer," Tovan hissed, "or we'd kill you now."

"Maybe we should," Nazarov said. "Dump her body for the Sunreaper to find. That'll set him off."

"Not the plan, but it could work," Tovan mused as the knife twisted deeper, deeper, deeper.

No. Astrea was so tired. So tired of them and this darkness and their threats. She grabbed onto her own terror and rage and panic and pain. *They cannot have me.*

Colors swirled in her mind's eye, the white terror and crimson rage and dark gray hate she felt for this place and the Paragon. *They cannot have me.* She pulled and pulled on those colors until she was sure she was going to explode, until her body could hold no more. And then she pushed them out. *They cannot have me.*

Every inch of Astrea's body burned and ached and crackled. The darkness was replaced by a radiance so blinding that Astrea couldn't see anything. A boom thundered through the tunnel again and again. Someone screamed. Was it her? Was it Tovan and Nazarov? The ground rocked underneath her.

None of it would stop her. Astrea pushed and pushed her magic out until finally, truly, she was empty. She slumped over onto the cold, hard ground.

No one said anything. No one tried to touch her or drag her back to her cell. Nobody sent visions into her mind. It was so silent that all Astrea could hear were her wheeze-filled breaths and pounding heart.

Maybe she was dead. Maybe that was why she couldn't hear Nazarov or Tovan or Ninette.

Maybe that was for the best.

Astrea stayed curled up in the darkness until her joints began to ache, and even then, she didn't dare move. Every inch of her body hurt. She couldn't distinguish the void fire burns from where Nazarov had stabbed her. She moved a hand to her shoulder. The knife was gone, but there was nothing she could do. She could not heal herself. She had nothing left to give. Even when she poked at her senses, they didn't respond.

Her magic was gone.

Maybe that was for the best, too. The Paragon couldn't force her to help if she had no magic. She would really and truly be useless to them. *Good.*

Pain coated her skin, the only thing she could feel besides the cold, hard ground underneath her. She lay there until her heart calmed. She couldn't stay, but where would she go? She didn't know her way around these tunnels. She had no light to guide her. And with her senses gone, there was no telling who she'd run into. *Doesn't matter.*

Slowly, Astrea uncurled her body. Pain lanced through her ribs, her shoulder, her back, as she pushed herself off the ground. She could barely breathe. *Doesn't matter. Can't stay.*

On unsteady legs, Astrea started forward. Every breath made her lungs burn. Her head wouldn't stop pounding. But she kept going, one foot in front of the other. Even if just to put space between herself and where Nazarov had last been. It would buy her time. It would give her a chance. *Stick to the plan. Find a way out.*

The unbearable silence broke as someone shouted, "Astrea!" The voice was far away, and her name echoed off the walls a million times.

Was this another one of Nazarov's tricks? Or had The One come looking for her? No, that wasn't The One's voice. It was feminine, familiar but foreign. Not Ninette. Solana, maybe?

"Astrea!" a more masculine voice shouted, this one closer. Tovan?

She pushed herself faster. *Please don't find me.* Each step was agony. *Please don't find me.*

Muffled voices bounced off the walls, joined by the occasional scuff of boots. Astrea's heart pounded so loudly she was sure the Paragon would be able to track her.

As the voices grew closer, Astrea forced herself to run. She was sluggish at first, but somehow, she found the will to push forward. And when a faint glow illuminated the wide tunnel, when the shadows returned and stretched unnaturally, almost reaching for her, Astrea sprinted.

Someone cursed behind her. They called her name.

The sharp pain in Astrea's ribs and lungs made her wheeze. Her heart pounded as she stumbled forward. She'd slowed too much. Her pursuer wrapped an arm around her shoulders. Astrea screamed, the piercing cry echoing off the walls so loudly she thought her own ears would burst.

"No!" she shrieked. "No!"

They tugged her back, gentle but strong. "Hey, hey, hey."

She strained against them, an inhuman sound coming from some-where deep within her. Everything. She'd given everything, and it hadn't been enough. Why was it never enough? Why couldn't they just kill her instead of taking her back to that cell? She couldn't go back, she couldn't—

They spun her around. Warm hands cupped her face, familiar. And the most beautiful golden eyes stared back at her.

Jin. His face was tired and beard scruffier than she remembered. Was this another trick? Just Nazarov tormenting her? She tried forcing her senses out, begging for some spark of magic to come to life. And it did, just long enough to catch a flicker of mint relief surrounding him.

Not the void.

"Hey, it's just me," he rasped. "I've got you, Az. I've got you."

Astrea fell into him, crying out as her knees buckled. But Jin caught her and sank to the ground with her. He was there. Jin hadn't abandoned her. He hadn't left her behind.

"Where's Nazarov?" Hot tears trickled down Astrea's cheeks as she choked back a sob. "The Paragon, they're—"

"It's okay. They're gone."

Gone? They couldn't be *gone.* "There were so many of them, and they—"

"The Paragon aren't here, I promise. It's just us."

Astrea finally took in the dimly lit tunnel around them. Obsidian stone glinted in the firelight, but there were no bodies. Nothing to suggest the Paragon had been there with her at all. But blood still leaked from Astrea's shoulder, warm and very real.

"But—"

"Hey." Jin smiled at her. "I still have eight birthdays and two gradu-ations to make up for. I can't do that if we don't get you out of here, okay?"

Adi approached behind Jin, flashlight in hand. Astrea paid little attention to their brief exchange, her focus solely on the darkness wavering around the tunnel. Jin hoisted her up and started back through the shadows with Adi as their guide.

Eventually, they made their way to those stairs Astrea had so desperately been trying to find. Jin carried her through those cozy hallways of the house and through a set of double doors. They emerged on a front porch, the bright lights of Talmaris visible in the distance. A few stars twinkled in the night sky above.

Talmaris? She'd been near the city this whole time?

On the wide tree-lined street in front of them, several trucks idled and guards in Ysabel's navy blue uniforms hurried about. Adi branched off from their trio. Jin brushed past everyone, then set Astrea down on a stack of blankets in the bed of a black truck.

"I'm sorry," Astrea started, then choked on a sob threatening to break free from her chest. "They were drugging me—"

"It's alright," Jin said. "It's alright, you don't have to tell me anything right now."

"It's not," she croaked. She had so much she had to tell him. To tell everyone. She had learned too much not to tell them. Had tried too hard to escape so that she *could* tell them. But the words still wouldn't come.

"I need to see what's hurt," Jin said. "Adi went to find Lucian. Can I look?"

Astrea nodded. He reached for her hands first, eyebrows furrowing as he turned her wrists over. With a trembling voice, Astrea tried to explain how they'd bound her after she retaliated against Nazarov. Jin removed the half-destroyed linen bandages from her arms with careful fingers. And as he moved to the wounds on her shoulder, barely pulling the sliced fabric apart to look, his jaw tightened.

"Can you heal yourself?" he asked.

She shook her head.

"I need to put pressure on this." He yanked a knapsack toward him and rifled through it. "Just until Lucian or one of the others gets back, alright? It's going to hurt."

"It already hurts." All she could feel was the pain. Pain as her shoulder pulsed. Pain where she'd never fully healed her ribs. Pain on her back.

"I know," Jin whispered as he bundled a cloth in his hands and pushed down on her shoulder. Tears sprang to Astrea's eyes. "I'm sorry, Az. I'm so sorry. We've been trying to find you."

"They told me you . . . they showed me—"

"I need a healer! Adi!" Jin shouted over his shoulder. When he turned back to her, he said, "You're shaking. You're practically blue."

"Well, I've been cold for weeks," she managed to say before Jin pressed into her shoulder again. She gritted her teeth.

"Weeks?" Jin hesitated. "What do you mean weeks?"

"They told me it had been two weeks since the attack at the palace, but that was a while ago."

"Az . . ." She didn't like the way his voice trailed off. "It's been five days."

"What?" Her voice cracked with the word. "No, they said . . ."

"I promise," Jin whispered. "I promise they didn't have you for weeks."

Astrea couldn't stop the tears even though she wanted to. The truck jostled as someone else joined them, but Jin didn't take the pressure off her shoulder.

"But . . ." Five days? The Paragon had said she'd been with them for weeks. *Weeks.* It had felt like months.

"It's meant to disorient you," Jin said. The truck bounced again.

The One had threatened to break her down. He'd already started to do that, Astrea realized, long before he made the threat. Long before he'd captured her. Wasn't that what the dreamwalking had been doing to her in Kalama? In Talmaris and Sezia?

"I thought you weren't coming," she whispered as she forced herself to look up at Jin through her tears. "They showed me . . . they said . . . I thought . . ."

"Hey, we'll talk about it later, alright?" Jin said. "Lucian's here."

"Don't leave. Please don't leave."

"I won't." Jin moved to Astrea's other side, then smoothed hair away from her eyes. "I'm not going anywhere, I promise."

Lucian's familiar face, soft for once, came into view above Astrea. "I know it hurts, but the good news is that none of this is fatal. Just give me a few minutes, alright?"

Astrea didn't even care about the healing. She just wanted to go back to the palace. "Just do what needs to be done now. The rest can wait."

"Astrea, you need—"

"I just want to go home." Anything was worth it to get away from this place. To go back to her friends. The Novarian palace wasn't exactly *home*, but it was all she had. "Please."

He hesitated, then said, "Alright." A soft glow flowed from his hands. He placed them on her shoulder, and Astrea's pain eased. "And some of this you tried to heal yourself?" Lucian asked when he finally pulled his hands away from her shoulder. His features had tightened. Surely he knew how much it had hurt, had felt all that ghost pain for himself.

"Yes," she barely managed to say.

"Let me finish what you've started," Lucian offered. "Then Marko will escort you back to the palace."

"And where will you be?" Jin asked.

Lucian's light flared to life again. Astrea flinched when his hand pressed against her abdomen. Grunting, Lucian slouched over, but the throbbing in her ribs died to a low ache.

"Searching the house for evidence and waiting for troops from Fort Gambit to help with the search."

"Nazarov." Astrea barely managed to get his name out as she focused on the cloudy sky. "He was there. I think he might've killed their leader."

"We found no bodies, but we'll continue our search," Lucian said. "We'll find them, Astrea. I'll see you back at the palace soon."

As Lucian stepped out of the truck, Jin helped Astrea sit up again. She sucked in one shuddering breath, then another, as static filled her body. She was so cold. She was so tired. Part of her still didn't believe she was outside in the fresh air.

Jin wrapped a thick blanket around Astrea's shoulders just as Adi moved around the back of the truck. Lucian's guards were entering and exiting the house at an alarming rate. It almost reminded Astrea of the Nikaphoros's townhome back in Kalama. The building was painted a deep green, dark wood trimming the windows, doors, and roof. It looked like any upper-class suburban home.

Questions. Astrea knew she should have questions about that house, but as she stared at it, she felt nothing.

Adi hopped up into the truck bed, then secured the rear hatch. He scooted past Jin and settled down behind them just as the truck rolled forward.

Jin took Astrea's hand, and she finally tore her gaze away from that house. He smiled at her and said, "Let's go home."

Chapter 43

The Novarian palace grounds were crawling with soldiers. Dozens of military trucks, including some mounted with large guns, and several tanks were spread out around the palace grounds. Even more soldiers milled about, their dark blue uniforms almost black under the cover of night.

"Where are the others?" Astrea asked as they returned to the guest house. Her senses hadn't returned. Other than the dull ache in her head and back, she felt nothing.

"Ellie and Nicos are probably with Ysabel," Jin said. "Cress is at the infirmary."

"Why?" Astrea asked. Wouldn't the palace healers have been able to patch Cressida up after that initial attack?

"She broke her leg and sustained a concussion," Jin said. "The healers have been spread thin and wanted to keep an eye on her because her headache never fully went away. Ellie's been with her."

"I need to see her." Astrea stopped in her tracks, unsure if she couldn't walk because of the fatigue or the need to see her best friend. But she had to see her. She had to make sure Cressida and Eliana were safe, see it with her own eyes. "Please. Can we go now?"

Adi's hand brushed Astrea's shoulder as he moved past her. She'd almost forgotten he was there behind them. He hadn't said a word the entire drive back to the palace.

Jin hesitated, then said, "Let's get you cleaned up first."

"I'll go tell her you're back, Az," Adi said. "I'll make sure the grand duchess knows, too." He hurried off without waiting for a response.

"Do you want me to take you upstairs?" Jin asked.

Astrea looked past him toward the wide, ornate staircase. Stairs she'd walked up and down dozens of times. She nodded; she didn't think she'd be able to climb even one step.

Jin scooped her up with no effort at all. What she wouldn't give to feel him there, relief and pain and panic and whatever else might be going on inside him. But she couldn't. Her vision wavered. Her head swam. Astrea tried to focus on what she could see and feel. *The blue and gray rug. The paintings of Talmaris. Jin's armor.*

Once upstairs, Jin took Astrea to their bathroom. He set her down, then turned on the shower. *Water hitting tile.*

"I need to go check on one thing." Jin's chest heaved. "Two minutes. That's all I need, but tell me if you want me to stay."

She wanted him to stay. She did. But Astrea nodded.

"I'll be right back." His hand brushed hers as he passed, and then he was gone.

Though it took several tries, Astrea managed to get the bloody, torn shirt off her body. She let it drop to the ground, a pile of white fabric and red blood. Her body screamed as she wiggled out of the loose pants next, and it screamed again when she barely stepped under the water of the shower.

Five days without a shower. Astrea was sure she smelled worse than just the tang of the blood still covering her shoulder and back. She realized, too, how bad her mouth tasted and how much oil clung to the roots of her hair. She wasn't even sure she cared.

Water soaked her front and the ends of her hair. It battered her, somehow both the greatest relief and most unbearable pain. Astrea squeezed her eyes shut.

The bathroom door squeaked. Had the hinges always made that noise? Buckles clinked and fabric rustled. Astrea forced herself to look, just in time to catch a glimpse of Jin's bare skin before he slid into the shower behind her.

"Is everything alright?" she asked.

"Everything's fine. Lucian's on his way back to the palace, and he'll come finish healing you if you aren't up for doing it yourself."

"Can't," she mumbled. "My magic's gone."

Jin spun her around and pulled her tight against him. She thought he might say nothing at all, but then his hands brushed the harsh, half healed cuts between her shoulders.

"Let me see." His voice strained. Astrea turned just enough for him to look. Jin sucked in a sharp breath. "What else?"

"My legs." The words were little more than a whisper. She didn't want to look, but Astrea forced her gaze down. Raised hives and small bruises covered her thick, pale—and usually unmarked—thighs.

Though his eyebrows pinched together, Jin said nothing. He worked meticulously as he washed days of blood and dirt from Astrea's body. When he said something about washing her hair in the morning, Astrea simply agreed. She tried to pretend it was any of their other afternoon showers together, fresh from training and covered in sweat instead of blood. Tired from stretching her magic, not letting it all go. Aching because of Adi's intense training routine, not because the Paragon had taken her.

"Let me dry your back," he said as he shut the water off. After instructing her to hold still, Jin pressed a towel in and around her shoulder blades. When he was satisfied, he wrapped a dry towel around her.

As Astrea stepped out of the shower, she stared at the fabric piled on the ground. Her Paragon clothing, stained red. Jin's black clothes that he wore under his armor, obviously dirty and rumpled. The blue towel he'd used on her back.

She shuffled to the vanity. Getting the awful taste out of her mouth was a priority. Astrea managed to avoid looking at the mirror mounted over the sink as she reached for the glass canister of mouthwash. It wasn't until she'd spit it back out that she caught her own reflection. An ugly purple bruise marred the right side of her head. She was pale. Too pale.

Her back. Her legs. Her face, arms, skin. She gripped her towel tighter as pain tore through her. And as the first sob wrenched itself from her throat, she sank to her knees. She couldn't stop it. Her body shook so violently that Astrea was sure she was going to crumble like drought-stricken earth.

There was no part of her untouched by the Paragon. She wanted to tear her skin off, find a way to abandon this body for a new one. One filled with her magic and one that hadn't felt the pain of needle or knife.

This wasn't supposed to happen. She should be at the observatory, home after a long day at work. Home after dinner out with Cressida at Ravintola, their favorite little restaurant. Home after visiting Sarsali and Balthazar for a day of food and gossip. Not here, in this foreign monarch's palace, broken on the floor.

"Breathe, Az." Jin's voice was almost unfamiliar, muffled by the roar of blood in Astrea's ears. Warm skin brushed hers. "Breathe."

Astrea choked, coughing on her tears and lack of air. Jin's hand slid to the base of her neck, his thumb drawing circles there.

"You're safe, I'm here." Jin repeated the words over and over, a prayer and a plea Astrea wanted to hear a thousand times. "I'm here, Az. You're safe."

Astrea hated how she cried. Hated how no matter how much she cried, it didn't feel like enough. Like her body had years' worth of tears to shed. She hated how she had so much she had to tell Jin and the others, yet her breath wouldn't come.

"Three things. Just three," Jin said as he pulled her closer. "Just think them."

The cold bathroom tile. The soft towel. Jin's warm hands. The knot around her heart loosened.

"Three more, Az."

Eucalyptus. Sandalwood. Lavender. Astrea sucked in a shaky breath.

Jin pushed her off his chest just enough to take her face between his hands. He brushed her tears away with his thumbs, those gold eyes burning bright with tears of his own. "Tell me what you need right now . . . if you can."

Astrea swallowed the last of her sobs. What did she need? Her mind was static, like someone had changed the radio to a far-off channel. "Can you braid my hair?"

Jin didn't move except for dropping his hands from her face. Astrea realized then that he'd pulled her into his lap, that she straddled his hips and his back rested against the cabinets under the vanity. Jin simply worked his hands through her damp hair. She let her head drop to his shoulder.

"What else?" he asked.

"I don't know." She barely got the words out, and she hated how small she sounded.

"How about we get dressed?"

Once Jin had helped Astrea into a pair of clean bloomers and one of the loose, wide-cut shirts he wore for training, he led her to the settee. He started a fire first, the logs roaring to life so quickly it was like they somehow knew Astrea was cold. Only once he'd gotten a blanket tucked around Astrea's shoulders did Jin leave the room again to use the phone.

Astrea curled her fists around the blanket. She wanted to feel silly or ridiculous or childish, sitting there like that. But she felt nothing. All she could do was stare at the flames flickering and dancing in the fireplace a dozen paces away. Deep orange flames. No shadows.

"Lucian won't be back for a bit," Jin said as he returned to their room. "We should go to one of Ysabel's other healers."

"No," Astrea whispered. Jin squatted down in front of her. Her thighs itched, and her back hurt, but she would live. "I can wait." She couldn't bear the thought of anyone else seeing her like this.

"I don't want to ask, but I have to," Jin said as he set one hand on her knee. "And if you can't tell me, it's alright. But what happened, Az?"

Names. She could give him names. "Nazarov, a man named Tovan, and a woman they called Solana . . ." Astrea wiped at a few stray tears as they fell. "I don't think they were supposed to . . ." She shook her head. "Another woman named Ninette said something about how their leader wouldn't be happy when he found out what they'd done."

"Did they do anything else?"

"Injections," she said as Jin squeezed her knee. "They were injecting me with blue lotus mixed with a sedative."

"How much did they give you?"

"Every time I woke up, they gave me more. And every time they gave it to me . . ." The words lodged in her throat.

"Hey," Jin said gently. "We don't have to talk about it, alright? That was good. Lucian can work with all of that."

"They took me . . ." Astrea focused on the flickering fire, on Jin's scruffy beard and worried expression. Had her magic been with her, she imagined she would see orange anxiety and mint relief dancing around him. How real that would feel. "They took me because they think you and I are the key to a prophecy they follow. They were trying to take both of us. Nazarov wanted both of us."

She had to get this out before she forgot. No matter how much it hurt. She had to tell him.

"I'm the moon and you're the sun. They want to take down the continental powers with our help. But I told them I wouldn't, and so they started with the drugs . . ."

She told Jin everything she could remember. Everything The One had told her about the Paragon's history, their prophecy, and their ideas. Trying to fight back. The fact that the Paragon didn't seem to know where this book was either. Nazarov and his crew rebelling against The One. Everything.

"Did you find anything in the house?" Astrea asked as she stared down at the rug beneath her socked feet. "Where did they all go?"

"Lucian's teams are out looking."

The knot around Astrea's heart tightened. If they didn't know where the Paragon had escaped to, that meant they didn't know where Nazarov was. He could come take her again.

Why? Why had Nazarov apparently killed The One? Why would he go through all the trouble to get Astrea, only to let her go? Surely the other void mages—at least some of them—could teleport the way Nazarov could. But why not return for her? Had she imagined all of them?

Was she even in the guest house now? Astrea squeezed her eyes shut. Was it another trick? Another vision? It felt real, too real, and neither Nazarov nor The One was talking to her. But could that be part of the ruse? Make her think she'd escaped so she'd let some information slip?

She couldn't be there again. She just couldn't. Astrea pulled the blankets tighter around herself. The floor creaked. A door opened. But Astrea couldn't open her eyes. She couldn't. She didn't want to know who was there. She didn't want to see Nazarov's face or Tovan's mask or hear those voices.

"Az?" Jin's hand brushed her shoulder. "Lucian's here."

The commander's voice was soft as he said, "Let's finish patching you up."

Astrea didn't want to look, but when Jin said something about lying on the bed, she had to. He guided her to the edge of the mattress, then had her sit down as he explained everything to the commander.

"Injections?" Lucian echoed. "May I see?"

Astrea nodded. Jin sat next to her as Lucian kneeled down to examine her thighs. In any other situation, she might be embarrassed to be sitting there like that—bloomers, Jin's shirt, little else—in front of the commander, but she wasn't. She barely felt anything except the warm relief of healing as Lucian's magic seeped into her bones. The commander healed her bruises next, then Jin helped Astrea lie facedown on the bed.

"I need to see your back," Lucian said. Lightbringers and Purifiers didn't *have* to see the problem to heal it, but in Astrea's experience, it made guiding her magic to the right spot easier.

Astrea stayed still as fabric moved and unexpectedly gentle hands settled on her bare back. More relief whispered over her skin and through her muscles. As frustrated as she may have been with the commander days before, Astrea hated that he had taken so much pain from her in the last few hours.

"I've done what I can," Lucian said when he pulled his hands away. "But your body was already doing a lot of the work for you. You will likely have some scarring. I can feel traces of the drugs in your system, too, but that should all wear off soon."

"You can't do anything?" Jin asked.

"No. Some things just take time."

"And will her magic return soon?"

Silence for one heartbeat, two, three. "It should," Lucian finally murmured. "As I said, some things just take time. Sleep. See if it's returned in the morning. And please, call me if you need anything else."

As soon as Lucian was gone, Jin wrapped his arms around Astrea and pulled her close. She tucked her head under his chin and begged her body to relax. Even if this wasn't real, she wanted to hold on to it. She wanted to hold on to him even if she woke up to find Ninette watching her again.

But how could this be fake when he felt so real? When she could feel his breath on her cheek, smell his soap, touch his skin?

"Jin," she whispered.

"Hm?"

"There's something I didn't tell you." She said it so quietly she almost didn't hear herself. Ignoring all of this would've been easier. Shutting down, not telling Jin, pretending it didn't happen, would've been easier. But Astrea so badly wanted—needed—to tell him.

"What is it?" Jin's fingers drifted up and down her arm, up and down. She focused on it, focused on the way his touch was both featherlight and impossibly heavy.

"I thought they were going to take me back," she said. "They came so close to taking me back, and I couldn't let them."

"I know." His voice was strained.

"I thought I was going to die down there." She swallowed. "I thought no one was coming for me."

"I would never let that happen," he said. "Never."

"I couldn't . . . I couldn't go back. I couldn't let them have me. If they come back for me, I don't think I can . . . I'd rather they just kill me."

"We won't let that happen," Jin said with such fierceness it broke Astrea's heart. "I can't promise they won't try, but we'll find a way to stop them. I swear."

"Okay." She didn't know what else to say. And even though Astrea knew there was no way to stop the Paragon from doing that again, she believed Jin. She believed he would try to keep that promise.

"I finally understand your visions," Jin said. "They showed me, too. Just once."

If she'd had the energy, Astrea would've pushed up to look at him. But skies, she was so tired. So impossibly tired. All she could do was stare at his bare chest. "What did they show you?"

"You. They showed me you, down there in the dark."

"When?"

"The fourth day we were looking for you."

"Why?"

"If the Paragon want me, too, they probably wanted me to figure out where they were."

"They showed me you. And everyone else. Sometimes dead, sometimes alive, in Talmaris . . . Nazarov threatened to kill me and leave my body for you to find . . ." Astrea's voice cracked, the memory of those void flames licking over her skin. Had she had the energy, Astrea was sure she would've started sobbing again. But she was spent. Exhausted. All that came out were a few tears and sniffles.

Jin's hold on her tightened, and she swore she heard him sniffle, too. "What do you need right now?" he asked, his voice hoarse. "What would help?"

What would help? Astrea wanted her senses to reawaken. She wanted to feel something good, feel it the way she always did. She wanted to go see Cressida and Eliana. She wanted to go home to Kalama, to Sarsali's garden and Balthazar's cooking and even Saros's brooding.

"I'm tired," she admitted.

"Then let's go to sleep."

"Can you tell me something good first?"

"Like what?"

"Anything. Please." Anything to make her mind stop thinking about that suffocating darkness.

Jin was silent for so long Astrea wasn't sure he'd answer. But then he asked, "Have I ever told you about the garage cat at Fort Avalon?"

"No."

And so Jin told her about the things he and Adi got up to at Fort Avalon. The garage tomcat Adi was afraid of and how he'd won the animal's affections with kitchen scraps. The first time they ever rode motorcycles. The first time Adi beat Jin in a spar. The awful beer Jin's other teammates got him drunk on several times.

Astrea couldn't feel any of it with her magic, but she imagined she could. Amusement. Fondness. Joy from old memories with a good friend. She knew what those felt like.

The tightness in Astrea's body began to loosen, Jin's quiet words making her eyelids heavy.

This was real. She was sure of it.

Chapter 44

On any normal morning, Jin's body heat would have Astrea throwing the blankets off herself. But as she watched morning sunlight dance across the bedroom wall, she reveled in the warmth pressing against her back. She also reveled in the fact that, weak as it was, her magic was seeping back into her body. The shift in energy was small, but it was there. Her senses refused to go out more than a few feet from her body, but she could *feel* Jin there behind her. That was enough.

He'd been there all night. He'd been there when the vomiting had started. He'd held her hair back as she dry heaved into the toilet, and he'd called Lucian. They'd theorized it was because of the lack of blue lotus in her system after so many days of being pumped full of it. Though Lucian had eased her symptoms, all she could really do was wait it out. Jin had stayed up with her for the entire night despite not sleeping for days himself.

She'd finally managed to get a couple hours of blissfully dreamless sleep. And exhausted as she was, she wanted to get up. She really needed to see Eliana and Cressida. She needed to tell Lucian and Ysabel about the Paragon. They needed to find a way to keep everyone safe.

As soon as Astrea started to move, Jin shifted behind her. Minty cool relief danced across her tongue. "Go back to sleep, Az," he rasped.

"Later. Need to talk to Lucian."

Jin was silent for one heartbeat, two, and then he sat up behind her. "Alright."

Another shower had Astrea feeling more like a real person. Jin joined her, taking his time washing her hair and body now that the rest of her wounds had been healed. He even braided her hair for her when they got out of the shower. All she could feel from him was that same cool relief. Maybe he needed to do this for her as much as she needed help.

As they got dressed, Astrea pulled on that faint energy pulsing through her. She didn't dare use much of her magic, but she needed to check Lucian's healing. She just needed to feel it for herself. Lucian's work was good, at least as far as she could tell. She wasn't sure if she was ready to ask Jin about the state of her back, though.

The rest of the guest house was silent as they slipped out of their bedroom. Astrea's senses still wouldn't push out far enough to find her friends, but all the doors in the second-floor hallway were closed. Nobody greeted them when they walked through the foyer.

"I'll call Lucian," Jin said.

As she entered the dining room, Astrea passed the long, empty table and moved toward the windows. She pushed the drapes aside and peeked out. Soldiers swarmed the palace compound, their gray and blue uniforms a harsh contrast to the green beauty of the gardens. They may as well have been in a war zone with the number of troops and trucks Astrea could see from the window.

Astrea opened the drapes on the three large windows just enough to let the morning sun in.

"Ysabel is coming, too," Jin said as he walked into the room. "I can talk to them. I can tell them what you told me."

That would've been easiest. But Astrea didn't want the details lost in translation. Didn't want Lucian to judge her for letting Jin handle things. As she sat in the empty chair at the end of the table, Astrea shook her head. "They need to hear it from me."

Jin's hand found her shoulder, and he gave it a gentle squeeze. "Of course. How about some coffee while we wait?" When Astrea nodded, Jin said, "I'll be right back," then disappeared out the door.

Astrea traced the wood grain patterns of the table with one finger. Should she have offered to go to the palace to meet Ysabel instead? Would that have been better?

She perked up when footsteps stormed through the foyer, but it wasn't Jin who stepped through the doorway. Cressida bounded in first, Eliana right behind her. As they crossed the distance to Astrea in silence, as the distance between Astrea and her best friends shrank, more of that familiar minty relief pulsed in the air and through Astrea's entire being. She stood just in time to be enveloped by both Cressida and Eliana. They collapsed onto the thick rug.

"I wanted to see you last night but Adi told me not to bother you," Cressida said as she finally pulled away. "I almost fought him, you know."

"Probably best you didn't," Astrea whispered.

"Best she didn't fight him or see you?" Eliana asked as she tucked a loose strand of hair behind Astrea's ear.

"Both."

"I don't know, I might pay to see her and Adi fight," Eliana said, drawing something between a laugh and a cry out of Astrea. "How do you feel?"

"Fine," Astrea lied. "Are you two alright?"

"Nothing a little healing couldn't fix," Cressida said with a wry smile.

"I'm so sorry I—" Astrea started, but Cressida grabbed both her hands.

"It's not like you didn't want to. He took you," she said. "There was nothing more either of us could have done."

"If I hadn't tried to go back to the dining room, maybe—" Astrea said, and again Cressida squeezed her hands.

"No," she said. When Astrea tried to protest again despite the lump in her throat, Cressida said, "We don't know if that's true at all, alright? So don't dwell on it. I'm not going to."

"And you're fine? You're healed?" Astrea asked.

"All patched up. Better than ever, really."

Eliana had started to say something when Jin cleared his throat. All three women turned toward the door, where Jin stood holding a tray laden with coffee supplies. "Maybe you'd like to let your best friend off the ground?" he suggested as he set the tray on the table. "Ellie, can I speak with you outside?"

Eliana got up first and followed her brother into the foyer. With Cressida's help, Astrea got off the floor and reclaimed her seat. She took a coffee cup when Cressida offered it to her, hot steam curling up and bringing with it the rich, layered smell of coffee. The good stuff, like what they had back home.

"What happened, Az?" Cressida asked, the words quiet, as she sat down across from Astrea. "Why wouldn't Adi let me see you?"

"I thought you were in the infirmary," Astrea managed to say.

"Yes, well, they'd kept me about two days too long anyway."

"I didn't ask Adi to keep you away."

"I know." Cressida smiled, warring mint relief and orange anxiety coloring the air around her. "I saw Lucian. He told me to let you be, too."

Astrea didn't know how to feel about that. Lucian had been so aggressive—downright mean—during some of their lightbringing lessons, but he'd also helped find her. Had healed a lot of injuries the night before.

"I think I can only say this once," Astrea whispered. Eliana wouldn't hear it, but Astrea assumed she wouldn't have to recount her injuries to

Ysabel. Lucian would surely have told the grand duchess. "You might have to explain it to Ellie for me."

Cressida nodded. "Whatever you need me to do."

And so Astrea told her, in hushed tones, what had happened. "And there's more," she said, "but I need to tell Lucian and Ysabel that part."

"Alright," Cressida murmured, worry and rage burning bright in her aura. "Of course."

Jin returned not long after with his sister in tow, and behind them came Zephyrine. Astrea hadn't seen the general in days other than a glimpse of her bright white hair the night before. Adi joined them not long after, as did Nicos. Noticeably absent were the twins, Lennor and Civan. Astrea didn't mind, just like she didn't mind that the rest of her friends talked only of Kalamian coffee and hoping that Ysabel had breakfast sent over for them.

By the time Commander Lucian and Grand Duchess Ysabel arrived—no breakfast in sight—Astrea had finished her first cup of coffee. Marko trailed in after them, then shut the dining room door. Astrea hadn't expected such a large audience. Not for this. It reminded her of the morning after they'd arrived in Talmaris, the morning when the Helosians and Novarians had first exchanged information about the Paragon.

But now, Astrea was the only one with information to share. The only one who had experienced exactly what the Paragon were willing to do. What they wanted and planned to do.

How was she supposed to tell all these people what happened to her? How she'd failed every time she'd fought back against the Paragon?

"I'm glad to see you're out of the infirmary, Miss Nikaphoros," Ysabel said once she settled in the head chair at the far end of the table. "And that you've returned safely, Miss Sovna. I am sorry for what you have been through."

Astrea swallowed. What was there to say?

"How about we start with what you can tell us, Astrea," Lucian said. "Then I can explain what my teams learned overnight, though that isn't much."

When Astrea swallowed again, it was like someone had shoved cotton into her mouth. *They need to know,* she reminded herself. *They have to.* Under the table, she reached for Jin's hand. He laced his fingers through hers.

"You all already know how the void mages are able to teleport between locations," Jin started. "That was how they got both Astrea and me out of the palace in the first place."

"When they brought me to that house, they had me speak with their leader, a man who called himself The One." Astrea plucked at a wrinkle in her dress with her free hand. "He explained what they want with me. What they want with both Jin and me." Through fits and starts, Astrea managed to explain what The One had told her about the prophecy, the Paragon's history, and their plans to dismantle the continental powers.

"Did he tell you how you're apparently supposed to help them?" Lucian asked.

Astrea shook her head. "No. He just kept saying I was supposed to help them restore balance to the continent and to magic. That Jin and I are. I asked another one of them about it, but all she would tell me was that we are the moon and sun, that we balance each other and must help the Paragon balance the continent."

"That's not very specific," Adi said.

"He called Jin the Sunreaper," Astrea said. "And he called me the Souleater. Do you know what that means?"

Around the table, everyone denied knowledge of Sunreapers or Souleaters. Astrea and Jin hadn't talked of it any more the night before after she'd told him, but next to her, he shifted in his chair and glanced at Zephyrine. Some silent question passed between them.

The Delian-Helosian War, Astrea realized. Jin had told her that he'd been able to create some kind of explosion with his fireweaving, something outside of normal fireweaving limits. *Sunreaper.*

Her stomach dropped. The Lightbringer ability she hadn't known about. The one Lucian had taught her. *Souleater.*

"I would like to have Mariya look into this further," Ysabel said. "Miss Sovna, what else did you learn?"

Astrea searched her cloudy mind, reaching through the fog to pull at whatever information she could. "One woman mentioned something to me about a 'true path' and how not every void mage follows the Paragon. And I don't think they know where that book the emperor wants is either." Yes, those were the things she had promised herself she would remember. "They kept asking me about the book."

"If they don't know where the book is, then who has it?" Cressida asked. "One of these . . . non-Paragon void mages?"

"We'll make the investigation a priority," Lucian said. "What else, Astrea?"

"Just what they showed me with dreamwalking," she muttered. "That's what the visions are. They can show you things whether you're asleep or awake."

"And they were dreamwalking to you?" he asked. When she nodded, he asked, "How often?"

"They . . . I don't know." The words died in Astrea's throat. Jin squeezed her hand. "They were drugging me. A lot of it is a blur. I think Nazarov tried to kill The One. Have you found either of them?"

"We have not," Lucian said. "Where were they keeping you?"

"I think that's enough, Commander," Eliana said.

Astrea ignored her. "In a cell under the house, in this system of tunnels. The furniture was small, almost child-sized."

Lucian nodded. "Did you notice anything strange about these tunnels?"

"Why?" Astrea didn't know why she asked.

"My people are mapping them out as we speak," he said. "There are a series of tunnels beneath the house, expansive tunnels that seem to run under a decent portion of the city." Lucian fixed his gaze on Astrea as he asked, "And you didn't notice anything else?"

"Just how dark they were."

"Nothing else?" he pushed.

"What is so strange about the tunnels, Lucian?" Jin asked. "Just tell us."

"Yes, please, Lucian," Ysabel said. "Let's not waste time."

Lucian dragged his fingers through his hair. "Last night, we were about a mile away from the house when I experienced an intense and overwhelming level of panic and pain."

"From so far away?" Astrea asked. She'd never been able to sense things so far from her body.

"It lit up the sky like a beacon," Lucian said. "But it disappeared. We headed that direction to investigate, and as Adi can testify to, he felt the earth rumbling. It came from the same direction."

"An earthquake?" Ysabel asked. "We felt no such thing here."

"Not so much an earthquake, Your Highness," Adi said. "I was the only one in the truck who felt it."

Panic and pain. Astrea swallowed hard, the edges of her vision going black and her veins filling with static. "That was me?" she choked out, half question and half statement. "There was one point where they jumped me from the tunnels to the leader's office, then back again. I just . . . I was just trying to get them away from me."

"Which brings me to my theory," Lucian said. "When my teams go into these tunnels, they cannot sense what is above them, though they should be able to. And I cannot sense them when they are in said tunnels."

"They're not too far underground?" Cressida asked.

"Deep enough," Lucian said, "but not so deep that a Lightbringer could not sense others above them."

"How is that possible?" Eliana asked.

"I don't yet know," Lucian said. "But there is something off about those tunnels."

Confusion drifted through the room, a low, steady pulse against Astrea's body. Her breathing quickened. Her head grew dizzy. She was going to be sick again.

"Have any of the void mages dreamwalked to you again, Miss Sovna?" Ysabel asked. "Have they tried to contact you?"

"No." That was one thing Astrea was sure of. The couple of hours of sleep she'd gotten overnight had not been filled with visions or images or dreams of any kind.

"How do we stop them from being able to dreamwalk?" Jin asked. "Or jumping us away?"

"I don't know," Lucian said, and Zephyrine murmured her agreement.

How, indeed? How would they stop Nazarov from finding Astrea? From taking her again? From taking Jin?

"Would you be willing to testify about this in front of the grand council, Miss Sovna?" Ysabel asked. "They need to know."

"Can it wait?" Jin asked. "We were up nearly all night."

"It would mean more coming from Miss Sovna as soon as possible," Ysabel said. "I know this must not be easy, but if they see you rally . . ."

"I'll do it," Astrea said quickly. "Can I just have an hour?"

Ysabel nodded. "Yes. I need time to gather them, anyway. Come to the palace when you're ready."

Chapter 45

Astrea stood there in the throne room, just as they had weeks before. She'd worn her lavender dress and a sweater over top. It wasn't exactly a stately outfit, but Astrea couldn't make herself do any more than that.

And now, as she stared up at Grand Duchess Ysabel, Crown Prince Veiko, and the councillors waiting on the dais, Astrea struggled to begin.

"Miss Sovna," said Councillor Reimo Tarsaya, the bald man who'd been reluctant to support Eliana at all. "I understand you've been through an ordeal, but please, enlighten us about this . . . Paragon."

Astrea sucked in a deep breath. "Well, Councillor . . ."

She'd hoped to get through the story in one simple go. No interruptions. But the council had other ideas. Jin, Adi, and the rest of their team gave their own testimonies, as did Lucian and Marko. So did Cressida about her brief altercation with Nazarov. By the time they'd finished, over an hour had passed.

"Thank you," Grand Duchess Ysabel said as their story concluded. "As you can surely see, Councillors, the Paragon and void magic are a threat to Novaria. The attack on this palace and our people was as good as a declaration of war."

"That may be," said another councillor, a plump woman with tawny skin and bright blue eyes, "but their targets were Miss Sovna and Prince Varojin, were they not?"

"Jade is right," Reimo said. "Novaria was not the target."

"Miss Sovna explained that this Paragon group wants to take down the continental powers," Crown Prince Veiko said. "That is a direct threat against us. Against this entire government."

The councillors all joined the conversation, trying to talk over and at each other. Astrea shrank back from the noise. Why did they have to be so loud?

"Councillors, please!" Ysabel called over the cacophony. "Please, for skies sake, let's just discuss this in a more orderly fashion."

"What else is there to discuss?" asked Councillor Sinni. "The Paragon may want to take down the continental powers, but their targets are Miss Sovna and Prince Varojin. While they are in Talmaris, we will *all* be direct targets."

"What are you saying, Councillor?" Lucian asked.

"We're saying we don't believe Prince Varojin and Miss Sovna should remain in the capital."

Jin looked at Ysabel. "You'd let them kick us out?"

Astrea held her breath. The council was influential, and Ysabel needed their support for certain things, but could the council really make that decision alone? Behind Ysabel, Lucian shifted his weight.

The grand duchess watched Jin and Astrea, her lavender eyes hard. Finally, she said, "I believe it's the best decision for all of us."

"After all of that, you think the solution is to make us leave?" Jin asked. "What about solving this?"

"Oh, it must be solved," said Reimo. "There is no doubt about that or the fact that your father possesses such magic. We cannot ignore his plans, whatever they may be. But we also cannot ignore the fact that your presence puts the grand ducal family at risk, Prince Varojin."

Astrea's knees nearly gave out. Where would they go? They certainly couldn't go back to Helosia. Around her, her friends' emotions wavered between shock, irritation, and outrage.

"What about my sister?" Jin asked.

"You are not a target, Your Imperial Highness," said Reimo to Eliana. "You may stay, and we will continue working together. Your other friends may stay as well."

"And Varojin? Astrea?" Eliana asked. "Where will you send them?"

The councillors exchanged a few silent glances, then Councillor Reimo turned to Ysabel. "We believe it's best for the grand duchess to make that decision," he said. "And best if very few people know where they go. We will see ourselves out, Your Highness. Do what must be done."

As the councillors shuffled out the rear door of the throne room, Astrea peeked up at the dome high above. Fluffy clouds drifted by overhead, almost cheerful. Wrong.

"Well?" Eliana asked once the door had been closed. Only their Helosian group, the Novarian royals, and Lucian and Marko remained. "How do we keep Jin and Astrea safe? Where are you sending them?"

Ysabel and Lucian huddled together on the dais, their words so hushed Astrea could barely tell they were speaking. But finally, Ysabel nodded and straightened. "Perhaps it would be best to split you two up and—"

"Absolutely not." Jin's voice may as well have been ice. Astrea's stomach dropped.

"Your Imperial Highness," Lucian said. "If the Paragon are—"

"I said *no*. I will go wherever it is you want to send me, but you aren't splitting us up."

Astrea swallowed hard. She could see Lucian and Ysabel's logic, but to be separated not just from Jin but most likely everyone else she cared about . . .

Lucian and Ysabel exchanged a few more whispers. The commander huffed.

"There is a recently decommissioned base in the northeastern part of the country," Ysabel said. "It's secluded—very remote, actually—and few people are aware of its existence."

"And both Astrea and I may go there?" Jin asked. Ysabel nodded. "You think we would be safe there?"

"I think it's the only option right now. You cannot go back to Helosia, and I don't think now is the time to try to rally other leaders to your side." When Jin said nothing, she added, "Between your team, Lucian, and Marko, you should be well-protected. There's another base about fifteen miles away blocking the only road to the old site. The only other way to access the base is by air or sea."

The grand duchess sending her captain of the guard? Did she not need him at the palace for her own security?

When they remained silent, Ysabel sighed. "I'll do what I can to ensure your safety, Varojin, but you cannot be at the palace right now. I simply cannot endanger my family or my people any more than I already have. If you don't like my plan, then you must find somewhere else to go."

After what seemed like an eternity, Jin nodded. "When do we leave?"

"Two days."

"I don't like this one bit." Eliana paced the length of the guest house parlor, hands clasped behind her back. It was just the six of them now. Astrea and Jin on the sofa, Adi and Nicos occupying the armchairs, and Cressida standing near the fireplace with arms crossed tightly over her chest. "I don't like it at all."

"I don't either, Ellie," Jin said. "And I really hate to say it, but I think Ysabel is right."

That made Eliana stop her pacing. "You cannot be serious."

"If the Paragon really think Az and I are the key to their delusions, then wherever we go will put people in danger. At least, if we're far away from the city, that lowers that number significantly."

Astrea hated to admit it, too, but Ysabel was right. Jin was right. Staying in Talmaris would put people in danger. Eliana, yes, but also all the palace staff and government officials. Children, like Helena and Leo. Civilians all over the city.

"No," Eliana said. "We need to stay together."

"It's temporary, Ellie," Cressida said. "It's just temporary until we can figure out what to actually do about the Paragon. We need to buy ourselves some time."

"But we don't even know if they'll be safe," Eliana said, midnight blue grief and orange anxiety twining around her. Astrea's heart cracked. "And I need help with Helosia. It's starting soon, I just know it. I need help."

"Then Zephyrine can stay with you," Jin said. "She knows far more about the state of the rebellion than I do."

"It's not the same," Eliana protested. In all the years Astrea had been friends with her, Eliana had never seemed small. But now, as she stood opposite them, she looked tiny. Scared. "It's not the same, Jin. It's too much for me to handle on my own. I need you both here."

"You won't be on your own, El," Nicos said. "I'll still be here."

"I didn't mean—" Eliana started, then stopped herself. She huffed. "I just need all of you here."

"We'll be back," Jin said. "You, Cress, Nicos, and Zephyrine can deal with Helosia."

"And what will the rest of you be doing?" Eliana asked as she looked at Jin, then Adi, then Astrea.

Jin shrugged. "Keeping a very low profile."

Astrea hated this. She hated that they had to leave, but they did.

Eliana let out a harsh, shuddering breath. "Then I suppose there's nothing left to discuss."

"We should talk about a few things," Jin said. "Let me help however I can before we leave. I need to talk to Ysabel, too."

"I can go with you," Eliana offered.

Jin leaned over and pressed a kiss to the side of Astrea's head before he stood. "I'll be back."

Eliana gave Astrea a hug, then led the way as Jin, Nicos, and Adi followed her out of the room. In the foyer beyond, Marko said something to them, then the front door closed. Lucian had assigned him to stay at the guest house with Astrea and Jin in the couple of days before they were to head out.

"Well?" Cressida prompted.

"Well." Astrea didn't know what to say. "I'm going to bed."

"Want some company?"

"Yes."

As they passed through the foyer, Marko simply nodded at them. Astrea was so winded by the time they got to her bedroom that she immediately flopped on the bed.

The mattress shifted as Cressida lay down next to her, their arms barely touching. "I had a lot of plans for this year," she said, "but helping start a real rebellion and tracking down a rogue group of void mages were definitely not on the list."

Astrea hadn't really had plans for the year. She was just going to do what she always did: work, spend time with Eliana and Cressida, and work some more. She would give anything to go back to that . . . right? Part of her thought that yes, her old life was better. But another part whispered the truth. That even though so many awful things had happened, she was glad her friends knew she was a Lightbringer. She was glad Jin was here. The circumstances were far from ideal, but at least she didn't have to hide that truth anymore.

"Do you think we'll ever get to go home?" Astrea asked.

"We'd better because I don't think I can take a lifetime of Novarian coffee."

Astrea smirked. "I don't think I can either."

Rough hesitation scraped Astrea's skin before Cressida asked, "Do you think Ellie's ready to lead the rebels?"

Eliana was smart. She'd been navigating the imperial court all twenty-three years of her life. But twenty-three was not old. Eliana wasn't that experienced. Could such a young person really lead a rebel group against the largest empire on the continent?

"Ellie is stubborn," Astrea said. "She's smart. I don't think she'll give up easily. And she has Zephyrine, Jin, and the rest of you."

"The rest of us, you mean."

Astrea didn't answer.

"Hey." The steel in Cressida's voice made Astrea turn to look at her. "You know you're part of that group, right?"

"I can't even sit up for more than a couple hours, Cress."

"That's temporary."

"I couldn't fight off the Paragon."

"Because they were drugging you and you don't have much training."

Somewhere, deep down, she knew Cressida was right. She was at a disadvantage. She'd had to hide her magic for the last fourteen years. Astrea hadn't had the same training as even Cressida, who still didn't have the same training as Jin or his team. They were both at a disadvantage going into a war.

"I just hate not being able to do anything." Astrea fingered the soft blanket beneath her, twisting the fabric over and over again. "I hate that I have to go hide, even if I know it's for the best."

"I bet it's only a couple weeks before we're all back together," Cressida said. "Are you going to sleep? Do you want me to leave?"

"Please, stay." The darkness beyond the windows made her skin crawl. "Stay until Jin gets back?"

Cressida smiled, peach amusement dancing around her. But her mood shifted, peach replaced by steely pain. "When he realized you were gone . . . in all the years I've known him, I've never seen him panic. Not once. Not until then."

Jin hadn't told Astrea anything about what happened in those five days she was gone. All he'd told her was that they'd combed the city looking for her and that he'd had one brush with dreamwalking.

"It was that bad?" Astrea asked.

"Yes." But then, Cressida laughed. "I threatened to kill him if he didn't find you."

"Of course you did."

"And he told me to do it if he failed. He adores you, you know."

Astrea's face heated. "I know."

"I'm pretty sure he would've torn the city—the country—apart brick by brick if that was what it would've taken to get you back."

Astrea's throat tightened, and she focused her attention on the corner of the blanket she kept rolling between her fingers. She was glad that, if they had to split the group up, at least he was going with her.

"You should get some sleep," Cressida said.

"You'll stay?"

"I'll stay."

While Cressida went to the bathroom, Astrea forced herself out of bed. She changed out of her dress and into one of Jin's shirts. The old Astrea would've been embarrassed for Cressida to see her like that, but the new Astrea couldn't be bothered to care. She needed this small comfort.

"You know," Cressida said as she climbed back into bed, "this feels an awful lot like the sleepovers we had when we were kids."

"Yes, because we stayed in foreign palaces and made plans to overthrow emperors when we were children."

"To my mother, we might as well have. Remember the time when we were what, eleven? Twelve? And she found us in the back garden going through my dad's workshop? I think she almost died when she saw me playing with one of the dummy grenades he was working on."

Astrea remembered. They'd both been generally well-behaved kids, but when they were high on sugar from whatever treats Balthazar gave them at sleepovers, well . . . that was a different story.

Yawning, Astrea settled into her side of the bed. "I'm fairly certain that happened more than once."

"Probably. You think they're alright?"

"I think so."

She had to believe that her family was safe. After all, they were on the other side of the continent. Far, far away from Jin and Astrea. From the Paragon.

Chapter 46

Outside the airship windows, the northern sea sparkled in the late afternoon sun. Below, a small fortress tucked near the base of the low mountains was the only thing breaking up the thick green forest.

"You've been quiet," Jin said.

Astrea shrugged. Saying goodbye to Eliana, Cressida, and Nicos early that morning had been hard. Cressida was staying behind to help Tomas in his research. Kostas had pulled multiple texts for them just before the dinner, and with The One's confirmation that Kostas had been one of theirs, it seemed like a good trail to follow. Lucian was staying behind with the twins for a couple more days to wrap up a few things, then the three of them would join the others at the base. Even though Astrea knew Eliana and Cressida were better off at Ysabel's palace, it had been just as hard as leaving Saros in Kalama.

"Let's just get settled in," she said.

It had been almost a whole three days since Jin had found her in those tunnels under Talmaris. Three whole days she'd had to recover. Her magic was back, but the very core of Astrea's bones ached.

Marko called something from the front of the ship, though Astrea had a hard time hearing it with the roar of the engines. The airship Grand Duchess Ysabel had sent them off in was small, just a single level. The fort below grew closer as the airship descended.

When the ship landed and the engines finally cut off, Astrea gathered her things and waited for Marko to unseal the door. Cool air streamed in.

"Right this way," he said, motioning for Astrea, Jin, and Adi to follow him. Then he picked up his suitcase and started down the ramp.

The fort was smaller than Astrea had originally thought; it wasn't much larger than the barracks back on the palace compound in Kalama. The walls had to be over a dozen feet tall even without the added height of the thick metal spikes rising up from the bricks. It looked more like a prison than a base.

A wide, open area separated buildings whose purpose she didn't know. Though if she had to guess, she'd say one was a garage, one was barracks, and another was some kind of guard house. The final building, tucked away on the northern side of the fort, was more like a house rather than a military bunker. It was close to the size of the Nikaphoroses' Sezian vacation home. Ivy and moss crawled up its gray facade, and columns held a portico up over the front porch. In the distance, waves crashed.

"We need to check—" Jin started.

"Can Astrea not check for intruders from right here?" Marko asked, one eyebrow raised.

Despite the lingering fatigue, Astrea pushed her senses out far and wide. She came up empty. The property was deserted except for the four of them. "It's fine," she said. "Nobody's here."

Marko pulled a silver key from his pocket and unlocked the front door of the misplaced house. Inside was a peculiar mix of utilitarian features and a more elegant touch.

"This is the old base commander's house," Marko explained as they stepped into the foyer. "Well, the officers shared it. Her Highness decommissioned it about two years ago in favor of the new fort up the road. Lucian personally knows the new base's commander."

Dark wood floors ran through the house. Wood paneling lined the lower half of the otherwise cool-toned walls. No paintings. No large chandeliers or sweeping staircases. When Marko flipped a nearby switch, the simple lights overhead flickered on.

Astrea trailed after the men as they went from room to room. Downstairs, they found a kitchen, dining room, and small library. There were also two separate parlors. On the second floor, there were six bedrooms—each with their own small bathroom—plus several storage closets. On the third floor, there were three more bedrooms, one of which had a terrace overlooking the forest.

"Is this where you'll be staying?" Marko asked as Astrea leaned on the terrace railing.

"Yes," Jin said.

As the men retreated into the house, Astrea turned back to the forest. She wished she could see the ocean, but she could hear it if she listened carefully. It was nice. Northern Novaria was far different than Kalama, of course; they were opposite ends of the continent. She was about as far away from Kalama as she could get, but still, knowing the ocean was so close made it feel a bit more like home.

Reluctantly, Astrea went back inside. A wide four-post bed sat in the middle of the bedroom's back wall, muslin draped between the posts. The rest of the room was as she expected: fireplace and settee, wardrobe, closet, small bathroom, and a writing desk tucked in one corner.

Jin returned. As he began unpacking their bags, Astrea checked the bathroom and found clean towels and extra blankets. The soft sheets covering the bed smelled like fresh laundry soap. Someone had definitely been there to clean.

"Do you think we'll be safe here?" she asked as she dropped onto the bed.

"We should be, at least for a while." He'd already emptied his suitcase and was finishing hanging her dresses in the wardrobe.

"And if the Paragon find us?" That question had been on her mind for days. What would they do if Nazarov found them here and brought that many void mages with him again? Or what if The One wasn't dead and came to find Astrea? They still didn't know how to prevent the void mages from dreamwalking or jumping locations.

"*If* they do," Jin said as he reached for her hand, "I'll do what I have to. So will Adi, Lennor, and Civan, and I'm fairly certain Lucian and Marko won't go down without a fight."

Astrea stared down at her lap, playing with the pleats of her black skirt. Every time she began to think back to the night of that fateful dinner, shame burned through her.

"I'm sorry, Jin."

Lavender surprise flashed in the corner of her eye as Jin asked, "Why are you sorry?"

"That you're in this position. That you might have to . . ." She shook her head. "I'm sorry I yelled at you that night. I shouldn't have. I thought . . . I thought I wasn't going to get to say—"

"Hey." Jin pulled her close as he sat down next to her. "Hey, you can say whatever you want to me now, alright? Anything. And I know you want to apologize, but Az, I'm the one who's sorry."

"What?"

"I'm so, so sorry that I ever made you think I didn't believe in you or that I didn't think you were capable of handling this." His hand brushed the back of her head as Astrea buried her face in the crook of his neck. "I know you can. I can only imagine how hard all those years were hiding who you really were and what you could do and feel. I'll never know what that's like. But I do know you're strong. You're so, so strong, Az. I've never, ever doubted that."

Astrea squeezed her eyes shut, though it didn't stop the tears. Her shoulders shook, and Jin held her tighter.

"I just get protective," he whispered. Warmth, soft like sunshine, settled on Astrea's skin. "Especially of people I care about. And I care about you so much, Az. So, so much."

"I care about you, too. I just need to know I can stand on my own." She barely got the words out. "Saros never even let me try. I need to know I can."

"You can. I *know* you can. I told you in Sezia that the thought of something happening to you makes me react in ways I don't like. I'll keep working on that, alright? I promise, I'll work on it. And I promise I'll let you stand on your own and do anything else you need."

She nodded against his shoulder, words lodging in her throat. Her appreciation. Her regret. Her apologies.

"I shouldn't have yelled at you that night," she whispered. "I'm sorry. It wasn't fair to you. Just because I was overwhelmed didn't give me the right to yell at you like that."

"Hey, it's alright." Jin hugged her tighter and pressed a kiss to her temple. "Maybe yelling isn't the way to go, but you know I sometimes need a kick in the ass to pull myself together. You were right."

Astrea laughed and pulled away, using the back of her hand to wipe at her tears. "Say it again."

"Which part?"

"That I was right."

A deep, low chuckle rumbled in Jin's chest. "Nice try." As his laughter died, he gazed down at her and cupped her face in his hands. "I'm not going anywhere unless you want me to."

"Stay."

They may have had things they needed to work on, but that didn't change how she felt about Jin. It didn't mean they couldn't figure it out together.

"Partners watch over each other," he said, "and we're partners, right?"

"Partners," she echoed, not missing the uncertainty in his voice. "Of course we are."

"Well, having a partner means you don't always have to stand on your own. I'll be here when you need me to hold you up, and I know you'll do the same for me."

Astrea tilted her head up to his, melting into Jin's embrace as his lips met hers for the first time in days. She wrapped her arms around his neck, one hand digging into his curls. And when they ended up tangled together in bed, Astrea drank in every color that danced in the room and every sensation that whispered over her skin. Everything he made her feel, and everything she made him feel, together.

Jin was unforgiving. Adi, Lennor, and Civan were unforgiving.

From her spot on the porch at the front of the house, Astrea watched the four of them train. She'd seen Jin and Adi spar before, but this was different. They were taking each other on three against one, and it was currently Jin's turn to take on his team.

Jin barely danced out of reach of one of Civan's water whips. Orange annoyance flared around the Tidebacker. Lennor kicked out, and Jin dodged something invisible. Air? But as he dodged, the ground under his feet rumbled. Jin managed to skip back again just as the earth cracked open.

None of that compared to the wave of fire Jin kicked out at his team. They all tipped off balance as they dodged the incoming flames. Jin pounced on Civan first, taking him down with two direct blows. Lennor went down next.

It was just Jin and Adi now, and the grin spreading across Adi's face said everything. How they could both still be so light on their feet after the last hour, Astrea didn't know.

Adi moved first. He went in with a cross. Jin dipped low. Uppercut. It didn't land. Jin bounced back and to the side. Adi circled to his other side, assessing. Light green focus swirled around him, but Jin's wall was tight.

"Oh, come on, Captain!" Lennor called. She'd sprawled out in the grass like she didn't have a care in the world. "Hurry up. We're tired!"

Adi punched. Jin blocked. Adi tried again. Jin blocked. Sugary amusement coated Astrea's tongue. What could Adi possibly find funny?

They continued in this dance of punches, kicks, and blocks for a couple more minutes. Their energy didn't seem to wane despite the sweat pouring off them.

Adi kicked, the blow headed straight for Jin's waist. Jin moved back half a step as he avoided the blow. Adi wobbled as his leg came back down, and Jin struck. It was quick. Three blows and Adi fell down onto his back. Jin immediately went to him and pulled him off the ground.

"And I think I'm done for today," Adi said as he wiped his forehead with his shirt.

Lennor and Civan pushed themselves off the ground and joined the other two, their voices low as they discussed something.

"Prince Varojin is impressive, isn't he? I've seen very few mages with that kind of stamina."

Astrea hadn't heard Lucian come outside, nor had she noticed his calm, steady aura. He'd arrived the night before with the twins, but Astrea had been avoiding him. She was fairly certain he was avoiding her, too.

"He works hard for it."

"Have you started training with Adi again?"

"No." Astrea kept her focus on Jin and his team, unable to make herself look Lucian in the eye.

"Why not?"

Every time Astrea thought about using her magic—really using it—her body froze. It took her back to that skies damned place. It took her back to when Nazarov was chasing her, when he'd found her in that tunnel despite the pitch darkness.

"Your barrier is down," Lucian murmured.

"I don't want to talk about it."

"You don't have to. I can see the pain around you very clearly, Astrea."

"Then what are you doing here?" she snapped.

"I was simply checking on everyone."

Anger flared in Astrea's veins, bright and hot, but she wasn't sure why she was even angry with him. Checking in wasn't wrong. And his Lightbringer—Souleater?—trick had probably saved her. She probably wouldn't be there if she hadn't had those few short lessons with Lucian, disastrous as she once thought they were.

These episodes had been coming in waves over the last four days they'd been at the base in northern Novaria. Sometimes she went hours without really thinking about what had happened, and other times, she could barely focus on what was going on around her. It was frustrating, confusing.

"I think you should keep training, Astrea. Both with me and with Adi. You know as well as I do that this is not the end of the Paragon. It's just the beginning."

Jin had started demonstrating something to Civan, something about the way he'd blocked Adi's kicks. Adi was working on the same thing with Lennor.

"I couldn't stop them," Astrea whispered. "I couldn't do anything against the void mages, just like I told you I wouldn't be able to."

"But you did," Lucian said.

"And it left me useless for days. That's not a good way to fight them."

"They were also drugging you. That's not exactly a fair fight. We don't know what you might've done if the circumstances were different."

"I do," she muttered. That was exactly what had gotten her in that situation in the first place: not being able to fight them off during the palace attack.

"Take some time," Lucian said as he set a hand on her shoulder. "Just don't take too long. We don't have the luxury of time right now."

As Lucian walked back into the house, Astrea leaned forward and rested her forehead on the veranda's thick stone railing.

The commander was right. It hadn't been a fair fight at all. But war wasn't fair, and they were about to be fighting enemies on two fronts. Astrea needed to keep training. She needed to find a way to fight the void mages in a way that worked for her magic. She had to be able to do something. Anything. Sitting around while her friends did all the work was not an option.

She'd fallen apart when Saros had chosen to stay behind. But she'd survived that. She'd survived the Paragon once. She'd been surviving in Kalama for years. Astrea didn't want to just keep surviving. She wanted to make it to the other side of this war. She wanted to make the most of her time with her friends, with her family, with Jin, as she could. She wanted to see what life might be like without the Paragon or Emperor Aelius standing in her way.

It was time for her to do something. It was time for her to take control.

It was time for Astrea to fight back.

To be continued

BOOKS BY H.E. BAUMAN

Forged by Flames: A Darkened Skies Prequel
Under Darkened Skies: Darkened Skies Book One
Into Whispering Shadows: Darkened Skies Book Two

ACKNOWLEDGMENTS

It's strange, having another book out in the world. I'm not sure I'll ever get used to the idea of people reading my work, but I'm so grateful to everyone who has encouraged me, helped me, and picked up a copy along the way.

To my husband, you already know how much your support means to me. Thank you for always being by my side and cheering me on.

To my family, thank you for your never-ending support, even when I get shy talking about my work.

To my friends, thank you for the long conversations about publishing and its joys and pitfalls, space to talk through plot points, and of course, trips to take a break from this work.

To Sarah and Kayla, you two know I literally couldn't have gotten this far without your help. Thank you for everything.

To my street team, your enthusiasm for this Darkened Skies universe and help spreading the work are both invaluable. Thank you.

To Hazel, you're a rock star! Thank you for all your help on my past few book launches and our ongoing partnership.

To Jeanine, thank you for the careful care with which you review my manuscripts. Your editor's eye is invaluable.

And finally, to all my readers, thank you for continuing on this journey with me, Astrea, and the whole Darkened Skies crew.

About Author

H.E. Bauman is a fantasy author fascinated with all things magical. After spending her childhood writing stories, she went on to receive her bachelor's in English and has continued writing ever since. When she's not reading or writing, she enjoys playing tennis, immersing herself in video games, and spending time with her family.

If you want to get in touch, visit H.E.'s website or follow her on social media.